OF GOD
AND
MADNESS

OF GOD
AND
MADNESS
A Historical Novel

T. Byram Karasu

ROWMAN & LITTLEFIELD
Lanham • Boulder • New York • Toronto • Oxford

Published in the United States of America
by Rowman & Littlefield Publishers, Inc.

The Rowman & Littlefield Publishing Group, Inc.
4501 Forbes Boulevard, Suite 200, Lanham, Maryland 20706
www.rowmanlittlefield.com

PO Box 317
Oxford
OX2 9RU, UK

British Library Cataloguing in Publication Information Available

Library of Congress Cataloging-in-Publication Data Available

Karasu, Toksoz B.
  Of God and madness / T. Byram Karasu.
    p. cm.
  ISBN-13: 978-0-7425-4689-9 (cloth : alk. paper)
  ISBN-10: 0-7425-4689-6 (cloth : alk. paper)
  1. Karasu, Toksoz B.—Family—Fiction. 2. Brain—Tumors—Patients—
Fiction. 3. Identity (Psychology)—Fiction. 4. Religious life—Fiction.
5. Middle East—Fiction. I. Title.
PS3611.A7773O35 2006
813'.6—dc22   2005034573

Printed in the United States of America

♾ ™ The paper used in this publication meets the minimum requirements of
American National Standard for Information Sciences—Permanence of Paper
for Printed Library Materials, ANSI/NISO Z39.48-1992.

To My Father,

The man who would be philosopher-king

CONTENTS

ONE

∽

Jesus cheers me, winks at me, and confuses me. I want to sin.

Istanbul

1905–1922

I was born into many languages.

I didn't speak until I was four years old. The doctors consulted considered me neither deaf nor dumb but pronounced me as having a bizarre case of speech impairment. Rabbi Nahum explained that this occurs in children who are too smart and shocked by their being born. A psychiatrist concluded that I had a speechless wish to be understood.

My mother said the first time I spoke understandable words, they came out in full sentences. I said, "Where is God?"

My mother, astonished, translated this into "Where is father?" and told me, "Your father is a very busy and important man. He comes to see you whenever he has a chance."

But I persisted, much to my mother's surprise, in asking more questions. "Where does God live? Does God talk? Does God have parents?" Mademoiselle Blanche, my governess, was the only one who took me seriously and responded by saying, "Just look at the world, really look, and you'll get a glimpse of God." I didn't stop asking these or similar questions throughout my growing-up years. She called me "my holy asker."

"Don't think of the how, why, or where of God," she always said. "Just accept Him as 'is'; the answer to your questions is promised in cognitive crucifixion." Did she mean I had to kill my mind?

Incidentally, I always spoke to myself; I don't know why, but I couldn't speak to others. I couldn't seem to translate my private language of experience into the common language of speech.

I did ask myself the question, "Where is father?" but I didn't really care where he was. I was more curious about God or Gods because the people around me constantly spoke of them and in conflicting ways in entirely different languages. My mother was a Sephardic Jew and spoke Ladino, my father was Turkish and a Sunni Muslim, my governess was a French Catholic, my history teacher was Shiite and spoke Arabic, my rabbi spoke Hebrew, my music teacher was Armenian, and I had a eunuch who practiced a version of Islam. They all spoke a sort of Turkish too. Each presented me with a world created by their language, as if I lived in many different worlds simultaneously. None of them, though, created a fitting home for me to live in.

Once I began to talk, I spoke all these languages almost fluently, and I wasn't easy to shut up. Because there were no other children to associate with, I talked like an adult and animatedly discussed adult subjects such as religion, especially religion, philosophy, and politics.

My mother told me I was a happy child. But somewhere along the line that changed. My ebullience ended, and sadness seeped in. When I was seven, I committed my first severe sin: I tried to kill myself. I put my hands tightly around my neck. Seconds passed. I heard my heart beating, felt it hitting my chest, getting faster and faster. More seconds passed. The urge to breathe was getting irresistible. I squeezed my throat with all my strength. I heard the sound of a click under my pointer finger, similar to the snapping of a chicken wishbone. The noise of my heart slowly dissipated; the beats became gentle. I felt as if I were watching myself from the outside. My arms turned limp, and my fingers released my throat, but I still couldn't breathe. I wanted to breathe, desperately. I just couldn't. Then all of a sudden, everything went black. I woke up to a harsh spell of coughs. I lay on the carpet and gasped as air entered my lungs.

Actually it was my second sin; the Bible says I was born a sinner, or, rather I was a sinner when my mother conceived me. My third sin was my ignorance. I chose an immature and uninformed method of killing myself: self-suffocation.

I knew that Jesus had suffered and died on the cross for me, that I shouldn't be taking my own life, but I had a very good reason. In losing my life, I could find Him because Jesus said I had to lose my life for His sake to find Him. But mine was simply an angry outburst, related to self-ish ambition, things Jesus disapproved of the most.

Why was I trying to kill myself? Because a son was just born to a Muslim wife of my father, Prince Vahdettin, the younger brother of the sultan of the Ottoman Empire. Being a *judenfürst*—a prince of Israel as my mother called me—was no consolation.

～

Up until my seventh birthday, mother and I played a little game that she made up. It was called *shehzade*—crown prince. I was the "crown prince" and sat on a "throne" of cushions, and she acted the part of the messenger who came with the news that the sultan was dead and I was to be the new sultan of the empire.

The birth of a son named Ertuğrul from my father's fourth wife, Müvedded Hanım, wiped out all my dreams of becoming crown prince. It undermined all my ambitious intellectual and physical preparations for the job: six hours each day—except Fridays—I received tutoring in Arabic and French, history, religion, literature, and music.

～

I didn't think things could get much worse for me than Ertuğrul's birth. Well, what followed six months later was worse. I was told I could no longer live with my mother. I know, Jesus doesn't want me to complain, but what do I do when bad things constantly happen to me?

"You are no longer a child," said our eunuch, Ahmed Agha. He told me that my father, Prince Vahdettin, had ordered that I move out of the harem—the women's quarters—to the *selâmlık*—the men's quarters. "From now on, if you want to see Şahhane Hanım," Ahmed Agha said and used the formal means of address for my mother, "you'll have to request to do so through me." He added, "Furthermore, Mademoiselle Blanche will no longer attend to your personal needs. I will."

I'm no longer a child? I've never been one.

Ertuğrul had taken away my hopes of being crown prince and sultan, and now my father was taking away my mother and especially my governess, Mademoiselle Blanche.

The entire scenario was painful and absurd since in our home there was neither a real harem nor a *selâmlık*. There was only my mother, me,

Mademoiselle Blanche, and the servants, who didn't count. So my mother was to live in one part of the house, and I was to live in the other?

Then I understood: father now wanted me to be caged. I guess that was God's punishment because of my corrupt nature: I am jealous and envious; therefore, I would never inherit the kingdom.

⌇

I couldn't wait to see Mademoiselle Blanche so I could tell her what I knew. I tugged on her hand.

"*Oui?* What is it?" she said. She frowned, worried.

I took a deep breath. "I think Vahdettin *Effendimiz* wants to put me in a cage and then kill me so that Ertuğrul won't have to do it when he becomes sultan."

Mademoiselle burst out laughing. Eventually, her laughter dissolved into giggles.

"Come on, no one is going to kill you, *mon petit*. First, never mind Ertuğrul or even your father becoming sultan. That's about as likely as my becoming president of France. The Sultan Reşat is in good health, and the young Crown Prince Yusuf Izzetin is waiting in line. Furthermore, unless Prince Vahdettin *Effendi* marries your mother, you'll not be officially recognized as his son. Somehow you seem to forget or are hell-bent to deny it, even though I told you dozens of times. Anyhow, who told you about cages?"

A sadness descended on me. "My history teacher, Muhsin *Effendi*."

"You are already caged," she said, gesturing to the house around us. "This is what they mean by 'caging' potential contenders to the throne. It's not a cage like one for zoo animals; it simply means you won't have much contact with the outside world. Don't let that old fogy of a history teacher of yours jumble up your young mind. Speak of the devil, here he is."

"Good afternoon Muhsin *Effendi*!" she greeted him. "Your student is eagerly awaiting your frightening stories."

"Mademoiselle Blanche, I beg your pardon, my stories are not frightening; they are lessons of truth," the man replied, drawing back and glaring at her through his pince-nez. "What is frightening is how many times in the glorious history of the Ottoman Empire demons taking the shape of foreign women have desecrated the principles of the caliphate—and continue to do so. The empire is failing because we didn't loyally follow the principles of Islam. The Qur'an warns you all: 'the unfaithful shall feed on the fruits of Zaqqum tree bearing the devil's head and they shall feed with draughts of scalding water.' "

"Well!" Mademoiselle Blanche turned and walked away and left me with him.

In the classroom, Muhsin *Effendi's* history lessons usually ended with larger lessons to be learned from them.

"*Mehmed II, the sickly son of Sultan Murad, had no chance of becoming sultan because his mother, Sara, was a Jew. Mehmed's chances were especially limited because there were two older, big and healthy half-brothers from a Muslim wife. But Sara arranged for both the elder brothers to be strangled by assassins. Thus, in 1443, at the age of twelve, Mehmed II took over the empire. Sara eased out the Turkish hierarchy and replaced them with Jews.*

"*You see, Adam, 'converts are always treacherous.'* "

Was he warning me about my mother or giving me hope?

⌇

I tried not to hate my father because the Bible says I should love and honor my father. But I hated his habits. He had this habit of touching his long, pointy nose when he spoke. His eyes darted around nervously, and he always complained about his health: his aching teeth, his acid indigestion, his throbbing fingers, his irritated bladder, his migraine headaches, and his backed-up bowel movements. He went to Karlsbad for treatment of a minor stomach virus and came back with a bad case of ulcers. Drs. Numan and Gunzberg were always on call. He talked infrequently and awkwardly and barely cracked a smile, except when he was with my mother. She, on the other hand, laughed and cried with abandon. He called her *gülen ağlayan Roxelana*—my laughing-crying Roxelana—after the woman who captured the gloomy heart of Sultan Süleyman the Magnificent.

Whenever I encountered father, he never looked into my eyes. He turned his face away from me whenever he spoke and half closed his eyes. Even worse was his habit of lighting one cigarette after another. Nicotine yellowed his fingertips, though he used cigarette holders. The lingering odor of cigarette smoke mixed with perspiration that emanated from his hands as he pulled at the set of worry beads he always kept with him.

I was as uncomfortable in father's presence as he seemed to be in mine. Initially, I thought his circumspect look meant that I should keep my distance. However, as I grew up, I realized that he was hiding his eyes and his words. He seemed scared, but why should he be afraid? He was a brother of the sultan.

My mother described my father's life in Çengelköy Palace before she moved out: eating, sleeping, praying, seeing doctors and dentists, visiting his wives, and playing with his jeweled guns.

I didn't know why he always frowned at me; there was also a disapproving, even punitive note in his voice. He certainly kept contact with me to a minimum. During rare meetings, I kissed his hand while holding my breath so as not to smell the tobacco on it. He, in return, touched my shoulder lightly with his cane, and as I turned to walk away, he very gently tapped my buttocks with it. That was the extent of any display of affection he may have had for me.

I was instructed by my mother always to inquire about his health. So I lifted my lips from his moist hand and quietly uttered, "How are you feeling, *Effendim?*"

"*Elhamdullullah*," he rumbled his thanks to God.

I wasn't allowed to ask any other questions since I was to speak only when addressed and in that case to be very brief.

Mother perpetually tried to find ways of getting me into his good graces, and I'm sure the following encounter was one of her machinations.

He asked to see me—an uncommon occurrence. He must have been in a good mood because rather than quickly tapping me with his cane, he held it there for a long while. He spoke to me:

"I gather you can recite the Qur'an by heart."

There goes my mother again, I thought. I stared at my feet as if modestly agreeing with her hyperbole.

"Yes." I couldn't be briefer. What I actually could do was tell the story of Jesus.

"Do you want to become a *mufti*—religious scholar?"

"No."

"Well, what would you like to be?"

"A Christian monk."

I saw my mother's face go ashen and realized I made a serious mistake.

"What?" He closed his eyes completely.

I shivered.

His eyes were still closed but his voice rose: "Is this the fine work of your Armenian music teacher?"

Vahdettin abruptly got up and walked away from me toward the harem; my mother trailed in his path. The servants and attendants scattered. I was left alone in the middle of the room, feeling dizzy and nauseated. Actually, I didn't know much about Christian monks. I just wanted what Soghomanian wanted to be.

～

Though confined to our luxurious compound, we got news of the outside world through newspapers—*Takvim-iVekai*; *Sabah, Akşam*; and the humorous *Karagöz* and *Akbaba*. If anything, at times I felt overwhelmed by the numbers of people visiting us.

One day I complained, "Mother, people are saying really bad things about what's going on here."

"Such as?"

"*Kerhāne!*—Whorehouse!"

"What?" she screamed. "Who are these people?"

Thankfully, without waiting for a reply, she stormed away.

I knew that we didn't run a whorehouse, and I believed that my mother slept only with my father. I couldn't figure out her relationship with Uncle Manny though. They always seemed to be whispering Ladino into each other's ears and laughing together. I tried whispering to her once:

"I'll see you at the will-o-the-wisp somewhere beyond the grasp of Jews."

Mother got irritated. "That is the coronation whisper of the new sultan in the ear of the Janissary chief and it is 'the grasp of Islam,' not Jews. We don't proselytize."

"Mother, isn't the mission of Israel to disperse Jews into the Diaspora to cultivate monotheism?" I asked.

"That too," she replied.

～

"Mademoiselle Blanche, is it true that the Virgin Mary was conceived through her ear?" I asked.

Mademoiselle Blanche shook her head dismissively. I shifted a little.

"Mademoiselle Blanche, what do you think I should whisper in mother's ear?" I asked.

"Anything you want." She wasn't that interested in my question. "But why whisper, unless you don't want someone else to hear it?"

"What did Jesus whisper in Mary Magdalene's ear?" I pursued.

"Ah, that is something else. He might have been telling her sweet little things." She coyly turned her right ear towards me.

"Sweet little things?"

"Ah *oui*. The ear is not that innocent you know; in fact, it is the ultimate sensual organ."

I think I love Mademoiselle Blanche. The Bible says, God is love, which must mean love is divine.

∼

During my growing-up years, our house was filled with visitors. There were the regulars, such as Uncle Manny and Rabbi Nahum; the finance minister, Djavid *Bey*; the prime minister, Talāt *Bey*; and Vladimir Jabotinsky, the owner of several newspapers. (Mademoiselle Blanche and I called him 666—the number of the beast in the Bible. She told me not to be afraid of him. Evil is only an obstacle course, a necessary ingredient of soul making.) I also met many others: Police Commissioner Deedes; Mr. Strauss and Mr. Elkus, the ambassadors of the United States; Senator Behar *Bey*; two other Jews who were members of Parliament; and young law students, such as David Ben-Gurion and Itzhak Ben Zvi, and other hangers-on, *schnorers*.

Even before I became "a man," I was an informal member of the *selāmlık*, the men's quarters, where the meetings were held. Mostly, no one paid much attention to me; I was just there. The evenings usually started with a low-key discussion about local political intrigues while everyone, with a few exceptions, such as Deedes and Rabbi Nahum, sipped *raki*, an anisette drink popular in Turkey, and nibbled on *meze*, a variety of Turkish appetizers, and smoked cigarettes or *narghile*, the water pipe. The discussions always progressed to who was trying to dominate the Middle East and what would be good for the Jews and continued until the early morning hours. Then one by one or two they departed, rubbing their foreheads or yawning behind their hands. I tried to stay awake until the last guest left; I didn't want to miss anything.

I liked Uncle Manny the most; he was a burly man whose piercing black eyes darted from one person to another without ever blinking.

Mother called him a Levantine Jew, not a Jewish Jew. But I think he is Christian because his name, Emmanuel, meaning "God with us," is Jesus' other name. She praised him as a gentleman of *le vieux jeu*—the old game of politics—and remarked how he played everyone's hand without revealing his own. Beneath his jocular, friendly demeanor, he was able to adopt any mood and wear many hats: as Karasu *Effendi*—the legislative representative from Salonika—he championed the transformation of the Ottoman Empire from a monarchy to a parliamentary regime; as Emmanuel Carasso—the lawyer—he defended luxurious foreign businesses operating in Turkey in their ongoing battle to maintain "the capitulation," which exempted foreigners from taxes and other Ottoman rules; and as Manny—the humble servant of Judaism—he ran Freemason lodges and tried to establish the Ottoman-Israelite Union to facilitate large-scale Jewish immigration to Palestine.

Uncle Manny was on a first-name basis with the leaders of all the competing as well as enemy camps: the Young Turks, the Ottomans, the Germans, the French, the English, and the various Jewish groups. He said that politics was like a tennis game: the one who makes the fewest mistakes, not the one who takes the best shots, wins. He summed up his philosophy, "I am not a very good player, but a very patient one."

❧

As I was growing up, mother recounted how Uncle Manny was instrumental in the way she and my father met. I must have heard the story dozens of times. I was always more than happy to hear it again and listened with awe and interest, curled up by my mother's feet.

Years before, when Abdulhamid was the sultan, she said, Uncle Manny had brought her from Salonika to Istanbul with the purpose of introducing her as a lady-in-waiting to Prince Reşat—the man expected to be the next sultan. He declined her service.

My mother was then introduced to my father, Prince Vahdettin, who accepted her rather reluctantly into his household because of her Jewish convert status.

"*John Cantazune, the grand chancellor of old Byzantium, gave his ten-year-old daughter, Theodora, to Orhan, the son of the first Ottoman sultan, and Prince Lazar of Serbia gave his twelve-year-old daughter, Despina, to Sultan Beyazıd to make peace.*

"*You see, Adam, 'the women are the best bargaining chips.'*"

෴

Although Ottoman history was full of examples of religious tolerance and interracial marriages, especially among the nobility, the times were different when my mother got to my father's household. Turkey was being besieged from within and without. Internally, ethnic minorities—Bulgars, Serbs, Greeks, Armenians, Arabs, and Jews—were trying to establish their independence by dismantling the empire. Therefore, every foreigner was suspect, and most were removed from important positions, especially at the palaces. Despite this, Uncle Manny arranged to install my mother in Vahdettin's palace, where, in no time, she became his concubine.

Because my father did not have any sons with his legal wives yet, the Sultan objected to his involvement with a Jewish concubine. So, an agreement was reached that Vahdettin would have no children with my mother. Further, he would immediately marry a Muslim woman to try to have a son. Within months, my father married another concubine-in-waiting, Neware *Kadın Effendi*. Ironically, she could not conceive, which forced Vahdettin to take a fourth wife: Müveddet *Kadın Effendi*, who eventually bore a son, "the darling Ertuğrul." Mother said word was out that military strongman Djemal Pasha was used for stud.

"*In 1540 a partitioned Hungary was ruled by the Hungarian, Zápolya, and the German, Ferdinand. Zápolya was ill and without a child, thus without a successor; Ferdinand was finally going to be the sole king of Hungary. A monk got a woman, Isabella, pregnant and had her marry Zápolya just a few months before he died.*

To stop Ferdinand from taking over, the monk needed Sultan Süleyman's support. So, he brought Isabella and her son to his court. She gracefully uncovered her breast and gave milk to the child in front of the sultan. The sultan took Isabella to his private room to see if she was really lactating. Later, the sultan granted Isabella the right to rule Zápolya's territory.

"*You see, Adam, 'The well is never too deep; it is the rope that is too short.'* "

෴

Just before the last wife came to the palace, my mother underwent two abortions. Then she was pregnant again. This time, her indignation raging, she refused another abortion. My father pleaded with her; he couldn't disobey the sultan.

To this impasse entered Uncle Manny, providing a solution that only an "unworldly prince could agree to." For public consumption, it was announced that my mother ran away.

In reality, my mother was housed in a highly restricted compound where she had me without any public recognition. Both she and I remained in seclusion until my father made a decision to relocate us either to France or to Palestine. In the meantime, Vahdettin visited her as often as he pleased.

The night of my mother's "disappearance," Vahdettin's most loyal staff member, Nessim Agha, the black eunuch of the harem, escorted my mother, disguised in men's clothing, to the gates of Çengelköy Palace. There, some of Uncle Manny's confederates waited to dash the escapee to Pasha Çiftliği, a compound owned by Dr. Victor Jacobson, the president of the Anglo-Levantine Banking Company.

The need for secrecy was a farce. The princes had many children from numerous illegitimate and illicit relationships. And no one ever explained to me why we lived where we lived and why most of our expenses were paid for by Uncle Manny.

∽

I was born at the Pasha Çiftliği on February 28, 1905, the day that the storks arrive in Istanbul. My mother, Şahhane—Hebrew name, Sheera—was the only child of Ethel and Moïse Cohen, a devoted follower of the Zionists, who inculcated my mother from a very young age with their extreme ideals. Ethel was the younger of the two daughters of Moshe Allatini, a wealthy businessman in Salonika. Moïse Cohen, originally from Batum, was a sought-after Russian and French literature teacher whose reputation—and introductions by my Uncle Manny—served to expand his social sphere. Through Uncle Manny, Moïse came to teach the daughter of Talāt Bey, an influential member of the Ottoman cabinet.

In the meantime, Talāt's daughter and my mother struck up a friendship, visiting each other's homes. It was during these visits that my mother—a stunningly beautiful girl: tall, full-bodied, and graceful, with pinkish-white skin; long, straight light brown hair; and hazel eyes that sparkled—caught Talāt Bey's eye.

Mother always smelled good; in fact, she was soaked in perfumes. She was always made-up, powdered, rouged, her hair done. She wore elegant, filmy clothes from Paris and bejeweled necklaces from Iran. Both her arms from her wrists to her elbows were covered with gold bracelets; her earlobes were stretched halfway to her shoulders under the weight of large overly jeweled earrings. Jesus wouldn't have approved of her way of dressing.

Men seemed to care about neither what she wore nor what she did. They were attracted to her. "When she locks her gaze on someone," Manny used to say, "the person would be obediently glued." While Talāt might have helped with my mother's introduction to the palace, it was she who eventually influenced the sultan into keeping Talāt in power as the prime minister.

༈

The Pasha Çiftliği, in which mother and I lived, was situated just outside Istanbul in the tiny village of Rumelihisari. It was a hidden compound on woody heights overlooking the Bosporus. The compound included the gigantic wooden main house surrounded by similar but smaller outbuildings, a barn housing Arabian horses, and a big garage that held three Mercedes. The compound was encircled by forest on all sides. The main house was surrounded by an extensive flower garden— wisteria, tulips, Judah bushes with pink rosettes, jasmine, terebinth, and a profusion of roses.

Slightly farther away, there was a working farm, replete with cows, sheep, chickens, and vegetable gardens, and a large piece of land punctuated with trees—wild cherry, peach, chestnut, and fig. The place was staffed with many farmers, mostly Albanians, who also functioned as guards. Then there was the chauffeur Abbas, an Anatolian, who became my friend.

༈

What is the name of God?

My mother's Jewishness was a strange mixture of inconsistency. I participated in her rituals wholeheartedly, even though I thought of myself as a Christian. As far as my mother was concerned, she couldn't recite the Ten Commandments, but she feasted and fasted with primitive zealotry and played the Jewish role with theatrical superstition. Aside from returning Jews to Israel, she had no other overriding convictions. She knew some of the rituals and complied with them in a totally exaggerated fashion. Every door, not just the main outside door, had *mezuzahs*; every room, including the bathroom, was garnished with cloves; and every outfit of mine, including my pajamas, had an amulet tucked in it, those blue glass bits supposedly protecting us against the evil eye.

On the solemn holidays of Rosh Hashanah and Yom Kippur, we outdid ourselves: fifteen days of penitence. During the full moon of the first month of spring, my mother had a lamb slaughtered and distributed to the staff; she dipped her fingers into the animal's blood and sprinkled it on the front doorpost and on our foreheads. At our Seder, no small procedure was neglected: Mother played the rabbi. Four cups of wine were sipped, and with each cup came a description of the four expressions of God's deliverance of Israel. We saved half of the middle matzoh and recited the Exodus with all its embellishments, and, of course, as the youngest, I got to ask the four questions. The Muslim staff—all women—were instructed to say "*Dayyenu*—It would have been enough," at the proper time during the meal. These reluctant participants were attired in the customary travel outfit of hat and overcoat and had bags tied to their backs. The women giggled throughout the routine.

On Purim, one of my favorite celebrations, I dressed like a sultan and acted the role of sultan and wise man for a day. Everyone else, including my mother, played the role of fool and wore outlandish outfits. I gave a mimic recital of the Sabbath benediction. I also imparted absurd answers to Mother's hilarious questions. She was at her best, offering silly gems:

"Is the endless toil, moil, and coil to serve creeps, freaks, and derelicts?"

To which I offered, "Keep your matzoh, keep your fish. Do you think I am not a Dervish?"

We went on and on like this, rolling with laughter on the floor.

On the Sabbath, we didn't switch on lights, didn't write, didn't read, didn't do paperwork, didn't carry anything, including an umbrella in pouring rain. Mother had a sweet, high voice; she sang religious songs at the end of our meal while she gazed at her fingernails.

After I closed the ceremony, she reminded me that the demons, who were temporarily confined during the Sabbath, would be out and I should be careful. "May God make you like Ephraim," she said, quoting the Torah as my father would if he were Jewish. She touched my head. She was my mother and my father.

〜

It was hard to be a Christian while being a Jew and a Muslim. It was harder still to be a man and only eight. That fateful day that my "manhood" was announced, a minor wound was intentionally inflicted on my penis, a form of circumcision in the Islamic tradition. Minor, because apparently I was born already circumcised. Perhaps I am like Edgar Mortara, that Jewish boy of Bologna, I thought. The Church found out he was baptized by a servant and made him a priest. I'll be taken away from the Jews by the caliph, never to be returned, and I'll become *sheyhul-Islam*—the head of all Muslims.

In a ceremony attended only by the male staff, I was seated on the lap of the local religious man who was selected to be my "*Kivra*," a kind of Muslim godfather. He locked my arms and legs with his own, totally immobilizing me while the Muslim *mohel* made that little cut. I was given a lot of hashish earlier so I barely felt any pain. I heard later on that day that my mother was accused of having me circumcised secretly on the eighth day following my birth, as is customary in the Jewish faith. I wouldn't have put it past her, but she vehemently denied it.

Afterward, everyone returned to their jobs, and I was led to the "men's quarters," of which I was the only permanent occupant. I sat on the divan alone. Ice cream dripped on my circumcision outfit, which looked like a girl's dress and was decorated with many gold coins, including one big one—a *Beşibirlik*, a five-coin piece—sent by Vahdettin. Hazily, I looked at the other gifts I'd been given: Uncle Manny had sent me a silver Browning pistol. Mother gave me an array of clay tablets, each with a plum pit pictured on one side and animals, like fawns and bulls, on the other. She also gave me a stamp seal: blue across the top, a solar design in the middle, surrounded by an inscription that I could not read. The case had a Jewish star on one cover and twelve men on the other. She said it was a gift from an archaeologist for whom she obtained the permit to excavate an old *Boğazköy* burial site.

I was crying from loneliness when Uncle Manny walked in. "Adam, you must learn to bear physical pain with stoic dignity."

"The pain doesn't hurt me, I just feel homesick."

"You are homesick at home, Adam?" he scolded me.

I was happy that he simply called me Adam.

～～

From a very young age, I was tutored at home by prominent teachers from Istanbul. But it seemed as if my teachers, in addition to what they were assigned to teach, wanted to teach me to hate various religious and ethnic groups.

"You see Adam, in long-standing arguments all sides tend to be wrong."

I have no long-standing arguments with anyone. Well, actually I do, I have a silent argument with Ertuğrul. But he has no arguments with me. He has it all; I am nothing. How sad to have no one to argue with. How sad not to believe in a cause to fight for with those who argue otherwise. Am I against Armenians? What about Kurds? Am I for Jews? How could I be for Jabotinsky? No, I am still for Jesus.

My Hebrew-Torah teacher, Rabbi Nahum, looked like a fat, scared mouse, yet his irregular, thick eyeglasses magnified his eyeballs, making him seem strangely likable. He was the second Jew I'd met, besides my Uncle Manny, who spoke fluent Turkish. He lisped when he spoke, and spit flew out of his mouth and all over me. Uncle Manny and the rabbi knew each other, and, of course, they knew my mother. All three were originally from Salonika and were, in one form or other, Zionists.

Rabbi Nahum was always saying, "Islam and Christianity are religions for illiterate men, but don't ever mention this conversation to your father."

I found that the rabbi's emotionally engaged deliberations in discrediting Islam and Christianity were more interesting than his instructing me in the Torah:

"Both Jesus and Muhammad were fatherless people. Jesus' mother just let him do whatever he wanted after he was six years old. Muhammad's mother died when he was six. Jesus spent his youth looking for succor; Muhammad actually moved in with a rich woman of his own mother's age. Both were neglected children. If these two had been taken into an orphanage, none of the world's troubles would have occurred."

I was horrified; was the rabbi recommending that I be sent to an orphanage?

My Arabic language and Qur'an teacher, Shayekh Omer, was an old man originally from Egypt (Egyptians were supposed to speak the most refined Arabic), and he was extremely dogmatic and unreasonable. During Ramadan, I wasn't supposed to swallow my own spit. His teaching was slow, laborious, pedantic, and repetitive and conducted in a semisomnolent state. The only time he was fully awake and interesting was when he unleashed his litany against Jews, Judaism, Jesus, and Christianity.

"The Scriptures were revealed only to Jews and Christians before us; we have no knowledge of what they understood. Had the Scriptures been revealed to us, we would have been better guided than they are. Hazreti Muhammad is the last of the Prophets. This is described in the Torah and the Gospels. He corrected all the wrongs of the previous prophets. Hazreti Musa picked the wrong people, Jews, to save; they were corrupt. Hazreti Isa was driven mad by the Jews; he began to say that he was the son of Allah and asked people to eat his flesh and drink his blood so they could live forever. Cannibalism is a sin; therefore, Allah punished him very severely. Just don't tell this to your mother."

What made me less inclined toward Islam the most was Muhammad urging me to trust in God but tie my camel first. It was a faith within reason that swallowed up faith.

My music teacher, Sağolan (his real name, Soghoman Soghomanian, was too cumbersome to use), managed to patronize both Judaism and Islam in between Jewish *neginots* (wordless songs), Turkish love songs, and Christian chants. He always dreamed about becoming a monk—the ultimate Christian salvation.

"You see, Adam, Judaism is the predecessor to Christianity, the way that infancy is to adulthood. Islam is the retarded cousin of Judaism. But don't ever tell this to your parents." I believed him because I liked him. In fact, I liked everything about Sağolan: his agile hands, the gentle way he looked into my eyes before imparting what he knew, and his sonorous voice that sang through me.

Sağolan was the only person ever to say something positive about my size. "You are like the mustard seed. Even though the mustard seed is one of the smallest seeds, when it is grown, it becomes a tree large enough for big birds to nest in its branches. Did you also know that Stephen the

Great, a fifteenth-century prince, who built a powerful Moldavia to stop
the invasion of the Ottomans, was a very, very short man?"

"*Turks believed in the gods of snow and sun, rain, earth, fertility, and
war, amongst many others. It was only after spiritually submitting to the
Arabs in the tenth century that they began to believe in Allah.*

"*Sultan Selim I in 1516 conquered Jerusalem. In 1517 he defeated
the king of rich Egypt. He took the standard, the cloak, and all other relics
of the Prophet Muhammad to Istanbul. Consequently, Selim became caliph,
the head of all Islam, thus automatically making all Turkish tribes Muslim.*

"*You see, Adam, who flies low, perches high.*"

To whom else am I supposed to submit? I couldn't fly any lower. I
wish Sultan Selim conquered Rome and became pope.

〜

My French teacher, Mademoiselle Blanche, and my Turkish teacher,
Tahsin *Effendi*, were the only ones who weren't attacking others, though
they wanted to inculcate in me their own interests.

Mademoiselle Blanche loved Turkish kilims. Not only did she collect them—her room looked like a carpet bazaar—but she also was
determined to impart every irrelevant bit of information about them
with all who came into contact with her: the best wools came from the
necks of castrated, fat-tailed, shaggy angora goats; the kilim lexicon had
a rectilinear and regular geometric, abstract visual grammar—hexagons,
squares, rectangles, triangles—in contrast to the curvilinear and irregular forms of nature and so on. I wasn't really interested in kilims, but I
listened to her intensely, as I loved looking at her mouth.

Whenever she bought or was given a kilim, we played a game of
finding the intentional imperfection and unintentional design flaws.
Mademoiselle Blanche explained that the Muslim kilim makers over-
estimated their threat of competitive perfection to God; the imperfections in the kilim were respectful recognitions that only God is perfect.
She kept reminding me that Jesus loved the imperfect, for only the
imperfect could be perfected.

I thought I had a chance then.

〜

My Turkish writing and reading teacher, Tokatlı Hafız Tahsin *Effendi*,
was an engraver who tried to engage me in the art of calligraphy.

He collected Old Masters' scripts and was eager to explain the fine distinctions among them: *Nesih* was written with a pen whose nib was one millimeter; *Sülüs*, two millimeters; and both were used for business transactions. *Tevkî* used a two-and-a-half-millimeter nib and only for governmental orders. All of this bored me. I was interested only in *Tuğra*—the sultan's calligraphic emblem—the imperial monogram.

∽

Of all my teachers, I liked Mademoiselle Blanche and Sağolan best. Through them I found Jesus. Christianity was a faith beyond reason and even against reason. I like the intimately engaged Christian God in daily life rather than some abstract idea of a Jewish God. In Judaism, it seems like I need to confront God to become a man. I didn't want any confrontation. Even if I did, how do I do that? Where do I find the God of the burning bush? YHVH is not even a noun; it is something that stands for a word that consists of entirely silent letters, so you can't even pronounce it. I loved being Christian, for there was a transformation to godlikeness through love and an optimistic expectation that all would be fine. Plus God approved of me without my earning it. Everyone else's approval required enormous effort on my part. Jesus understood things that other children his age and even adults didn't. He carried on long conversations with teachers in the temple. He was a genius. My mother had told me I was a genius too. Furthermore, I liked the idea of Jesus: the son not of his own father but that of God. Jesus figured out that he was the son of God when he was twelve and got involved in his Father's kingdom. I had a few years to go then before I become involved in my father's kingdom.

I had a little statue of Jesus, a gift from Mademoiselle Blanche, hidden in my room. I prayed to it every night before going to bed. "Please, little Jesus, make me the crown prince so I can become the sultan." Then I'd get scared: Oh, my goodness! Jesus says selfish ambitions are not good. So, what do I do? If I have no selfish ambitions for myself, will someone else have them for me?

∽

When I was twelve years old, Sağolan left us to become a monk in Armenia, where they changed his name to Komitas Vartabed. He wrote me countless letters, all about his spiritually fired life as a monk and about how I should become one, and I wrote him back double his letters, saying I was considering running away and joining him in Armenia.

A year later when he got back, I was ready to be spiritually fired, but he seemed to have abandoned the religion. His eyes seemed glazed over. Before he left for Armenia, he had a sunny disposition. Now he was very serious and determined to save me from Jesus, of all things!

"Adam, Jesus wasn't the Messiah. He just thought he was. He wasn't even a priest. Moses said no priest would ever come from the tribe of Judah because it is an ignorant tribe. The Messiah isn't someone who needs to quarrel with rabbis or to allow Roman soldiers to arrest and crucify him like a thief to fulfill his destiny. Nor is the Messiah someone who would cry for help. Once Jesus was nailed to the cross, he realized that he was just an ordinary man. He moaned pitifully on the cross, '*Eli, Eli, lema sabachthani?*'—'My God, My God, why have you forsaken me?'"

"So his father abandoned him."

"No, God was never his father."

Obviously, I should stop moaning pitifully about my father's lack of interest in me.

"As for those twelve so-called apostles, they were simply fast-talking salesmen who weren't even embarrassed by their circular reasoning: If Jesus didn't come back to life, then there was no meaning to their message. Yet those who died as believers with Christ no longer existed. Still, they preached that people should be baptized because the dead would come back to life. But the dead can't come back, so why do people get baptized as if they can come back to life?"

"But where was I before I was here?"

"Nowhere. You just didn't exist, and when you die you'll be equally and permanently nonexistent. The cemeteries are the best witnesses."

He was sure fired, but not spiritually.

"After Jesus died, the so-called apostles came to their senses a little, especially Paul and Peter, the real villains who invented Christianity. They revised Jesus' idea that you are saved by God for having faith alone. These two said the opposite. Faith by itself is a dead end if it doesn't motivate you to do good things."

"So which is it?" I asked, more confused than before.

"Am I wasting my time with you, Adam? Neither! Where was I? Yes, the source of all the world's problems is Jesus. He said so himself. 'I didn't come to bring peace but conflict. I came to turn a man against his father, the daughter against her mother . . .' And he did. He was a confused man who preached love and acceptance while negating his own mother, brothers, and sisters. One moment he blessed Peter, in another, made him Satan. How could he not be confused? He grew up in a house filled with deception. His mother concocted the most audacious story ever told—that she got pregnant by God. But she conceived her other four boys and two girls from her legitimate husband, Joseph. So Jesus assumed all sorts of omnipotent fantasies to the point of delusion, and he negated all paternal figures, the rabbis, government, teachers, and almost God himself. Jesus was clever enough to settle with the Son of God title."

"Did Joseph refuse to accept Jesus as his son?"

"No, no. You don't understand. Joseph swallowed the whole concoction and even agreed not to sleep with Mary until she gave birth to Jesus."

"But Joseph slept with Mary and had his own sons with her, right?"

"Yes, I told you, he had four sons with her."

"Did Joseph love his own sons more than he loved Jesus?"

"Adam, what is this orgiastic appetite for reality? Come on, you must ask better questions."

I was being embalmed alive in his crusade against Jesus.

⁓

I missed the Sağolan whom I knew. He had changed not only his name but also his disposition: he lost his optimism, the rhyme of his face. Now he was always in a somber mood, preoccupied with establishing an independent Armenia with the city of Erzurum as its capital.

He raised funds, gave concerts, and solicited for the Armenian cause. I gave him two gold coins. Then the Armenian uprising occurred in Anatolia and Istanbul. Under the leadership of two Armenian representatives from Erzurum, insurrectionists bombed a few banks in Istanbul and killed a number of civilians. All the bombers were arrested and sent on foot to the Ayash military camp outside Istanbul.

When mother heard that Sağolan was among the detainees, she immediately arranged for his release through Talāt Pasha's office. Mother said he returned, totally devastated, within ten days. Sağolan, in fact, became crazy, and within a few months he was admitted to the Hôpital de la Paix in Şişli. He spent years in and out of there under the care of Dr. Mazhar Osman.

During that interval, Sağolan continued to teach me, but his criticism of Christianity grew stronger; in fact, he began a sarcastic litany against all religions. "Jesus didn't suffer for us; we are suffering because of him," he declared. "All three children of Abraham are, in fact, misleading liars. Their religions are variations of the same untruth. The priests are all bribable. You don't believe me? Go see the mosaic in the south gallery at the Santa Sophia. There you'll witness King Constantine giving a bag full of money to Jesus."

I was devastated. Christianity obviously drew him into insanity. What do you expect? A woman sleeps with God, not just a sultan, and has a son who is ultimately deserted by his father. So he went crazy; so did people like Sağolan, who followed in his footsteps.

"Christianity is part paganism, part Judaism," he told me on another occasion. "Have you noticed that churches face east? That is because on judgment day, Jesus will come from the sunrise. In fact, Christians worship the sun. Don't you wonder why Easter, their most important religious day, remains linked to the Lunar calendar, the Jewish calendar, and tied to Passover?"

Stop, I said to myself. Don't doubt. Faith needs the faithful, those who speak the language of angels. Sağolan is only speaking the language of humans. He simply must be confused. I should be patient with him and never stop believing. He'll eventually see the light. I should never stop hoping. Jesus wants me never to give up.

~~~

I knew everything and nothing else.

After a while, I came to understand that I didn't live in a whorehouse but a spy house. I surmised, from the activity I observed, that *all* these people, working on such an elaborate scheme, couldn't simply be interested only in Jerusalem and facilitating immigration of Jews to Palestine as Manny said frequently; they were after something else. But what? Were we agents of the British? Manny seemed to have set that up—but wasn't that treachery against Sultan Reşat, who was pro-German?

Outside of my lessons, I had nothing to do, especially during late afternoons and evenings. I read whatever there was in the library, sometimes rereading books many times, books about spies like *Kim*, by Rudyard Kipling, and *Secret Agent*, by Joseph Conrad, or books like

Tancred, written by a baptized Christian Jew; *Rome and Jerusalem,* written by a German Jew; and *Auto Emancipation,* written by an English Jew. One day there'll be a book written by a Turkish Jew, I decided. But was I a Turkish Jew? How does one know who one is? Who was to say I wasn't a Christian since I still read from the New Testament and longed for Jesus' friendship? Each day I recorded my thoughts, my discussions with Chevalier D'Artagnan (my childhood imaginary friend), and the conversations of those I eavesdropped on in my journal. I became very skilled at listening, and I decided to become a spy myself. Jesus said I should be as cunning as a snake.

I knew our living quarters better than anyone else with the exception of Ahmed Agha because people who worked in the harem weren't allowed in the *selâmlık* and vice versa. I was the only one who had lived in both quarters, though sequentially. I knew that on the first and second floors of both the *selâmlık* and the harem, four small closets were aligned back to back and on top of each other. For the best spying, all I had to do was remove small pieces of the partitions in the closets, making sure to replace the bits in a nonpermanent fashion. I also knew I had to make any adjustments invisible to the occupants of the rooms and the housekeepers. How difficult could that be? After all, the Count of Monte Cristo had dug a hole one meter deep through a stone wall to escape his prison.

Actually, my project turned out to be very difficult. I couldn't remove any part of the partitions, let alone cleverly replace them. I was a little demoralized, but I also realized that I could easily do without the spy holes. After all I wasn't trying to escape; all I wanted to do was overhear. I didn't need to see who was in the harem because only my mother and father were there. I could easily hear all the conversations by sitting in the nearest closet. As for the *selâmlık,* mostly I was allowed to come and go as I pleased, but during those rare times when I wasn't welcome to stay in the meeting room, I could easily stick my head in for a few seconds to see who was there if I couldn't identify them by their voices.

"You see, the eyes are better witnesses than the ears."

I was transformed into a gigantic ear, except I couldn't figure out for whom I would be spying. I knew on whom to spy. Then it became obvious: I should be spying for D'Artagnan, who, in return, would know where to pass the information. Or maybe I'd do it for Mademoiselle Blanche, and she, in return, might share some of her secrets with me.

⌒

Jabotinsky and Uncle Manny were, as usual, early arrivals; a little later, Rabbi Nahum joined them. I sat in my usual corner in the *selâmlık* and pricked up my ears.

"You feel powerless, you see, because you hanker for the flesh pots of Turkey, the same way that our ancestors did in Egypt," Jabotinsky accused Uncle Manny.

"And you," he launched onto Rabbi Nahum. "You exalt in that powerlessness in a person, my dear rabbi, because you purport that is what makes him the suffering servant of the Lord."

The rabbi sounded exasperated: "I don't want the disruption of the Ottoman order. For one thing, the Turks have been very good to us, even before the expulsion from Spain. Great-grandchildren of Greek-speaking Romaniote Jews can tell you how life for Byzantine Jewry changed for the better with the Ottoman conquest of Constantinople. For another, without the Ottomans, the presumed Israeli state would be adrift in a sea of Arab nations."

"Even in a country as tolerant as Turkey, anti-Semitism can never be eradicated," said Jabotinsky. "They hate us."

"If the Jews do not shed their particularism, they will never become genuine citizens of the country," replied the rabbi. "If Jews spoke fluent Turkish and worked in good faith for the well-being of the Ottoman government, do you believe that prejudice would still perpetuate?"

"Yes, it would. If we assimilated, we would be in an even worse position. Real assimilation would mean the end of the Jewish people. It is already happening in France and in America and even a little bit here. How Jewish are you, Manny? You even observe Ramadan."

"Observe Ramadan?" Manny laughed, patting his abdomen, "I fast—kind of—all year round. But I also think it's in bad taste to eat or drink in front of Muslim friends and colleagues during their holy month."

"Fine, fine," said Jabotinsky, "can you get your Muslim friend Vahdettin to request that the sultan recognize him as an alternate crown prince?"

"First of all, there is no such a thing," Manny replied. "Second, why create a situation that will fuel people's suspicions when . . . I mean if something happens to Crown Prince Yusuf Izzettin? Everyone would believe Vahdettin was behind it."

The rabbi looked confused. "Gentlemen, what are we talking about exactly? Sultan Reşat is alive, Crown Prince Yusuf Izzettin is alive; why are we talking about Vahdettin's succession to the throne? Furthermore, he said himself that he has neither the interest nor the disposition for it."

They talk, they talk, and nothing ever happens here. They eat, they drink, and they talk more; they eat and drink more, and they talk. Each has a set of ideas and never diverges from them. They all try to convert each other to their own views. It never happens. They only get louder and more emotional but say exactly the same things over and over again.

How come I have no point of view about Palestine, the Ottoman Empire, or even ruling the empire? I just want to be the sultan and live in the Yıldız Palace. That'll make my mother the Valide sultan. She'll protect me with all her schemings.

⌇

"Mademoiselle Blanche, I think Jabotinsky is going to kill Sultan Reşat and Crown Prince Yusuf Izzettin."

Mademoiselle Blanche burst into laughter.

"Adam, what a phantasmagoric story. Jabotinsky couldn't even get close to either of them to talk with, much less kill them. You see, *mon chou*, you have to differentiate your wishes from reality. Otherwise you'll become like your music teacher. Think about becoming a fine gentleman, an educated, sophisticated young man with much potential. You may even be appointed the ambassador to France. What about that? And you'll hire me as your assistant. Hmm?"

Hire her as an assistant? I'll marry her.

⌇

The Zionists' overbearing rhetoric was getting a little too repetitive for me. I decided to extend my spying activities beyond the harem and *selâmlık*, paying special attention to Mademoiselle Blanche's bedroom.

To get there, I had to shimmy through a crawl space beneath the floor. This was no easy job. The first day I tried it, I held my breath as I maneuvered through dirt, insects, and dead mice. I overheard Mademoiselle making the same noises I had heard my mother make when Vahdettin was with her. "Ah—aahh, uf—w—ufuf—ah." Except she was alone.

I must have been breathing hard, and old dirt and dust, mixed with mouse and rat excrement, nearly clogged my nostrils. Oh my God, I thought. Please don't let me sneeze. I squeezed my nose as hard as I could and held my breath. No chance. I sneezed so hard I hit my head on the top of my hiding spot (Mademoiselle's bedroom floor). It hurt so much that I yelled.

"Adam?" Mademoiselle called out, obviously startled. "Are you all right? Come out, immediately."

"I don't know how to come out at this end." I sneezed again, this time holding my head down.

"Well, follow that old pipe; it will get you to the storage area next to the kitchen."

I wondered how she could have known that. Of course! She was spying for France!

I kept crawling, using the pipe as a guide. Suddenly, the space enlarged to a gigantic room full of sacks of grain, potatoes, sugar, ginger, and coal; huge pickle barrels; jars of jam, honey, and poppies; and cans of *halvah*. Mademoiselle Blanche stood near a door that opened to the kitchen. Her white complexion was even whiter. Once I climbed out, she took me by my ear and walked me to her room, closing the doors behind us. I was not only embarrassed but also scared. I knew that my mother would kill me. Still holding me by the ear, Mademoiselle dragged me to her bathroom. I kept sneezing.

"Look at your face," she said, pushing me toward the mirror. "See if you can recognize yourself."

I was covered from head to toe in soot.

"How are you going to get back to the *selâmlık* in these clothes? Take them off and get into the tub. If you're going to behave like a child, then I'm going to treat you like one. Take off, off, off all your clothes, underwear too," she commanded. "I'll have a fresh pair brought to the kitchen."

I had a sense of comforting familiarity with her. In my first seven years, she washed and dressed me, put me to bed, told me stories, and sang me lullabies. I let her wash me, including my genitals. "Remember, your body is your temple, treat it accordingly." Her body was my temple.

◡◠◡

"Crown Prince Yusuf Izzettin Commits Suicide" was in all the newspaper headlines. I got scared and was also intrigued that mother seemed nonplussed at the news. In the article that followed, we read that he was found in the bathtub of his house at Hekimbaşı Farm in Çamlıca on the Bosporus. Both wrists were cut deeply, almost severing his hands. Apparently, exactly the same thing had happened to his grandfather, who was once a sultan. While visiting my mother that day, Dr. Numan volunteered his medical opinion that no one could have cut both his wrists to that degree. My mother vehemently objected.

"Of course you can, all you need is a sharp knife. He was a hashish addict and lunatic enough to amputate his own head, not only his hands. Did you ever see him? He used to show up on some occasions with those frightened eyes, which he covered with dark glasses, even when he was inside. It took him five whole minutes to say 'Thank you, I am fine.' It was painful to watch him walk around the room—he tried not to step on any lines in the floor. The last few years he routinely accused his own staff of poisoning him, and those so-called Karlsbad cures turned out to be nothing more than drug accessory shopping trips."

What was going on here? Why would a crown prince kill himself? And why was mother so emotionally asserting her view against that of our doctor. They killed him. I am sure.

〜〜

"Mademoiselle Blanche, didn't I tell you Jabotinsky was going to kill Crown Prince Izzettin?"

Mademoiselle Blanche was perplexed. "It is just a coincidence. You read the story, Adam. He suicided. No one kills another person by cutting his wrists. They put a knife in his heart."

Was she stupid?

"You told me that Jabotinsky couldn't get close to him, right? How could he put a knife in the prince's heart? No, they poisoned him first by bribing one of his eunuchs, and then they cut his wrists. You see, only when a person is already dead or in a coma can you cut both of his wrists."

She was looking at me curiously.

"What an imagination! You could write detective stories. But Adam, I wouldn't go around talking about your theory as-to how the prince died if I were you. You heard your mother's reaction to Dr. Numan. And he was qualified to make some inferences."

Why was she not impressed with my figuring all that out?

That night in the *selâmlık*, to my surprise, the gang didn't even discuss the matter. What should I make of it? After all, the crown prince of the empire was dead. Weren't they hoping for this? Vahdettin, my father, their man, was now the crown prince and one step closer to the throne. Were they speaking in codes?

"I heard from Mademoiselle Blanche that you fell into the milk barrel," Ahmed Agha said, smiling mischievously. "She asked me to bring a new set of everything, including shoes. The same thing happened to me when I was your age. I didn't have anyone to pull me out, though. As a matter of fact, my stepmother jumped in with me. So my father crushed my testicles by twisting them with pliers, and he didn't offer me any hashish. Afterwards he sold me to a slave trader, an Italian Jew who brought me here ten years ago. I'm most grateful to him."

I hiccupped. "You're just trying to scare me. I know Negroes are castrated with clean knives. And Jews don't trade in slaves."

"Well, you're wrong, Adam *Effendi*," he replied. "Jews are the main slave traders. They bring Circassian women to Arab countries and take back Negroes. I know because I lived through it. I saw beautiful, young, blue-eyed white women sold for one hundred gold coins each. In return the slavers bought one hundred Negroes, at one gold coin each. The castrated *Zenci* were worth two gold coins and used as eunuchs in the Middle East."

I was having severe pain in my testicles and felt faint and nauseated. I lay down. "What happened to their penises?" I managed to ask.

"They don't cut the penises, but from then on they are only useful for peeing." Ahmed Agha smiled contentedly. "Oh, dear, you look sick. Would you like me to carry you to your room?"

"Yes, thank you," I said, holding my stomach.

Ahmed Agha carried me away and gently laid me down on the couch, putting a pillow under my head.

"Listen, I am sorry, I didn't mean to frighten you. But 'if you don't eat raw, you won't have a bellyache.' That means, there are consequences for one's behavior. What have you done anyway? Did you poke

Mademoiselle Blanche? You can tell me. I didn't see your old clothes, were they bloodied? What happened?"

The more Ahmed Agha insisted, the more I recoiled.

"Okay, let me ask you a question, are you having wet dreams?"

"No."

"Do you know what I am talking about? Do you wake up in the middle of the night with your underpants and bed wet? And I don't mean peeing. A creamy stuff."

"No."

"Never? You are almost fifteen years-old."

"Never."

"Do you play thirty-one?"

"Thirty-one?"

"I guess you don't know. Well, of course, who was going to teach you? When you pull thirty one times on your penis, a sticky, creamy stuff will come rushing out, and you'll feel incredibly good. Much better than anything you've ever felt in your life. You should try it sometime. The bathtub is a good place to do it." Ahmed Agha never went to any school or read any book, but somehow he knew the essence of everything innately. I wondered how he reconciled the "eunuchness" of his body with the power of his mind.

⌇

I woke up in the middle of the night with an excruciating pain in my lower abdomen. Ahmed Agha brought me a hot-water bottle and gave me a little hashish. It helped for a couple of hours, until I got up to urinate. I couldn't, but my bladder felt as if it were bursting. Ahmed Agha called my mother, and she looked frightened when she arrived. "Get Dr. Numan or Dr. Gunzberg," she ordered, and she sat next to me.

"*Anne*—Mother, I think I am dying. I can't pee."

"No, no, my love," she tried to reassure me. "The doctor will be here soon, and you'll be fine. Take a little bit more hashish; you look exhausted."

The crotch of my pajama bottoms was bloodstained. The doctor turned me over and put his finger in my rectum. "What are you doing?" I shrieked. He turned me back, took my penis into my palm, and squeezed. The pain shot right up from my penis to the roots of my hair.

"There is a little kidney stone," the doctor explained, "stuck in his penis. The only thing we can do is try to dilate his urethra and wait. I may have to empty his bladder with an abdominal syringe. Wrap hot towels around his penis, and when the towels begin to cool, change them."

It seemed all house protocols were abandoned—everyone, men and women, were gathered around my bed as I lay there totally exposed.

"Just wait?" my mother asked nervously. "Couldn't you try fishing the stone out?"

"No," the doctor replied. "The only other treatment I know of is to try suctioning the stone out. I've seen it done . . . once."

"Okay then," mother said, "suction it out. Do you have a suction machine with you?"

"Well, there is no such machine. Someone has to do it. In the case I observed, the mother did it."

"Now, now doctor."

Why were all these people laughing? The hashish clouded my mind; I couldn't focus my eyes. Faces overlapped, words jumbled, movements slowed. Someone's head settled against my stomach. Suddenly the room went silent; no one spoke or laughed. Something warm, wet, and smooth tugged softly at my penis, going down over it again and again. The pain seemed to subside into the background, and I had a delicious shuddering sensation of release where, just moments ago, it hurt. I was startled back to reality by the sound of applause ringing around the room. I opened my eyes to see women hugging each other, dancing about, and congratulating one another. I was disappointed. I wanted the wonderful sensation to go on forever.

"Oh God," I heard my mother's voice, "he is drowning in his urine. Ahmed Agha, take him into the bathroom. Let's clean him up. Thank you so much Mademoiselle Blanche. I will never forget the generosity of your soul."

I heard a lot of little giggles as I was taken away.

Some people, including Vahdettin's eunuch, occasionally called me "midget." Even my mother scolded me using that word. I hated that. I wondered if I was just short or if I was also cowardly. And why was it that I was so short? Mademoiselle Blanche said my male hormones hadn't kicked in yet and that as soon as they did, I'd be as tall as everyone else. Ahmed Agha kept suggesting that I would get taller if I thought of women's bodies and kept masturbating.

"Adam *Effendi*, how is it going, the thirty-one?" Ahmed Agha asked.

"It hurts and nothing comes out."

"Well, maybe you don't know how to do it. If you use spit or soap or olive oil to lubricate when you rub, it won't hurt. It's better to use olive oil than soap because soap can get into the little hole, and afterwards, when you urinate, it hurts like hell. Look, would you like me to show you how it's done?"

"I suppose so."

"Okay, off to the bathroom. I'll join you in a few moments."

As I waited in the bathroom, I wished I had never started this whole sex thing. Ahmed Agha soon showed up carrying a bottle of olive oil in one hand and a French magazine in the other.

"Take out your penis. Oh come on, you don't have to worry. I've been seeing your private parts since you were born. Come on, sit here. Okay now, look at these actresses' pictures and imagine what they look like underneath their swimsuits. Imagine their breasts and think of Mademoiselle Blanche's body, too."

"Ahmed Agha, I don't want olive oil," I groaned.

"Well, do you want to try with spit? Spit in my palm. Come on, you can do better than that. Good. Okay, now look at the pictures and visualize Mademoiselle Blanche's ass."

Ahmed Agha fondled my penis, stroking it back and forth. "Spit more in my hand."

I couldn't; my mouth was totally dry. Ahmed Agha looked despairing, spit on his palm, and kept going. Meanwhile, instead of becoming erect, my penis shrank until it almost disappeared into my abdomen.

"What's the matter?" Ahmed Agha asked, discouraged.

"Ahmed Agha, you don't like boys, do you?" I managed to ask. "Once you said, 'The boy's penis is the man's *Tesbih* [bead-string]. Don't let anyone else play with your penis.'"

Ahmed Agha replied calmly, "Well, I am not a pederast. But I see why you weren't really relaxing or enjoying the experience. Maybe we should stop for now. If you like we can try again some other time. Perhaps we can arrange for a woman to teach you. Maybe that will be easier on you."

"But Agha, Jesus says: If you have illicit sex you'll never inherit the kingdom."

"Jesus? Sex is the kingdom," he tersely replied.

I quickly pulled up my underwear, retreated to my room, and closed the doors. The thought of remaining short and being called "midget" all my life was very depressing. Then I began to wonder which woman Ahmed Agha had in mind. Definitely female spit was what I needed.

∼

The mood in the *selāmlık* was very down. The whole influential Jewish contingency was present.

"Thanks for coming on such short notice," began Manny. "I have bad news, from all the newspapers' reporters in the field. Djemal Pasha has ordered the evacuation of the Jews from Jaffa, Haifa, Acre, Beirut, and Jerusalem. Over 10,000 Jews are being forced to travel on foot toward the Syrian hinterland. All their possessions were appropriated. Jewish homes have been sacked. Thefts and extortions are reported to be rampant."

"Thousands of Jews are being forced into the Syrian desert on foot?" asked Rabbi Nahum. "This is an extremely serious accusation against our own government. It is unbelievable that Talāt, as the grand vizier, would allow it to happen."

"It's the Sultan Reşat, not Talāt, who is behind this nationalistic movement," explained Manny. "Talāt tried to remove Djemal from Palestine, but the sultan refused to give the order. In fact, we have information from a very reliable source that next week the sultan is planning to remove Talāt as grand vizier and replace him with Djemal."

"Then, we have no choice?" asked Jabotinsky.

Rabbi Nahum got up, agitated: "May God have mercy on us all."

As the rabbi left, an uneasy silence filled the room.

Manny said, "Vladimir, are you sure that your news reporters aren't exaggerating?" He looked as if he knew they were.

"*The battle of 1571 in the Gulf of Leganto became famous because of one fighter on the Christian flagship: Miguel de Cervantes. Most of the Christians were killed trying to board the Turkish fleet. Cervantes escaped death by converting to Islam on the spot. After he was released, he kept writing and bragging even more than his famous character, Don Quixote, about how valiant a soldier he was and how he triumphed over the Turks. The battle itself was just another skirmish on the Mediterranean, but the difference was there was a writer present.*

"*You see, Adam, 'The tongue is longer than the arm.'* "

❧

"Mademoiselle Blanche, I heard it last night. Jabotinsky is going to have Sultan Reşat killed. Please don't look as if I am making this all up. I am telling you, they are going to kill the sultan."

"Adam, you are becoming paranoid. Keep thinking like this, and you'll end up in an insane asylum, like Monsieur Soghoman."

This time she looked utterly unamused; she spoke sternly with a flavor of a threat. I wondered whether she was also a part of the plot. Why else would she be spending her life with us?

"Adam, you are not listening. You are on a slippery slope; nothing good comes out of these crazy thoughts except inflaming your young mind. Stop it. You know I am talking for your own good."

Was she? Her eyes were scaldingly cold.

❧

I've been having agonizing pain in my groin for the past two weeks. I guess I'm passing another stone. Dr. Numan doesn't think so, but as a precaution he has restricted my diet, eliminating halvah, cheese, milk, and yogurt, but it's to no avail—the pain remains. Ahmed Agha keeps bringing me hashish. I stayed in bed most of the time, hot-water bottles held to my side. I got up only to spy. Today, after examining me, the doctor went to see my mother. I positioned myself in the spying closet.

"I think Adam is suffering from neurasthenia, *Hanım Effendi*," Dr. Numan pronounced to my mother.

"What do you mean? Isn't that some kind of woman's craziness?" asked my mother.

"Well, it's a sort of a weakening of the nerves. It affects mostly women, it's true, but it is not uncommon in boys during puberty. I also think Adam is a little too isolated. Aloneness at his age inflames the brain, which, if left unattended, may cause schizophrenia. I'm especially concerned by the fact that he is taking so much hashish and looks totally unaffected by it. You should reconsider sending him to a French boarding school. Anyhow, I'll stop by again on Thursday. Instruct Ahmed Agha to keep checking Adam's urine. If he sees any blood in it, let me know immediately."

After the doctor walked out, Ahmed Agha, who was present during the conversation, approached my mother. *"Hanım Effendi?"*

My mother glanced her consent for him to continue.

"Adam is not suffering from craziness; he suffers from innocence," he explained.

"I know what is wrong with him. He misses Mademoiselle Blanche."

"What do you mean, Ahmed Agha? He sees her every day."

"He doesn't miss seeing her. You, uhmm, know what I, err, mean."

"No, I don't," my mother replied tersely.

A rush of heat came over me as I sat in the closet, and I broke into a sweat. I guessed the neurosis wasn't a legitimate suffering.

"Well, you know . . . he misses how, ah . . remember the first time he had to pass a stone? He did it with . . . ah . . . you know, her help."

My mother sounded both amazed and amused. "Ahmed Agha, are you insinuating that he wants her to? Ah—you're out of your mind! No, let me say this quickly. Are you trying to tell me that he's been malingering with a kidney stone these last fifteen days just to get Mademoiselle Blanche to . . . well . . . suck his little penis? I've never heard such a devious and disgusting thing in my life. Well, that isn't exactly true. I have heard worse. But where does that midget get such a twisted mind? Oh, never mind. I know that, too."

I always felt that Mother had a tender contempt for me. Maybe I was responsible for her failure to become the Valide sultan like her father wanted or for her failure to get me legitimized. How would I ever be able to look into her eyes again?

"Ahmed Agha, how on earth did you come up with such an idea when the famous Dr. Numan threw up his hands and identified him as insane?"

"Well, *Hanım Effendi*. I don't believe that he is really in pain. You see, he hasn't been taking the hashish I bring him. He's been putting it away in his cabinet. He isn't even trying to hide it that well."

Oh, how humiliating all this was. I hoped they'd never tell Mademoiselle.

My mother mused, "Ahmed Agha I must say, you're a smart man. Thank God you have no education, or you would be incorrigible. Now, I want you to find out, gently, if that is what he wants, needs. If it is, then you two figure out something. But it cannot be with Mademoiselle Blanche; she is his teacher."

"Yes, *Hanım Effendi*. With your permission I'll go now."

I wanted to run away, never to be seen again. But I couldn't move. I also noticed I was no longer in pain. I needed to find some dignified way to get out of this. I should get rid of all that hashish. Then a brainstorm—ah, of course, I'd have them find some blood in my urine pot.

That night, I took a razor blade and pressed it against my wrist—it was going to hurt. However, the few drops of blood from my finger might not even show, so I closed my eyes and, firmly holding the razor in my left hand, forced it into my right wrist. I began to bleed a little. I pressed harder; it felt as if I was cutting a tough meat. Still not much blood, except my little finger went numb. The knife would not go any further. I think I hit bone. I began moving the knife from side to side, like a bow on a violin. There was pain, but it was a strangely pleasant pain. Then all of a sudden, the blood gushed. The yellow liquid in the basin turned reddish in no time. That was plenty, but the bleeding wouldn't stop. I put my hand on the wound, but blood still oozed out, and the moment I relieved the pressure, blood pulsed out, as if pumped. I got panicky. The contents of the basin were turning almost completely red and were at the point of overflowing. I felt dizzy. I lay down, still pressing on my wrist, but my hand was getting weaker. I'm going to bleed to death, I thought. I left my room, crossing the *selāmlık*. I heard some noises in the distance. I couldn't keep my hand pressed on the wound. I let go. There is no way a person can cut deeply both his wrists, I thought. The crown prince was definitely murdered. I must have fainted. I don't know how much time passed, but I woke up to my mother's voice:

"Why would he want to kill himself, doctor?"

"Well, it isn't all that uncommon in adolescence; symptoms tend to be miscarried communication. He might be imitating the late Crown Prince Yusuf Izzettin. On the other hand, we might be dealing with schizophrenia. He has too many unrelated neurotic symptoms, like disabling headaches, chronic indigestion and stomach pain, voyeurism, stunted physical stature, lack of sexual maturity, and now self-mutilation—a type of pan-neuroses. As to spitting out of tomato seeds, I don't know what to make of it."

"Oh my God, my poor child," my mother lamented. "It's all my fault. Vahdettin was right, I shouldn't have had a child under the circumstances."

I had a familiar sinking feeling in my stomach. I knew she regretted having me.

"There is a Jewish doctor in Vienna who is a world-renowned expert on these conditions. If you send Adam abroad for an education, he could also get psychoanalyzed."

"Freud's Jewish disease? I thought that had something to do with boys being in love with their mothers? Do you think Adam is suffering from that?" mother asked.

"Honestly, I don't know. It may be more than that. You know, a number of people in the ruling class went to visit Freud. He even treated Herzl's children."

Mother was aghast: "Herzl's kids? His daughter is a drug addict, and his son suicided. You must be kidding! Anyhow, there is no way Vahdettin would allow him to go to Vienna. He doesn't even permit him to go downtown. Are there no specialists in Istanbul with whom we could consult?"

"There is a young doctor trained in Germany—Mazhar Osman—you know him; he is the one taking care of Soghoman at the Hôpital de la Paix. People swear by him."

"Oh, come on. Isn't Soghoman still as much of a lunatic as ever?"

"Well, there are no other choices. In the meantime, Adam has to resume his outdoor activities, riding and walking and keep taking the palace pink juice. There's to be no more taking hashish, no more collecting urine, no more staying in bed or even in his room. Can he swim?" the doctor inquired.

"Oh yes, he swims in the Bosporus. In some ways he is so brave, in others he is a very scared boy. Is that what you mean by schizophrenia?"

"Yes, in schizophrenia there is a personality split. His talking to himself and his D'Artagnan; his fears about being assassinated and the stories he tells Mademoiselle Blanche about Zionist plots, which he is willing to share only with Mademoiselle Blanche, border on paranoia; curious, isn't it? She confessed his confidences under duress, but I think she believes him. Maybe you should think about sending her away."

"One night in 1788, the incompetent Emperor Joseph of Austria, after crossing the Danube, mistook a force of his own for the Turks, and his soldiers started firing blindly in all directions. In the light of daybreak, they realized that they had been firing at themselves, and thousands lay dead or dying. The emperor raised the white flag and surrendered to himself.

"You see, Adam, 'Any return from losing is a gain.' "

I must become sane fast.

~~~

Ahmed Agha pulled back the curtains roughly. "Good morning, Adam *Effendi*. It's almost nine o'clock. Why aren't you up? Are we still suicidal or just embarrassed by a scheme gone awry?"

"I'm not talking to you anymore. I'm not suicidal or embarrassed. Everybody thinks that I'm crazy. Well, you're wrong. That *thing* was just an accident, not a scheme."

"A scheme turned accident?"

He was such a weasel.

"Get up, we're going to swim in the Bosporus before your classes—doctor's orders."

Was it my imagination, or did I hear glee in that weasel's voice?

That day I asked Rabbi Nahum how one knew whether one was crazy. He said he wasn't really expert on the subject. But he said that one is most likely crazy if one goes out at night all by oneself, hangs around cemeteries, and walks about aimlessly.

"Do you think Sağolan did all that . . . walking around aimlessly?" I asked.

"Well, your music teacher was wandering aimlessly in the world; he was single, which is never good for one's nerves. He checked into a monastery to get help, not really to be a monk. There, he became isolated and confused. Such a life inflames the vulnerable mind."

I know I am not crazy. Definitely not paranoid. The schemes in our house are real. Oh Mademoiselle Blanche! How could you betray me even under torture? Now I feel really alone and confused. On the other hand, wasn't Jesus betrayed by Peter, whom he loved the most?

~~~

During the following six months, Dr. Mazhar Osman came to our house to treat me, which consisted of his inquiring about every minor detail of my life. I spoke; he wrote down. He asked question after question, encouraging me to describe how I felt, what I thought, and why I thought so. Of course, I said nothing about the killings going on. Let him find out for himself. On every visit he kept repeating the same questions:

Did I think I was the son of God?

Did I think that there were people trying to poison me?

Did I really see and speak with Chevalier D'Artagnan?

Did I think that my mother was a spy for the Zionists?

The answer to all these questions was the same: "Of course not. That is ridiculous. I am not *that* crazy, doctor."

After these interchanges, he stared at me and said, "Well, at least you know what is crazy and what is not." A few times I wasn't all that sure. Could I be fooling a famous psychiatrist?

"If you want to be cured, forget about your body and get interested in someone else's body. Do you know what I mean?" Doctor Osman's eyes stared at me, unblinking: "You were very close friends with Komitas, weren't you? You must miss him. You call him Sağolan, right?"

"Yes, how is he?"

He replied briefly to my question: "Doing well, but we may be sending him to France for special care."

Did that mean I should get well or what? What am I supposed to be getting "well" from? Am I supposed to deny that Prince Izzettin was killed or that Jabotinsky was planning to kill the Sultan Reşat or even that my own father is going to poison me and have my wrists cut to protect his Muslim son? Would denying this make me well, or do I really have to believe what I say?

Doctor Osman stared at me again for a long time, then got up, and as he left, he said, "Maybe you cannot bear too much reality for now."

But what was the reality? Mademoiselle Blanche said Jesus means "He who saves." I knelt and repeated ten times, "Blessed is the one who comes in the name of the Lord." Mademoiselle Blanche said that is the best prayer to recruit Jesus.

～

Uncle Manny made an urgent visit to my mother in the middle of the night and announced Sultan Reşat's death. They hugged each other. I knew it! I knew it! I hung around behind the door to my mother's room and listened to them discuss it.

"Well?" my mother said.

"No one on the Turkish side gave a damn whether Sultan Reşat was dead or alive. The Germans are quite happy that Vahdettin will ascend to the throne; they think he is a more ambitious partner and will put up a better fight against the Allies. The Allies think that they have him in their pocket," answered Manny.

"The grand vizier held a war council with his commanders, discussing how to take over Vienna. Ibrahim, the pasha of Buda, suggested a step-by-step encroachment instead of a full-frontal attack on the city. He told the fable of a king who placed a pile of gold in the center of a carpet, then offered it to any man who could take it without treading on the carpet. The winner was the one who rolled up the carpet from the edge, until he was able to grab the gold.

"You see, Adam, 'Smart people, not strong people, will inherit the world.' "

Then I thought, I had a shot. But how smart was I really?

∼∽

The following morning, I awoke to a frenzy of celebration. People gathered in front of the house and hugged and kissed each other. Donizetti's *Ottoman March* blared from the gramophone. Ahmed Agha shot his tiny Browning into the air. I walked outside. Mademoiselle Blanche wrapped her arms around me, and I realized with a mixture of joy and disappointment that she still considered me a boy.

"Sultan Reşat is dead," she cried joyously. "Our Vahdettin Bey will be the next sultan."

"Why should I care then if he becomes the sultan? Only Ertuğrul will benefit from it. He will be the king. What is in it for me?"

"Adam, you are not born to be pleased, but saved. Don't you remember what Jesus said: 'The Kingdom of God is within you.' Furthermore, can you not see how fortunate that is for your mother?"

"Sultans used to order strangulation with a bowstring of their own brothers, unless they were little sacred beings—a little crazy, to prevent conflict over succession. In 1590, Mehmed III, after his ascension to the throne, had his nineteen brothers strangled by mutes, and he also ordered his brothers' pregnant women sewn up in sacks and thrown into the Bosporus. Such fratricide is condoned in the Qur'an: 'Kill them wheresoever you find them, even if they offer peace, as they may return to sedition and subvert therein.'

"You see, Adam, 'Assassination is preferable to sedition.' "

This must be the time for the sultan to have me killed to protect Ertuğrul, as I always knew he would. But then will that mean that I am his son after all?

⌇

Abandoning all my hopes brought me no freedom.

Two weeks passed. Father, now the sultan, never showed up for a visit. Two weeks turned to two months. I read in the newspapers about his coronation, his receiving Omer's sword, his arresting Young Turks, and his going to his brother ex-sultan Abdulhamid's funeral.

Meanwhile, I began spending time with our mechanic and chauffeur, Abbas, who was different from all other people I knew. He said what he meant; what he meant, he said. I never doubted his sincerity or loyalty. He laughed, he cried, he got angry so comfortably.

Dr. Osman always asked me about my feelings. How did I feel about something? I saw others feel, especially Mademoiselle Blanche and Abbas. I only had *felt thoughts*. I had linguistic feelings. I rarely cried. Other than that, I had no other *felt reference*. Whenever I talked about myself, I spoke about what I did. The doctor would stop me and say, "No, no, tell me how you felt." He accused me of emotional self-continence and using language to protect myself from feeling. Actually I was simply an emotional illiterate. But we had no books to read on emotion. So I wrote my own. Sad: when I feel like not getting out of bed, not having the desire to eat halvah, not wanting to talk. Anxious: when I feel a pit in my stomach, eating a lot of everything, talking a lot but not being able to listen. Happy: not being sad or anxious.

⌇

Abbas could dismantle a whole car engine, then reassemble it. He could quickly figure out what was wrong with a car and fix it with highly improvised parts (since genuine Mercedes parts were hard to obtain). Abbas and I used to play at troubleshooting: he would intentionally disrupt the car's function, and I was to figure out the cause and correct it.

Like me, Abbas didn't have many friends around the compound. Abbas was from Hasankale of Erzurum, the most suspect of all cities for being populated with Kurds. He resented the Kurd title that people gave him and tried at every opportunity to explain that he wasn't a Kurd but a Mamluk, from the Hittite tribe. I didn't care one way or the other. I just liked him.

Both of us liked to bet. Winning versus losing bets were limited to information about Mademoiselle Blanche. He drove her to the French consulate on Saturdays and all Christian holidays for social gatherings, parties, and frequently to various other places during weekdays for shopping and sightseeing. He accompanied her during her forays into the covered bazaar, translating her bizarre Turkish to an understandable one for the merchants and bargaining on her behalf. The task shouldn't have been too difficult because in the covered bazaar they only went to the Kilim auctions. She picked; he bid.

I was interested in two specific pieces of information. First, was she a spy of the French government? I had to ask that question very circumspectly to avoid creating unnecessary suspicion and hurting her. Second, did she whisper sweet things in his ear? If so, what?

Abbas talked about the whispers in his heart and soul, which were his memories and yearnings for his hometown, Hasankale. I found his stories so intriguing that I wished I were Abbas or that I could live in Hasankale. The town sounded magical, and after hearing so much about the place, I felt I knew it.

Hasankale was a small village. It leaned against a mountain and spread down a valley that was crossed by a tributary to the Euphrates River, the Karasu River. On the mountaintop was a deserted castle, in ruins.

In the spring, the Karasu River was wide and deep, with whirling riptides, and thus it was quite dangerous. Abbas amused himself with the other children, wrestling, swimming in the river, and exploring the old castle.

One day while exploring, the children discovered a path hidden at the bottom of the mountain that led inside the castle. The children also found a path from the castle to a cave on the otherwise inaccessible granite south face of the mountain.

Abbas then told me a mystical story about jumping from the cave. Hasankale's most revered religious leader, Ibrahim Hakkı Hazretleri, had many sons; the youngest, Molla Şakir, was a steady, thoughtful, hardworking, obedient boy, and the oldest, Molla Fehim, was a *çeng çalan* (harpist), a slightly lazy, drunken man known as "*Karada gezici, denizde yüzücü*" (walked the land, swam the sea). Because of his imperfections, Fehim was despised by many, especially by his brother. One day, Ibrahim Hakkı took a walk with Şakir to the castle, and they stood at the cave's edge. Şakir asked his father if the time had come for enlightenment and, if so, how would he, Şakir, join the angels.

Ibrahim Hakkı shook his head yes. It was time. He ordered, "Jump!"

With that, hundreds of white pigeons appeared, hovering above them.

"Jump!" Ibrahim Hakkı repeated.

But Şakir looked down the deep granite cliff and hesitated. Suddenly, Fehim, who had followed them to the cave, appeared and asked, "Shall I, father?"

"Go, my son."

With that, Fehim jumped from the lip of the cave into the midst of the pigeons, which spread their wings like a white carpet and caught him. In a shout of purest joy, they all flew away. After Fehim disappeared into the clouds, Şakir, still shaking with fear, wondered how such a drunkard could join the angels. His father replied, "Don't look down on the downtrodden. There are ruins with hidden treasures."

When the time comes, I thought, maybe Ertuğrul won't be able to jump into being the sultan and I will.

~~~

One day, father, now the sultan, accompanied by a large contingent of guards wearing bright red uniforms and white toques with black trim, soldiers, and Agas—companions of the sultan in different services—arrived in a four-horse-driven magnificent but noisy palace carriage. He was resplendent in a long, jeweled, fur kaftan. He carried a sword decorated with emeralds and the sultanate's insignia and looked big and even handsome. As he stepped from the royal carriage, a few of our staff tried to kiss the tail of his scarf, but they weren't allowed to get close to him. He didn't even notice me. "You are condemned to hell," I said under my breath (Jesus says so if you allow yourself to act arrogantly). He went right to the house. His eunuch carried a large package covered by a rug.

He hurriedly went to the harem. My father's voice had a dark tone.

"Don't give me the silent treatment, woman. You're never satisfied unless you get everything you want."

"But, you're the sultan now," my mother spoke plaintively, "the lord of the time and age, the caliph of Islam, the lord of Mecca and Medina, Baghdad, Damascus, Egypt, Yemen, and Arabia. I've been your loyal servant for eighteen years, you never recognized Adam. And this golden table, what is this supposed to mean? Are you trying to emulate Sultan Selim by his table, his naked face, and his quirky sexual interests?"

"It is a gift." He must have started eating. "I told you not to put in too much hashish. I don't like the taste. It gives me indigestion."

"Everything gives you indigestion," she retorted. "Do you realize whenever you are here you have indigestion?"

"That's because you are always peddling something, woman. Now you are enmeshed in the totally inappropriate dream of Adam being recognized as a *shehzade* of the sultanate. Manny told me about it. I cannot do this. I cannot endanger Ertuğrul's life. Don't look so innocently surprised. If there were any chance of Adam's becoming sultan, you wouldn't hesitate to have Ertuğrul eliminated."

I heard my mother's angry breathing.

"You are throwing *that* in my face? If it were not for me, you would be still sitting in Çengelköy, eating your own stomach. You ingrate! All I wanted was for Adam to be recognized, legitimized."

"Enough! Now leave me alone. I am tired. Wake me in two hours."

According to my book, I was neither anxious nor sad but not happy either. I was watching myself listening to these frightening conversations as if they had nothing to do with me.

༄

"Allies Declare War against Ottoman Empire," the newspaper headlines screamed. The Italians landed at Antalya, and a few months later the Greeks took Smyrna. Meanwhile, the sultan retreated to Yıldız Palace like his older brother had done.

In the *selâmlık*, Manny and Talāt were smoking. Judging from the expressions on their faces, they were discussing something quite serious.

"Manny, we have been friends for a long time," Talāt spoke with a deliberate slowness as if he wasn't sure how to proceed. "And I haven't interfered with anything you've done. . . . You haven't even hesitated to cut the throats of your allies to actualize the asinine idea of a state of Israel. Even if you accomplish it, sooner or later it will drown in a sea of Arabs. I give its existence one hundred years at best.

"The Allies, as well as Germans, support the idea of Israel not because they care about Jews; on the contrary, they hate you, and they think that by sending you all back to the Middle East where you belong, they'll be rid of you. They welcome Zionism as a deliverance. At a dinner party at the German embassy, I heard the snickering snide remarks about what a lovely sight a country populated only by Jews would be."

"Dear Talāt," Manny smiled, "you should be the last person to criticize physical unattractiveness. As for Jewish traits, yes, we males do have peculiarities that the Germans may not wish to contaminate their gene pool with. However, I don't think the Turks have similar reasons to be concerned. You're not a homogeneous group. I'll bet that you—and even the sultan—have no more than 1 percent Turkish blood. I am sure he has more Greek and Ukrainian blood than anything else. Where do you think Prince Abdulmecit got those blue eyes, not from Anatolia. Anyhow, we both happen to know one extraordinarily beautiful Jewish woman, right? I wouldn't mind living anywhere where there are thousands of them."

They walked to the dining room arm in arm, laughing and joking.

What did Manny mean? Were they talking about my mother? Did he mean knowing her in a biblical sense? My mother is definitely good-looking. How come I am not?

I looked in the mirror for a long time. I was short. My sloping shoulders made me look even shorter. My head was too big, my eyes too narrow, my nose too long. My upper lip was cracked in the middle and always getting infected. My front teeth overlapped, and my skin was darkish. I was ugly. In Palestine at least I could easily blend in. There I could easily please Jesus by bragging about my weaknesses.

∿

The newspapers heralded the disgraceful departure of three major figures of the empire for Germany: Talāt, Djemal, and Enver.

In the harem, my father and mother were screaming at each other. I watched them from behind the slightly open door to my mother's room. I was by now a master spy: invisible, silent, and invincible.

"Tell the truth, woman!" my father confronted her. "You knew it and chose not to tell me, didn't you?"

"I swear, no," my mother countered, clearly upset. "I had no idea. Why would I hide it from you anyway? I like Talāt, but the other two, Enver and Djemal, can go to hell as far as I'm concerned. Stop and think for a second. Who would gain by keeping their exile a secret?"

"What about Manny; he had no idea either? That's odd since he seems to know even who fathered whom and where."

"How come you didn't know that your top three generals were defecting in the middle of the war?" Mother replied. "Talāt was your right hand, your prime minister, for God's sake. Didn't you suspect anything when he gave up his most prestigious post voluntarily? What happened to your suspicious nature? Is it only directed at me? What are you doing, really? Rumor has it that you spend most of your time in the harem. Are you so blinded by that little bitch that you're unaware of events in your own government?"

Father slouched into the sofa, looking totally exhausted as he mused, "What kind of an ally is Germany when it provides a means of defection for the most important members of my cabinet—three generals of the all-powerful Ottoman Empire, who sneaked out in a German submarine like thieves in the night just to save their own dirty skins."

"Let me set up your *narghile*" (their code word for hashish), my mother soothed, when she realized that he was simply frightened. As she prepared the pipe, she kept talking: "Did the German government approach you at all—I mean to try to save you from a potential revolt here?"

"Of course not; what sort of silly question is that? Would anyone dare even to suggest to the sultan of the mighty Ottoman Empire that he desert? A deal is about to be struck with the Allies. Once the issue of sovereignty is settled and the borders redefined, we'll go back to our usual lives." He inhaled laboriously at the *narghile*, then sat back. "Why are you trying to scare me? Did you hear something? Listen, the most valuable part of the empire is here, in Istanbul. Who cares about Syria, Iraq, Palestine, or Bulgaria? We have everything we want here. Honestly I don't understand your Jewish obsession with Palestine. Speaking of your Jews, what are Manny and company scheming these days? Now that I have nothing to say about immigration, they rarely talk to me. I have a hunch that they're trying to figure out how to own Istanbul. Am I right? You filthy rats."

"Okay, that is it," mother admonished. "You're going home to the palace of mice."

He was already asleep.

"Napoleon Bonaparte wanted to learn skills in the Ottoman army, in which he applied as a technician in 1792. When he became the emperor of France, he sent a letter of gratitude and support to the sultan, writing that

anything that shall happen, whether fortunate or unfortunate for the Turks, will be fortunate or unfortunate for France.

"*You see, Adam, 'In politics there are no permanent friends, there are no permanent enemies. There are only permanent interests.' "*

Well if there are no permanent friends, I shall not be unhappy for not having any, and if there are no permanent enemies, I should not be so scared. But what exactly is my permanent interest, if not becoming the sultan?

～

I must have dozed off over my assigned reading of the chapter "*L'idée Fixe*" by Paul Valéry.

"Your dinner, Adam *Effendi*," Ahmed Agha gently woke me. "We have cabbage rolls, yogurt soup, shepherd salad, and baklava. Incidentally, you're overdoing the hashish again. You forget the doctor's order. You are taking it even when you don't have any pain; you're becoming like your father. You two use it as if it were a cigarette. Well it's not. I am telling you, Adam *Effendi*, hashish is a medicine. You don't take aspirin when you don't have a headache; it's the same with hashish. Now, then—do you want the soup first?"

"No, baklava."

"You see, only an addict would eat sweets first. You have to stop it."

Actually, the sweets weren't even that sweet. The baklava was made with tasteless American flour; the milk was replaced with some imported donated condensed milk powder. What happened to our wheat fields, cows, and the foods from ships that had fed this nation for centuries? One war, and we ended up at the mercy of enemies for food? Hashish was the only homegrown product left; why not take it? What could a eunuch know about the highs and lows of emotions? He was emotionally castrated too. Homer! Now he, he knew: "Hashish banishes all pain, sorrow, and sadness."

～

I finally mastered ejaculation. Thirty-one strokes as Ahmed Agha suggested were definitely not enough; more likely it was about one hundred thirty-one. Of course, it depended on how many times I masturbated in a day. Other factors also weighed in the process, for example, time of day. The process seemed to go more slowly during the day than at night. Equally important was whether I had a full stomach or was hungry. Either extreme was not good for masturbation. I found what one ate had relevance: meat and cheese took desire away, making me want to nap. But pasta and sweets were fine, providing that I didn't gorge on them. I must bring all this information to Ahmed Agha. His ignorance had cost me a few years of hormone building, and I hadn't grown according to my age. What should I have expected? How stupid of me, trying to learn about sex from a eunuch.

༄

The darkness surrounding Manny grew into deeper shades. He was alone with mother.

"They condemned Djavid to fifteen years in prison. The Allies are pressuring the sultan to arrest people at will. I can't risk staying any longer. This is a real good-bye; I'm leaving tomorrow for Salonika. Incidentally, you should buy some stock in the Standard Oil Company. With the American Jewry partnership we have acquired land in Mesopotamia that is believed to hold large oil reserves. So this is my bit of parting."

"Manny, my dear, I'll miss you." Mother hugged him. "Would you like to say good-bye to Adam? You know, he really loves you like a father."

"Well, of course. I intended to do so," he replied.

I quickly returned to my room and waited. Manny walked in, in a much lighter mood.

༄

The sultan and Mother sat on the sofa.

"I am frightened, I am frightened," the sultan said.

I had seen him nervous—even scared—but I'd never seen him like this. He sat rocking back and forth. My mother held his arm.

"They are going to hang me," he continued. "The Patriots are swarming over Istanbul, killing people who are against them. Meanwhile, the Allies want me to sign the Sèvres agreement, which gives me a meager subsidy—even less than the British gave to the *Seyh* of Mecca, Sharif Husayn ibn Ali.

"The Allies who took over police activities in Istanbul are scaring my loyal representatives. More than one hundred have departed for Ankara to join Kemal, who has declared himself the president, whatever that means. Kemal is killing anyone who is an obstacle to him. He is going to come here and hang me in front of the Dolmabahçe Palace. Don't shake your head. He said that in Parliament, where those self-appointed representatives are even cursing me, their sultan and caliph. And where is my grand vizier brother-in-law during all this? He's gone to the baths in Karlsbad.

"I'm left here with Deedes and that Frau, the pederast English priest, who constantly bring me the names of people to be arrested, killed, or exiled to Malta. There is no one in the palace upon whom I can rely. I made too many mistakes. I know I'm going to pay dearly for all that."

"Listen," Mother shook his arm, "speaking of mistakes, why don't you get in touch with Kemal Pasha? You've known each other a long time and even traveled to Berlin together. Why are you taking the English advice so exclusively?"

"I've tried, actually, to contact Kemal. He and the Patriots want me to give up the throne. I cannot betray nine hundred years of history. Now, I have to get back to the Palace," said Vahdettin. "These are my personal notes and journals." He handed over a large folder. "Do whatever you like with them. They are mostly related to the machinations of your Jews. Maybe Adam can write a book on how to bring down an empire. Anyway, good-bye."

Mother remained motionless at the doorstep long after he left. I snuck in and opened the top folder, which contained a draft letter to General Harrington, chief of the occupation forces, requesting immediate, safe transport to London.

"In 1889, four medical students in Istanbul founded the first organized secret society, which eventually set the stage for the Young Turks in Salonika. In 1909, the Young Turks enlisted support from the Freemasons, Jews, and Dunmehs (Jewish converts to Islam) and revolted against Sultan Abdulhamid. He was brought late at night to the railway station, with two young princes and four chosen favorites from his harem. He was deported to Salonika, where, through the connections of Rabbi Nahum and Senator Emmanuel Carasso, he was given a house—the Villa Allatini—belonging to the family of Ethel Cohen.

"You see, Adam, 'Better to be killed off by your friends than to be saved by your enemies.' "

But how do I know who is my friend and who is my enemy?

❧

"Are you all right, Mother?" I asked. Should I tell her about the draft letter?

"*Canım*—dear, I don't know what it is. I get these awful headaches after rotten coughing spells that aren't helped by Dr. Numan's medications, and I just have to sleep them off. Why are you looking so worried?"

"I thought, maybe the sultan upset you, that is why." Obviously mother never even opened the file.

She let out a short laugh. "Ah, men always upset women, my dear child, because our inner space has an opening to the outside. Anyway, this is my fate, and, unfortunately, it's also yours."

"*Anne*, everyone seems so scared."

"I know," she replied. "You know, the country is engaged in a major battle of wills between the sultanate, which is supported by the British, and the Patriots, who are hell-bent on abolishing the sultanate. The people are divided, either for or against one of them. Depending on where they cast their luck, the result could be felicitous or totally disastrous."

"We're with the sultanate and the British these days, right?"

"For the moment, yes. If the British succeed in throwing Kemal Pasha into one of their famous dungeons, we'll be free of worries, at least for a while. But if the Patriots win, well, we'll have no choice but to wholeheartedly support the new republic. Jews have survived over many millennia by being reasonable, adaptive, and submissive to the reigning power until it cracks, then we jump on the opportunity to build a new government in which we have a greater say. You'll see; if the Patriots win, all of our Jewish friends will return and take up important roles in the transition from Ottoman Empire to the Turkish Republic. Even the Patriots need money and brains: rhetoric can go only so far. They've got to deliver goods to the public, and people don't care about ideologies; they care about food, comfort, and security.

"Now, are you ready to hear a confession, you little spy? Don't look so shocked; remember whose tummy you came from. I know what you've been up to. This house is like a training camp for spies. There's no reason you shouldn't benefit from it."

I was curious to know how she knew and for how long. Primarily, I was hurt that she called me *little spy*. I was little, but not a little spy.

She continued, "Well, here is my confession. Where do you think I've been going every Saturday morning?"

"To the Beth Israel synagogue in Şişli."

" Şişli yes, but I don't go to the synagogue every Saturday. Once a month I pay a visit to an old lady, "the white rose"—*Zübeyde hanım*. You couldn't by any chance guess who *Zübeyde hanım* is, could you?"

I didn't even try guessing, and my mother went on.

"She is Kemal Pasha's mother! I bring her gifts and food, but most important I bring gold and money to give to her son. And why does she think I'm being so generous? She believes I'm a mole in the sultanate-British web and really a Patriot. Hah!"

I was dumbfounded and relieved.

She got up and coyly walked away. "I think my cough is coming back. I have to rest for a while."

"In 1711, Turkish forces surrounded Peter the Great and his army at the banks of the Pruth. He was so afraid of being captured and enslaved, he began to have hysterical fits. He confined himself to his tent in total panic and was willing to give up everything, including his beautiful wife Catherine, to escape.

"Catherine agreed to his rescue plan. She went to the grand vizier Baltacı Mehmed Pasha with proposals for a truce, bringing her own jewelry and a collection of gold rubles from the Russian officers. She spent the night in the grand vizier's tent and later returned her pimping husband to St. Petersburg. The grand vizier was exiled first to the island of Lesbos and then to Limnos, and there he died. A few years later, the stronger Catherine demanded the right to intervene on behalf of the Orthodox Christians who, until then, saw the Ottomans as the protectors from the Latin Catholics. Empress Catherine even prepared her second grandson for the throne of Constantinople, christening the child Constantine, giving him Greek wet nurses, and teaching him the Greek language.

"You see, Adam, 'All wars are religious in nature.' "

This was the last lesson of my history teacher, Muhsin *Effendi*.

ᚙ

For weeks we were totally isolated. No one visited. All of my teachers, except Mademoiselle Blanche, had disappeared. Mother explained that because the sultan couldn't send money, we were behind on paying the teachers but that things would be ironed out once everything settled down.

I spent most of my time in my room, sitting in front of the window, as if waiting for someone. One day, while at the window, I saw my mother covered head to toe in *tcharchafs* hurrying into the car with Ahmed Agha and our driver, Abbas. I wondered where she was going all covered up.

~

Mother returned four hours later, disheveled, eyes red and swollen from crying. I met her in the entranceway and she signaled for me to follow her into an inner chamber. As she ripped off her *tcharchafs*, she talked while sobbing and hiccupping incessantly.

"He's leaving! The sultan is going to defect." Mother was still very surprised? Had she never read his letter to General Harrington? "I went to see him at *Dolmabahçe*. This is permanent, Adam; the sultan is leaving the country and all his loyal people and us without even saying good-bye. Only a few months ago he derided his brother-in-law Ferit Pasha for doing the same thing. I was hoping that as the sultan of this glorious empire, Vahdettin would stay and face his fate on his own sacred soil despite his fears, if only for the sake of his soul."

She threw herself face down on the sofa, crying. Then, lifting her head, she said, "I don't even know why I'm crying. In truth I really don't give a damn whether or not he said good-bye or that he didn't even ask us to go with him. I would never have gone. I don't think he even loved me. Well, I don't love him; if anything, I'm disgusted by him. Oh, my child, I didn't mean to leak this to you. Maybe I'm crying for the Ottoman Empire and its death. I'm crying for the end of an era, a romantic, unreal era."

Mother talked and cried for a long time. I sat next to her on the sofa. I wanted to touch her hands, but I couldn't bring myself to do so. How could she be crying over the parting of this awful man and the death of the empire she conspired to bring down?

~

If God is with me, why has all this happened to me?

Mademoiselle Blanche looked as if all the blood had drained from her face. She brought me a few French and Turkish newspapers. They all had gigantic headlines:

Mehmet VI Defects
Sultan Abandons Throne
Goodbye and Go to Hell Vahdettin
Emperor Flees Turkey Aboard English Destroyer

One newspaper published a picture of the sultan, one hand holding a cane, the other placed on Ertuğrul's shoulder. Both looked happy.

"So Ertuğrul went with him too?" I asked.

"Monsieur Adam," answered Mademoiselle Blanche, sounding disconcerted, "at times you behave like an admirable, mature man, yet at other times you act like the silly two-year-old boy you were when I first met you; it's as if you haven't grown up at all. Is your competition with Ertuğrul more significant than the sultan's defection? Which, need I remind you, has enormous implications for you?"

"In view of your attitude about the sultan's departure, I'm sure you aren't going to be too disturbed by my next announcement. The French embassy has asked that all nonessential personnel return to France immediately. I am moving to the embassy today, and I hope that tomorrow I'll be on the Express d'Orient on my way home to France.

"Adam, your French is impeccable. At worst people may think you are from Alsace. Remember, Jesus will always be with you until the end." As she gently touched my lips and walked away, my heart ached. Jesus will always be with me? Some consolation. Did I really care about Jesus or French, or did I become Christian and learn French just to please her? Jesus was abandoned by his disciples and even by his father but never by Mary Magdalene. That day I threw my little Jesus into the lake and made a reverse sign of the cross three times to undo my Christianity. I thought about how the water would feel, closing over my head. Religion, instead of anchoring me, was drowning me. Could I detach myself from my convictions and free myself from faith?

～～

The following morning, my mother woke me up. I slept very late because I no longer had classes.

"Get up, Canım. Governor Refet Pasha is here; he wants to talk to us both."

I quickly dressed and in ten minutes was standing in front of a stern-looking, stocky man in a brand-new uniform. Mother, her face ashen, slowly rose from her chair and brought me to sit next to her.

Refet Pasha, who wore medals on his jacket, shifted in his chair, then began to speak. "I've already mentioned this to your mother, but I wanted to repeat it briefly for you. The Parliament has abolished the sultanate but will allow the caliphate to continue. Your cousin Abdulmecit *Effendi* will be appointed thus soon. Members of the household of Vahdettin *Effendi*, who disgraced the country by his defection, will be relocated from their present residences, Yıldız Palace, Dolmabahçe, Cihannuma, and others, to the Feriye Palace and Nişantaşı Konaki. You two may join them, or, if your mother prefers, you and she may live among the commoners. We have a small apartment in Şişli that is about to be vacated by Kemal Pasha's mother. You are both welcome to move there. *Zubeyda Hanım* is aware of the situation and has made it clear that she will gladly leave the apartment furnished."

He continued, now addressing my mother. "You have exactly forty-eight hours to decide. My chief of staff will take over the termination arrangements of your workers and ensure their safe return to their villages.

"This property is being confiscated, though the American embassy claims to have bought it from the Anglo-Levantine Company-British partnership. The matter will be resolved in the courts.

"If neither relocation option is to your liking, you are free to exercise your own options, just advise my office of your whereabouts—we'll need your address to deliver your monthly pension. There are no charges against you, and you will not be detained in any way by the government. You are free, like any other member of the republic, to live and do as you please. But you must vacate this property by the deadline. You can take only your personal belongings because all the furniture, rugs, and other things came with the buildings. I'm terribly sorry, *Hanım Effendi*, for the message. Believe me, it gives me no pleasure to be its messenger."

Refet Pasha clicked his heels, gave a military salute, and left.

❧

That night, Mother coughed so harshly and incessantly that it could be heard in every corner of the house. The sound of hurried footsteps echoed through the hall; I guessed the servants in the harem were rushing to attend to her. I went to her doorstep and watched Ahmed Agha pleading with her for permission to fetch Dr. Numan.

"I'm fine, Ahmed Agha. Please go to sleep, all of you."

Ahmed Agha protested, "*Hanım Effendi,* you are spitting too much blood."

She was equally determined, "What can a doctor do, especially at this hour? You men get too scared off by blood. We women are rather accustomed to it; in fact, we see it at least once a month. Right girls?"

She seemed in a peculiarly good mood, in the midst of her hacking spells.

"Adam, my goodness, did I wake you up also? I am sorry. Look, I'm okay. The cough has stopped, and I would appreciate it if you all would leave so that I can get some sleep. Good night, everyone; good night, Adam. Oh, Adam, come back for a minute; give me your hand. . . . Oh my love, you are so innocent. I'm sorry, I am so sorry."

She closed her eyes, and pinkish tears ran down her cheeks to her mouth. She let my hand go.

～

Ahmed Agha opened the curtains with uncharacteristic quietness; a dim light seeped into the room, even though it was almost noon.

Ahmed Agha said calmly, "Adam *Effendi,* last night your mother happily joined her creator; may you live a long life. Rabbi Nahum is here and has ordered the burial to be this afternoon.

I watched Ahmed Agha as he spoke; he was cool and collected, almost indifferent.

"All the preparations have been made. She'll be buried in the *Yahudi Mezarlığı,* the Jewish cemetery, in Eyüp. Put on your dark suit and come to the reception area."

"All right," I said, imitating his even voice.

I arrived at the reception area, waiting to hear the sounds of grief. It seemed as if everyone was unaffected. The women of the house who tore their hair and howled in pain at Vahdettin's defection showed no emotion at the death of their *Hanım Effendi.* And I was no different. As I walked toward her closed casket, I felt nothing. It was as if she hadn't died. Was it possible that this was another plot of hers? Had she orchestrated her death and fled so that the Patriots would not be able to pursue her? Of course, otherwise how could all these people, who loved her so much, behave as if nothing had happened? But why weren't they including me in on the plan? Why didn't she fake my death while she was at it so that the two of us could have fled together?

"Rabbi" I said, "if mother really died, would she now be freed from all her sins?"

The rabbi shook his head. "Adam I don't know how to answer that question, but let's talk about some urgent practical matters."

I had other pressing questions on my mind. "Rabbi, do you think death is the last enemy and Jesus will destroy it?"

"Son, this is all nonsense," he said dismissively. He took me aside. "Listen, this jewelry case is for you, as is this key. It was in your mother's lockbox. All the contents of the case are yours. Most likely there is nothing else for you to inherit. I'm leaving the box and key with Ahmed Agha for the time being. Don't worry about your mother's burial expenses; she was extremely generous to the *shul* and to me personally. The staff, with the exception of Ahmed Agha, will not be coming to the cemetery, as there is only one car."

The staff may have already known these details; they all came to kiss my hand. "May you live long." I was taken to the cemetery, in a fugue state, sitting between the driver, Abbas, and the rabbi. Ahmed Agha sat in the backseat, one hand on the casket—which stuck out of the car's back door—the other holding the jewelry case.

The streets were crowded with people, soldiers, cars, horses, carriages, and trams, of which until that day I had only seen in pictures. Street vendors hawked their goods, porters shouldered people with shouts and warnings. It was very noisy and bewildering; I had to cover my ears and close my eyes. We drove past buildings that seemed to lean on each other. No land surrounded them, and no fruit trees, cows, lambs, or chickens were in sight. What did all these people eat?

When we arrived at the Jewish cemetery, beneath the curve of the Golden Horn, men were still digging the grave. We had to wait an hour before the casket was interred. Rows of small white stones were laid out on a bare hill, a stark contrast to the Muslim cemetery on the other side, with its decorated mausoleums, gilded railings, soft shade of poplar, horse chestnut trees, and umbrella pines. I asked the rabbi on which side I would be buried if I died. He corrected the *if* to *when*. He asked me to pray with him. All I wanted to do was go to my room and close the door. I don't think I believed in praying anymore. I know now that we are not born to eternal life in death the way Jesus described. I guess I am truly no longer a Christian. Maybe I never really was because when Jesus played music for me, I didn't rejoice; now he is singing a funeral song, and I show no sadness. It is obvious Jesus didn't work a miracle for me because of my lack of faith. The rabbi is right. All this is nonsense. If Jesus miraculously had made me the crown prince, of course, I would have faith.

When we returned, the staff was gone. Waiting for us in the *selāmlık* were one young blondish officer who looked as if he came from the Laz people, near the Black Sea, and one soldier. They smoked cigarettes and chatted with each other and laughed. One of them asked the rabbi, "Master, in your religion where do people go when they die, heaven or hell?"

The rabbi replied with a kind smile, "Neither my son; they just go to the cemetery."

The two smirked.

The Laz-looking officer continued, "It is Refet Pasha's order that Adam *Effendi* be brought to his office immediately. Adam *Effendi* should take only his personal belongings."

The rabbi looked at me. "Can Ahmed Agha accompany him?"

"I'm afraid not. We have strict orders to bring him only."

Ahmed Agha respectfully addressed the officer, "But Commander, Adam *Effendi* never has lived alone. He couldn't prepare his meals or wash his clothes or even . . ."

The officer cut him short, "Well, he'll learn. At his age I was fighting the French in Syria."

I stared at the Laz, wondering why the belt he wore crossed over his chest on the left became thicker and wider at the belly. It was because it supported a big gun on the right and a flat thermos-canteen on the left. Both officers wore brand-new green uniforms.

I tried standing stiff, upright, like an officer. I tried to smile.

The Laz said, "Look, he is laughing about our asinine conversation. It's ridiculous, isn't it, kid? Now prepare his luggage, one suitcase with only what is essential for the next few days. Get going."

Ahmed Agha took me to my room; the luggage was already prepared.

"Listen, and listen very carefully," Ahmed Agha instructed as he placed a coffer into the luggage. "In this box is your mother's jewelry—and I'm sure, some gold coins and money. I want you to put the key in your sock, right here. But don't forget it. Open the box when no one is around and hide its contents somewhere else very carefully. Remember, this is all you own in life. You will be fine. Okay now, *Allaha ısmarladık*—go with the will of Allah."

As I walked out of the house with the officers, I felt as if I was watching someone else go through it all. I felt eternally lost. Even if God didn't exist, that would change nothing.

∾

The Laz and his soldier hurried me into the car, and we left the rabbi and Ahmed Agha standing in front of the house. Ahmed Agha yelled, "Forgive me, Adam *Effendi*."

Why should I forgive him, I wondered. He served me for my whole life. I should be the one asking for forgiveness. Abbas stopped us at the gate. "Adam, remember, 'In high tide the fish eat ants, in low tide it's the reverse.' Come to Hasankale, my hometown. We only have mountains there. No one eats the other."

"Fuck off," the Laz sneered at Abbas. "Don't make me run over you, you asshole Kurd."

∾

Refet Pasha spoke firmly: "We have someplace in mind for you; it is a hostel. Maybe there you will have the opportunity to make some friends while continuing your schooling. For the time being you're entitled to a small pension; later you may apply for a scholarship, get a job, enlist in the army, do whatever you like. What do you say?"

I wondered how long it would take to become a pasha if I enlisted.

"Thank you, general."

"All right, that's settled." He chuckled.

Refet Pasha turned to the Laz. "Take him to Madame Sakızlıyan's place in the Süleymaniye district. She is holding a room for us."

Refet took my arm. "I am not sure that this is the best use of the republic's money, but here we are. Your monthly pension will be delivered regularly to Madame. She will take her share as it relates to her expenses and give you the rest for food, clothes, or whatever you need.

If you decide to make any change, discuss it with her. Son! You are not listening."

When we walked out, the skies looked the same.

⌇

In Jerusalem, the French were disputing with the Greeks and Russians as to whether the Latin monks should possess keys to the Church of Bethlehem and the doors leading to the manger itself, whether they could place in the sanctuary of the Nativity a silver star with the arms of France, or if, at Gethsemane, they could retain their right to a cupboard and a lamp in the tomb of the Virgin.

Two

~~~

Atheists unground me, sneer at me, and make me depressed. I want to die.

Istanbul

1922–1926

I have to grow out of religion.

Madame Sakızlıyan was a heavy-set old woman with a dark mustache.

"Oh, you are so small," she said, looking me over with piercing eyes. I flinched.

She picked up my luggage and began climbing a flight of creaky stairs to her third-floor apartment in the large, old, weather-stained wooden house.

"Would you like some tea and *smit?*" she offered. A large ornamented brass samovar was percolating near a tray of sesame pretzels.

"No, thanks." I was fascinated by the views from her windows. From the side window, I saw the enormous Mosque of Süleyman and the dozens of small domes of its *madrasah*—religious school. The view from the front window was of a large iron gate guarding the University of Istanbul's back entrance. Pictures had never conveyed its awesome presence.

"Okay, then, I'll take you to your room. You must be tired."

We walked down the stairs again, this time going all the way down to the basement. Once there, she dropped my luggage on the floor.

"There are four rooms here," she began. "This one is yours. There are three other students like you who live in the other rooms. The bathroom is in the garden. We all take turns bringing water from the mosque's fountains when the city water is cut off. You will have a chamber pot in your room for night use, but you'll have to take care of it yourself in the morning. I'll prepare hot water for you to wash your underwear. You can hang it out in the courtyard to dry. Our electricity comes and goes, mostly goes, so I'll leave you this lamp. I'll check its oil frequently to make sure you're not without light. I have a locked cabinet for your valuables. Don't keep them in your room."

The room was very small and smelled of moss and decay. The cement walls were damp to the point of dripping. Overhead, a narrow, curtainless window faced the street. Because the room was below street level, the only view from the window was of people's legs.

Madame instructed, "Open the window if you want fresh air, but always close it when you leave; otherwise, if it rains, the room will flood. I'll clean the room and change the sheets once a week. Keep it neat, though; I'm an old woman."

"Did you know the architect Sinan was an Armenian from Kayseri?" I asked, stammering. My face and the palms of my hands were sweating.

"What is this Sinan business? Are you talking about him because I'm Armenian? Don't worry about things like that. I'm Turkish, and so are you. Also we're both 'Muslims,'" she winked. "Do you understand? You're not to tell anyone about your Jewish mother, and you're always to use your middle name, Zakir. In Turkish, "Adam" means "person," as you know. It makes no sense as a name, and if you use it, you will unnecessarily attract attention. Similarly, my name is Sakız *Hanım*, not Sakızlıyan.

"I want you to trust me. I was ordered to watch over you by Refet Pasha. You need me. If you decide to put anything in the safe, let me know. Maybe you should just go to bed. Young man, I must tell you that I am impressed by the way you've maintained your dignity. You're abandoned completely, and yet you're still standing. Are you sure you don't have a little Armenian blood?"

I couldn't stop talking: "You know, I'm not the first or only one abused by fate and abandoned by his parents who survived by grounding himself in separation. You know, both Moses and Romulus made something really big from their abandonment."

This time she looked at me with trepidation and left.

The real world wasn't fitted to my mind. I sat on the edge of the bed and gazed at the flickering light of the oil lamp as it played across the repetitive design of the old kilim that covered about one-third of the irregular cement floor. The kilim was from the Erzurum area; it had red hexagons and yellow rectangles on a dark blue base and was geometrically regular.

Allah-u-Akbar-Allah-u-Akbar!!

I was startled awake by the sound of a *muezzin* loudly calling the faithful to prayer. He sounded as if he were in my room. It was pitch dark, and for a sleepy moment I thought Ahmed Agha was playing a trick on me.

Such a loud devotional coercion only left me with a deeper conviction of God's absence.

The *muezzin's* demanding voice for communion was over.

"Zakir *Effendi*, wake up son, it is past noon," a strange female voice hollered through my door. Zakir? No one ever called me Zakir. Oh, yes, of course. It took me a while to recognize the voice of the landlady.

I opened the door, and she eyed me. "Ah, hmm, did you sleep with your clothes on? I guess you were too tired to change. I want you to meet some of the other tenant students. This is Mete *Effendi*; he is a second-year law student from Kars."

He was the first person I had ever met who was even close to my height.

Sakız went on, "This is Nurettin *Effendi*. He is also a law student— third year he says. He is from Malatya."

He was well built and older and had a black mustache fringing large lips.

"And this is Doğan *Effendi*—what do you study again, Doğan? Anyway, he is from Diyarbekir."

Doğan was tall, blond, and very handsome and had an innocent, winning smile. All three men wore the same dark gray outfits with minor variations.

"Gentlemen," Sakız explained, "Zakir *Effendi's* parents recently passed away. He is from Şişli, but now he can only afford to live here, like the rest of you. He'll be going to the—ah—the medical school. Yes, the medical school."

"Welcome," everyone chimed.

"Join us, we're going to the cafeteria."

❧

We entered the large cafeteria, in the basement of the old building of the war minister of my empire. My empire?

There was a short line of students waiting to eat. As we joined the line, Mete handed me a tray. The smell of meatballs, rice, and white bean salad made me dizzy.

"I'm sorry, I forgot to bring money," I managed to say.

"What money? Food and clothing are free for poor students. Tomorrow I'll get your *meccani—gratis* card," Doğan offered.

A burly man behind the counter filled my plate with food while cheerfully teasing my companions, "He doesn't look poor like you hooligans. I think he is a real gentleman."

"Shut up," Nurettin muscled in. "He was just orphaned and he is a medical student."

The burly man turned to me: "Don't hang around with these kids; otherwise you'll never finish school."

There were about one hundred students in the cafeteria, eating, laughing, and talking to each other across the room. The noise hurt my ears. I couldn't focus on eating, let alone the discussion at the table. I realized that my companions were finished with dinner and waiting for me, but I wasn't even halfway done.

"Actually, I'm finished too, not hungry enough, I guess," I muttered.

I followed them out. They were smoking cigarettes and seemed to be heading in a direction opposite the house. It took them a while to realize that I was trailing them.

"Oh Zakir," Doğan noticed, "we're going to the coffeehouse, to play a few hands of poker. Do you know how to play? No? You'll learn."

We entered a small coffeehouse filled with students, all noisily playing backgammon or cards and drinking tea. Our group squeezed in among the others, took over a table, and settled in to play poker.

They played all night, teasing, at times arguing, even cursing each other. How strange, I thought; they were so highly engaged with each other and the game. They were hardly aware of my presence until the closing time, when they asked if I had learned the game.

"Not yet," I said. I hadn't been watching the game. I was watching them. In the past, I only had an imaginary friend. How does one relate to real friends?

◡◠◡

If I don't believe in God, can I believe in anything else?

That night I finally opened my luggage. It held one suit, some underwear, socks, shirts, a few ties, my Hittite seal and clay tablets, and, of course, the jewelry box, which I unlocked with great curiosity. The box was half empty but held three brooches, two necklaces, a bunch of earrings and rings, two women's watches, four *beşibirlik* worth five gold coins each, twelve single gold coins, a few uncut emeralds and rubies, and two hundred English pounds. Also an ancient flint knife! Some of the treasure were jeweled pieces, several encrusted with diamonds and made of gold or silver. I didn't recognize any of the jewels. Mother had worn entirely different pieces.

I individually wrapped the gold coins so that they wouldn't jingle, cut a small hole in a corner of the mattress, and hid the money and coins.

At midmorning the next day, only Doğan was home. I showed him the jewels. I trusted him more than Sakız, who, after all, was connected to Refet Pasha.

"Do you want to sell them? I know someone from my town in the *Kapalı Çarşı*—the covered bazaar. He won't cheat you," Doğan offered.

The *Kapalı Çarşı* was a ten-minute walk from our house. I'd heard about it but never imagined it would be like this: hundreds of shops selling everything from jewelry to rugs to clothing to furniture, all crowded into one place. The scents of cinnamon, saffron, nutmeg, licorice, and cloves mixed with the smells of leather and sweat. A young man beat coffee beans in an enormous iron bowl. He lifted a heavy iron pestle and hit the inside of the bowl with all his strength. He repeated the process to a tempo of a "*homm*" sayer—an older man sitting in front of him and making encouraging noises, a sort of cheering. The *homms* were equally powerful and sonorous. The two tunes mingled, sending the men into a sort of dervish haze, but instead of twirling around like a Sufi dancer, the younger man bounced vertically to the older man's monodic, monosyllabic music. Both men were in a deep trance, totally indifferent to passersby. Actually, I was the only one watching the duet; no one else seemed to notice them either. I was so dazzled that Doğan led me by the hand to his friend's shop.

Once we arrived, the townsmen hugged, kissed each other on both cheeks, and chatted with enthusiasm. The shopkeeper offered us hot tea, and finally we sat down to talk business. The man looked at the jewels and, unimpressed, said, "Second class, the gold is fourteen karat, the diamonds are D-grade, mostly chipped, and of too large a size to be valuable. I would say the whole box is worth no more than four hundred Turkish lira. If I could sell them for more, I would be happy to give you the difference. But I doubt I'll be able to do it. Are you sure you aren't holding onto the really good pieces?"

Of course, I didn't believe him. Once you free yourself from believing in God, you never need to believe anyone. I accepted the deal.

⌇

For a long time, God had become simply a superstition for me. I couldn't dismiss it, the same way that I couldn't dismiss my other superstitions like stepping on cracks on the pavement or putting on my left shoe first or my left arm first in my coat.

In the morning I made the point of putting on my left shoe first.

The whole city seemed to be jumping with nervous deprivation as it was teeming with an impoverished army of people. Streets, stores, houses were all festooned with oversized pictures of Kemal Pasha and black, white, and green banners. Food had been scarce for weeks. Coal was in short supply, streetlights were turned off, and the cable cars weren't functioning well. In the cafés, tea, heated over wood fires, was being served with raisins in place of sugar. Everyone wore overcoats and hats indoors. The streets were clogged with garbage. Rats were unfazed as they competed with people rummaging through trash heaps trying to find something to eat. There seemed to be more beggars on the streets than passersby. The beggars were mostly young men recently discharged from the dismantled army. Many wore at least a piece of their uniform. They filled every mosque in the city.

Outdoor walls were covered with graffiti insulting the defected sultan. "Vahdettin Betrayer!" one read. Was I also a betrayer? A terrible sensation stuck to me. I guess this is what it means to be frightened.

Newspaper boys hawking their papers screamed, "Vahdettin stays in Italy! Vahdettin is in San Remo!" I wondered why he was staying there. Did the British betray him, as Manny always believed they would? I didn't speak Italian.

～

The university was set in a vast, well-landscaped area. U-shaped stone buildings encapsulated a large cobblestone courtyard. Hundreds of *alafranga*—foreign-clad students—moved around energetically, while others, huddled in small groups, engaged in serious, lively discussions. These students looked softer, well-fed and bred, and quite different from my shabby friends, who seemed interested only in having a good time and not at all in a hurry or eager to discuss any current topics or even their classes.

From the courtyard, I entered the main building. It was palatial: gray stone floors; high, ornate ceiling; huge marble columns. I followed the flow of students through a wide door that opened into an enormous library. The room was airy and well lit, tall windows almost replacing all of the south and east walls. Heavy oak tables laid out across the length of the room were made cozy by leather chairs on either side of them. There were a few newspapers, in Turkish and foreign languages. I've found my place, I thought.

I picked up a copy of an obscure journal *El Judeo* and settled into a light corner. The headline read, "Jews to Have a National Army." The article then went on to explain the need for such a force, noting why the British could not guarantee Jewish safety in Palestine. Even the Vatican supported the idea of an independent Jewish state. An article quoting Monsignor Marchetti conveyed the instructions of Pope Benedictus XV, confirming that the Holy See's interest in the subject was unwavering.

There was a statement from my Deedes, now chief secretary to the high commissioner of Palestine, Herbert Samuel, denying that the British took ancient objects, structures, or works of art from the Ottoman Empire.

I felt at home for an instant.

Having finished the newspaper, I surveyed the bookshelves. This section was related to the medical sciences. The books were all in French or German. I picked up a French anatomy book and began to read. I don't know how many hours passed until someone gently tapped me on the shoulder:

"It's closing time now," said Canib *Effendi*, the librarian. "Unfortunately, we are open only during daylight hours." Canib *Effendi* was a skinny man with silver-white hair who wore multiple pairs of eyeglasses simultaneously. More than a librarian, he lived and breathed books.

"Remember! We are operating on the Gregorian calendar now, not by the lunar one," he called after me.

Soon, I had a routine. I woke at no particular time, walked over to Agop's shop for a honey and heavy cream sandwich with tea, went to the library, and sat next to the coal-burning Dutch stove in the study room where I read until noon, had lunch with my house friends in the cafeteria, went back to the library, attended some classes, then went back to the cafeteria for dinner or met my friends and went somewhere to have something to eat with them. Doğan got me the *meccani* student card, so between the cafeteria and the library, I settled into the periphery of university life since I was not a legitimately registered student. Occasionally we went to the Tepebaşı Cinema, one of the two theaters in town that played silent movies.

Nothing was stable in Turkey. The joke was that the country was being run by a drunkard, Kemal, and by a deaf man, Ismet. Kemal Pasha, now the president of the republic, was more autocratic than the sultan had been. How could Kemal abolish a more than thousand-year-old structure without any regard for its constituents, ordinary Muslims in forty different countries? And what if he abolished my pension?

One evening, Sakız greeted me with a concerned look: "Tomorrow you are expected to report to the local governor, Kaymakam's office in Çağaloğlu, to have your photograph taken. I don't know why. But they asked me to make sure that you be there at nine o'clock in the morning."

The following morning, after I had my picture taken, I asked the security officer the purpose of it. The officer said, "This is for passport purposes." Passport? I returned to the library.

⟿

The penis is like a pump made of muscles, the text explained, and an erection occurs when arterial blood gushes in and the venous return is blocked. Accordingly, its muscles must enlarge, I thought, by exercise, in the same way that arms and legs are strengthened. Therefore, the longer and more frequently one has an erection, I reasoned, the bigger and stronger the penis will become.

As I was spending a lot of time sitting and reading, I decided that I could simultaneously exercise my penis muscles while studying. Initially this was quite distracting, but later on I managed to apply the double-bookkeeping technique I had mastered for mental activities to the body. I found that I could study well and maintain an erection—without any visual or mental stimulation—for an hour, but not much longer, as the penis muscles were liable to fatigue and needed at least twelve minutes of rest before commencing the next round of exercise, which could last only a half hour. After that I needed a twenty-minute rest. Thereafter, there was a steady diminishment on return. Even without an orgasm, I found there was a cumulative fatigue or a decline in interest in the subject. Was my mind exhausting itself in a field of substitutions?

⟿

The neighborhood was filled with the lyrical calls of vendors announcing the sale of sour cherries, plums, and cucumbers. The spring sun washed over the cypress and sycamore trees. The new flags of the republic—red with a white crescent and star—hung from every shop and house window. The Greeks had been thrown out of Izmir and the Italians from Anatolia, but we had lost 80 percent of the empire. What was the reason for this euphoria? Was it because we hadn't lost everything? Newspapers were praising Nahum Bey (there was not a word about his being a rabbi) for his helping Ismet Pasha negotiate highly favorable terms for the republic at Lausanne.

Every day, Kemal Pasha, who renamed himself Atatürk—the father of the Turks—gave new orders or issued declarations: no more wearing of the *fez*, no more *tcharchaf*, no more religious activities in governmental and school properties. While Atatürk was at it, why didn't he cut prayers—*namaz*—from five times to once a day? His disbelief is not absolute in order to be effective atheism. He erroneously tried to shackle Islam to some utilitarian chains, like better use of time. Pragmatism cannot forestall faith.

~~~

Newspaper headlines announced the Parliament's decision to abolish the caliphate. Doğan, who came from a very religious Islamic family, was especially interested in hearing what the *imam* of the Süleymaniye Mosque would say at the evening prayer service. So we all went. Even though I lived across the street, I had never visited the place about which I had heard and read so much. My mother's pet namesake Roxelana was buried here, and so was her husband, Sultan Süleyman. I glanced at their mausoleum, now covered with overgrown fig and mulberry trees. Had they actually lived?

The mosque was packed with praying people and homeless soldiers. The *mufti*, in full regalia, took his place and delivered a passionate speech. He associated the abolishment of the caliphate by the republic with the negation of Islam.

"Who were the soldiers Kemal Pasha relied upon to fight the enemy?" cried the *mufti*. "The sons of Muslim families. Why were these poor people willing to risk their lives? For jihad, and why did Kemal Pasha go to the peasants of Erzurum and not to the fancies of Tarabya to recruit fighters? Because Muslims, while on their deathbed, can be awakened to fight the enemy for Allah's cause. What was the battle cry of the handful of Turks who charged the invading Greek army in Izmir? Allah—Allah!

"Now that the enemy is defeated, Kemal Pasha wants to get rid of Islam. Doesn't he realize who brought him to power? Anyone who is a full-blooded Muslim knows. Only blue-eyed devils can betray the God who saved them from total disgrace. Look around you, my brothers, do you see any blue-eyed, blond-haired people in this mosque?"

Doğan was the only one. People elbowed him and hissed at him, but he was unfazed and would not leave. Eventually they settled down to hear the rest of the speech.

"My Muslim brothers, how do you think we happen to be praying here in Istanbul, the city of Constantine? It is because of the army of Islam. How do you think this mosque came to be built? It is because of the army of Islam. For more than a thousand years, God delivered us victory upon victory, stretching our power all the way from the sandy deserts of Yemen to the green grasses of the Danube. How can anyone deny or negate this heritage? Islam is not just a religion; it is the texture of our lives; it is our law, our community, our family, our sorrow, and our joy; it is with us from birth to death, and it can take us from hell to heaven. And the caliph is the father of our faith. Who can remove the father from his family? You know who, my friends? The one who is not a father of any child. Who throws away the headgear of our men, tears away the *tcharchaf* from our wives! Who, my friends? The one who doesn't have a wife! Who, chosen by his people to lead, would reject the title of caliph, the deputy of the Prophet? You know who, my friends? The one who isn't even Muslim! But don't be dispirited, my brothers; remember our real ancestor's saying: 'At gider, meydan kalır, the horse dies, the course remains.' "

I was stunned. Not only was this my first visit to a mosque, but it was also my first exposure to an Islamic sermon. In a spiritual drama, they all held their fists in the air and shouted, "*Allahu akbar!*" God seems to provide personal sedation, organized atrophy, and social agitation simultaneously.

                                        ~

"Out!" One newspaper was especially adamant in reporting the National Assembly's decision to deport all members of the Ottoman family. The men and women—all princes and princesses—their spouses and children were given forty-eight hours to leave the country. Each person was to receive one thousand Turkish lira, a diplomatic passport, and a one-way ticket to a desired destination. It then occurred to me that was why they took my picture. Not everyone received a passport.

I left the library and ran home. I was scared and excited. Exile meant that I really was considered a member of the Ottoman family.

Sakız was noncommittal. "Two officers brought you a passport and a thousand lira. That's a lot of money. It should last you a few years, wherever you go." I looked at the passport.

Name: His Excellency Adam Zakir *Bey*
Birth date: February 28, 1905
Religion: Yehudi
Mother's maiden name: Sheera Cohen
Father's name: Vahdettin, Mehmed VI

Why Yehudi? Who enrolled me in the Jewish race? Why father's name, Vahdettin? When the name was really worth something, it was denied me. Now, with the exception of the pension, it wasn't a good thing to be labeled. There was enormous hatred against the sultan and the whole Ottoman family.

During the next few days, I stayed at home—except for going out to eat—waiting for someone to come and take me to a train. What would be my desired destination? France? I'd find Mademoiselle Blanche, who would take care of me. Meanwhile, I waited and kept examining my passport. It was a diplomatic passport and had visas, with undetermined residence permission, for Italy, France, and Switzerland. Return to Turkey, however, required special consent by the Turkish consulate and the host country.

Days passed, and nothing happened. So what was I to do? Had Refet Pasha charitably decided to condemn me to internal exile? I felt I was living in a foreign country anyway. After the initial disappointment wore away, I was relieved. So seemed Sakız *Hanım*. I carefully hid the passport and gave the thousand lira to her for safekeeping.

The school year ended. My three friends and most of the students went home. I was very lonely. A small cafeteria was kept open for the *meccanisgratis* who remained, but even the library was closed. I spent my time in the university gardens, sitting on benches or lying in the grass, watching the leaves and branches of the chestnut trees move. The sound of the rustling trees was similar to that of the trees that had surrounded my old house. Occasionally it seemed that I almost heard Mademoiselle Blanche calling me, "*Monsieur* Adam . . . *Monsieur* Adam."

One day I decided to try to find my old house. I knew it was in the vicinity of Robert College. By transferring on and off a series of cable cars, I managed to get to the *Beşiktaş*, where the line ended. From there I went on foot, following a street that paralleled the Bosporus. Every now and then, I stopped in a shop to ask directions. Almost all of them knew of Robert College, and nearly all of them were Sephardic Jews and Greeks and had accents.

Finally, I got to the college entrance. I passed sloping gardens and large, sprawling buildings that were interconnected by carefully designed pathways. It took me a half hour to climb a steep hill, after which I hiked through a forest of old, high pines and cypresses. Then, there it was—our compound, except that it was almost leveled and was surrounded by bulldozers, tractors, and other machines. At the far end sat three workers. I approached them, my heart beating hard, hoping that they would be some of the Albanians who had worked for us.

"*Merhaba*," I greeted them.

They looked at each other, hesitating for a long moment before one answered, "*Merhaba, Bey Effendi*. Sorry, we thought you might be from the American School."

"What are you building here?"

"*Vallaha*—I swear, we don't know; we were just instructed to take down all these wooden houses, then take away the rubbish. I guess they want to make it plain land."

"Do you mind if I walk around a little?" I asked.

"Not at all *Bey Effendi*, just be careful."

As I walked away, they respectfully stood up.

Doors were piled up in one area, windows in another, wood from the floors and walls were in yet another pile, as were the remnants of banisters and pieces of broken furniture. The rest of the house looked junked. The perimeter of the main house's first floor was exposed. This had been the *selāmlık*—men's quarter—and that the harem. Walking from one room to another had never been a major ordeal, but now I could not only walk through the house but also see through it. This one had been Mademoiselle Blanche's room. Some remnants of the yellow walls still were visible. The basement beneath what had been her room looked very shallow. How had I fit through it? I lay down in it, face up. I remembered the insects crawling on me, felt the basement's dampness in my bones, even on such a sunny July day. I closed my eyes and heard, "Ah, ahh, ahhh." No, it couldn't be, I couldn't be hearing her voice. I opened my eyes to find all three workers standing above me.

"Did you fall, *Bey Effendi*? Are you okay?"

"This used to be the room of Mademoiselle Blanche. When I was a child, I used to crawl under her floor boards and listen to her make sweet noises," I explained, beginning to cry.

The men didn't know quite what to do, so they lifted me to my feet and sat me on a low stone wall. "Do you want a cigarette?" one asked. I shook my head no. Still sobbing, I took a small piece of yellow plaster from Mademoiselle Blanche's bedroom wall and began to walk down the hill. I turned around, and I saw the house as it always had been. I waved good-bye—the three men took off their hats in response.

∽

I woke up in total darkness to the sounds of a commotion in the house. It sounded as if things were being thrown around or as if someone was being thrown down on the floor. A garbled male voice was being drowned out by a woman screaming:

"Is there anyone here?"

I heard someone running down the hall, banging on doors. Suddenly, a woman fell through my unlocked, half-open door.

"Help!" she yelled. "Is anybody here?"

"Yes," I said. "What's going on?"

"Oh, thank God! Please come! My boyfriend fell on the floor and lost consciousness. He's still breathing though—"

She spoke with a heavy accent. Russian?

I didn't know who her boyfriend was since all the usual occupants were away, but the noise was coming from Doğan's room.

I made my way to the room and turned up the lamp. On his back on the floor was a man whose entire body was twitching. His mouth was full of bubbling saliva and blood, his pupils were drawn sideways and up, and he smelled of urine. Was it a stroke or a seizure? I wondered a second—the symptoms were in both sides of his body, and he was a young man.

"Your boyfriend is having a *grand mal*," I pronounced authoritatively, after a moment's hesitation. If people saw me as a doctor, I might as well sound like one, even if I weren't really a medical student.

"What is that?" she asked.

"It's an epileptic seizure, nothing to worry about. He'll fall asleep in a few minutes."

I turned him over carefully, pulled his tongue out (the way my medical textbook directed for *grand mal*), and placed him face down.

Then the woman and I realized that she was naked. She was mon-strously beautiful, with light hair and a pale complexion. Hers was a lus-cious body. She grabbed the man's jacket to cover up and looked even sexier. I couldn't help but stare at her, open-mouthed.

"I'm sorry. I panicked, and I forgot to put something on. How come you're all dressed in the middle of the night?"

"Oh . . . I . . . look in his pockets, see if he has any pills."

As she searched his pockets, her body slithered in and out of the jacket.

"Here's something," she said, handing me a silver pillbox with some blue tablets in it.

"I guess we'll have to wait 'til he wakes up," I suggested.

"Listen, he was supposed to get home before midnight. We lost track of time. He's terrified of his father, who constantly threatens him with disinheritance if he doesn't stop seeing me. How long will he sleep?"

"We could wake him up, but how will he get home?"

"He has a car parked outside."

"But how can he drive in this condition?"

As we talked, the man awoke.

"What happened? Oh, no! Did I have? . . . I guess I did. Oh, what a mess. I'm terribly sorry. Is there a place where I can wash up? Who are you?

"My name is Zakir. I live here. At the end of the hall there's a wash basin. Take one of these lamps."

The woman spoke as she took off the jacket and quickly put on her own clothes. "My name is Tatiana. We've been sneaking around, trying to meet somewhere private. You know, it's very difficult.

"Your friend sublet the place to David—the man you just helped—for the summer, so I hope we'll see you often—not like this, of course."

A few moments later, David reappeared. He walked me to my room and, while shaking my hand, squeezed a bit of folded money into it, thanking me profusely again. He left in a hurry.

Fifty lira! Oh my! That was the same as my monthly income! Was this a fee for medical care, an apology for an embarrassing, disturbing situation, or simply hush money? I lay down on my bed and for much of the night visualized Tatiana's body moving in and out of the jacket.

Any restraint of bodily instincts is an abuse of the body and a violence against the mind. It'll stunt all creative growth.

∿

I need a secular theology.

I was living with a stranger who was almost myself. But do I have
to be the same person all my life?

The summer days were passing too slowly. I missed the library and
the guys. Were they friends? What is friendship anyway? The love of
another person stems from the fear of aloneness. Friendship is finding
your friends' fears—your mutual fears. It is the union of fears of aloneness within this immense universe. All encounters between friends are
witnessed by the dread of separation.

∿

I thought maybe I could sit and read at the *madrasah* of the Mosque of
Süleyman. When I tried to get in, however, I was harshly scolded by a
softa, an Islamic theological student, who lectured me at length about
the qualifications required to read their books. While he was pushing me
out, the thread of his *tesbih* snapped, and its prayer beads scattered all
over the stone patio. He pushed me again when I tried to collect them.
An older *imam*-teacher saw me stumbling out of the door and asked what
I was looking for. I told him that I just wanted something to read.

"I'll lend you a book, but you cannot read it here, and you have to
promise to bring it back."

I thanked him as he handed me a book that looked like it was about
to fall apart.

"Be careful," he warned, "it's a little old."

The gentleness and generosity of the older man didn't totally undo
the sense of harsh rejection I had experienced a few moments earlier. It
seemed as if I had no real or permanent ties to anyone anywhere. Why
didn't Atatürk at least throw me out of the country? How long would I
be able to hang around like this?

I sat on my favorite bench in the university park and opened the
cover of the book. The title page read, *Marifetname—The Declaration of
Skill and Wisdom.* The book was written in the eighteenth century by
Ibrahim Hakkı Hazretleri, from the Hasankale town of Erzurum. That
was Abbas's town! What an unbelievable gift, I thought. Abbas could

not have read this, but he had a certain wisdom about him. I wondered if it was the water, the air, or the soil of that town that generated such a man of wisdom. I glanced at the first chapter—"God's Intention in the Creation of the Universe." I then randomly picked a stanza:

Mevlā görelim neyler—Let's see what God will deliver.

Neylerse güzel eyler—Whatever He delivers, it will be grace.

I can't seem to get away from God. I opened the astronomy section. I was so engaged in the book that I didn't notice two young girls leaning behind me, trying to see what I was reading. Only after they began to giggle did I jump, startled, scaring all three of us. Then recognizing how silly the situation was, we all started to laugh. Two little girls with bright, innocent, black eyes had frightened an older guy.

"Hi," ventured the younger one, who, I assumed, was seven or eight years old. "I am the daughter of the Kaymakam, the district governor, and so is my sister."

"You know, you two really scared me. How long have you been here?"

They both giggled again. "One hour . . . okay . . . just a few seconds," replied the younger girl. "What are you reading?"

"Well . . . ah . . . I borrowed this book from the madrasah. It's about almost anything that God created," I replied.

The older one, about thirteen or fourteen years old, asked, in a slightly deprecating tone, if I were a softa—a religion student.

"No. I'm a medical student."

"Oh, really?" she responded, changing her demeanor. "In the fall I'll be starting high school. You know, we see you all the time. We live in the new building—on the second floor. Our windows overlook the street. You come home at almost exactly the same time every evening the whole summer, from the direction of the cafeteria, always alone and always whistling the same tune. Gülderen and I occasionally make bets whether it'll be a few minutes before 8:00 or after. We make a commotion at the window, but you never notice."

"What is your name? Mine is Zakir."

"Mine is Gülseren. We've got to go now. Good-bye, good-bye."

Gülderen, Gülseren! Rose spreader and rose collector, what beautiful names. They looked like baby deer as they ran off, playfully tugging at each other and tripping each other. A sadness came over me. Why do even happy events bring some sadness to me?

⌇

I finished my dinner at 7:50 in the cafeteria. I planned to be in the girls' view and whistling at exactly 8:00 P.M. to see what would happen to their bet. I waited by the side gate—7:58, 7:59—and jumped into the street right in front of their window, whistling. I saw them peeking between the curtains, one girl hovering over the other's head, pulling and pushing each other away from the window. Could they be competing for my attention? The thought of it gave me a disquieting sensation.

I wanted my relationship with Gülseren to remain a potential relationship rather than a real one. I want our relationship to be in seed form like in the unconsummated marriage of Greek mythology. She is my Persephone, and our eight o'clock whistle/curtain encounters are our pomegranate seeds full of promises never to be allowed to ripen their fruits. You see, actualized life is an extended form of plagiarism.

⌇

Sakız had been away for six weeks. The sheets on my bed were so dirty that fungus was growing on them. I didn't have access to fresh sheets because Sakız had locked her area and hadn't left any instructions. I took the sheets off the bed and began sleeping on the bare mattress, using the blanket as a cover. In our old house, I had slept in a bed with a silk coverlet embroidered with flower emblems.

Summer in Istanbul is very hot and humid, and my basement room was like a Turkish bath. All my clothes were wet. Every morning I had to spend at least a half hour standing fully dressed in the sun trying to dry. My underwear was no longer wearable, my socks looked like they were made of rubber, and, when dried, they wouldn't even fold. My shoes had holes in them, and I had no shoelaces. Nevertheless, I was on the right track. I was becoming.

As Sağolan used to say after he gave up Christianity, only through self-deprivation, isolation, and alienation could one achieve self-formation. He urged patience, that becoming was not something one could study; it was something that would unfold in time. I must steel my mind, go into total stillness, and take refuge in myself. As a secular man, I have to make myself. The frontier lies within me; it is there that I must hammer and forge myself. But by cutting myself off from both the natural order below and the supernatural order above, was I railroading myself into craziness like Sağolan?

∾

I left my room only to go to the university cafeteria, even though frequently I had no appetite. I lay in bed, my eyelids glued open most of the time. I had nightmares while I was fully awake. The last time I visited the local barber for a haircut was two months earlier, and I had no energy even to shave. Mirrors no longer reflected me. I had no interest in the news, food, or girls. I was alive only during my literary knitting about the pain of my existence. It was too slow to call it writing. I should stop talking to other people. I don't want to and cannot live with people. Self can be conceived only in the mind alone in the community of solitude. The one who is given inner voice must hear no other. The outer silence is required for self-revelation.

∾

You see, life is an esoteric instructional handbook of blank pages. You fill it with the pain of life's time-released traumas. So it is obvious that life is a slowly acquired illness. Then what was the point of living? I need a philosophy to justify my subjective impasses. I had learned to speak four languages, yet I was silent in all four. Once I had been important enough to be denied formal recognition by my father; now I was totally insignificant. I had learned history, literature, music, and philosophy, and they all made me something less. I should stop learning and forget all I had learned. Only the negation of knowledge brings self-cohesiveness. That is it! Abbas possessed such an ignorance and was a very good man. Obviously, one's goodness resonates with one's depth of ignorance; learning causes moral mutation. Knowing is a veil that portends finality, making disproportionate profit of loss.

∾

Once I lived in silk-and-feather luxury where even ants weren't allowed to disturb me. Now gigantic rats ran round the house without any fear. I had met and conversed with the rich and the strong. However tangentially, I had been part of international intrigue and power plays. Now I wasn't part of anything. I am like a coin that has lost its image and is now just metal. Even in the cafeteria I was a fraud, not a real student. I could tell from the expressions on the faces of the cafeteria workers that they had begun to wonder about me. When I went to the cafeteria, they tried to load up my tray with more food than I was supposed to have. I should stop eating; only self-denial heals one's basic faults. I ate alone, while other students sat together, often, I was sure, talking about me, speculating about who I really was and what I was doing there. I should stop going to the cafeteria. They could call the police and have me arrested for trespassing, using false identity, and cheating the republic. Anyway, the cafeteria food was giving me indigestion. After each meal, I had a burning sensation that went from my stomach all the way up to my throat. But if I didn't eat, a pain hit me midstomach, as if a cat was clawing inside me. Agop's milk or cream were the only things that soothed my stomachaches for a while, but the pain always came back. Agop told me that I was losing weight and should see a doctor: "You look awful. Get a haircut and go to a bathhouse. Clean up; don't let your lady friends see you this way." Lady friends? Friends!

∾

I've noticed that people always looked at me strangely. I shouldn't let people observe me: they might influence me into clarity; only obscurity is self-revelatory. If the mind, which is never free from its own illness, is kept still, the sediments of incoherence eventually settle and make room for the self to retreat. Furthermore, knowing oneself is a contemptuous urging for self-domestication; at best, it is promoting a systematic self-deluding for pseudo-intelligibility. The only knowledge is in the making of a quantum leap to unknowing—that, at least, secures the meaning of provisional existence.

∾

All of a sudden, the whole of reality burst into lucidity. I made a secular leap of faith. The religions' cunningly devised fables that fill people's minds with illusions cause the descent of the mind. If you are predisposed to religious emotion, faith will be planted in you, you will perpetuate a sham belief, and your duplicity will pervade the rest of your life while you live a thoughtless life. You see, you can exist truthfully only without believing.

Religion is morality touched by a fixed feeling of fear, a heavy yoke of forced conviction, a resignation to its duplicity. Simultaneously, salvation comes neither through man nor through God. It comes from the rejection of both and the negation of all sameness.

Everything is self-evident, and the reason is the divinity—the ultimate revelation. I must avoid false solutions. It is not enough to wind the clock—you also have to set it. If the clock is working, it tells the time. Otherwise, it is a collection of metals. Worse than that, it'll give false information.

∾

There was runaway inflation in the country, and even the cash inside the mattress wouldn't last much longer. Everything already was four times more expensive than it had been a short time ago. Agop's breakfast used to cost twenty-five *kuruş*—pennies; now it was one lira. Everything was going in the wrong direction. The solution: I should try to make everything worse. Only at the far end of despair is the self revealed. Didn't Sağolan say the ultimate stability is obtained through total instability? I didn't appreciate him and his ideas after he denigrated Christianity. I thought he was just crazy. He said in order to find yourself, first you must lose yourself.

The killing of God was easy; all I needed was some irony. But killing myself demands self-irony. That, in return, requires a sense of self, which I don't have. So how do I get there? Not by impotent philosophy—an examined life is not worth its termination; furthermore, *what* and *why* questions do not supply answers to *how* questions. Of course, every passing day, there is one less day to live. But that is too slow a process to feed one's ambivalence to self-extinction. So let there be . . . let there be what? Being through nonbeing? Maybe the fault lies in the question? When there is no God, killing oneself is not only permitted but also required as a sign of self-ascension. One must live in such a way as not only to be unafraid of death but in fact to welcome it.

I think the vocabulary of death is inadequate if not misleading. Dying is a deliberate resignation, not an apathetic one; it is fueled with energizing pessimism, to free oneself from the prison of living. Now I must cast off this worn-out body to assure myself that life is only a journey to death. When purpose ends, so should existence. Nothing is to be gained in losing moderation. You see, you can attain a higher grade of nature only by total loss. Only extremes provide salvation.

Options: I could try to hang myself, though there are no exposed beams in the house. I could throw myself under a cable car, though people seem to survive that with broken arms and legs. I could rent a boat at the Kumkapı shore of the Marmara, row out, capsize the craft, and drown myself. That sounded more like a death I could author, if I cannot be an author of anything else. I thought about my little toy Jesus that I threw into the lake.

I finally had reached an intolerable abyss of myself. Is nothingness also endless?

Everything was getting clearer. You see, the philosophy of the continuous is practical expediency in self-world relationships. It prevents inner dissolution in the immediacy of the discontinuous and extends the installment of self-legitimation by way of concealment of the unfamiliar and unintelligible.

∿

The *muezzin* of the Süleymaniye Mosque was reciting the Friday evening prayer. I remembered that I hadn't returned the *Marifetname* book to the old *imam*. I quickly went to the *madrasah* and caught him just as he was about to leave for the mosque. At first he didn't recognize me and mistook me for a beggar. He scrambled to check his pockets for something to give me. When I handed him the book, he looked as if he couldn't believe his eyes. Then he recovered and, with pity on his face and pain in his voice, said, "Oh my God, what happened to you?"

At this moment the younger *softa*, who once threw me out of the *madrasah*, came on us on his way to prayer and must have thought that I was bothering his elder. He pushed me away, saying, "*Allah versin*— God should give it to you, get going, the master is in a hurry. You should be ashamed of yourself, such filthiness is a sin against God." I suddenly realized why I had not been cleaning myself and my clothes. Because there is no God, therefore, there is no sin in being dirty.

My bringing back the book was a self-betraying attempt to seek a false solution to my sense of disconnectedness.

∿

Someone knocking on the window of my room woke me. Two voices were quarreling:

"How do you know for sure he lives here?"

"Everyone knows."

"Don't knock so hard; you'll break the window!"

From my basement room window I could see people only from the knees down. I looked up and saw two pairs of white-socked legs and the edges of navy blue skirts: Gülderen and Gülseren! I stood on a chair to get closer to the window. The girls were bent down, hands cupped to their foreheads, straining to see inside. When we came face to face, Gülderen let out a shriek.

"Oh! An old, ugly monster!" and ran away.

Gülseren lingered for a few seconds, looking shocked. Slowly, she withdrew from the window, and I could see her legs as she hesitated, trying to decide which way to go. Then she disappeared.

Old, ugly monster? My mother had always told me that I was a young, beautiful treasure. Had she really meant it? I was ready to sink the treasure into the Marmara, but I just didn't have the energy to leave the house. I wished that one of Istanbul's infamous earthquakes would bury me here and now. I wondered how long it would take to starve to death. It had been two days since I'd eaten. My breath smelled foul. I guessed that was why the rats walked freely around me and even jumped onto my bed. I didn't have the energy to shoo them away. I had to get up and finish it today. It was getting late. I took all my cash and left for the Marmara. I'd buy a boat if necessary. I left the jewelry and the gold for whoever was going to clear out my room and be clever enough to search the mattress.

∾

I am not afraid of dying, but I am worried that death may not be final. What if life ends but doesn't stop? No, no, no. There is no God; therefore, all is final. Then I must give an aim to my death—my finality. How can I give an aim to dying when I didn't have an aim for living? Well, one thing, I must be free of self-pity and confusion. Self-pity, if one takes the world as real rather then as metaphorical; confusion, if one seeks relation with a nonreal entity; and together they preempt the real despair. If, however, despair is carried to term and not aborted, it might give inner birth to an embryonic serenity. This is a meaningful aim to give to one's death. Any other death is simply an inadequate litany of contentment.

✧

I no longer want to know the why's and how's of my being flung into this world. All these questions make me helpless and impotent. I need to act without further thought. Killing myself will be the ultimate proof of God's absence.

The boatman saw me approaching and shook his head:

"There are no boats left now. Come back tomorrow and early. Early!"

"How about this one?" I asked, pointing to a large boat that was pulled aside.

"It's a fisherman's boat, kid. You couldn't even maneuver it out of the harbor."

"I'll buy it from you." I took a wrinkled one-hundred-lira bill out of my pocket.

"Are you crazy or something, kid? Where did you get all that money anyway?"

He glared at me. But his eyes shone when he looked at the bill in my hand.

"If you're so determined," he said, "I'll have my younger brother come with you. You know, you may need someone to steady the boat if you swim. But it'll cost you ten lira an hour."

I agreed. He hollered a few times for his brother and, getting no response, walked to the boathouse. He returned with a man who looked more disheveled than I did but rough and muscular—hardly a younger brother.

The two of them pushed the boat into the water and asked me to jump in. The fisherman took the oars, and we swiftly moved out—a little too far out—of the harbor's crowded area. As we moved, I noticed Gülseren and her friends, including some boys, in a boat. My heart sank.

"This is a good place to swim," the fisherman advised. "The tide is going out, so don't lose sight of the boat."

It was clear to me that he had an agenda—robbing me. Even before I had gotten into the boat, I saw the fisherman and the boatman giving each other not-so-subtle glances. A paranoid novice at scheme detection would have seen it. I smiled to myself. I felt happy, not the kind of happiness that God and people promise. Unwrapped from its romantic camouflage, this real happiness is an ever-incoherent state of mind—a prelinguistic, primordial warmth. There is no place better for it than being dissolved in the ocean.

I got undressed and jumped naked into the warm waters of the Marmara. As I surfaced, I could see the fisherman rifling through my pants pockets.

"Hey! What are you doing?"

"Where did you steal all this money?" he demanded.

I was upset, but I was more upset that I was upset. What difference did it make who took the money? I was planning to drown—with or without the money. Was I tagging a drama into my trivial death? Nevertheless, it was disturbing to me that he was stealing my money while I was vulnerable in the water. What if I didn't want to die?

"You're the thief!" I screamed. "You just stole my money right in front of me. I know Governor Refet Pasha. I'll have you put behind bars!"

What was I doing? Not leaving him any choice except to abandon me here?

"You know Refet Pasha?" he laughed loudly. "Did you steal the money from him?"

"What of it?" I shouted.

He began rowing toward me. I saw the side of the boat and him above it. When he got up beside me, he lifted an oar and hit me. Before he did it again, I dove so that I didn't take the full impact of the blow. He came after me, trying again and again to hit me. I kept diving to protect myself. Why, I wondered, was I not letting him kill me? Isn't this what I wanted, to die? What better situation could I have imagined? If he struck me, then I'd be unconscious while drowning.

But his determination to kill me infuriated me. I wasn't going to die *his* way. Is justice reducible to the rightness of the will? The tide pulled me out, and the fisherman, being sure that there was no way I could be seen from the shore—let alone being rescued at that late hour—rowed away.

そ

This was a most bizarre situation: I had just escaped a murder attempt while trying to commit suicide. Only God is supposed to be paradoxically true. Exhausted, I lay on my back, floating, strangely enjoying the delicious moment of watching the sunset over the Marmara. Every part of me—back, arms, and legs—hurt from being hit, and I had swallowed a lot of water. I felt as if I had left my body. I felt unburdened and sort of cheerful. In fact, this was the most magnificent moment in my life. No god can offer such a feeling. If anything, a god would interfere with "it," especially at the time of dying—"it" being to see your dying through to the end, truthfully.

You see, primarily you die for others; your own death cannot have any effect on your own life but only on the lives of others. Your death has meaning only for them—actually not a meaning but consequences in the forms of regrets, guilt, satisfaction. Others bring God into the the-ater of funerals and burials so as to give a meaning to the absence of a person in their lives. But if you have no presence in other people's lives while you are alive, then you may as well not die.

I felt myself drifting out to sea. There were no boats around, and it was getting very dark. Isn't it too bad? I thought. I could have become a doctor, married Gülseren, practiced medicine in Erzurum, and raised children, or I could have gone to Palestine, helped the Jews establish a state, and become a wise rabbi, like Nahum. I might even have joined Atatürk. I wondered what it would have been like to make love to Tatiana. Sakız would rent my room to another poor student. The gang would give me a thought or two. The cafeteria would have one fewer mouth to feed. Would Gülseren miss me? I began to whistle, the same tune that called her to the window. I imagined I saw her silhouette through a little opening of the curtains.

Self-made calamity doesn't offer self-pity. Actually it offers absolutely nothing except prolonging itself. In his devotional phase, Sağolan used to preach that Calvary be prolonged for truly experiencing one's potentials in Divinity. If you believe that, then slow down—you deserve all the pain you can get. Slow down and savor the taste of death.

༄

All of a sudden the drifting stopped. For a few moments I felt an inti-mation of immortality. The water was flat, not moving in either direc-tion. I was alive in this glorious moment, in this incredible universe. This must be the feeling of ecstasy—a state of being outside of oneself. I neither wanted to live longer nor die. I just wanted this moment to be frozen in time.

Slowly the drift began to move me toward the shore. I began to back-stroke without wasting too much energy. I knew then that I would make it, if I didn't drown in the weltering sea of emotions. By the time I washed up on shore, the sun was about to rise. I sat naked, exhausted, hungry, thirsty, and cold in the harsh sands of the Marmara. The only sound was the *muezzin's* morning prayer call from the Valide Mosque in Aksaray.

Was this the common scheme of "*Deus ex Machina*" of Greek tragedies where God appears at the last moment of a potential disaster and saves the desperate hero or heroine? No. This was a preordained chance. If there were a God, he could have drowned me.

Thankfully, the streets were nearly empty. Still naked, I ran to the mosque and explained my situation to the puzzled *mufti*. He kindly let me borrow an overcoat and gave me some hot tea, both of which helped me get home.

I must have slept more than twenty-four hours, waking up totally energized. I then took a *beşibirlik*—five-in-one gold coin—from the mattress; sold it in the covered bazaar; bought new sheets, shoes, shirts, and pants; got a haircut and a clean shave; went to a restaurant—where I ordered grilled lamb and rice washed down by beer—came home; and fell asleep for another five hours. I jumped out of bed just in time to travel from my backyard through the university grounds and emerged from the side gate at 8:02. I whistled.

Yes, there she was, alone by the window and so delighted to see me. She waved, waved until I got out of her sight. I skipped down the street, blurting the words from an old love song my mother used to sing to me: "*Yasamak sevilmektir*—to live is to be loved." I experienced having a seed of my emotional self—the promise of things, however small.

⌒

God is not, and all is.

I went home, but I couldn't stay put. I went to the coffeeshop that the gang frequented and sat and talked with strangers; I ordered tea and coffee for everyone in the shop—on me. At midnight, everyone had left, but I was still full of energy. The café owner suggested that I go to the Kasaplıyan's *meyhane* a few blocks south. When I got to the bar, it was also closing. There were a half dozen customers getting ready to leave. I offered to buy them all drinks, so the barkeeper let me stay for another half hour.

I walked back toward the house and decided to settle myself in front of the university's side gate. From there I watched Gülseren's house. I quietly began to whistle to myself, and low and behold, Gülseren appeared at the window. I stood there, as did she, motionless. I finally signaled her to come down; she shook her head no. I repeated my request again and again. She finally signaled something like "one minute." The request for the promise of restraint, that's what God is.

She opened the door. Right in front of me stood the angel of all angels, dark-black eyes fringed with long, soft lashes set against the whitest skin, in her most adorable pajamas. Her innocence excited me. I walked into the entrance and closed the door behind me. We leapt into each other's arms, our lips sealing in a long, long kiss. I felt her nakedness under her thin pajamas and moved my hand over her small, soft bosom. I caressed her silky hair; her long eyelashes danced with mine. The beauty, that's what God is, and the goodness is the distilled essence of God.

"Please go now," she pleaded after we exchanged several more breathless kisses. "My parents may wake up." She gently pushed me out of the door while still kissing my lips. I couldn't talk; I couldn't breathe. Why breathe or talk anyway, and what is there to say? Love is the last breath and last sound. Is this the first fluttering of silken wings or simply the fever of the mind? I walked around the university grounds near where she lived, inhaling the roses and hugging the gently rustling chestnut trees. You see, it's the promise of the seed, not the delivery of the flower, that matters. God is the innocence of love.

I dipped into a real feeling, maybe for the first time in my life. Crying didn't count as it is merely an expression of self-pity. I guess this is what Dr. Osman was trying to have me experience, however small it could have been then. Yes, I feel, I do. I got home and couldn't sleep. I was feverishly excited. Eventually, I must have dozed off because I was awakened by a call for morning prayer from the mosque. The chant that usually irritated me now sounded melodious and inviting. I quickly got dressed, walked all the way to Aksaray, returned the overcoat to the *mufti* of the Valide Mosque, and dropped one hundred lira into the collection box. I walked to Agop's place in no time, ate three portions of his heavy cream and honey plate, and left him a big tip. He was delighted to see me happy.

I now had excessive energy. "Gülseren, Gülseren, Gülseren," I said to the bed, the lamp, the chair. I repeated her name to all the people I saw on the streets; some of them smiled; one shook his head and tapped his forehead with his fingers. I bargained one of the bazaar's rug dealers down to nothing on a big rug, then paid its original price and carried the rug back to my room with no help at all.

The seed suddenly sprouted. I was destined to make a difference in the world. Perhaps I could rescue the land of the Jews from the British. I must visit my mother's grave, I thought.

At home, I noticed an envelope on the floor that apparently had been thrown in through the half-opened window. The envelope contained a picture of Gülseren. I should definitely marry her.

I wrote a poem to her:

Manevi hazza yakındır
Closer to the pleasure of the souls
Maddi olmaktan ırak
Far from the world's bowels
Gāh Gülserenden gül kopardım
At times I picked from the joyful a rose
Gāh gönlümden ihtirak
At times from my heart alienating fools

I couldn't stop writing every minute for days; I wrote pages and pages with ceaseless energy and expansiveness, filling one pad after another, until the skin of my fingers frayed and bled. I can author far more than my own death. I was inebriated with the poetically inflated flow of my own thoughts. Frontiers lie within me. All of a sudden the same words had too many meanings. I have a steady urge to trespass all restraints of thought and reason.

My mind is unbound. It lifts itself, provided that it is free from the hope of external help, including that of God. God is a rendered helplessness. Only poetry can redeem the mind from decay of religious irrationality and insidious rationalism. Poetry reminds me that I am the center of myself and confirms my self-ultimacy.

❧

During the rest of August, I sold a few of my mother's gold coins and bought things: twenty suits, dozens of recordings of Italian and German operas, medical textbooks with large sections devoted to treating the female patient, and several spy novels. I ate out in restaurants night after night, drank lots of beer, and frenetically smoked two packs of cigarettes a day. I was drunk on life. I didn't know how to put on the brakes, nor did I really want to. There is no God; therefore, everything is permitted. The striving for satisfaction of all visceral appetites is the basis of life. I couldn't control my mind, but for the first time in my life I felt life. I didn't need to understand it.

Understanding is an old, outdated phenomenon. What is the purpose of examining the source of my well-being? You see, the more you understand life, the less certain you'll become your own self. The imposition of patterns of life on the self conflicts with acquiring degrees of being because there is no end point. Thus, if being is not an end in itself, then life must be lived as is, not studied or patterned.

～

One night after David left, Tatiana remained at the house. I told her how much I missed her. The lines of poetry just rolled out:

> *Dildai sevda eylemekte mazurdur halim*
> In yearning my love I am only in pain
> *Boynunda kalır yad etmezsen sonra vebalim.*
> My sins will be yours if it is all in vain

"Ohh! A poet-doctor!" she giggled. "I am a musician. In fact, I was quite well known in Russia." She had this afterglow of a sexualized life.

She poured some of the wine that was left over from her evening with David. I gulped it down. When she leaned over to pour more wine, her shapely breasts softly bumped each other and jiggled from side to side. She knew she was beautiful and playful. She looked long at me with her erotically hypnotic eyes. "I think something happened to you since the last time. You met a girl, huh?" The verses poured from my lips:

> *Gurur ile yükselen gögsün olgunlukları*
> Pridefully rising, your bosom in fullness
> *Değdikçe can alıyor, zehirden mi okları?*
> They become alive, in touch, are arrows poisonous?
> *Ben onları kendime mehtap yaptığım akşam*
> The night that I make them my moonlight
> *Saadetim kudurur, sana taptığım akşam*
> My happiness will rage when I worship you that night.

"It's so beautiful it hurts to hear it," she declared. "For which lucky woman did you write it?"

"For you."

"No, no," she protested. "But when?"

"Just now," I murmured.

"Right now? You mean it came out just like that? My God, you must be a genius. But . . . why do you look so sad all of a sudden?"

"I don't know," I replied. It was true. I didn't know why, but the sinking feeling took over.

"Come over here," she invited me to sit near her on the sofa.

She put her arms around me and lightly kissed my face, eyes, and lips as if I were a child. I wanted to be kissed again and again.

"You know, I could easily worship you myself," she whispered.

You see, the impracticality of poetry is not all that seamless.

I continued reciting:

Beni sen sev, kanayım zevkine hep ağlamanın
Love me, so that I would indulge in the pleasure of pain
Böyle bir kahrını çeksem, sana bel bağlamanın
Thus to suffer in the extreme of attachment to you

As soon as I got into her bed, I fell asleep. My own loud snoring woke me in the middle of the night. Tatiana's arm was pressing against my throat. I gently moved out from under her and sat on the bed watching this exquisite creature reclining naked in front of me. I didn't want to go to sleep; I wanted to admire her the whole night. The supremacy of beauty is uncontestable.

I'm not sure what woke her, but she rolled over, pulled me under her, and began playing with my penis, trying to insert it in her vagina. Nothing. My penis shrank. The more she tried, the worse it became. What was the matter with me? I should get on top, I thought; after all, maintaining an erection against gravity would be more difficult. Again nothing. Was I too awed, able only to observe and admire, restrained with the intensity of my desire?

Although I never recovered from the former, I eventually overcame the latter and became Tatiana's lover. We met almost every day for several weeks, and though I didn't learn much more about her, I learned how to make love and not to be too serious. Her love made life light.

She possessed an erotic intelligence. "I love making love, I love giving all myself," she said. She didn't need to know more than that. Exuberant with my success—she thought I was great—and guessing that poetry was the key to approaching women, I began to offer my poems to anyone who was half willing to listen.

~

Sakız and the boys returned from summer vacation, and the house again was full of noise and laughter. They all hugged and kissed me as if I were a long-lost relative. I was happy to see them but also felt a sense of emptiness.

The boys quickly settled into their usual routine of reluctantly attending classes for a half day, then spending the rest of the day and night going to coffeehouses, playing cards and backgammon, getting drunk, and searching for women (unsuccessfully, except for their girls in the red-light district). I, on the other hand, was living a life in an intoxicated sex haze with a grown-up woman and was romantically involved with a young girl.

Is love a self-assertion through lust, or is it a self-ascension through self-restraint? Do I need them both? My mood seems to soar on the wings of them.

I felt and behaved differently from day to day, if not hour to hour. One moment I was an orphan, a lowly student, eating free meals at the university cafeteria with the rest of the poor kids. The next I was a poet-physician, hobnobbing with the wealthy, elegant class of Istanbul. I even had two separate wardrobes. Neither life, of course, was real or realizable.

~

I had a ferocious appetite to read. I spent the day either studying in the library or attending advanced-level classes at the medical school. The first two and a half years of medical study—the predoctoral period— didn't interest me because the classes were oriented toward basic science. Only in the third year did students begin to learn the clinical sciences, and I was a stubborn presence in those classes, despite my nightlife. Because I had read the medical texts from cover to cover rather than chapter by chapter as in formal classes, teachers occasionally called on me to engage in playful inquiry, and students would encourage me to challenge haughty teachers. But I was a large-class-only student. I couldn't participate in the smaller, clinical clerkships, which were organized by rotating assignment, because one had to be a real, registered student.

I avoided making friends with other students to prevent close questioning. Nevertheless, someone occasionally asked where I was doing a specific rotation, upon which I mentioned the name of one of the hospitals and quickly disengaged. A couple of times their excessive curiosity almost blew my cover.

"I never see you in hospital," one observed. "Where do you hide?"

My secret nearly escaped when another student, Rebecca, the daughter of a wealthy and well-known entrepreneur, invited me to a party:

"I told my father all about how you know more than some teachers. He said you must be Jewish. I'm having a party in Kuzguncuk. Why don't you come? No? Maybe you could come for a Sabbath dinner."

Although I had managed to put off other inquiries by offering some disdainful explanation, I felt a strong urge to confess to her.

"Actually I'm not a medical student, I just read medical textbooks and attend seminars."

She laughed. "Oh, what a strange sense of humor you have. I've got to tell this to my father."

I have mastered the art of counterfeiting myself.

～～

The Hotel Claude Farrère was a five-story building in the Çağaloğlu district overlooking the Sultan Ahmet Mosque. David's father owned the hotel. David's father was a dark, heavy-set man who usually sat in a dark corner of the hotel reception area or in the restaurant with his feet up on a table, smoking cigarettes, drinking tea, pulling incessantly at worry beads, and chatting with people. He sat in stunning contrast to the hotel manager—who really ran the place—a middle-aged, skinny, nervous, Jewish man whom everyone called Schwarz—as if it were his first name. Schwarz lived alone in a small room at the hotel and was on duty day and night. Accordingly, he was always running from one task to another, scolding workers, buttering up clients, and making notes. I never saw him outside the hotel or with anyone other than guests of the hotel.

The hotel guests were mostly artists and young tourists, most of whom didn't pay well, on time, or at all. The other occupants were

Kurds, permanent residents of the top floors, who paid their bills well and ahead of time.

David introduced me to his father: "This is my friend Zakir, Dad. He is a doctor and a poet and speaks French and Arabic."

"Listen, David," he turned to his son. "I want you to make friends with people like Doctor Bey, not all those *züppes*, who pretend to be westernized . . ."

Schwarz, unabashedly eavesdropping, cornered me on the way out and noted conspiratorially, "Trade follows the bride. . . . He has a beautiful daughter!"

~~~

In time I became the physician of the Turks and the Kurds at the Claude Farrère and also the exiled *nouveaux pauvres* Russians. By now I had an almost perfect grasp of book-knowledge medicine. But I had no way of getting practical experience with real patients because I couldn't attend the university clinics, which were limited to legitimately registered students. Therefore, the Hotel Claude Farrère became my clinic. I now carried a regular doctor's bag containing the standard contents, including a stethoscope, blood pressure cuff, and reflex hammer. I treated headaches, colds, sties, sore throats, diarrhea, and constipation; I stitched cuts and offered remedies for other pains and aches and, of course, indigestion.

If a patient's situation was over my head, I knew exactly where to refer him, sending him along with a note from me written on hotel letterhead. It worked like a charm.

My female Russian patients paid me with private musical evenings— oh, how I missed Sağolan. Male Russians offered pimping services and occasionally some inherited, ugly, antique jewelry. Almost all of the seminoble Russians were amateur musicians. I presumed that as members of a privileged class, they all had musical training. But with the exception of Baroness Taskin and Mademoiselle Timchenkov, they were simply bad. Still, I didn't have the heart to refuse their offers; they had nothing else to give. And what had I provided them anyway? Faux medicine—a fair exchange.

My Russian patients were afflicted primarily with the disease of holding on to their pasts. Their nostalgia was for a lost paradise that had never existed. Theirs was an incurable disease in ever-changing, smallest detail. Yes, they occasionally had boils, hemorrhoids, and back pain, but these never disturbed them as much as the diseases of "what might have been," "if," and "one day." For the latter condition I had the right skills: listening.

~~~

There was an elusive leader of the Kurds, Molla Seyyit, who was also staying at the Hotel Claude Farrère. My Kurdish patients spoke so idealizingly of him, as if he were their god. I had to meet him. But he never consulted me like the others. I decided to send a note, through Schwarz, the hotel manager, to Molla Seyyit:

Nöbetçi Zakir, beklemekle tektek kelām et
Zakir is on call, every step of his waiting is written
Huzura kabul etmez ise, benden bir selām et
If an audience isn't granted, could his salutation be forgiven

The following morning, I received a written invitation:

Physicians are accepted with reluctance but poets with open arms.
Come have lunch with me at C.F. today.

When I arrived, a light-skinned man with partially gray hair, dressed in the old Ottoman style, displaying upper-class manners and an impressive presence, called a greeting:
"Young poet! I gather you are interested in our struggle."
He rose from the table in the hotel restaurant where he had been having *narghile* with David's father.
Seyyit looked and behaved differently from all the other Kurds I had met. He looked me over with eyes that seemed to absorb every detail. Apparently satisfied, he said, "Sit down."
I sat, and he began speaking:
"I have been preoccupied with the Atatürk government's atrocities. They hanged forty of our brothers in front of the Elazığ Mosque.
"Atatürk recruited our help by deceiving us that he was fighting to save the caliphate, establishing a European government and society. Did you know that on the streets of Diyarbekir officers are taking away men's fezzes and tearing off women's *tcharchafs*? And if that is not enough, Atatürk blamed the killing of the Armenians on the Kurds. So guess

who is now helping in our mission for Kurdish independence? Our old enemies—the English and the Greeks!"

"You know, the British can't be trusted," escaped my mouth.

"Nor can any other nation," he smiled. "Look at the Jews. Until the empire fell, they supported us Kurds directly and indirectly. They needed us to destabilize the sultanate to gain concessions for their Zionist ambitions. Now, they want us to destabilize the British, their strongest ally. But one day, this all will come to a dead end. America will be Spanish, Europe will be overrun with the Negroes of Africa, the Jews will be wiped out by the Arabs, and the Kurds will inherit the old Ottoman Empire. The date? My crystal ball says 2084!"

David's father winced.

"How will Kurds inherit the empire?"

"If we Kurds do not gain our independence actively in the next few generations, we'll end up inheriting the whole of Turkey in the long run. Did you know that real Ottomans make up less than 1 percent of the Turkish population? The rest are original inhabitants of Anatolia: Hittites, Arabs, Greeks, Lazs, Circassians, Bedouins, Armenians, and Gypsies. Kurds are the largest homogeneous population in Turkey. In the next two hundred years we'll multiply faster than any other subgroup and passively invade the whole country. Your grandson will walk in these streets and hear again Kurdish songs. Turks will become a semi-European, decadent people, godless and rudderless. Don't let me go on. You are not only a great physician and a poet but also a good listener. Speaking of poetry, maybe you should write our national anthem, ha!" He laughed, for the first time in our long conversation.

There is no God; therefore, there is no truth or lie. You are who you say you are, or not. All are equally suspect.

∾

Am I myself?

My mood reflected the seasons. The last three summers I had been filled with ceaseless energy, expansiveness, and certainty, even in my fabrications and exuberant productivity. I would go to extremes with an unbridled visceral force and regularly wake up around 4:00 A.M. and not be able to go back to sleep. During these accelerated days, I felt the pulse of time: I wrote dozens of rambling poems and philosophical essays, only to discard them during my dead days. Of course, by now I knew from reading the type of craziness I had: mania in the summer, depression in the winter. In the medical texts, Kraepelin, the famous European psychiatrist, didn't address such a subtype of mania.

I was bored not only with medicine but also with women, food, music, Palestine, and Kurdistan. I bought a radio, a Granfunken. It remained in its original box. Looking back on it, I believe I didn't have much interest in any of those things during my manic months either; I only thought I did. Poetry and philosophy remained the only relative constants in my life—those and the idea of death: especially the poetry, which drugged the pain of reality and vacated the hollowness of the search for relevance in living and dying.

❧

Whenever it was cold, I went to the Law Library. I was embarrassed to be seen in the Medical Library, or worse, to be questioned about my graduation status. I would enviously watch the law students' eager and lively engagement with each other even in the library. They had futures. Mostly, I read newspapers and recent legal briefs published in conjunction with the creation of the republic's new constitution. A totally new system was being developed and formed, but what relevance did it have for me?

Again I began to think of various ways of killing myself. I imagined starting a fire in the library and staying there to burn with the books. Perhaps first I would stab a few of the cocky guys—especially the tall one with the thick, curly hair and wealthy demeanor. Go to sleep with the charcoal fire on? No, I couldn't stand the smell of it. Overdose with opium? It was no longer easy to find opium. I couldn't cut my wrists. I wouldn't. Furthermore, I didn't want to kill myself; I just wanted to die.

❧

It was about midnight when I returned from the hotel after an emergency visit. I walked back to my place through dark, narrow, steep, and empty streets. The profound quiet of the night was occasionally punctured by the screaming whistles of the *Bekçis*. Why were these police assistants blowing their whistles? I wondered. Were they obligated to show their presence, or were they comforting themselves? Were they scared in these lonely, haphazard, ancient labyrinths?

I wondered why I wasn't scared. I guess you've got to be real to get hurt. I wasn't totally real. I was like a ghost. I walked parallel to the old

Byzantine wall, which seemed equally unreal. People had built this enormous wall with their hands and sweat to protect themselves from invaders. Other people tore it down and called it victory. Now others were dismantling it stone by stone to build houses for themselves from its ruins. I ached. I ached for the Byzantines.

I turned the corner. Gülseren's house stood in total darkness. I whistled, again and again. No movement at the curtains.

~

Atatürk was imprisoning and executing anyone he considered an enemy of Turkey, all potentially powerful people who disagreed with him. Every day his list of enemies grew. I was surprised and pleased that he had his own man, Refet Pasha, arrested. The word was that he had Djemal assassinated in Tiflis and Enver killed in Bukhara. He wanted the same for Talāt in Germany, but the Armenians got him first.

Reading the list of people arrested became a daily activity of mine. One day I saw a familiar name on the top of the list: Emmanuel Carasso, ex-member of the Ottoman Parliament.

I must have screamed because everyone in the library turned toward me. I got up, made apologies, and left crying. Oh, my Manny, my Uncle Manny! I thought he had escaped to Salonika. Why did he return? I don't remember how I got home. I sat on the bed. I hadn't thought about Uncle Manny for years, and I couldn't understand why I was crying so copiously. He wasn't my real uncle, and looking back, now that I knew something about the relationships between men and women, I guessed he was my mother's lover. Why hadn't I looked for him?

I walked to Gülseren's home and began pacing in front of it, whistling our signal. It was Saturday, and I thought she might be at home. There were no activities going on in the house. About two o'clock I saw Gülderen coming home with her nanny. She gladly informed me that her sister had gone boating with some friends off Kumkapı.

I was out of breath by the time I got there. I saw a number of boats in the distance and decided to rent a boat myself. The fisherman who had tried to kill me didn't even recognize me. As I rowed toward the boats, I saw Gülseren with two other girls and three boys. I wanted to turn away quickly, but she saw me. We looked at each other for a few seconds. I felt caressed by her black eyes, but sadly, as if we were saying good-bye. Then a tall boy with full, curly hair took her chin in his hand and pulled her toward him. He was that rich law student I had seen in the library. She looked as if she resisted momentarily, then flung herself into his chest, laughing. Her long, straight hair fell over his shirt front.

〰

You see, there are no permanent lovers, only temporary desire with a double inscription: read vertically, it is the anxiety of the discontinuous; read horizontally, it is the sadness of remembered oneness. Neither my anxiety nor my sadness had anything to do with her. I didn't even know her. No man can truly know another, especially a woman. The pain in seeing her betray me was so excruciatingly painful that it was peculiarly pleasurable.

〰

Again I was spinning wildly. I wrote frenetically. In the ardor of my longing to be incarnate of God, I ended up losing myself, whatever little of myself I had. I must ascend to myself; descending from God is not enough.

I didn't feel at home with my own ideas and feelings and behavior. I slept with Tatiana, and still I looked for other women. The ordinary human immediacy bored me; only the exhaustive was interesting; even then, I couldn't be with anyone for a long period of time. Every relation was a sort of prison from which I wanted to escape. I couldn't sit still and listen to my favorite music; I couldn't follow my own thoughts, let alone those of others. Thoughts are worthless sensations. They rush, churn, and thresh in profusion of frameworks and force my words to choose their own meanings. I was too aware of everything. Sounds and colors were too vivid, conversations were too loud and too slow.

〰

In the late afternoon Doğan and Mete came home with a young Dutch girl of no more than sixteen years old whom they had picked up on the university grounds. She was a high school student interested in a college education in Istanbul. The boys, who didn't speak much of any foreign language, brought her to our house under the premise of introducing me to her as a translator. She kept gazing longingly at Doğan, who looked more Dutch than Turk.

The girl, Majbritt, was plump and full of enthusiasm. She talked incessantly as I tried to translate her hybrid French to Turkish. Apparently, she was the daughter of a recently appointed consul of the embassy of the Netherlands and was already enamored with Turkish culture. "I hope I can go to Istanbul University after I graduate high school," she said earnestly. She drank raki as if it were water. The boys were all over her, touching her scantily dressed body and caressing her hair, with no objection from her. She soon was totally inebriated, singing Dutch songs, dancing around, pulling up her skirt, then sitting—or rather falling—onto the guys' laps.

The sun went down, and Doğan finally signaled that the rest of us should make ourselves scarce, but no one listened. So, with a wink, he took her to my room and closed the door. An hour later, Doğan emerged and announced that the girl wanted to talk to me.

I walked in. Her white body was a stark contrast to the darkness of the room. She reached out for me, then held me tight. We both fell on the bed. It was all wet. Had she urinated? I wondered. Was she that drunk? I definitely was.

She kissed me, and I kissed her back. She pulled off my shirt. Did I make love to her? I don't know. I sobered up to her screaming.

"Oh my God, it's twelve o'clock. My parents must be so worried. Oh Jesus, what has happened to me?" She got up, shakily but quickly dressed, and staggered out.

When I came back to Doğan's room, the boys, joined by Nurettin, were wringing their hands.

"What did she say? Is she all right?" one of them asked.

"What are you talking about?" I said, confused.

They dragged me into my room. They brought a lamp, and the sight was unbelievable. The sheets and pillows were all soaked in blood. The lower end of the wall, next to the bed, was covered with her bloody handprints, as if she had struggled with an ax murderer.

Nurettin took charge: "Okay, you two take off your clothes, put them in a bag, and then shower. Mete and I will clean the walls. We'll get rid of the sheets. Tonight and the next few days, you and Doğan sleep elsewhere, maybe at the dormitory. All right, everyone get going."

Doğan took me to his jewelry store friend's house. The man and his wife were most gracious. They accommodated us in their living room, without asking any questions, though Doğan said a few things in Kurdish.

The following morning, Doğan and I both thought that Nurettin, a law student, had overreacted, and we went straight home. My room was squeaky clean, but my mattress was gone.

Nurettin stumbled in. "How do you like it?"

"Where is my mattress?"

"Oh, it was unsalvageable. Mete and I dumped it over the Galata Bridge with the rest of the stuff."

My arms and knees felt weak. "Did you notice—I mean were there any things. . . . Oh! Forget it."

I was ruined. Obviously they could not have known that I had all that jewelry and money hidden in it. Now I was penniless. Reality, I guess, is what one comes up against. All I was concerned about was the loss of money and the fear that I may have done something wrong and would be punished for it. I had no internal active conflict with the wrong itself. If anything, I was even intrigued to be living a little outside the law.

⁓

You see, virtue is self-condemnation—let the law take care of the wrongness. That is enough. There is no need to insert the laws of the soul. The conscience is the misjudgment of the darkest inner tribunal. It is the chronic self-accusation, always paying homage to goodness, and it is an ever-present incorruptible witness against self. The conscience doesn't operate with the rule of expediency, which is the essence of survival. Secular morality is just that, the rule of expediency. But can I be the standard of good and bad and still not be God? The Talmud says, "If I am for myself, what am I?" Simply an unbeliever, who is supposed to worship himself. But I am neither god nor man.

The belief in God, thus living forever in eternity, contributes to living honestly, sort of. What if you don't believe in eternity? Then it doesn't matter whether you are honest or not. Is it all a matter of expediency? I saw Rabbi Nahum's disappointed eyes glaring at me as he said, "Son, good doesn't exist without God."

In Sağolan's Christianity, I was always and at the same time both just and sinner.

My thoughts were interrupted when the front door flew open. Four policemen forced themselves in and without any explanation hand-cuffed all of us, dragged us outside, put us in a police wagon, and took us to the Tevkifhane. We were placed in different cells. I began to shiver with fear. I guessed I deserved what I got.

Hadn't the old guy in the cafeteria warned me not to associate with these vagabonds? But then again, what was I myself?

I must have been there for a few hours before the officers took me to the commissar's office. He was an enormous man with a hefty black mustache covering half his face. He sat next to Majbritt and her equally blond father, who was a towering figure, handsome, and courtly.

"State your full name and address."

"Adam Zakir. Süleymaniye Caddesi, Number 2."

"Your father's and mother's names?"

"Vahdettin Sultan and Şahhane Hanım."

"Are you making fun of me?" the commissar growled. "You know, you're in deep shit here. If you don't behave yourself, you'll be in prison for a long time, and I am telling you, a pretty boy like you will be enthu-siastically received by the other prisoners. Now, try again. What is your father's name and his address? What is so funny anyway?"

"Nothing," I said, continuing. "I was told by my mother and every-one else I knew in my childhood, even Rabbi Nahum, that the sultan was my father, though he never wanted to acknowledge it because my mother was Jewish and he didn't want that to interfere with his becom-ing the sultan. You see, my mother left him when she was pregnant and he was just a prince . . ."

"Hold it, hold it." The commissar got up. "Are you nuts or some-thing? You're being charged with the rape of a minor, a foreigner, a daughter of a consul, and you're telling me this tall story. How is this going to help you?"

Meanwhile, both Majbritt and her father were trying to figure out what was going on through the quasi-help of a young translator who said, "This man says he is a prince of the empire and claims immunity."

At that moment, a well-dressed civilian entered. The commissar stood and saluted him. "The kid is unmoored, if not totally deranged," he said. The man shook hands with the consul and Majbritt, who throughout the interview looked at me with pity. The man instructed the commissar to "continue."

"Where were you on the evening of April 20?"

"In my room."

"What were you doing?"

"Nothing."

"Have you been with this young lady?"

"Yes."

"Yes? All the other three denied ever having seen her. Did you have sex with her?"

"I am not sure."

"How can you not be sure? Did you know that she was underage?"

"She looks sixteen or seventeen."

"So, you confess that you raped this young virgin girl?"

"I don't know."

You see, the truth is the safest lie.

I found myself reciting a poem:

Hayatın sırrını oku, mısralara kıl nazar
Read the secret of the life in your verses
Sahte söz bilmez Zakir, her zaman doğru yazar
You always write the truth Zakir, only the truth.

What happened to my rule of expediency?

The well-dressed civilian interrupted. "This man is clueless. Look *oğlum*—son, think carefully. Maybe you should consult a lawyer, especially before you go any further."

The commissar said to him, "I think he is crazy. He thinks he is the son of Sultan Vahdettin, though he mentioned Chief Rabbi Nahum's name."

I felt a crying fit coming. Until now, I had bravely faced the inquiry. Suddenly I began to sob. Was this a manifestation of criminal sorrow or self-pity? How embarrassing, I thought, but I couldn't stop the tears from pouring down my face. The consul extended his handkerchief. I took it. It smelled of perfume.

Majbritt shouted in French, "He didn't rape me, he is innocent."

My sobbing got worse. Now all of them, except the civilian, were trying to soothe me.

"Okay now, you'll be okay," the commissar said. "But why were you confessing to a crime that you didn't commit? Are you some kind of idiot? Stop crying; soon you'll go home."

The civilian was on a different track.

"Not so fast. I need to check his claim of royalty. I thought all these leeches were exiled in 1923. Send him back to the cell until I discuss this with the *Vali Bey*, the governor. If this is true, Refet Pasha will turn in his grave. It wouldn't bring much praise for us either. Let's hope that he is either a lunatic or a hoaxer."

That evening a guard brought me a bowl of yogurt soup with a piece of bread. I curled up into the corner of the cell and fell asleep.

In the morning, a guard took me out to a toilet, and when I was finished, he gave me a cup of tea, five black olives, and a loaf of bread. The guards, for the most part, were very nice to me and didn't seem to take my crime too seriously. Each time they encountered me, they asked the same questions: "How was it, kid? "I hear *gavurlar*—the unfaithful— don't shave!" One of the guards, though, had something else on his mind. He kept twirling his mustache, winking at me, insisting on shaking my hand and then tickling my palm with his finger (a Turkish expression of sexual interest).

"*Senin davununu patlatayım*—I would love to thorn your drum," he kept saying.

I wasn't scared, just disturbed. Why would he treat me as if I were a homosexual when I was in jail for raping a girl?

As soon as I finished my breakfast, the civilian arrived, accompanied by an older man. The civilian asked the guard to open the door.

They led me to the commissar's office, and just before we entered, he said, "I'll give you one more chance to negate your earlier fabrication. On the other side of this door there is someone who, if he contradicts your story, will cause you to pay dearly for making such an outlandish claim: the son of the sultan! Well?"

I stood frozen. I wondered who might be on the other side of the door—Mademoiselle Blanche perhaps?

"Come on, let's get it over with," said the older man. "Don't you see he is laughing at us?"

The civilian opened the door, and I came face-to-face with Rabbi Nahum. We looked at each other for a long while. Finally he said, "I am glad to see you, Adam *Effendi*. You have grown up quite a bit. How do you come to be involved in an unspeakable act such as this?"

"So you know him?" asked the older man.

"Oh yes. He is Adam *Effendi*, the son of Şahhane *Hanım*. I have not seen him since his mother's death."

The older man needed him to be more specific: "Şahhane *Hanım* and Sultan Vahdettin?"

"Yes sir."

"Eh, listen, rabbi," the civilian pursued. "Let's say that you've never been here and we never had a discussion about the identity of the prisoner, understand?"

"What are you going to do with him?" the Rabbi asked. "He is a very good boy, just a little lost soul."

"Well, all I can tell you is that he won't be able to reside in Turkey. That is the law of the republic. He'll be treated the same way the other members of the ruling class were treated three years ago. He will be settled in a host country that will give him exile status." I smiled. Finally they had noticed me, enough to kick me out of the country. "Look, he doesn't seem to be worrying about it; why should you?" said the civilian.

I was fascinated by both their recognition of me as belonging to the ruling class and the idea of exile in a host country.

Rabbi Nahum gently took me aside, "Adam, you escaped the punishment of the law but not the punishment of your soul. Sin penetrates the soul and carves a deep sense of loneliness in man. Self-exile . . . that is what is meant by the saying, 'We are punished by our sins and not for them.' Guilt and remorse are the tortures of the soul. The only redemption is to welcome this divine dispensation and live a life, thereafter, with only the lesson to be learned from the sin: no longer needing to sin."

I had heard this rhetoric of morality frequently in my childhood and half believed it. But I didn't realize how much I enjoyed the rabbi's devotional language. He continued, "I don't know what exactly occurred between you and this girl in that house. But the truth between people has its roots in God. Sin is simply unbelief. Believe in God and confide in Him. Even the darkest violence of human nature can be woven into spiritual wholeness."

As we parted, Rabbi Nahum shook my hand warmly. "Don't look so sad. It is okay to leave this country. I am going to Egypt myself. *Dina de-Malkhuta-dina*—The law of the land is the Law. Anyhow, son, you've got to restrain yourself. I'll pray for you. You look cold and distant. You have some secret sorrow? You seem lost. Have you lost your faith? That would be spiritual insanity—if not spiritual death. You've got to seek deliverance from sin, the restoration of your soul into its original purity and goodness. God called Israel out of Egypt into his service. Maybe he is calling you out of Turkey for the same purpose."

I watched him walking away as if time had stood still the past four years. Was he right? I am definitely lost and badly in need of restraining myself.

But I can restrain myself only within the limits of the comprehensible. Faith is not comprehensible. On the other hand, wasn't faith to be simply apprehended? Have I exiled myself from myself? How could this person whom I hardly tolerated as a child have touched me and animated my soul? Did I say "soul"? I hadn't even used this word for years.

I remembered an old childhood prayer of mine that Rabbi Nahum had taught me and kept repeating whenever I resisted: "I'll bend my mind and my knees like tree branches in the wind; I'll bend my mind and my knees."

I bent my knees and my mind.

I spent the rest of the morning wondering what happened to my friends. The guards weren't much help, saying only that they were still being questioned. The civilian, accompanied by a police officer, returned in the early afternoon, bringing my luggage to me.

"Only your clothes are allowed. The rest of your belongings have been given to the owner of the boardinghouse. You were about a month behind in your rent, and the owner said you had nothing in her safe. You obviously spent your original thousand lira on girls. Here is another five hundred, but that is it. This is your diplomatic passport with French and Italian visas. This is a one-way ticket, second class, to San Remo, Italy. I am sure Sultan Vahdettin will welcome you at his villa, at least until you take charge of your life. The horny old crook owes you and your mother that much. This officer will accompany you to the police dorm where you can wash up. Then put on your fresh clothes and be ready to leave by four o'clock. They'll pick you up and put you on the train."

～

The train was packed, the compartments and corridors filled all the way to the doors. People had to be lifted from the station platform and pulled into the cars through the windows; it was impossible to get in any other way. There was a mass of humanity—peasant Turks going to the border city of Adrianopolis, Greeks returning home, Italian merchants, impoverished Istanbul inhabitants heading to anywhere in Europe, and Jewish families on their way to America. No one paid attention to the distinction between second- and third-class tickets. The train was unbearably hot and humid and smelled of sweat, *sucuk*—cured lamb—and overflowing toilets. Luggage was everywhere, including in the bathrooms.

My cabin-mates were two elderly gentlemen—one plump like a plum and the other shriveled like a prune—a middle-aged Jew traveling with his teenaged son, and other assorted characters. One of the two officers who had brought me to the Sirkeci station stayed with me, forcefully preventing anyone else from entering. The older men were dressed as if they belonged to Ottoman times past. They gave grateful glances to the officer for his protection, but they also were obviously curious about his relationship with me. Without asking permission, the officer cleared the overhead luggage area, piling baggage between the seats. Then he helped me jump up on the rack and gently instructed me to go to sleep. I wasn't sure if he had noticed how exhausted I was and felt sorry for me or if this was his way of removing me, thus avoiding potential conversations with the others. This strategy did not, however, prevent the Jewish man from asking the first question:

"Is he sick or something?"

I saw the officer glaring at him. He didn't respond, but the man wasn't discouraged. "He isn't contagious, I hope. I have a very weak constitution. Whatever he has, I'll have it by tomorrow."

The officer ignored him.

Finally, the train slowly pulled out of the station. In the midst of the cacophony of noises, cries, and whistles, a song began playing over the loudspeakers:

Yolculuk var yarına
Tomorrow we'll travel
Sevenler diyarına
To the world of lovers

How could that be? Whoever was playing this music obviously had never been in one of these trains. The plump man opened his sack and pulled out a knife, a loaf of bread, and a big piece of *sucuk*. As he sliced, the delicious smell of the seasoned, cured meat rose to my perch. He graciously offered some to everyone; they all politely declined. I hoped he would offer me some, but I guessed I wasn't part of their group.

"So," said the Jewish man, "where are you taking him?"

The officer looked at him for a little while before talking: "Where are *you* going?"

"Oh, we—my son and I—are going to Salonika for my nephew's bar mitz—"

"And you fellows, where are you heading?" the officer said abruptly, addressing the two elderly gentlemen.

The plump man quickly swallowed his last mouthful and coughed.

"God willing, we'll be visiting Sultan Vahdettin Hazretleri in San Remo. We were both *katips*—secretaries of the sultanate—for a long time, you see."

"What are you hoping to get from that big leech?"

"Well sir, we're hoping to be beneficiaries of his generosity. We know some people who visited him and were recognized kindly."

The officer smiled. "Fine," he said. "Now listen. Here is the deal. You see that kid up there? He is Vahdettin's son from a concubine. I'll be getting off the train very soon because we are approaching the Greek border. If you two take him to your sultan, he'll be even more generous. What do you say?"

The other men stopped rolling cigarettes and jumped to their feet: "*Başüstüne Kumandan*—It's our over-our-heads top priority! We'll be most happy to deliver him to his father."

All of a sudden, the dynamic in the cabin changed. The plump secretary pulled out a big pastrami sandwich and offered it to me. Meanwhile, the officer got ready to disembark as we pulled into a small border-town station.

I closed my eyes. The images of the teenaged Dutch girl's bloodied hand marks on the wall were stuck to the insides of my eyelids.

Sultan Ibrahim had an illegitimate son, Osman, from a concubine. While on a Turkish galley on their way to Egypt, both mother and child were captured by corsairs from Malta. The sultan besieged Crete for twenty-four years to get Osman back, spurred by the fear that the Europeans would use Osman against his legitimate sons and the empire. But he couldn't succeed. Osman grew up and converted to Christianity. In fact, he became a Catholic priest. Père Osman was recognized by Europeans as the pretender to the throne of the joint Byzantine and Ottoman empires.

THREE

**Moses oppresses me, stares at me, and makes me anxious.
I want to rebel.**

Paris
1926–1941

My whole is less than my parts.

The two old secretaries took charge of me, and the three of us stayed together until we arrived in San Remo.

The plump secretary negotiated a fee with a taxi driver to take us to Villa Parodi, where the sultan was living with his entourage. The taxi driver demanded payment before we got in his car and then embarked on the hour-long trip to the villa. He sped through a warren of alleyways and narrow, steep, cobblestone streets, shouldered by old houses with verdant terraces, not unlike those in old Istanbul.

"Why would the sultan of the Ottoman Empire choose a place like this to be exiled?" the plump one wondered aloud. Both secretaries looked very disappointed.

All of a sudden, the streets became wider and cleaner, and there were houses surrounded by formidable walls and gardens. The whole area was scented from roses, mimosas, and carnations. The driver asked if he should wait for us since it would be hard to find a taxi to take us back to the station. Of course I had no such need, and clearly the two secretaries had no plans to return that day. Finally, we stopped in front of an enormous iron gate; the driver got out of the car, piled our luggage on the sidewalk, and pulled away. There were no guards at the gate as I had expected. In fact, there were no signs of life at all. The place looked deserted. Pushing the doorbell button at the gate seemed useless because we had no way of knowing if it rang somewhere in the compound. I tried my hand at unlocking the gate.

We waited there for hours, sitting in the heat of the noonday sun, hungry and thirsty. Had the driver cheated us and left us at the wrong villa? Finally a car passed us, continued down the road for a few hundred feet, and turned back. The driver was wearing a fez.

"You're in the wrong place," he said in Turkish. "If you're looking to pay your last respects to the sultan, his house is about a half mile farther up the road. It is called Villa Manolya." He sped away.

We shouldered our belongings and headed in the direction that the man had pointed. Last respects? I wondered. Was father dead?

As we got closer to the Villa Manolya, the scene changed from serene to pandemonium. There was a large crowd, mostly Italians, screaming and shaking the gate as if to break it. The shriveled secretary—the Prune—translated the Italian for us. The crowd was irate because the sultan had not paid them for supplies and services for more than six months. Therefore, they wouldn't allow the sultan's casket to be moved until they were properly compensated.

I thought about the days when the sultan had thrown gold pieces into the crowd. Now the last sultan of the glorious empire couldn't even get a proper burial.

At the gate, a drunken Turk welcomed my companions. "Oh my good fellows, what on earth are you two doing here? Did you come for the funeral? My God, that is loyalty. The sultan would have been so happy to know you were here. Who is the kid?"

The secretaries were beyond consolation. They had spent their every last penny to get here, only to find their last resort, the sultan, dead. I was unaffected by the situation because I knew that for me, my father was as good dead as alive.

"Zeki Bey, the boy is Prince Adam. Do you remember?"

"Of course, of course, and thank God there are so many princes," the drunkard said, glancing at me and sneering. "Listen shehzade, do you have any gold coins with you? You must!" It was the first time anyone had called me by that title.

In the house, people were milling about, whispering and wringing their hands. The sultan's body wasn't to be visited. The woman, I presumed to be Nazikeda *Kadın Effendi*, older wife of the sultan, briefly spoke to my companions, gave me a quick glance, and turned away. A younger woman, Müveddet *Kadın Effendi*, was inconsolable. She literally was tearing out her hair. Recognizing that there was no way to get anything from her, both secretaries settled down in a corner. Eventually, a young Italian woman in her early twenties brought us Turkish coffees.

"Natali!" screamed Nazikeda at the young woman. "There are many noble guests here to be served first. Don't you have any manners?"

Natali, obviously disheartened, gave up and sat next to us.

"You should pick up your things and go home anyway, Natali," continued Nazikeda. "There is no longer a reason for your presence. The same goes for you." She looked at us disapprovingly.

"Is Ertuğrul here?" I dared ask.

"You mean His Majesty Ertuğrul *Effendi*? No. He is on his way to Egypt to be crowned the sultan and caliph of the Ottoman Empire. Now, kindly leave us, as we have a great deal to do. You may take your coffee and drink it in the garden."

I was happy to leave the overstuffed, airless, crowded room. The four of us moved outside and sat near the veranda in the garden. The Prune, in mixed Italian and French, tried to converse with Natali, who told him she had been Vahdettin's last concubine and was three months pregnant. The drunkard, Zeki *Bey*, spotted us and staggered toward the veranda carrying a suitcase. Natali pulled something from her belt, got up, and walked over to Zeki, then tried to grab the suitcase, but he wouldn't let go. Because both spoke fractured French, all I could garner from their animated conversation was that she needed money to give birth and take care of the child. He was trying to take a paper from her clutched hand. After a struggle, he fell down. She picked up her luggage, ran toward the gate, and signaled me to follow.

I had no reason to stay at the villa, and the secretaries encouraged me to go after her. I grabbed my suitcase and followed Natali. We ran outside the gate.

At the bus station, she told me her strange story.

She had been given to the sultan as a welcome gift from the king of Italy, Victor Emanuel. Natali tried to serve the sultan, but he was depressed and agitated, and all he wanted to talk about were his wives, ex-wives, and the concubines he had left behind in Istanbul.

"Their arrival ended my relationship with the sultan," she said. "I became a servant to his women and a mistress to both Zeki *Bey*, the drunkard gambler, and the gentle doctor Reşat Pasha. Those two always quarreled about money and a document in the doctor's possession. The doctor was worried that the drunkard would kill him, and that is exactly what happened. The night before he was killed, the doctor gave me the document for safekeeping.

"After the sultan died, I told Zeki I would be willing to sell the document to him. That was the struggle you witnessed. You see, he wanted it for free. Although he said it was worthless, he still tried to take it away from me. Worthless or not, I wasn't going to give it to him. It's written in Arabic. Do you want to see it?"

Natali pulled a piece of paper with the sultanate letterhead on it from her belt and gave it to me. It was a map and some directions.

My heart beat so fast I thought I was going to faint. So they hid treasure before being exiled! How else could the sultan of the centuries-old empire become bankrupt in four short years? His people had hidden gold and other valuables, hoping either to recover the bounty for themselves or to return from a short exile with the sultan to be rewarded for their foresight.

"What is it?" I heard Natali's voice as if she were far away.

"It is a sort of hidden treasure map." She burst into laughter. "Well, then, go get it."

I divided half my money and squeezed it into her reluctant hand.

⁓

I needed a place to stay. The narrow curve of the main road was backed up with traffic because of a stalled Mercedes. Drivers flickered their car lights and blew horns; truck drivers cursed and yelled.

In exchange for fixing the stalled Mercedes, which belonged to an American doctor and his wife, the Steins, they let me drive them through Monaco and on to Paris, where they planned a visit to the Lugners, old friends of theirs.

We parked right in front of the Lugners' house since there were neither cars nor people around. Dr. Stein jumped out of the car and locked an obese, balding man with an unsightly tangled face—Dr. Lugner—in a bear hug. They held each other, swaying, then drew back to look at each other's faces. Tears ran down each face.

"Harvey, you haven't changed a bit!" exclaimed Dr. Stein.

The wives hugged each other briefly. Mrs. Lugner was exactly like the caricatures of aging Jewish women that appeared in Turkish magazines: dark, frizzy hair; leathery copper skin; heavy makeup covering every inch of her face; too-large eyeglasses; circumflex nose; a thick gold chain around her neck; dangling earrings; a fat diamond ring on a bloated finger—loud, wealthy, and vulgar.

Then there was fourteen-year-old Sara! Porcelain skin, light brown straight hair, penetrating green eyes, and tiny breasts that just barely nudged her dress out. She looked indifferent to—if not sullenly bored by—all the commotion.

"Come in, come in," Mrs. Lugner waved. "Sara, show the chauffeur where to put the luggage before he leaves."

Dr. Stein interjected, "Actually the car is ours. We bought it in Rome, and we're going to ship it to New York from London. It's much cheaper that way. And Adam here is a fellow Jewish traveler who saved us from all sorts of *tzuris*—troubles. He says he's a medical student from Istanbul University, just a *luftmentsh*—a sort of drifter—but he's a good driver and mechanic.

"Well then," Dr. Lugner said. "Come in, son. Join us. Eat something. Do you have a place to stay? It's awfully late. There is a little room in the basement. You are welcome to sleep there tonight."

Then, as I came in and the light fell on me, both Doctor and Mrs. Lugner stared at me; Mrs. Lugner's face contorted, while Dr. Lugner stood open-mouthed.

"What is it?" I said, the perspiration beginning to drip from my armpits.

Her pupils glazed, Mrs. Lugner came toward me, gripped my shoulders, and started to cry. She pulled me into the house.

Dr. Lugner's face was ashen. "You look a little like our dead son," he said hoarsely.

◆◆◆

Thus began my long-term enmeshment with the Lugners. The Steins left for London. The next few days, I chauffeured Mrs. Lugner around town. In return, they treated me like a houseguest, paying for my dinners and loaning me some of their son's clothes, which fit perfectly. Meanwhile, I disabled their old Peugeot—a four-horsepower car parked in their makeshift garage—a few times, then fixed it quickly to show my competence and also to assure them of my indispensability.

Dr. Lugner offered me the summer job of driving him and his wife (Mrs. Lugner worked in the office on some afternoons) to the office and back many times a day. In between the driving from home to office and back, I was available to take Mrs. Lugner and Sara wherever they wanted to go or to run errands for them. In August, I was to house-sit while they were on vacation in Le Levandou, in the south of France. In exchange for these services, I would have bed and board, plus twenty-five francs a day. Misreading my grateful silence at the offer as a bargaining posture, Dr. Lugner added, "We'll fix up the basement room, and you can take Saturdays off, paid of course. In the fall you should try to get a scholarship to continue your medical studies. I hope your transcripts are in good shape. Transferring from foreign schools is not all that easy."

I wasn't negotiating at all; if anything, I was glad I was in a Jewish home. For years I had been totally removed from anything Jewish. It was as if when I became a man, on my time schedule, God had died. I paid no attention to the Sabbath or high holidays. I sinned—lied, cheated, stole, and slept with women.

Rabbi Nahum's parting words were reverberating in my mind: "You've got to restrain yourself." I can do that only by maintaining spiritual sanity. This was the home to come to, my spiritual home, not like my home in Istanbul, where everyone had a different idea as to what religion was or even what God was. Here, everyone was Jewish, and all was clear. The Lugners seemed to have a true sacramental bond of unity—the essential cell of faithful society—real marriage.

Mrs. Lugner apparently got over her initial terrible reaction to me.

"After she met you, she told me she was devastated," Sara told me. "Your name is the same as my brother's, you're the same age and height as he was, and you have his complexion. Even your face, except for your eyes, is a bit alike. You have the same drooping shoulders and short-guy sway. That first day, when you wore one of his jackets, she told me she could have sworn that you were he. That's why she asked you to take it off before dinner, even though you were trying so hard to be polite and appropriately dressed. I knew we were in trouble when I saw my mother fix her eyes on you in that dreamy way she does when she talks or hears about my brother."

Now I was staring at Mrs. Lugner, hypnotized, thinking about how I had never really believed in Judaism, nor had I given it a chance.

Faith, the Rabbi used to say, has to be absolute in order to be faith. Any doubt or faint resolution undermines its power and supremacy.

When I saw Mrs. Lugner spread a white cloth on the table, carefully arrange the challah bread covered with ornate napkins, and light the Sabbath candles, I felt shame and yearning.

"Bless the Lord who has wedded us to Israel and commanded us to kindle the Sabbath lights," she intoned.

My soul is stunted and my character nonformed. Both my soul and character were supposed to be by-products of a devotional life. I didn't live a real worldly life either. So in that sense I have nothing to give up to return to faith. I do have a conscience—my judgment of myself, albeit a fallible one. It just needed a shelter to evolve into infallible faith. Maybe one finds true faith in average households, not in intrigue-infested palaces. Mrs. Lugner warmed her hands over the flames and touched her eyes—the way my mother used to touch mine. I was in a Jewish home, a Jewish home! Maybe this would end my exile.

Then we all sat for dinner. To my surprise, Dr. Lugner and Sara plunged into the meal unceremoniously. Dr. Lugner took one of the embroidered napkins and blew his nose on it. Mrs. Lugner must have been accustomed to this behavior; she gave me a helpless look, cut one of the challah loaves, and passed it to me.

At the end of the evening, there was no Habdallah to commemorate the end of the Sabbath, except that Dr. Lugner took his glass, which was filled to overflowing, and drank down the wine in a single gulp. He allowed a little wine to spill over into the saucer for Mrs. Lugner to gaze at so she wouldn't, as old custom had it, grow a mustache.

"This in spite of *teo-yerinkeh*—my dearest growing a mustache."

All three of them laughed. I was dumbfounded and disappointed. I wondered if this was the custom of the Jews in France or if it were some kind of cruel joke—otherwise, why would they be laughing? My stomach felt leaden.

Even if the Lugners' home were not a devotional shelter, I still could have faith. The devotion is the shelter, by itself, the Rabbi used to say. Why am I questioning the spiritual relativity of the Lugners? I have already gratified many vile excesses and frenzies of cravings, only to encounter counterfeit ecstasy in lust. Who am I to doubt the devotion of these people? I already tasted the death of my body in the waters of the Marmara and the bleakness of my thin soul in bed with Majbritt. Nothing good came out of these events except a spiritual stagnancy. I have to guard my faith from being defiled by raising the question about the purity of other people's religious emotions.

～

The following week was Passover. I had no idea what to expect. I was hoping for that feeling of warmth and family, for that feeling of being taken in out of the cold and dark. The first night, Mrs. Lugner prepared a traditional Seder meal: eggs, matzoh, horseradish, chopped fruits, and nuts. We all sat at the table, and Mrs. Lugner dipped a sprig of parsley in salted water. Again Dr. Lugner and Sara quickly ate their food. Dr. Lugner drank all four glasses of ceremonial wine while disregarding the rest of us.

"Shouldn't Sara be asking, 'Why is this night different from all other nights?'" I inquired.

"No, Adam," said Dr. Lugner. "Not only does she know that tonight is no different from all other nights, she also knows that these wicked questions are no more than a litany."

Sara got up and left without a word. Dr. Lugner retired to the parlor and reclined on the sofa. From there he held court: "We adopted not only pagan practices but also the Christian ones—so it is backward and forward appropriation. For example, on the Feast of Booths you're supposed to point the Lulav or a branch of a bush to the left and then to the right, then up and down while murmuring 'Hosanna.' What does that look like to you? Christians crossing themselves.

"All these high holidays are just a concoction of the rabbis to justify their existence so they could make a living. I don't deny their genius for attaching some religious or historical meaning to every pagan celebration. Passover has nothing to do with the Exodus; it is simply the beginning of the spring and the season of the sowing of the new grain. The Pentecost gives believers permission to gorge themselves silly after the harvest. It has nothing to do with Israelites' arrival at Mount Sinai from Egypt. The Feast of Booths marks the beginning of the fall and is the season of the reaping of the fruits. It has nothing to do with the Jews' wandering through the wilderness."

"But what about the Jews slaving away in Egypt?"

"No, no, no," he interrupted. "Jews weren't even in Egypt, except for one small tribe, that of Jacob, and Jacob chose to leave. You see, the Jews were traders; they kept moving. Usually an unmarried man sought his fortune in a frontier town neighboring his family's and married a local, non-Jewish woman. This helped him to be accepted in the new town and also to have a better sex life. Then his sons repeated the pattern in the next town. With the exception of the ultraorthodox in Jerusalem, there is no such a thing as a pure Jewish race. The rest of us are matrilineal descendants of local women. Look at Sara's green eyes."

He continued, "The whole Seder ceremony is a pagan ritual. Do you know why half of the middle slice of the matzoh is preserved to be eaten at the end of dinner and shared by everyone? It's because we were dirt poor and had no dessert. And the unleavened bread is the ultimate cover-up. Jacob's wife forgot to put yeast in the dough. Instead of apologizing for the fuckup and sparing us from eating that tasteless crap, they make up a story of hurried departure.

"Furthermore, be careful with the Torah, it can screw up your mind, Adam. Do you know the root of the word 'Torah'? It is 'harah,' which means impregnation of mind, that is, mind-fucking. It puts a dark glass between man and God, so when you turn to God, you find yourself. That's how Jewish Jesus thought he was God.

"Jesus was just a Pharisee Jew who got circumcised on the eighth day of his birth. When he got older and couldn't make a living as a carpenter—mind you there are no forests or trees in Palestine; it is all rock and stone—he found himself twelve more Pharisees and began to peddle his product that had nothing in it. But you see, it's the illusion that sells best because people are bored with realities. And the poor Europeans were so starved for some divine message that they believed all those bizarre stories."

My hope of becoming a good Jew and, with that, living a normal life was disappearing in a merciless, irony-soaked litany against God and religion by a Jewish man. Is hope a great falsifier?

"But what do I do if I want to be Jewish?" I asked.

"The most Jewish thing you could do is to become a Catholic," he said.

〰

Dr. Lugner's run-down office was on the first floor of a large building in Le Quartier de la Roquette, not far from La Place de Voltaire. He was a general practitioner, serving primarily immigrants of the eleventh arrondissement. The neighborhood immediately around his office was hardly distinguishable from a Turkish bazaar: it was settled with artisans, rug merchants, kosher delicatessens, and other commercial enterprises. In fact, there was a large contingent of Ottoman Jews who had their own synagogue in the rue de Popincourt.

Dr. Lugner employed a young woman, Denise, as a receptionist and an older woman, Renée, as a nurses' aide. Mrs. Lugner was the book-keeper and filled in for the other two. The outer waiting room was always filled with patients, mostly women. The four inner examination rooms were always occupied, and Dr. Lugner relentlessly moved among them with lightning efficiency. On Thursdays, fertility patients' day, Denise and Renée were off, but Dr. and Mrs. Lugner continued to work.

Except for Thursdays, I was allowed to haunt the reception area (primarily enjoying the scent wafting from Denise) to try to figure out the patients' problems. Could they be suffering illnesses similar to my Kurdish and Russian patients? I wondered how French medicine treated them. I was a little surprised that Dr. Lugner wasn't interested in using my medical skills. Instead, he limited me to driving and other chores.

༒

Denise smelled womanly any time of the day or month. When she spoke to me, her soft hazel eyes lingered on my eyes. Her smile was equally lingering. She was an unmarried mother of a four-year-old boy, the product of a relationship with an Algerian musician who jilted her. She swore never to become romantically involved with any man again. Renée more or less hinted that I should stay away from her because "you know, Dr. Lugner . . ."

I couldn't believe that. When I managed to ask him if he was involved with Denise, I guess a little disapprovingly and hoping that he'd deny it, he said, "Look, at my age if my *shlanger* gets a little something here and there, is it so bad? Even my wife sort of knows about it. As long as you stick to the principles of *Kashrut*: you know, the milk here, the meat there. You see, Denise isn't Jewish. My wife would never tolerate it if I were sleeping with another Jewish woman. Now that is adultery and a no-no. Not that I am religious at all, as you well know, but it just isn't done, period!"

"So non-Jewish women, single or married, are not sin?"

"Stale sin, I think it says in the Talmud, as long as you sleep with the wife, too."

I asked Dr. Lugner if he ever sat down and read and understood the Talmud.

He replied, "What is there to understand? In there are *bubba meisses*—grandmother's tales—my son. Ha, ha, ha."

Denise herself advised me, "You should marry a young nurse; all doctors do. Don't waste your time on an old receptionist with a kid."

She was only two years older than I.

"Even better," she continued, "marry Sara and become Dr. Lugner's partner."

Sara, beautiful though she was, didn't smell womanly; if anything, she smelled like men's sweat. She talked in straight short sentences, coloring her speech with "*merde!*" and "*je m'en fiche*—I couldn't care less!" She considered herself a "communist" as opposed to her parents' "duplicitous pacifist socialism," an affiliation they had adopted after the death of their son, who had been an active member of the Pacifist Party.

Sara quickly became my defender, objecting vehemently to my sleeping in the basement when her dead brother's upstairs room was empty and kept as a shrine. Some nights she battled with her parents, especially her mother, until late. I often heard them screaming.

"He's dead mom. Almost two years. Let go!"

"That's easy for you to say. Wait 'til you become a mother and see how you feel if you lose a child."

"Lose a son you mean."

"So that's what's behind all this altruistic stuff about our giving the room to our boarder," Mrs. Lugner said. "You think that we loved your brother more than we love you. You were always jealous of him. Isn't it horrible enough that he's gone? Do you want us to erase his memory, too?" she said and started to sob.

What was the aim of Sara's chronic psychological mutiny, I wondered. Was it possible that beneath her inhospitable, thorny facade, this beautiful cactus nursed sweet juices?

I didn't care where I slept. In fact, this basement was similar to my basement abode in Istanbul, including the humidity and vermin. Even the weak electricity and light were familiar. I wished the place had a door, though.

One day when her parents were at the office, Sara gave me the tour of the house, with the special intent of showing me her brother's "shrine." I was more interested in seeing her room.

According to Sara, Adam's room was kept exactly as it was on the day he left for Israel, except now every inch of the walls were covered with his pictures.

Adam had constantly complained of headaches and nausea. He saw a dozen physicians, and he was given all types of medication, but nothing worked. Everyone was convinced that Adam was just a lazy, spoiled kid who, though very charming and funny, wasn't that smart. At length, Adam, failed and dispirited, decided to go to Israel to study Hebrew.

Apparently, on the night Adam arrived in Jerusalem, he began to vomit violently. Adam's entrusted local doctor—Helena Kagan, a childhood friend of Dr. Lugner's from Lithuania—gave him something to calm his stomach. The young man claimed to feel better, ate a big bowl of soup, and went to sleep. They found him unconscious the following morning and took him to Sha'arei Tzedek Hospital, where he died the following day. An autopsy showed a brain tumor.

"He was her everything," explained Sara as we sat on her dead brother's bed in his room. "I think my mother is a little demented as a result of her pain. I feel bad for her. I don't think she really cares much about my father. In fact, I think she hates him. She won't forgive him for not only being unable to diagnose his own son's illness, but also for accusing Adam of being a hypochondriac and lazy, for treating him harshly for so many years, and for leaving him in the care of an 'unlicensed physician,' Helena Kagan. In reality, Kagan practiced without a license from the Muslim government, which would not issue her one because she was a woman. She was a fully trained physician.

"On the other hand, Dad said to Mom, 'How did we produce such a son? No one in my family in ten generations of rabbis is like him,' the implication being that all the bad qualities were inherited from *her* family."

"Your father must also feel awful," I said.

"Yes and no," Sara replied. "He felt a little guilty, but mostly he was afraid of Mom's reaction, so he went along with the crying and mourning and self-flagellation. This may seem callous to you, but he was really upset that his line of heritage ended with his son's death. My father is really a liar and deeply clever. He'll never accept that he was relieved he won't have to endure his son's failures for the rest of his own life. I think Dad was embarrassed by having a son like Adam and disliked him. Though he seems to heap scorn on everything, my brother got the worst of it. Occasionally I see a little glimpse of unburdened joy in the corner of my father's eyes for having gotten rid of Adam. Believe me, I can tell."

"What about you, Sara?" I inquired. "Is fighting with them your way of mourning?"

Sara's green eyes got colder. "I really don't care. I had nothing in common with my brother. To me he was sort of weird. I didn't feel a real sense of loss, if that is what you are asking. Mom would have preferred that I died instead of my brother. Dad? I don't know. Do you see how vacant his eyes are? He doesn't relate. He says he loves me, but I'm not sure he has any idea what that means. All he seems to be interested in is hoarding money, which is more of a malignant obsession as he does nothing with it. He would do anything for money. Look at our house. Does it look like a successful physician's house? If you put our furniture out on the street, no one would take it. At night he follows us around, turning off the lights. His obsession makes him look foolish. He buys cheap food in bulk, which ends up spoiled.

"My mother, as you see, is sort of a collector of secondhand jewelry and furs. She always wants more than she has. Incredibly enough, she has made a dent in my father's tightfisted budget, especially since my brother's death. What kind of woman would adorn herself while allowing the house she lives in to look like a tenement?"

Sara continued speaking and shifted to a more comfortable position on the bed. "My parents are not lovable or likable people. My mother thinks that I'm secretly happy about Adam's death because I'll inherit everything. It isn't that the thought hadn't occurred to me, but it wasn't something I'd considered much. It's just an example of how they think. For me it's worse. I wouldn't have minded if all three had died during my childhood and I was sent to a foster home. Now let me ask you a question. You seem to be a well-educated, well-bred man. You're obviously intelligent—why on earth did you check in with us to become a 'shabbes goy'—to do our dirty work? You seem to be sad, if not depressed, after being with us for just a few weeks. My parents are poisonous. Get away before they permanently encapsulate you in their neuroses and cripple you, too."

Do overly familiar people always come to detest each other, or do their contentions simply serve to fight their loneliness?

"I am sad, Sara, even when I am happy. What is that wispy, inadequate 'happiness' with which everyone is so preoccupied anyway? What you observe in me isn't false incoherence; it's sheer groundlessness. I'm looking for a safe psychological bubble in which I can reside, the lowest possible standard. I can't afford to share your exuberance about independence, virtues, or even love. I'm a minority within the minority, the immigrant of all immigrants. I wasn't at home even when I was home. I can neither lament the past nor glorify the present. As for the future, for me it's an abstract concept. Adapting to the indignities of life and trying to contain the unexpected constantly validate my failures. It may seem rather measly to you, but for me I am just living out of time. The only serious question I have is when and how I can bring eternal death to myself." Was I trying to ward off my craziness by escalating a display of brilliance?

"What nonsense! Did you prepare this speech or read it somewhere? So kill yourself," she said coolly, "you have access to all those poisonous medications. Why don't you swallow a bunch of them?"

"Because I am not like the subordinate characters in Shakespeare's plays, who succumb to external forces, but like tragic heroes who are allowed to die from within. It isn't that I want to kill myself. Don't you see? I want to die, die of death."

"This is fucking bizarre. Enough with this fake enigmatic profundity. You are not a tragic hero but a pathetic one. Your waiting to die is to legitimize your noninvolvement. Do you get a kick out of this philosophical exhibitionism of yours? Do you want to experience a long natural death? How about rolling up your sleeves, getting your medical degree, becoming a physician, having a family, and living your short life?" she scolded me. "You simply got depressed here."

"My state of mind has nothing to do with your parents. I seem to go in and out of some tedium of existence. What you see is a plausible imitation of a person. When I feel better, I am even worse."

With a cold intellectual fury, she laid on me: "You litter the world with your intellectual debris; you explain at length obscure matter with more obscurity. You may be having fun with your psychological decadence, but for the receiver it is like verbal bewitchment. Adam, you are so subliminally irrelevant that you sound profound. In fact, you are simply spouting gobbledygook. You seem to be exchanging words and not their content. You treat concrete things as though they are abstract."

She had me all figured out. Of course, language can only talk about itself in the end. My back was against the wall, and I was trying to impersonate myself. Well, that was the most honest lie I could have told.

∾

I am in disharmony with myself.

I drove Mrs. Lugner, a widow friend of hers, and Sara to Le Levandou, a town on the Mediterranean in the south of France, where the family had been renting a two-bedroom seaside apartment for a number of summers. Dr. Lugner was scheduled to join them in August.

All the way to the shore, Mrs. Lugner and her friend sat in the backseat talking incessantly about people they knew. Sara, in the front seat with me, complained about being taken away from Paris and her friends for two months and dragged to a godforsaken, boring, middle-class resort where nothing ever happened: "Le Levandou," she sniffed. Apparently her friends from Lycée Claude-Bernard all went to St. Tropez. She mocked her mother's and the widow's way of talking, their loudness, laughing, subjects of conversation, and frequent need for bathroom breaks. She read loudly passages from the leftist newspaper *Rampart*, which attacked bourgeois Jews. Sara insisted on driving and, failing to persuade her mother to allow her to take the wheel, demanded that I drive faster "to spare her the torture of being in the car." She intimidated everyone with her aggressive and exaggerated truthfulness.

We arrived in Le Levandou long after sunset, and I had to leave by sunrise. Nevertheless, I got a glimpse of the place. It was a charming town with a large fishing harbor and a not-so-fine sand shoreline that reminded me of the beaches of Kumkapı in Istanbul.

The return trip to Paris was joyful for me. Church bells seemed sonorous and exuberant, a contrast to the muted, apologetic churches of Istanbul. I was happy to be driving alone, stopping along the road whenever and wherever I wanted, including sightseeing at some castles with large gardens bursting with peonies, marigolds, roses, and morning glories.

I pondered taking the car, going to some other city and working as a taxi driver, or going to Strasbourg and finding and marrying Mademoiselle Blanche and living a "bourgeois life." It seemed such an attractive idea. I wondered why Sara was so much against the middle class. In between my suicidal moments, I yearned for the stability, pre-dictability, and even utter boringness of such an existence.

It was almost midnight when I arrived home, and Dr. Lugner was up, waiting for me.

"Adam. Listen, you told me you have medical skills, right?"

"Right."

"Can you assist me in a little procedure tomorrow? I know it's your day off, but I've never noticed you doing anything special on your days off. You are going to be off for the whole of August, right?"

Without waiting for my answer, he went on: "I usually don't sched-ule these procedures when my wife is away, but this came up today, and I couldn't say no. I don't want Denise and Renée to know too much about it. So, what do you say?"

"Of course," I replied.

He seemed pleased. "I'll make breakfast, and we'll lunch at the deli. You know, if you like, we could work together during the month of July. Believe me, you'll learn more medicine from me in a few months than you could in six years of medical school. By the way, there are two rules for tomorrow: cut your nails very short tonight and don't ask any ques-tions in front of the patients."

᠆᠊ᢍ᠊᠆

In the usually overcrowded waiting room, there was only one patient, a young, obviously pregnant, very shabbily dressed blond woman in her early twenties. Dr. Lugner introduced me to her as "my assistant, Dr. Adam." He then asked me to go to the procedure room while he spent the next few minutes alone with the patient in the waiting room. Soon he escorted the patient to the next room and helped her get undressed, as she was rather unsteady on her feet. He must have given her a sedative.

The procedure room was set up for cervical dilation and curettage—I recognized the instruments from the textbooks. Once he helped the patient to the examining table, Dr. Lugner spread her legs, washed her vulva area thoroughly with soap, then put cream in his hand and began to expand the patient's vagina using a circular, stretching motion. We left the patient for about five minutes and went to scrub our hands and arms with soap and hot water, followed by an alcohol hand dip. We fin-ished by drying off with steamed-dried towels and put on surgical gowns. By the time we returned to the procedure room, the patient was snoring.

Dr. Lugner moved with the confidence of someone who must have done this hundreds of times. He explained the procedure step-by-step. He inserted a speculum, followed by a long instrument to grab the cervix. I heard a harsh clipping noise and winced. He pulled out the cervix and instructed, "The cervix has no nerves, as you know Adam, so this doesn't hurt. Now, hand me dilator number 4. No, don't give it to me like that. Place it flat on my hand. I open my palm, you hit it with the instrument I request."

He kept asking for thicker and thicker instruments for dilation, and eventually blood began to gush from the woman. By the time he began to curette, the catch basin was filled with blood.

Although the patient seemed totally oblivious to what was going on, Dr. Lugner was becoming agitated and rattled off a series of orders.

"Adam, empty out this goddamned basin. Put your wrist on her abdomen, right here over the pubic area; now stay there and put pressure on it. Oh, nuts. Get some ice from the icebox. Damn! You're contaminated now. Don't touch the instruments. Go scrub again. Is she okay? Check her eye reflexes."

I wanted to ask what was going on, why the pregnancy was being terminated. Then a big splash occurred. A squash-sized mass of tissue fell into the basin, painting Dr. Lugner red. The tissue moved its parts—it was a live fetus.

"*G'vald*—Oh my! Now, Adam," said Dr. Lugner, as he filled two large towels with ice and rolled them, "put one of these on her abdomen and the other against her *k'nish*. Hold them tightly in place. I'll be back in a minute."

He picked up the basin with the fetus and left the room. He didn't come back for more than five minutes. I was getting exhausted, but if I tried to ease my muscles, the patient began bleeding profusely. I had no strength left in my arms and decided to put my head against her abdomen and my shoulder against her vulva. In a little while Dr. Lugner walked in, took one look, and began laughing.

"This, I've never seen before."

"She is going to die." I said. My teeth chattered.

"*Shat, shat, hush*—don't get excited!" he replied and calmly took over. "You go to the front; press the towel with both your hands or your head if you have some special preference for that. I'll squeeze her uterus from the abdomen. He dug his hands into her abdomen, literally lifting the uterus and holding it tightly, as if checking a melon. This time it was I who got washed with blood and urine.

"You're hurting me."

The faint female voice disoriented me totally. I was so engrossed with the anatomical aspects of the procedure—abdomen, vagina, and uterus—I'd forgotten that all these parts were attached to a person.

"Hang in there, dear," Dr. Lugner said to the patient, "it won't be too long. When we relieve the pressure I want you to stay in this same position for one hour. Take it easy for the next week. No walking around, no lifting, no hot baths, no forcing bowel movements, and definitely no sex."

I didn't know about her, but I didn't think that I could ever have sex again, never mind the next week.

As soon as I cleaned up, I had to get out of there. Once outside, I kept vomiting on the sidewalks. I attracted glances from passersby, glances that ranged from pity to disgust. I don't know how and when I got home. I was physically and psychologically exhausted, but in spite of my cursing, I found the cause of my fatigue interesting. I slept the whole afternoon. I woke up to Dr. Lugner touching my arm and chiding, "Don't tell me you're one of those doctors who are afraid of blood?"

"Dr. Lugner . . . how is she?"

"Oh, she was fine," he replied with a dry matter-of-factness. "This is her third. Don't be deceived by her fragile look; she's tough as nails."

"Why is she having so many abortions?"

"Because she's sleeping with her married boss, who doesn't want any scandal."

"In Turkey, doctors wouldn't abort a viable fetus."

"The fetus wasn't viable."

"Yes, it was. I saw its fingers moving."

"No, she was no more than two months along, and the fetus was already dead. She had toxic fever from the decaying fetus."

"All three times?"

"Come on, Adam." He changed the subject. "I've got delicious corned beef, coleslaw, pickles, and rye bread. Let's celebrate your first assistance to a major surgical procedure."

"I thought you said it was a minor procedure."

"Major, minor, what's the difference? You get more money with majors. Now do you want dinner or not?"

"No thanks, I'm not hungry. I'm too tired. I just need to sleep. I can still smell that patient's urine and placental fluids. Dr. Lugner, I feel awful. Not that I have not sinned before, but this?"

⌐◠◡

Dr. Lugner was a very, very competent physician. There was nothing he couldn't handle. He pulled teeth, stitched wounds, circumcised adults, set dislocations and fractures, unblocked impacted bowels, cleaned ears, removed foreign bodies from eyes, gave enemas, cauterized cuts, attached leeches, taught contraception, delivered babies, certified the dead, drained abscesses and hematomas, and removed moles and warts. He wrote prescriptions in specific milligrams with combinations of ingredients for pain, infection, cold, anemia, diarrhea, bed-wetting, hemorrhoids, insomnia, skin diseases, seizures, and any other malady that could be named. Dr. Lugner was like a one-man hospital. But he was mainly an abortionist.

I taught Dr. Lugner a thing or two, too: the treatment of heartburn, impotence, and vaginal discharge, to name a few.

To female patients with infertility problems, Dr. Lugner offered the same old prescription—menstrual cycle and coitus timing and positioning. This method resulted in the same old high level of failure. Although Dr. Lugner suspected that males were responsible in half these infertility cases, if the men had no venereal disease and were able to have an erection and ejaculate, there wasn't much he could do for them. When I told him about an Eastern technique, though—a placebo that produced great results in which the *imam* writes a sacred message around the woman's vulva—Dr. Lugner burst into laughter.

"Most likely while writing, the *imam* was inserting his own semen into the woman! Who could prove otherwise? I'll bet the two of us could get much better results with our improved technology. Instead of just smearing the vagina with semen, we can mechanically insert it into the woman's uterus. If you masturbate into a cup each time we schedule an insemination, I'll give you one hundred francs for each pregnancy!"

Dr. Lugner smiled with the self-contentment of evil. His life of privation of faith must have rendered him this perversity of mind. Only through faith do all virtues enter. There is a lesson for me here. One can learn faith from someone's heedlessness to good, one can learn faith from someone who doesn't know it, and one can learn to be virtuous from someone who is not.

"That is a serious crime, you know. But illegality aside, don't you think to inseminate women with sperm other than her husband's is a monstrous cheating, a *shanda*—a sin against God?" I was not really taken aback by his suggestion; I guess I just wanted to confirm that it was a sin.

"Adam, sober up from this God-drunkenness. God is a superstition. Even if God exists, who do you think taught us to cheat? God himself: he lied about our beginning and our ending. Furthermore, he took our two loaves of bread and in return gave us two tablets, which supposedly made us his chosen people. The religious people aren't honest; no one is. You know the story of Diogenes. He went around Athens, holding his lamp in his noble quest to find an honest man. I imagine when he got to Lithuania, a very religious country, someone stole his lamp." He had a full belly laugh.

"Drunkenness?" I said. "God fills my mind with fortitude. It is only when God *is* that all is well for me. Your taking delight in sin is drunkenness. You should desire for others what you desire for yourself. That is goodness, the goodness of God that binds and rules all men. I am not God-drunk, I am simply trying to be a religious humanist." Why was I so intensely preaching and advocating goodness?

Dr. Lugner said, "Do you know why you Sephardic Jews have songs for every fruit? Because you're best represented by nuts. You're all nuts, and the hardest ones are the Orthodox Sephardic Jews. You need detoxification from the Jewish religion." He shook his head in disbelief, then went on: "Money rules man!" he said. "And the global marketplace is its synagogue. This is sane, reasonable, practical, and invulnerable. Don't be a professional victim."

Did he have a rubber soul? Please someone deliver me to insanity, unreasonableness and impracticality and victimhood, and help me claim my vulnerability.

He badgered me about his fertilization plan for days until I suggested that we smear women with his sperm; that way he could save himself the 100 francs he was going to pay me to do it. "Besides, we know that there'll be a better chance of impregnation since you've already been proven fertile," I said.

"No, you should do it, Adam. I'm too old. This is your chance to be a seed sower—a godly man." he said.

The man was like a dancer; he kept shifting his position to keep his balance.

"But all the kids may come out with Mongolian eyes," I joked.

I wondered whether God in His personified incomprehensibility had witnessed this encounter and, if so, why He allowed me to make this joke? Can wittiness displace morality?

Of all the things Dr. Lugner did, abortion was the most troubling to me. I don't know why. Was it because my mother was forced to abort a few pregnancies or didn't abort me? In any case, one day when Dr. Lugner operated on a third-trimester woman, I refused to participate, and he lashed out at me:

"Oh God! You'd better find some other line of work, boy. You'll never make it in medicine. This field of merciful ruthlessness requires a male, not a female, mind. As to the badness issue, despite all your literariness and intellect, you have a total ignorance about life."

Just like my father, Dr. Lugner found me unfit.

◦∿◦

I wasn't completely surprised when I was ready to resume "my career" a few days later. After all, I might end up being useful to Dr. Lugner, which is more than I can say about myself regarding my father. In fact, I had this strange exhilaration. Helper's high? You see, we need a moral moratorium, a kind of emotional and cognitive atheism: a detachment from our convictions as to *a priori* truths whose strong footholds are in the emotional substratum. Any meaning endowing such innate ideas of the mind is accepting its tyranny, which would force the constant into the foreground. What moratorium? I had no morals; who was the real Lugner? The more I observed, the more obscure things were getting.

The old jackal accepted my recovery with an "of course" attitude. "People who ride high horses are eminently corruptible," he said slyly.

But to my surprise, that day and the following four weeks were extraordinarily satisfying learning experiences for me, even though he was alternating bullying me with trying to arouse pity, both annoyingly.

◦∿◦

During August, after Dr. Lugner left on vacation for Le Levandou, I didn't even leave the house. More and more I stayed in bed, not even bothering to undress. Again, I was drifting inward. I couldn't visualize

Istanbul, my mother, my friends, Gülseren, or my Kurds and Russians. I tried to evoke the *muezzin's* prayer calls, the scrappy gardens of Istanbul University, and even the lackadaisical students with their dark, well-trimmed mustaches or the smell of *simit* and halvah. Nothing came to me, as if somewhere in becoming myself I disappeared.

You see, if living is a well-disguised form of dying, there is no reason to live. To praise the virtue of seeing one thing through to the end—a malpractice of life—is to live in linear time. In omnidirectional time, there is no one thing: there is no beginning and no ending. Everything is arbitrary punctuation in recognition, which perpetuates one's life lie.

Who can deny the supremacy of reason? It even explains God. Reasoning protects man from getting lost in bleak stretches of interstellar space vacated by God. I feel I am again straying away from the sacred precinct of Divine splendor. But, of course, I should.

Only total alienation and estrangement from all that is familiar allows a pensive self-interrogation toward fixing the basic fault in one's self-complacency.

I was losing my substitute for reality. Was I really teetering at the edge of insanity this time? Was the prolonged isolation forcing me to self-reflection? This time my mind wasn't free enough from its illness. It was actively inattentive. I couldn't tag an aim to it, not even a simple one, like suicide. I was drifting inward—to inner deadness.

I am okay in a nonfunctional, nonrelational existence. This experience of emptiness isn't that painful for me because I don't feel lonely in it. Nor am I bored or restless. I am not aware of the possibility of really being with someone. The adaptation to life would not be too time-consuming if one thinks of neither past nor present nor future, and especially not feign difference and I mean difference to one's existence, falsely.

～

I dreaded the Lugners' return. I didn't want their precious "normality" intruding on my insanity.

Well, the normality arrived, and for the next few weeks I contemplated eliminating the Lugner family. The plots ranged from burning down the house in the middle of the night to poisoning them one by one over time.

Meanwhile, in a surprising change of heart, Mrs. Lugner decided to allow me to sleep in her son Adam's shrine, provided I made no changes to the room, especially the walls. I was permitted to wear all his clothes since "there is no virtue in shabbiness" and use his radio. Was the change attributable to Dr. Lugner's report of our successful collaboration in July, a practice he wanted to continue? He made it clear, however, that my increased responsibilities would not be matched with more than a minor increase in my salary, as my room and board far exceeded monetary compensation. "You'll make more money, Adam, if you cut some corners rather than adding new ones." His gold teeth sparkled as he spoke.

So I had a real bed (and board) plus thirty francs a week and one day a week off—Thursday or Saturday or Sunday—depending on the family's needs for an assistant doctor, chauffeur, escort, or porter. This was fine with everyone except Sara, who vehemently objected to my minuscule salary, irregularity of hours off, and restrictions imposed regarding my room's decor. I couldn't figure her out. Was she using my cause as a pretext to fight her parents—illustrating an individuation rite? Was she tormenting them for having loved her less than her brother? Or was she a genuine communist, indignant about the inequality and injustice to which she believed I'd been subjected?

Sara seemed puzzled with me. "On the one hand, you're like a lion with an enigmatic strength—as if nothing can touch you; on the other, you look defanged; no! more like a dandelion. Puff! You no longer exist."

I didn't think I existed in a way that she could have perceived as existence, that is, having real intentions. I believed I truly existed only in isolation because in others' presence, I took on any assigned role.

My new room overlooked the small backyard, in the middle of which stood an old chestnut tree. With the exception of the window, every inch of "my" room was covered with pictures of Adam. I had to look at them all the time, and, eerily, they seemed to be looking back at me. His hair was parted on the right side, curling up. He had long, dark sideburns, a contrast to his barely visible eyebrows. In some pictures he was laughing, throwing his head back, with a hand on his hip. There were a couple of pictures where he had a dreamy, unfocused stare. It was a look I'd been accused of having.

From talking with Sara, I learned a bit about Adam and the symptoms that turned out to be early signs of his pituitary tumor: dry skin, chronic headaches, lack of interest in sex, a nasal tone of voice, frequent throat clearing, and loss of peripheral vision in both eyes, indicating invasion of the *sella Turcica*—Turkish saddle—in the brain by the growth. Sara suspected he was a homosexual, but he hadn't sought relationships. Apparently, he didn't even have a vicarious sex life; there weren't any pornographic pictures of either men or women in his room. His reading materials were limited to brochures and newspapers on pacifists. His drawers were full of headache pills, bismuth (for his stomachaches), and creams and lotions for his skin.

Sara's classmates were always shocked whenever they met me. They all momentarily believed that her dead brother wasn't really dead.

Sara occasionally teased me about my having been possessed by her brother's ghost. Mrs. Lugner adopted me fully, which included rubbing lotion onto my hands and my feet, as I myself had developed very dry skin. I regularly took pills for my perpetually aching head and bismuth for my cramping stomach. My surrogate mother and I went to pacifist rallies and meetings. Dr. Lugner told his wife that she and I should see the same psychiatrist and definitely not live under the same roof.

～

The following day Dr. Lugner told me that it is about time that I should find someplace else to live but that I was always welcome for dinner or to visit. He had already arranged a room for me in a hotel on La rue Lepic in Monmartre: Hôtel Beauséjour.

"You have to pay for it from your own income, Adam. I am sorry, I know that I am breaking our contract, but that is life. You just have to accept it. You know damn well that I have the right to revoke what I might have forsworn in the past. That is why we have *Kol Nidrei*—the formal abjuration of our vows."

His capacity to seriously invoke a Judaic principle for the support of his argument was the ultimate *chutzpah*.

"Is it your moral obligation to be so immoral?" I asked.

He grinned. "Adam, you can't compensate for common sense with wit. I know you think that I have holes in my soul, but I do really care about you."

"It is all right, but get off the moral low horse. I'll move out."

Did I have a soft spot for this unabashedly cunning and devious person?

"Moral low horse," he repeated, chuckling.

"It's only temporary," he tried to reassure me. "We'll find a nice apartment for you, decorate it to your taste, you know, with Turkish rugs. Don't look sad. You'll love it. You'll be able to bring your girlfriends home. Once you get your working permit, you'll have even greater freedom. You'll see."

∽

My beliefs don't even require a real religion. I believe in primacy of self-interest, not the primacy of truth or lie. I thank Dr. Lugner for not possessing any trace of goodwill, acting on his unchecked instincts, and displaying no moral restraints. He is guilt free in the sight of God, for he is invisible. He has a world-weariness, though, which is very unbecoming to an atheist.

As a child, I never warmed up to my Jewishness, partly because Jews were relegated to second-class status in Turkey and I had enough of being second class in all other ways, and partly because of Rabbi Nahum's teachings. He wouldn't even allow me to mention the word "God." The whole thing was so complicated, if not convoluted, that it was almost impossible to discuss God.

Furthermore, the Torah was the law or, more specifically, teaching of the law. I didn't want more restrictions on my already restrained life; I certainly didn't need another teacher. The Jewish God seemed always ready to exact retribution for what he considered wickedness. There was no affectionate tolerance or understanding of human frailty or forgiveness. So what difference did it make to which religion one belonged? Both Judaism and Christianity were ancient cisterns defiled with slime.

∽

As much as I disliked both Dr. and Mrs. Lugner, in some perverse way I was content living with them. At least there was some semblance of family and home, for which I yearned. Checking into the Hôtel Beauséjour invoked all the feelings of anxiety and sadness I had felt when I was moved to Sakız's dorm for Anatolian students.

Why is it that the worst possible hotels have such beautiful names; there was nothing beautiful about the Hôtel Beauséjour—a seedy residence owned and operated by another Armenian, Mr. Varham Dökmejian, whose doctor was Dr. Lugner.

"There isn't much light—the room has no windows—but it's our quietest room," Mr. Dökmejian said with a heavy accent. "When you become a doctor, you won't have to live in this neighborhood. Incidentally, many famous people have stayed in this hotel; of course, that's before they became famous writers, singers, painters. The most celebrated Armenian musician used to stay in your very room whenever he was in Paris. Have you ever heard of Father Vartabed?"

The room suddenly lit up in my mind; it was very small, with a narrow bed, thin mattress, and a stool turned upside down atop a three-legged table. This was a sort of monastery.

"You mean Komitas Vartabed stayed here?"

"Until he had lost his marbles. He now lives in the Villejuif Sanitorium."

"He was my music teacher," I said. Tears welled up in my eyes.

Mr. Dökmejian flipped through my passport: "Diplomatic. Ha! Across the hall there is a black eunuch with a little white girl—an Indian princess, he says. He claims she is exiled royalty too."

〜〜

The theaters were warmer than either the churches or my room, and in a counterphobic way, it was comforting to be in the midst of a crowd but not to be with them or for them or against them. Cartoons like Mickey Mouse or Popeye always preceded the films. The theater owners never vacated the movie house after each show, so I stayed, found a better seat, and sat through the whole show once or sometimes twice more. In some ways, I never saw the same movie twice, as I was never fully present. I had my own internal reel playing simultaneously to the one on the screen. The newsreels were less news than propaganda, the focus of which changed daily with the political sway of the country. One day newsreels railed against the Germans, the next day they were pro-German, but always they bragged about the strength of the French military and were anti-Jewish and anti-American. Both Jews and Americans were one and the same to Europeans when it related to business. One newsreel production company always began its pieces with "Uncle Shylock wants your money." The crowd reacted to the newsreels with shouts of anger, hurling insults against whomever the newsreels intended as targets. Afterward the audience settled down and enjoyed the movies. Ironically, they were mostly American movies—the Marx Brothers,

Tarzan, or cowboys and Indians. I was able to experience neither anger nor joy. The movies simply and temporarily distracted me from folding in on myself, thus allowing me to be a legitimate observer without being a participant. Other moviegoers seemed interested in engaging their seatmates or even those across the aisle in animated conversation.

～

Contrary to the prophesies of Dr. Lugner and Mr. Dökmejian, I never moved from the Hôtel Beauséjour or its neighborhood. I stayed there for many years. Of course, I didn't become a real doctor either, but I became as competent in the practice of medicine as Dr. Lugner. We were almost interchangeable in the office. More significantly, they even let me use my old room occasionally.

As I was now capable of filling in for Dr. Lugner, we no longer had to close the office in August. In fact, Dr. Lugner occasionally deferred to me in front of the staff, perhaps purposefully, to emphasize our collegiality.

"If Adam had been born in this country, he would have become one of its best doctors," he was fond of saying.

This recognition and praise resulted in only minor financial compensation. But there were other privileges associated with being a "very good doctor"—women's interest, mainly. Women in Paris, as those in Istanbul, threw themselves at doctors. I was alternatingly either too interested in sex or totally indifferent. Most women preferred giving me oral sex, I presumed because it was safe. This suited me well, as I couldn't maintain an erection when I attempted to have intercourse. I noticed that a lot of French women in Paris had their teeth extracted, and initially I wondered if this was somehow related to fellatio. Then I realized that many of them also had no appendixes, no tonsils, and frequently no gallbladders or veins in their legs. I finally acknowledged that they were simply victims of medical overpractice.

I was a bundle of contradictory emotions. At one moment, in an intoxicated mood, I felt light, zestful, confident, expansive, and willing to take on any risk with ceaseless energy. I recited poems and stories with the acceleration of association and dazzled everyone. Then at another time, even on the same day, my certainty disappeared, to be replaced by unknown dread and suspicion accompanied by a profound darkness of mood. A tailing emptiness of testosterone-poisoned relations left me paralyzed, as if my mind were going to turn on me and grind to a halt.

⌣

Sara, in her first year of law school at the Sorbonne, became engaged to Gerald Weinstein, an internist twelve years her senior. Both were members of the same communist group and had been dating for more than a year. I received the news of their betrothal with a tinged mixture of jealousy and envy. Once again, I felt defeated. Not that I wanted to marry her or anything like that. It was just that another man was chosen to be more desirable, deserving, and legitimate. First there was Ertuğrul, then there was Gülseren's boyfriend, now there was Gerald, an attentive, soft-spoken, well-bred gentleman who belonged to a third-generation Jewish family living in Paris. He was one of the few Jews allowed to specialize and had a successful practice housed in a very elegant office in St. Germaine, in Paris proper. Whenever he came to visit, he and Sara listened to the gramophone and played cards in her room. I never heard the sounds of kissing, nor did they talk like lovers, whisper in each other's ears, or hold hands in public. Hellos and good-byes were three little pecks on both cheeks. Once I asked Sara whether she had fallen in love with Gerald. She coldly replied that she "never falls."

"To 'fall in love' isn't the right term to describe the relationships between men and women of my generation. It's more of a synchronicity in commitments to a cause," she asserted.

"Well, is making love part of it?"

"Having sex is. Didn't you say love is an extended form of plagiarism?"

"Well, have you had sex with him yet?"

"It isn't your business, Adam! Do I ever ask whom *you* fucked today? For you, sex is a matter of daily discharge, the recipients of which are totally interchangeable. This has been going on for years; I see no growth in you. If anything, you seem to have become more immature with age!"

Was her irritably self-assured attitude related to being an innately pent-up girl, or did she want me in spite of my fig leaf of sanity? She continued her litany against me with an escalating intensity. "Sex is neither a looting game nor a compulsive sickness like that of Casanova. He called women in his life by letters, but for your play there aren't enough letters in the alphabet. You should give your women numbers. You treat women as sexual commodities, as means, but to what end? A cult of *self*, like Casanova? Serial and simultaneous adultery isn't going to help you to find yourself. Yours is a case of sexual incontinence."

Sara's heterogeneous intelligence was untouched by tenderness. I wasn't trying to find myself through others, sexually or otherwise. If anything, I watch my sexual behavior as it happens. I was simply making myself felt to myself through my excesses.

When Sara was a teenager, the closest she and I came to sexual play was wrestling, which she always initiated. Her parents strenuously objected to our getting physical, so Sara usually ambushed me when we were alone. Sara was a strong girl—a Polish pony, her father called her. However, after a long and harsh struggle, she would end up on the floor, under me, both of us face down. We would stay in that position for a long time, ostensibly catching our breath. Inevitably I had an erection, and she, sensing the tightness, made room for my penis between her clothed legs, all without either of us uttering a word. Then we got up and carried on as if nothing had happened, only to repeat the scenario again a few days later. In between, she didn't tolerate being touched, even casually. I wanted to tickle her all the time and dared to attempt it, only to be rebuffed with a most hostile glance. She willed a steady and impenetrable emotional obtuseness.

∽

I lack a self-coherence.

Sara referred her schoolmate, an older Turkish student, Cemil Karasu, and his French-Jewish wife, Sabina, to our fertility clinic. The couple had been married for two years, during which Sabina had been trying desperately to get pregnant. She was frenzied to the point of threatening divorce or suicide if, within the next two years, her husband didn't give her a child.

Before I met Sabina, I thought that such a statement would be enough for a man to be rid of her, and I was ready to advise this to my countryman. Then I met her; she was a younger, sweeter, more beautiful version of Mademoiselle Blanche.

She agonized during our consultation. "When I see children on the street, I want to wrap them up in my arms and squeeze them tight. I cry when I can't do it. I'm essentially a mother. If I can't be a mother, I'm nothing."

Twice she had been diagnosed with false pregnancy, including lactation. She even had become a wet nurse for a neighbor's infant. Cemil had typical Mongolian features. He was overweight, bald, and jovial and always had a ready pat on the back (or backside, depending on the recipient's sex) for everyone, including Dr. Lugner.

"You give me a child, I'll give you my kingdom! Here is the baksheesh," challenged Cemil, throwing a gold piece on the doctor's desk. Cemil, the son of a wealthy man from Erzurum—the town of my former chauffeur, Abbas—bragged that his family literally owned the town. Erzurum again!

As Dr. Lugner pocketed the gold, he didn't miss the opportunity to put Cemil in his place: "Then, you may know Prince Adam, the son of the last king of Turkey."

"No, I don't. Are you the son of Padishah Vahdettin? I thought his name was Ertuğrul?"

"I'm his son, though illegitimate," I clarified.

"Oh, I'm sorry. If I hadn't been told, I would never have guessed that you were Turkish, well, except for your eyes. When I saw you in the waiting room, I thought you might be French-Vietnamese. Do you speak Turkish?"

"Of course."

"Ayağına düştük—we fall at your feet, Doctor Bey. Please help us."

Dr. Lugner examined Sabina and mischievously asked me for a second opinion. Sabina's vagina was so dilated I couldn't palpate its engorged walls. A pinkish fluid dripped from her bulging, red vulva, whispering, "Come in." Dr. Lugner looked at me. "Today is the day," he said. "It would be a *mitzvah*."

He called Cemil into the room and explained that if he could masturbate into a cup, then the sperm could be injected into Sabina's uterus. "No problem," Cemil assented and disappeared into the bathroom. I excused myself to the other room. Filling my cup was no problem either; just thinking of Sabina's dilation was stimulation enough. While Cemil sat in the waiting room, thinking that it was his cup that was being used, Dr. Lugner and I were in the examining room, injecting my sperm into Sabina.

That evening I left the office in turmoil, not because we hadn't really performed a *mitzvah* (and our treatment was, in fact, fraud, dishonesty, and dishonorable trespassing) but because I somehow perceived impregnating Sabina—my substitute mixture of Gülseren and Mademoiselle Blanche—as my pitiful way of possessing them.

Of course the whole exercise might be moot since I might not have had viable sperm and Sabina may not have been in a fertile state.

That night at the dinner table, Dr. Lugner and I couldn't look into each other's eyes. When Sara asked if her friend's wife could be helped, Dr. Lugner said, "Who knows? Let's hope so," and changed the subject.

The following day I found myself utterly possessed, but not for the reason I had feared. I was obsessed with Sabina. I dreamt about her and fantasized about her at all hours of the day. I spent any free time I had hanging around their apartment, just to catch a glimpse of her. They lived in the posh neighborhood of Passy on the Rue de Vignes. Many nights I passed under their window and whistled the tune I used to for Gülseren in Istanbul. Sabina, though, never opened the curtains.

On my tenth day of watching for her, in the early afternoon, as I was again passing in front of the building, Sabina stuck her head out of her door and signaled for me to come in. I walked into the foyer of the building. She motioned for me to follow her, and we began climbing the stairs, until we entered her large apartment. Her cotton dress clung to every moist crevice of her body. I was drunk with the aroma of her.

"I've been watching you," she said. "I'll . . . if you promise that it'll only be once and that you won't hang around anymore."

My fevered senses promised all and everything. She quickly took off her dress as I stood in awe. I tore at my clothes and, with the awkward urgency of a new lover, plunged into her. She smiled gently and whispered in my ear:

"*Ne hāte pas, cet acte tendre*"—Don't hurry, this is a tender act.

Was she reciting Paul Valéry? I dissolved in her. I had been waiting to be emotionally seized for such a long time, or was this just a delirium of desire?

∿

Not to want her again was the hardest promise to keep. I restrained myself by walking around her apartment in my imagination, paying attention to the smallest details. I learned the art of inner dissolution with a lover. All was fine, except that I was losing weight and not sleeping. I found the cause of all my sufferings: desire.

You see, every love relationship is a quest for the original loss, whatever it was—not the love of that person. For me, the original loss is the father. But man is collectively fatherless; what we have at best are abortive substitutes—symbolic fathers. Finding them requires their absence: a father becomes a father only when he is dead. One doesn't have to be literally dead either.

~~~

For the next eight weeks, I vacillated between being as hopefully excited as an expectant father and as anxious as a prisoner awaiting a parole decision. Then one day, Cemil showed up in the office carrying a case of expensive champagne. Once confronted with the finality, I felt nothing. I had fathered a child. Now I have to die.

~~~

Sara and Gerald got married. She moved to his spacious apartment in St. Germaine, just a few blocks from his office. I helped her move. Why was it so very painful? I never had loved her, and a marriage to her—even if she had wanted one, which she didn't—would never have worked. I chose to be her dead brother, as she rightly accused me. But does one ever fully recover from an incestuous fantasy, no matter how undesirable it might be?

The Lugners invited me back to live with them; I guessed they were lonelier than I was. Now I was reluctant to give up my hotel room. It was peculiar not to have Sara at home. The house was uglier. Her parents were very much at a loss, though they had campaigned hard to marry her off.

Now the two remaining Lugners and I dined in silence thinking of different things. Dr. Lugner read investment tip sheets and mulled over them. Mrs. Lugner looked at outfits in fashion magazines. I contrived when and how to kill them. Sara had been the only decent person in the house. Her absence made it clear that there was no reason for the Lugners' existence. What about me? Why was I still alive? I ate enough, I read enough, I fucked enough.

Meanwhile, I fell into the Lugners' routine, but I moved as if in a fog: I got up early in the morning, had a quick breakfast, went to the office (where I didn't function particularly well), broke for lunch, went back to work until dark, and went either to the Lugners' for dinner and stayed there or went back to my hotel.

On my days off, I hung around the cemetery or visited with women. Père Lachaise Cemetery was within walking distance from the house. With its hills and trees, the cemetery looked like a deserted historical park. I walked around the tombstones, touched them, and read the inscriptions. There was a grave for Alexander Walewski, Napoleon's bastard son from a Jewish wife, who became minister of war. The largest mausoleum belonged to the smallest man buried there: Adolph Theirs, who became a powerful politician. I usually ended up in my favorite northeast corner of the cemetery near Le Mûre des Fédère, the communal grave. I lay down on the ground and stayed there for hours at a time.

This was the right place to gaze into infinite distance—the actuality beyond the reach of the senses. The sediment of my ever-present consciousness wouldn't allow me to partake of the eternity of God. If all transient things are permanent in God, only by getting rid of my consciousness could I partake of the eternity. I yearned for nothing else. The women, my primary interest in life were totally interchangeable.

You see, sex, in its idea of union of desire, takes away the "I-ness"; in fact, it is bait, for no object is worth desiring. In sex, one seeks self-confirmation in the negation of the other person, and one longs to be revealed by an imaginary one.

～

I always behaved as if I related to people, but I didn't; I couldn't. I expressed interest in their lives, but I wasn't a bit interested. I looked into their eyes as if I were listening, but I wasn't. Occasionally I couldn't remember with whom I was, forgetting not just a name but also who she was, how I met her, and how long I had known her. I presumed the same would have happened with men, but I had no male acquaintances besides Dr. Lugner and Dökmejian. Sara accused me of having conversations that had the quality of observation. Well, it is true because, for me, all relationships are separating experiences.

～

Ironically, the Lugners, Denise, and Renée all interpreted my withdrawal to Sara's marriage. I couldn't protest the wrongness of their presumption because I had no other explanation except to declare my insanity.

At the end of one workday, Dr. Lugner called me into his office for a private chat.

Before he began, he cleared his throat several times.

"Adam, I'm no psychiatrist," he began, slowly. "It's difficult to say this, but there's something wrong with you. You are either sick or behaving like one who is sick."

"Behaving like sick?"

"Well, let's just say, in the way of King David. In order to escape from Achish, he pretended to be insane, letting his saliva dribble all over his beard and clothes, bumping into others as if he didn't see them."

I didn't want to correct some of the details of his story.

"You look like a ghost. Your eyes have sunken into their sockets and seem to tremble. You say things that sound very profound but actually make no sense. Having a conversation means what you say must have some relevance to what the other person has just said. You leak literary quotes to us and then relate them to yourself. If I didn't know you better, I'd say you're a self-referential maniac."

I had tried to articulate my obscure experiences, hoping that someone else would make sense of them. I should stop talking, I thought. My thoughts should remain invisible.

He continued, "Actually, it's worse than that; if you made no sense all the time, it would be easier. We could just dismiss you as *meshugana*—crazy. But at times you say very meaningful things. Even Sara commented on it. I guess you're reading my books up there and remembering enough to repeat, without giving credit. I mean, where else could these things be coming from?"

"I quarry in our collective inherited memories."

"This is exactly what I mean. You drop these one-liners all the time! There is something called conversational postulate: the spontaneity and relevance."

I didn't realize that. What I said had nothing to do with any idea or any relational concept that I wanted to convey. It simply represented my inner state, to keep in check my intuitive dissonance.

I tried so hard to be spontaneous. But I was too busy figuring out my semantic strategies. Even words became real only after I said them. I am always worried about providing the wrong lexicon. Furthermore, there was an incompatibility of meanings between my formless inner experiences and the outer world.

"And I hear you spend a couple of hours every day at the cemetery. What is that all about?"

"Oh, that. You know the story of King of Pontus? Who, fearing that his enemy would poison him, took small doses of arsenic every day?"

"So, do you have an enemy who is planning to kill you?" he asked with a crooked smile.

With his limited knowledge in the field, he was trying to figure out whether I was paranoid. "Yes, myself."

"Adam, I don't need further proof of your confusion. You walk around as if you're a shadow; you actually bump into other people. You're physically here, but you're not here."

Did he not know that presence is never reciprocal?

"Am I doing my job practicing medicine?" I asked.

"Yes," he replied. "I am not talking about some malpractice of medicine. You can do almost anything here using only one-tenth of your brain. I am talking about your malpractice of life. Furthermore, it isn't just mental promiscuity. I hear from the girls that you've been sexually involved with many of our married patients. Depression, if that is what you have, cannot be warded off by sex. You're always disheveled, and you smell of something, I'm not sure what. I smelled that scent only when I was doing clinical rotations in the insane asylum. I think you need to go and see a psychiatrist."

His urging me to see a psychiatrist sounded like "You need a good beating."

He continued: "You pay half for it. I'll pay the other half, all right? For all I know, I might have been at least partly responsible for what you're going through. Sara's husband swears by the analyst, Dr. Lacan, without whom he says he couldn't have gotten married. Dr. Lacan's office is on the same street as Sara's husband's office."

I broke into a cold sweat. I felt naked, frightened, but also relieved.

Dr. Lacan's waiting room looked like ours; there were many patients. They sat quietly, staring at each other, and were not pleased to see me. I approached the receptionist, telling her I was there for my ten o'clock appointment with Dr. Lacan. She shook her head in affirmation, explained that everyone was there to see Dr. Lacan, and pointed me to a chair. I sat. Now I understood why these people were staring at each other. They were competing for Dr. Lacan's time. I soon found myself staring at them. An older, highly perfumed woman in an elegant hat and an overweight middle-aged man were each called in turn to the inner office. Each spent no more than fifteen minutes in the office. A preadolescent boy with his doting mother seemed to stay in the office forever. Finally, the only people left in the waiting room beside me were a pale, twentyish, tall, underweight, young woman with a boyish hairdo and her companion-nurse. The young woman glared at me. "How can he keep me waiting like this? I am James Joyce's daughter for God sakes." After just ten minutes, the young woman stormed out of the office, and the receptionist called me in.

To my surprise, Jacques Lacan looked no more than a few years older than I. Lacan's writings, of which I'd read a few in anticipation of the interview, sounded like the work of an older man. He spoke:

"What kind of doctor are you?"

"The 'imposter' kind."

"So, what is bothering the imposter?"

"Was she really Joyce's daughter or another imposter? It's the duplicity that bothers me," I replied.

"Oh, that is a true universal symptom. Where do you live?"

"In my thoughts."

"Listen. Psychotherapy is not the demonstration of excess wittiness. Well, at least not on the part of the patient. You are too short; has any doctor recommended bovine serum injections for you?"

"No, you're the only psychiatrist I've seen."

"You haven't done the rounds with Doctors Fontain, Maier, and Forel yet?"

"No."

"I see, a psychiatric virgin. Would you like to be analyzed? A low-cost analysis?"

"Do I have to be admitted to your Asiles Hospital?"

"No, not at all. You'll come here three times a week, lie on the couch, and tell me whatever comes to your mind."

"For how long?"

"Until you remember the sourness of your mother's breast milk."

Was psychoanalysis an exercise in insensitivity training?

"I wasn't breast-fed by my mother; she didn't believe in anyone tugging at her nipples," I said and immediately regretted my concreteness.

"I meant your remembered oneness," he said with a pitying smile. "*Alors! Bonne journée.*" With that, he got up, took his hat, and left.

My treatment with Dr. Lacan lasted four months. I felt experimented on in sessions as if he was after proving some theory, and I was resisting. Finally, Dr. Lacan decided that I was not ready for psychoanalysis and explained, "You are unengageable in a transferential relationship with me because you have no prototype relations from the past, not even metaphorical ones. Craziness is not the loss of reality, as there is no such a thing (any scarecrow could frighten reality away), but rather the loss of its metaphorical substitutes, of which you have none. One can recover from the loss of reality by participating in the delusion of normalcy or by transcending the norm, but you are seeking sanctuary in the invisibility of thoughts."

How come he was allowed to be so obscure? As if the banality and the mutually subversive quality of this commercialized friendliness were not enough, I was again found lacking.

~~~

I entered our office, and there, on display in the reception area, was a case of champagne with a note attached to it: "Thank you for helping me to come into the world. Nevim."

A prophet! They had named the baby "prophet" in Hebrew. We were all invited to a reception in celebration of "our collective success."

The large apartment was packed with their friends and members of Sabina's family. She welcomed me with joyful kisses on the cheeks while holding the baby in her arms: "Ça alors!" I kissed the baby Nevim, too. Both smelled of a mixture of powder and old sweat. Suddenly my interest in Sabina disappeared: not only had her smell changed, but so had the expression in her eyes. She looked at me with maternal eyes. I felt strangely resentful and wanted to get away quickly. Shortly thereafter, I lost my desire to conjure up vivid images of Mademoiselle Blanche and Sabina. But I felt better. I knew all along that only the loser takes all. Dr. Lugner said, "Adam you look great. Discharged from the asylum?"

"No, Dr. Lugner. Just a long furlough." The man was just a big, ugly, emotional callus.

~~~

My own insecurity was compounded by the growing anxiety of the French and France's Jews. The Lugners were very anxious. Since Hitler became a chancellor of Germany, Paris had been transformed into a city of strikes and demonstrations. The talk on the street was about either a war with Germany or a socialist revolution. Every week there were demonstrations and bloody confrontations between rival groups of communists and nationalists. It was as if the city had plunged into a civil war. The newspapers fueled the hostilities with their disparate headlines. *L'Action Française*, the fascist gazette, encouraged riots against communists, socialists, and especially Jews, noting that they were manipulating the political system. Newspapers such as *L'Humanite* and *La Republique* portrayed the ordinary worker fighting fascism. *Lu*—an apolitical paper—lost its readers to various virulent camps.

What was I? To which group did I belong? Why was this happening to me again? In Turkey, I had been for neither the sultanate rightists nor the semileftist patriots, and look where it had gotten me. How was it that two countries in which I lived had turned into battlegrounds? I had thought that France was a safe haven. It had emerged from the Great War as a victorious country, rich and civilized. What was the problem?

Meanwhile, every day Paris became more and more a once-powerful-but-decaying place. The "illnesses of war" were reappearing in a new generation of men partly because of the reality of an impending war with Germany. Although the next war with Germany had not yet been declared, the idea that there could be one created a siege mentality in Paris. The constant air-raid sirens seemed to be requesting some bombing to occur. Besides being contentious, people had become more mistrustful of each other and the government. The red socialists, white pacifists, and red, white, and blue nationalists were all disgruntled and querulous within and outside their organizations. The communists were mostly recruited from among the recently immigrated Eastern European Jews.

The older, more established Jews, such as the Lugners, abhorred the newcomers, though they couldn't prevent their children from joining them. The nationalists were the "real French." They wanted the Jews out of the country but didn't know how to bring that about. They still brooded over their encounter with the Germans in the previous war: "We should have eliminated those Germans when we had the chance" was common rhetoric. As inflation increased, people began to accuse the various factions of bad faith if not outright thievery.

Meanwhile, the value of the franc kept declining. Food became scarce, and water was barely drinkable. Dr. Lugner had long stopped depositing money in French banks and advised me to do the same. I had barely graduated from using my mattress as a safe deposit box to using a local bank.

～

I have no self to retreat into.

What is the meaning of my life? A Dr. Lacan might be helpful in unraveling the uncertainty and obscurity of my mind, but my unglued core was what I had to take care of.

You see, only the negation of outer certainty and the inarticulateness of the obscure brings out an inner coherence—a gnawed innocence.

My thoughts began bubbling up, semicoherent at best. First, why did I need to have a purpose in my life? I should find a way to make the question of meaning irrelevant. Meaning was simply a series of incompatible schemes of the mind, and they constantly mutate. I should also stop being the victim of introspection. It only brings one to the abyss of the self. Life was hard enough without its being examined. I must stop my relations with women. What I desired was desire itself, not women—nothing out there was worth desiring.

The quest for the self in another's gaze is never reciprocal; at best, it serves a temporary anxiety-lowering dependency. If you ground yourself in separation, you will never have to experience yourself as being abandoned but rather only confirmed. I also must stop believing in anything; all must be doubted. I must resign from the cult of suffering. Despair is a major ingredient of maturity. Confusion is another imaginary entity. I am confused because I think I should not be. All this is the tyranny of the norm. In reality, life is normless and formless.

I must reassemble myself on the basis of the above principles, then edit myself for general consumption. I shouldn't be so stuck on truth. Like everything else, the truth is in the service of self-coherence. I must muffle the messages and voices within me. I didn't need to have a real self. All I needed was to come to terms with my life lies. Because I didn't just tell lies—I *was* the lie—there was no deliberate act committed. What stories I told in the process of existing were like landfills, to set ground—no matter how artificially brought about—so that structures could be erected. I could build real, self-like selves atop the unreal but still solid ground. My life lie is the largest frame of mine, encapsulating all other frames that may or may not contain truths.

﹏

Had I moved from one sick man of Europe to another? France seemed as much in distress as the Ottoman Empire had been. People talked only of being invaded by the German army or being besieged by immigrants from Eastern Europe. It seemed to me that France was trying to make itself unworthy of invasion.

Inflation was so extreme that people were hoarding anything they could. Prices were posted on every item in shops, obstructing the goods for sale from sight. Salesgirls and some housewives began walking the streets at night, offering discount prices.

Contagious diseases, such as tuberculosis, gonorrhea, and syphilis, were rampant. Children were dying in disproportionate numbers from untreated infections, and there seemed to be no major protest. The marriage rate declined, and those who were married were reluctant to have children. The number of couples seeking abortions in our office tripled. Dr. Lugner even aborted nonexistent fetuses. "I can feel an inseminated egg the size of a filbert," he boasted. Who was the real nut? Simultaneously we sold more quinine pomade (a contraceptive) than any other product we carried.

Of course, even advocating abortion, much less performing it, was a criminal act. One day, Denise found a newspaper clipping posted on our office door announcing the arrest of Madeleine Pelletier, the well-known psychologist, for her pro-abortion advocacy. Someone was obviously sending us a message. It wasn't all that difficult, of course, to figure out what Dr. Lugner was up to, as his practice openly shifted toward abortion. I gradually became the caregiver for the rest of the patients.

When I confronted Dr. Lugner about the possibility of both of us getting arrested, he dismissed my concern: "The French don't mind Jewish infants being aborted!"

"But Dr. Lugner, you also operate on non-Jews."

"How should I know? Women don't get the tips of their clitorises clipped. I practice in a Jewish ghetto. If a non-Jew sneaks in without my knowledge, is that my fault? Am I to ask every patient her faith? Wouldn't that be a rather unethical, if not illegal, act in itself?"

﹏

Dr. Lugner finally succumbed to his wife's chronic badgering and decided to buy a new car, a six-horsepower, light-gray Peugeot 201, to replace his old Peugeot. Since Sara left, the car was the only new thing the Lugners had bought. Nothing else was touched in the house. Moths had eaten so much that the designs on the oriental rugs weren't identifiable. The battered sofa and chairs were covered with throw covers, unstable doorknobs were removed and never replaced, and burnt-out lightbulbs went unchanged. The windows, which the Lugners wouldn't ever open—"the breeze causes pneumonia!"—were glued shut from nonuse. The window curtains, so long kept closed "to prevent the sun from bleaching the rugs," couldn't be opened without the danger of breaking their pulleys. The shower handles came off with a minor pull, leaving the surprised victim burning or freezing while trying to put them back. Still, the refrigerator was always full with bulk-sale abundance. Frequently, food rotted and had to be thrown away after a few days of frugal hesitation.

Sara, during her infrequent visits, lashed out at her parents, reprimanding them for the state of her old home and threatening never to visit again. She accused me of having a bad influence on them because I didn't care how or if I lived.

"Adam, you're one of the most knowledgeable men I've met in my life, but you treat life as discrete bits, with no continuity. You're in some self-defeating reverse *Echternach danse*; you advance one step forward, then take two steps backward. You live in squalid turmoil while systematically pursuing the derangement of that beautiful mind of yours."

Sara's righteousness was insufferable.

She continued, "I want to know your pain and to know you and be known to you."

"Sara, I cannot really know you; I can only reflect. Any human interaction requires lengthy rehearsals on my part. I hardly manage to live a missing life. I am appearing to be, but I am never actually being.

"I have finally managed to invent a strategy in order to live in an unlivable world. At best, I can experience myself. I am sure I am not alone. Every person is isolated and permanently unknown and unknowable. Therefore, every person has to become sort of a philosopher, methodically or haphazardly. There are no existential scaffolds hiding my personal issues. You see, when I am truthfully speaking, I cannot be understood; if I am understood, I am not being truthful. Therefore, to know me is to leave me alone."

Sara answered impatiently. "I have, Adam, for so many years. Why do you want to be left alone?"

"To make sure that nothing worse happens."

"I don't know what you mean by worse, but believe me, Adam, you're about as bad as it gets. Please say something that I can relate to."

"Okay, a full goblet must be carried very steadily."

"Full of what?"

"Nameless dreads."

"Adam, empty them to me," she said.

"Sara, do you know the predicament of the Norse god Thor? He tried to empty a goblet, only to find that it was refilled by the sea."

⌁

At the bottom section of the newspapers there was an announcement of the death of Atatürk—the president of the Republic of Turkey. A jealous French husband who killed his wife was given four times more space. "Mustafa Kemal, the yellow rose," I murmured to myself. He never would have married my mother. My mother's image flashed through my mind. Why wasn't I thinking of her more often?

⌁

Dr. Lugner was hovering over me of late. He was tentative and uncharacteristically deferential, paying for lunches, inviting me to dinners, or complimenting me for one thing or another. I sensed he wanted to talk about something but couldn't bring himself to do so.

One day, finally, he spilled: "Gerald is afraid of being drafted. You know, only men with young children or pregnant wives are excused from the draft. That is, of course, why our fertility clinic is surpassing the abortion clinic these days. I've sent Sara to the best fertility specialists in town—I don't know if she's told you—but nothing has come of it."

Dr. Lugner mopped the sweat from his face with his handkerchief. "Adam, I need your help. I need you to get Sara pregnant. Please don't look at me that way."

I had no idea how I looked. In fact, I wasn't surprised, shocked, or anything of the sort.

"We'll do it. Stop squirming," I said.

"No, no, you'll have to do this by yourself. I can't even be in the office. What I want is for you to offer Sara your help as if I didn't know anything about it."

"Okay, but what do I say to her? What technique could I offer her that hasn't been suggested so far? And Gerald? He *is* a doctor."

"The Eastern technique!" Dr. Lugner interrupted, looking very pleased.

"What are you talking about?"

"You told me, remember? You write something around her vulva a few times within one menstrual cycle. Gerald will understand the psychological, if not mythical, power of healing."

"But that is a technique used by *muftis*, not doctors," I countered.

"Adam, stop quibbling over titles. It's true you're not a *mufti*, but you're not exactly a doctor either."

I'd been reduced to a sperm donor. What convinced me to do it wasn't his despair and his willingness to do anything for his daughter. No, it was the opportunity to impregnate Sara. She would have my child, not Gerald's. It was a victory—the high sperm count over the low, the potency of the otherwise impotent.

My father had been the caliph—the leader of all *muftis*—an inherited title. I was, therefore, a contender for the grand position of caliph—or at least a measly *mufti*.

~

I surprised Sara on her way home from where she worked, a small law firm in Montmartre. She was meeting Gerald and going to the international exhibition to see Picasso's *Guernica*.

She seemed pleased to see me. We chatted on for a few moments, then, after her low-key acknowledgment of Gerald's predicament and her failed attempts to get pregnant, I told her that I knew some special oriental remedies she might want to try. She stopped, turned, and looked into my eyes with her deep-green ones, which had become darker over the years, and said, "So you want to fuck me, huh?"

I turned away and began walking, my head down, as if she had made a joke. She put her hand on my arm and stopped me.

"Adam, what fucking oriental remedy do you know that no one else does? Do you think that I'm an idiot? Why don't you say it? If someone other than Gerald fucks me, I may get pregnant, and you're willing to be that obliging gentleman. Isn't that it?"

"Well, not exactly," I demurred.

"Well, what exactly?" she insisted.

"It's like this: I can insert live sperm from a donor into your uterus."
The agony of asexual reasoning about a sexual matter was unbearable.

"What a lapse in taste! Whose idea is this? Your mind doesn't work
that way, nor do you care whether Gerald is drafted or not. Is it my father?
Tell the truth. This is his kind of scheme, isn't it? No, don't tell me, I
know it is. Okay, who is this donor with the live—or is it lively—sperm?"

"Me," I sputtered.

"Well, I would rather be fucked. I mean, why not? At least you'll
get something out of it too. Now, if you don't mind, I must be going.
Bye Adam, this *faux-naif* sensitivity of yours cannot be abstracted into
kindness. Oh God! I sound like you."

She quickly turned away, and I felt shamed by my compliance with
Dr. Lugner's scheme and Sara's honesty. As I began walking toward my
hotel room in the winter drizzle, the rain started falling hard. The wind
was beating on me. I didn't want to seek shelter. Icy water hit my face
and head, and as rainwater swallowed my feet, I slowed my pace.

᪲

The newspapers not only depressed and confused me but also reminded
me how helpless and impotent I was about my own fate. I began to lose
my interest in women as well for more or less the same reason. Plus my
erection problem now was compounded with a pleasureless if not
uncomfortable orgasm—I was ejaculating backward to my bladder. Was
this self-seeding a penalty for my misdeed of seeding others, or was it a
self-prohibition against its potential repetition? I guess, empty of God,
I'll be permanently unsatisfied in sin.

Furthermore, in my sexual interactions with women, I found a negative balance of the transaction developing for me. In exchange for a measly
orgasm, I had to listen to their medical, psychological, and family problems before sex, after sex, at times even during sex. I found that occasional
visits to the Sphinx brothel on Boulevard Edgar Quinet or The Colony
(at rue Fontaine in Montmartre), a whorehouse run by an aging American
dancer, were fairer deals. Their *filles de joie*—joy girls, as prostitutes were
called—tended to be moonlighting housewives, jobless dancers, singers,
and actresses. By sleeping with prostitutes, I was trying to make sex finite.

A few times I went to church. At the end of each service, there was a
prayer for the conversion of Jews to the "true faith." Well, all right then,

I will. But will this not be considered a sham conversion? Conversion from what?

༄

Gerald was the most enthusiastic of all the Lugner family members about the reality of the "Eastern solution." Of course, it could be said that he had the most to lose if Sara didn't become pregnant soon. He reasoned that if Jewish boys were willing to deform their hands to prevent being drafted, it wouldn't be so horrible to have his wife artificially inseminated by "a decent fellow" (as he patronizingly described me) who had no special agenda. Nevertheless, Gerald had two concerns that required my further cooperation: first, that I would allow him to be present during the procedure, and, second, that I would never claim or even speak of fathering the child.

I reassured him on both counts, though I was disappointed about his request to be present during the procedure. He was taking away the pleasure of intimacy—however mechanical—to which I was looking forward. Thankfully Sara objected to his (or anyone else's) presence. On the appointed day, she showed up at the office on time and immediately took charge, announcing, "Okay, let's go."

That morning I had to open the place, and I was just getting it set up.

"Can we just get on with it, Adam?"

She was already undressed from the waist down, pacing up and down the office.

"Wait a minute! My God! You are the most demanding patient I've ever met. If you need to go to the bathroom, this is a good time to do it; after the procedure, you're going to have to lie flat on your back for at least two hours. Okay. Now lie down on your back on the examination table; put your feet in the stirrups and move your bottom to the edge of the table."

I gave her the full spiel: "I'm going to the next room to fill this jar with sperm; I'll then draw it into a syringe, which I'll insert into your cervix and inject the contents."

"Not on your bloody life! I told you a month ago, Adam, that if I were to do it, it would be the natural way. So, take off your pants. Do it! What's that look? You've been fucking everything that moves since I've known you. Are you on to the letter Z yet?"

"Sara, I am hardly a Casanova. It is the human proximity for which I am yearning." Why was I lying to her?

"Oh, no! You are not yearning for a human proximity; in sex, you annihilate women as people. You are an emotional annihilationist. You behave the same way with me. You look at me as if I am an object. As if that is not enough, you give the impression that you don't even recognize 'the object.' Do you know how that makes me feel? Ashamed. Because in your eyes I only see a reflected appraisal of me. Can you look at me, for once, as if you have seen me for the first time? Just experience me as I am, as a distinct individual."

Sara wore her brain on her skirt. Whatever sexual interest or simple curiosity I had anticipated about this encounter with her evaporated.

"Sara, I can't have an erection with you. I need to be desired. If I can even masturbate next door—knowing that you are here and knowing what I am doing it for—it will be success enough for me."

"Do you want me to jerk you off?"

"Sara, would you please just let me do this on my own?"

I went to the next room, but no matter how hard I tried, I couldn't have an erection. I tried fantasizing about Denise, Sabina, and Mademoiselle Blanche, but Sara's face kept popping into my mind. I guessed the saying was true: the harder you try, the less likely you are to succeed.

Sara knocked on the door. "Adam! It's been more than half an hour. What are you doing? Let me help you. Listen, Gerald has the same problem. I know how to fix it, you fussy lion. Trust me: all you'll have to do is sit on my face and jerk off on my breasts."

I was willing to try anything. It felt awkward at first, but when she put her tongue gently around my anus, I succeeded. I quickly collected the discharge into my hand and, having no other method of delivery, haphazardly pushed it deep into her vagina. This was obviously a technically inferior method. I thought it would never work, especially because Sara refused to stay in the prone position for more than two minutes. She quickly got dressed and waved good-bye, calling out, "You Jewish doctors are all latent homosexuals you know!"

～

Sara was not pregnant. One day she stopped me in a bookshop. "Would you like to go to the Luxembourg Gardens and watch Guignols—the puppet theater?" she asked. "They are playing a funny imagined encounter of Napoleon with Hitler and Stalin."

"No, but would you like to go to Père-Lachaise cemetery to visit Napoleon's grave?"

At Père-Lachaise, I pointed toward some of the graves. "Do you think all these corpses that are lying here under the ground really had selves? What do you think these granite and marble memorials are all about? Aren't these pyramids, obelisks, ziggurats, basilicas, and menhirs defensive assertions of doubted selves? Do you think all these altars, urns, columns, stone owls, *cippi*, and sarcophagi simply serve the fear of bourgeois mortality?" Sara couldn't be bought. "Don't patronize me, Adam. Why do you come here anyway? Is this solemnity of eroticized death, or is it because no one any longer dies here?"

She quoted Baudelaire casually.

"No, because this is where one is never evicted," I said.

I thought that instead of burying people lying down, if they buried them standing, the cemetery would accommodate tenfold more dead. The headstones still would identify where the heads are, of course, if one is buried feet down . . .

Sara was impressed with the depth of my knowledge of the cemetery.

"This is the grave of Samuel Hahnemann, the father of homeopathic cures, and here lies Honoré de Balzac," I said. "You should read *Père Goriot*."

"I've had enough of fathers with their schemes, but you could quit medicine and be a guide here," she joked.

I showed Sara my favorite spot, "of the unknowns," and I lay down as usual over the grass-covered tomb.

We were in front of the small mosque next to a huge, baroque crematorium.

"How on earth did the Muslims get enough of this precious real estate to build a mosque here, prince manqué?" she asked.

"It was an exchange between Napoleon III and the Ottoman emperor for the Crimea. It was a trade, one square block for a whole country. Do you see that walled-in tomb with R on it? It stands for "Rothschild." He is the fellow who snookered both Ottoman and French emperors in that deal."

Sara laughed. "You know that can't be true. It's too outrageous a story."

I couldn't join her in laughing. I was wondering what would have happened if the Ottoman Empire wasn't squandered like this.

We were supposed to repeat the insemination "procedure" a few times, which we did during cemetery trysts. Sara was unlike any other woman I'd ever met. She was the only person I had ever known who was sexually weirder than myself. Sex with her was a peculiarly empty experience.

During intercourse, she stared at me as if she were asking a question without expecting an answer. I wanted to get the act over with; she seemed to need it to go on forever, riding on top of me without the specific interest in having an orgasm (which she never seemed to have). I asked her whether she even got dilated or wet with Gerald. She, in return, would go into a rage, accuse me of being "*un malbandeur*"—a bad fuck—and storm away, only to return to the cemetery on our next meeting with lots of food and wine, hollering, "A *la bouffe!*—grub's up, *le basduc*—short ass!"

Sara mocked the issues I considered deadly serious. "Tell me more about the Ottoman Empire," she insisted. As soon as I uttered a word, she would collapse over a gravestone, laughing: "*C'est vachement bolan*—this is side-splitting hilarious." I couldn't join in her newly found playfulness because I didn't know whether I could come back from it. I was a finite player.

Then, all of a sudden, Sara refused any contact with me. I wondered whether Gerald had found us out. Artificial insemination was one thing; trysts were quite another.

<hr/>

One day, Dr. Lugner called all of us staff members into his office and proudly announced that he had very good news: Sara was pregnant. The women broke into applause, offering congratulations. I was as much puzzled by such a public display of a private matter as I was of being treated as an employee who had nothing to do with her pregnancy. I thought Dr. Lugner and I might have had a private discussion, but no.

The announcement was made, and that was it. During the coming months, I waited for some invitation from the Lugners or some indication of thankfulness from Sara or Gerald, but there was none. If anything, in the next seven months, Dr. Lugner became more distant, avoiding informal contact with me. He began to go home for lunch—just to avoid being alone with me.

Then one Friday, Dr. Lugner casually told me that it was time to ter-
minate our professional relationship. "Your illegal status is endangering
me," he said. "Besides, I'm going to phase out my practice soon anyway."
I wondered what the real reason for the termination was. I walked into
the hotel, lost in thought, exploring my options—I had none, but I did
have some money in the bank. I didn't notice how empty the hotel was.
The place was usually filled with Armenians, Moroccans, and Algerians—
talking, smoking, and playing card games. Mr. Dökmejian, the hotel
owner, ran over to me, panic reflected in his eyes:

"Dr. Adam, the police are looking for you. They took your passport.
You must go immediately to the police station. They had me lock your
room and told me not to open it for you until you report to the station.

"They asked where you work; I didn't tell them. I would never. I
don't know what to advise; you're a good man, but you can't come back
here. I'm terribly sorry."

I was trembling. My memory was flooded with images of Turkish officers tearing me away from the only place I knew and felt safe. This time,
though, I didn't even have a small piece of luggage to take with me.

～

I knocked on the Lugners' door. It was late.

"Hello Adam." Dr. Lugner was frowning. After a long silence, he
said, "Come in, my wife has a few hard-boiled eggs strewn with ashes."
He began imitating a Limbing dance, a dance I'd seen my mother do, a
Jewish ritual dance of mourning to ward off gloom.

"Oh, I am sorry, Dr. Lugner. I had no idea of the timing. I definitely
didn't mean to bring gloom to your house," I said.

I wanted to turn away and never see them again. Instead, I ended by
explaining my situation, expecting to be helped. That night, Dr. Lugner
offered me my old room temporarily—emphasizing the temporary—until
I found an alternate plan. Mrs. Lugner was much more welcoming. As
we sat down to eat, a commotion in front of the house, followed by loud
knocking on the front door, jolted me from the table.

"Police! Open the door!"

Mrs. Lugner scurried to let them in. That son-of-a-bitch Dökmejian
must have given them the address—or was it Dr. Lugner? Perhaps he
wanted to get rid of me and remove all evidence of shame about his
daughter's pregnancy.

Dr. Lugner and I remained frozen, looking into each other's eyes. I tried to find some sign of misdeed in his expression. Mrs. Lugner returned with three young officers. Dr. Lugner arose and gave a military salute.

"It's just a routine survey," the sergeant explained. "We have a few questions. It won't take more than a few minutes. How many people live here?"

"Only three of us," replied Mrs. Lugner. "My daughter got married four years ago. Her husband is doctor Gerald Weinstein—"

"Fine, fine, let's see your IDs."

Dr. Lugner still stood in the middle of the room, heels locked in the salute position. Seeing him scared made me less so. If anything, it should have had the opposite effect.

"Also bring the men's military service documents," the sergeant instructed.

Mrs. Lugner charmingly attempted to take charge. "Would you boys like to drink something or taste my delicious pot roast? Sit here, I'll get our IDs."

The officers didn't sit, nor did they accept Mrs. Lugner's offer of drink or food. They looked around the room, with undisguised smirks on their faces. One laughed, shook his head, and muttered, "A typical Yid house."

I contemplated making a quick dash out the front door when Mrs. Lugner disappeared into the back of the apartment. She soon reappeared holding a bunch of documents.

"This is my ID, this is my husband's ID and his military papers, and these belong to our son, Adam."

I turned toward Dr. Lugner, whose face was so distorted I couldn't tell if he was scared or furious.

"How come you both, father and son, received medical exemptions from active duty?" the sergeant snickered, after reviewing the documents.

The sergeant then said, "Get the daughter's address and meet me in the car." Abruptly, he turned and walked outside.

Brave thus far, Mrs. Lugner now visibly shook and began to equivocate while writing Sara's address on a piece of paper:

"Please, she's nine months pregnant. She'll get scared. I'll give you all the information that you need about her. Can you at least visit her during the day? Sara is not even Jewish—she is an atheist."

One of the officers pulled the paper from Mrs. Lugner's hand. Then the officers left, leaving the front door open. I went to close it and saw them knocking on the door of the Rabinowitzes' house across the street. When I returned, Dr. and Mrs. Lugner were having a deadly staring contest and talking in low, cold voices to each other.

"Are you crazy?" Dr. Lugner said. "If they ever find out that we lied to them, they'll kill us. Do you understand?"

"How will they find out? We never registered Adam's death certificate."

"What about the neighbors, my staff?"

Now Mrs. Lugner was sobbing loudly. She made no effort to keep her voice down. "I don't know, I don't know, please do something. Why are they collecting all that information. Do you think they'll deport us? Sara was born in Paris. How could they do that to her? Please tell me they couldn't."

Dr. Lugner turned to me: "Adam, there is no way you can take my son's identity and get away with it. Sooner or later the truth will come out, and we'll all be in serious trouble. If you want to take his documents and leave town, it's okay with me. But you can no longer stay here or work for me. You have to disappear and fast. Sara—you know how honest she is—would never be a coconspirator to such a crime, even though she cares about you and owes you one."

I only heard "owes you one." This was the first time anyone acknowledged that I did them a service, ugly as it was.

"You can stay here tonight, but tomorrow you're on your own. I suggest you go to Marseille and get lost there. Marseille is a haven for illegals. Now, I must go to bed. I don't feel well—a little dizzy. What did I eat?"

"Nothing," I said, "maybe that is why; sit down, have some roast."

"No, you two eat. I feel nauseated. I just need some rest; this has been an awful night."

Dr. Lugner staggered out of the dining room. Mrs. Lugner and I couldn't eat either.

That night, in his sleep, Dr. Lugner had a stroke; he woke up with right arm and leg paralysis and speech impairment. The following day, Sara gave birth to a boy—three weeks prematurely. As for me, all bets were off about my leaving: the office had to be maintained; Mrs. Lugner had to be helped. Suddenly I was indispensable. Dr. and Mrs. Lugner's concern that Sara would reject my taking the identity of her brother proved wrong. Sara asserted that I behaved more like a brother to her than her own brother ever had, "including the sibling incest." No one found that even mildly amusing.

Sara named her son *Amiti*—the "truth teller," in Hebrew—as a long-delayed response to the insult a German immigration officer inflicted on her unsuspecting father when the guard renamed the doctor "lugner," or "liar." *Yomtov* would be the child's middle name in spite of everyone's objections. It meant "celebration" in Yiddish; Sara couldn't think of anything more fitting.

"Don't give the child such an unusual name," Mrs. Lugner pleaded. "He is going to be mocked."

"It couldn't be worse than my last name," replied Sara.

Amiti was an ugly baby. Mrs. Lugner thought that he looked like her father—blue eyed and blondish haired. It was as if she were attempting to erase his connection to me. She must know that every baby is born with blue eyes.

～

Like the Ottomans, the French really didn't want war. In turn, the French leaders pretended, bluffed, and appeased but to no avail. The Germans were coming. But unlike the Istanbul papers, some French nationalist newspapers reported on the successes of the German army as if it were an extension of the French army. A number of stores displayed the swastika along with the French flag. The signing of a nonaggression treaty in Munich was celebrated as if it were a victory. Paris looked like the elaborate stage of a shabby theater putting on a farcical show about war. Some Parisians began to speak French with a German accent; women wore camouflage outfits and hats and dresses printed with the French and German flags. Men added epaulets to their coats, grew moustaches similar to Hitler's, and parted their hair on the side, leaving a thatch of hair half covering their foreheads.

People blamed Jews for fomenting hostilities between France and Germany. The two movie theaters I frequented were ransacked because of the suspicion of Jewish ownership. At the pâtisserie where I used to breakfast, a "No Jews" sign was posted next to the "No Dogs" sign. Such signs began appearing even in very common places, such as public urinals. Would someone check men for circumcision before letting them use the facilities? I walked into a public urinal, curious to see what would happen. The attendant was interested only in his *pourboire*—tip. But I couldn't urinate no matter how hard I tried and left the place with my bladder distended. Was I obeying the new rules?

∽

The Lugners decided to leave Paris for Le Levandou a few months before their usual time. Sara, Gerald, and Amiti were to travel with them, as Gerald's car recently had been requisitioned by the military. Dr. Lugner responded to a similar requisition request by claiming that his car was nonfuctional. He then asked me to make it such. I sufficiently dismantled small parts of the car's engine and hid them in boxes in the basement. Meanwhile, no one came to verify the claim. In any event, he now wanted me to restore the car and buy an extra tank of gas and a spare tire.

After dinner, we loaded the car with mere essentials. Even so, the trunk couldn't hold everything, and some supplies had to be tied to the top of the car. They all began to say good-bye to me, kissing me three times on the cheeks. "Take good care of the place. We'll see you soon, hopefully," said Mrs. Lugner. Sara acted indifferently. Gerald took the wheel. I opened the garage door. As the car pulled out, only Amiti looked at me. What was he seeing? I wondered.

My reveries were short-lived: within an hour, three cars came to a screeching halt in front of the house—two police cars and Dr. Lugner's sedan. Gerald and Sara, with Amiti in her arms, stepped out of the first police car. A policeman shoved them toward the door of the apartment. Two other policemen from the other car began unloading the Lugner's car, throwing their suitcases on the sidewalk. I ran downstairs and opened the door.

"Who's this?" the chief officer asked, pointing to me with his stick.

"He is a Turkish doctor visiting us," Gerald offered in a trembling voice.

"You Jews leave your guest at home and try to run out of town? Ha! That's a good one! Bring all your junk back into the house." Turning to me, he continued, "Now, let me tell you, fellow, what sort of people you are associating with. These rats were fleeing in a requisitioned car in the middle of the night. I want you to watch the kid. These two are coming to the police station with me." He jerked his head at Sara. "Her parents are already there. You are not to leave the house under any condition, until we come back. Do you understand?"

"Yes," I said.

Sara looked at Amiti, then at me with pleading eyes.

༄

When I went to the office on Monday morning, I took Amiti with me. The women there were delighted to see him and immediately understood the situation. Several of them said they had seen Jews in their neighborhoods being picked up by the police. Denise easily took charge of Amiti, who, with equal ease, sunk his head between Denise's breasts.

I canceled my afternoon appointments and went to look for the Lugners. There was a mob scene at the police station. Dozens of people, mostly women, were inquiring about their family members, crying, and begging for information. A few of the younger women aggressively demanded to know the whereabouts of next of kin and were promptly arrested. Finally, a senior officer appeared in the doorway and announced that "missing" family members could be searched for at the detention center at Vel' d'Hive—the indoor sport arena in the seventeenth arrondissement.

A young clerk at Vel' d'Hive confirmed that the Lugners and Weinstocks (including Gerald's parents) had been detained there until Saturday and then had been moved temporarily to the Drancy apartments.

I was physically and psychologically exhausted. I walked in a daze for a while and finally lay down on a bench at Parc Monceau. As I fell asleep, I imagined that the whole matter must be a dream, a nightmare from which I'd soon awake.

༄

I needed to go home to regain my strength before I could make my way to Drancy, but when I arrived at the Lugners' house, I found it padlocked and sealed, with a sign posted on the door: "L'entrée interdite! Par l'ordre de Police—No entry, by order of the police." A number of houses in the neighborhood bore similar locks and signs on their doors. Two synagogues in the tenth and eleventh arrondissements had been burned to the ground.

I spent the night at the office, restlessly sleeping on and off in Dr. Lugner's reclining chair. On this very chair, I thought, he had fucked Denise. The following morning, Denise, carrying Amiti, found me in the chair. On hearing my story, she offered to let me stay at her apartment until I found a place of my own. Because her son, François, was in the military service, I could use his room. Until I shopped for myself, I could wear some of his clothes. Amiti seemed to like being held by her. He was smiling.

Before I did anything else, I had to secure a stable home for Amiti. I wondered if Sabina would keep him: she didn't work and had another young child in the house.

⌇

Sabina opened the door and screamed with joy when she saw Amiti, who let her take him in her arms without protest. Since giving birth to Nevim four years earlier, she had been trying to become pregnant again, without success. Even our foolproof method failed miserably and inexplicably. For two years, Sabina and her husband Cemil had sought to adopt a child. She obviously thought I had brought her one. When I explained the situation, she made room for a glimmer of hope in her disappointment. Cruel as it sounded, I knew she hoped the child's Jewish parents would never be freed.

"What is his name?"

"Amiti. It means the 'one who tells the truth' in Hebrew."

"Why?" I heard little footsteps upstairs.

"Who is that, Mama?" called out a small, childish voice.

"Nevim, come downstairs, dear. It is little Amiti!"

⌇

I am free of faith; that is why I am lost.

The transit camp at Drancy, a gigantic, concrete, town-sized complex still under construction, was a three-quarter hour's taxi ride from Paris. I was astonished by the activity around the complex: workers were installing ten-foot-high wire fences, behind which lay massive rolls of the wire fencing. Big buses and police vehicles were hurriedly coming and going, nearly running over the people gathered in front of the narrow gate. An officer at the entrance was willing to take letters, food, or other amenities if the intended recipient was on his list of detainees.

I wrote a note on one of Dr. Lugner's prescription pads, which I always carried with me, "To Dr. Lugner and Dr. Weinstock: Please advise me on how to proceed."

The officer looked at the note and his list, then at me:
"Okay, move on."

~

It wasn't long before I moved from Denise's son's room to Denise's bed.
I felt enveloped by her soft contours, long, almond-colored hair and
whispering snore. She wouldn't make love to me, instructing me instead
to "just hug me."

This was fine with me. I liked wrapping myself around her luscious
naked body, placing one arm under her, resting a hand on her breast and
the other on her thigh.

"Are you upset about Dr. Lugner?" I asked.

"Go to sleep."

While awaiting Dr. Lugner's return, Denise and I kept running the
office as usual. Denise and I also acted like a couple, going to the office
together, having lunch together, and going home together.

Denise and I even went to Drancy together. There was now regular
bus service to and from the prison. We brought Dr. Lugner's favorite
foods: herring *bilinisi*, kasha, gefilte fish, and *gefillah kishkeh*, hoping they
would bolster him. We left many messages but received no reply. I began
to wonder if he was even there. One day the officer at the gate refused to
take the food and our note. He informed us the Lugners were no longer
at Drancy.

~

The German army formally entered Paris. The French now understood
that German occupation meant savoring the bitter taste of defeat. The
mood turned black overnight: streets and cafés emptied, shutters
snapped shut, and the once-proud faces of French citizens began to
resemble those of the confused and guilty Istanbul Turks during that
occupation.

The Germans' arrival lifted all French pretension and restraint
regarding how they really felt about Jews. New dictates emerged. All
Jews were to register with their local police, stores were to display a
sign of Jewish ownership, and Jews were to travel only in the last car
of the Metro. Jews could enter non-Jewish-owned stores only during
prescribed hours. Each day new ordinances identified and restricted Jews

in their freedoms. Each Jew had to buy a yellow cloth Star of David at the police station and attach it to the left side of his or her outer garments. Any Jew caught not wearing or hiding the insignia was immediately sent to Drancy. Radio commentators happily propagated the Vichy government's views on Jews: they were corrupt, contemptuous of God, promiscuous, and lustful—especially in pursuit of Aryan women—contaminators of French blood, black marketers, anarchists, and incestuous pederasts.

Fueled by such provocation, angry mobs and opportunists looted and burned synagogues, Jewish stores, and homes. When I went back to the Lugner house, the door was wide open. There was absolutely nothing left inside—all amenities had been professionally removed; there were no curtains, not even lightbulbs. The interior doors were gone. Adam's pictures were strewn across the floor—the frames had been taken.

～

The world was closing in on me. I moved only between Denise's apartment and the office. German *feld polizei* arrested immigrants, people without work permits, and anyone who broke the 6:00 P.M. to 6:00 A.M. curfew or anyone who didn't look French. Our office, along with all other businesses, was served an order to identify foreign employees and provide justification for their continued employment within twenty-four hours of notification. Dr. Lugner received—in absentia—an order from the *commissariat général d'ordre de medicine* to cease practicing medicine because his parents hadn't been French. Where did I stand in all this? I didn't have French parents, I didn't have a working permit, and I didn't look French at any hour of the day.

That night in bed, I tried to talk to Denise about my options. She listened politely as I laid out plans and obstacles. She made it clear that our relationship could not go up to the altar, and, more important, her concierge had already issued her an ultimatum to get rid of me—he did not want to harbor "an undesirable" in his building. I thought of converting. However, priests were suspicious of conversions under duress, and the police weren't at all convinced of the authenticity of these "epiphanies."

"What will we do about the office?" I asked Denise.

"Oh, that is all taken care of. Dr. Lavalle will be taking over the practice."

I was shocked. Dr. Lavalle was Dr. Lugner's competitor. They hated each other. "When was that decided and by whom?"

"Actually, I spoke to him myself. Adam, we need to work. Dr. Lavalle graciously agreed to help out until Dr. Lugner is released. I wanted to tell you earlier, but you were preoccupied with your own safety. I'm really tired. Let's go to sleep and think about your situation tomorrow."

Why was I trying to survive; because Germans were trying to kill me? She turned her back to me and pretended to fall asleep immediately. There was innocence in Denise's deception. I couldn't be angry; I couldn't even be disappointed. Yet how could she, after years of working with me and feeling affection toward me, so easily end our relationship as a matter-of-fact practicality? The mercy of ruthlessness may not always be useless.

⤳

When I woke up, Denise was gone; there was a note on the table: "Dear Adam, You're welcome to take some of my son's clothes. Best of luck."

I walked toward the office, then realized I would no longer be welcomed. I had spent fifteen years of my life there; overnight I was banished. From a distance, I watched the office door. Patients went in and out as usual, looking content. Was I so easily replaced by that drunk Lavalle? Once Dr. Lugner told me that if I ever left, I'd leave such large shoes to fill that no one could ever fill them.

I walked away in a daze. I bumped into a few people and was cursed for my inattentiveness. Suddenly, I found myself standing in front of Sabina's house. They would happily hide me, I thought. After all, they owed me a big favor.

As I ran for the door, an old woman dusting a rug that hung from the second-floor window hollered, "What is it you want?"

"I'm looking for Sabina and Cemil."

"Oh, they left for Turkey yesterday. They say the wife is Jewish, so they got scared, especially for their two children."

Their two children! I had to go to Turkey. I'd withdraw all my money from the bank and pay a smuggler to get me through the Vichy zone, maybe to Marseille, then on to Istanbul. I felt a sense of excitement I hadn't experienced for a long time. It would be easier for me to adapt and become invisible in Turkey than in France. I had enough money to live a quiet, modest life and frequently visit Nevim and Amiti. They were my children after all.

Feeling elated, I made my way to the bank, striding past other customers to the cashier window that served important clients. Madame Boulanger, who had been working there for as long as I had been their customer, glanced at me over her reading glasses.

"*Bonjour docteur*, are you here to deposit money?"

"No Madame. Actually, I would like to close my account."

"Oh! I'll have to discuss that with the manager. I'll be back in a minute."

Her usual accommodative expression turned formal. Madame Boulanger returned trailing a thin, tall man I had never seen before.

He asked, "May I see your bank book and a separate identification, *monsieur?*"

"I have been a customer at this bank for more than ten years," I replied, irritated. "Madame Boulanger can testify to that."

"Your account is frozen by order of the government. Furthermore, you still have to produce an ID now; otherwise, I'll have to turn you over to the police."

"All my papers were lost when my house was broken into and looted," I said.

He stopped me with a vicious smile: "Is that so? I was informed that all your papers are still at the Hôtel Beauséjour. If you care to collect them, the police would be most happy to escort you there. *Ça te la bouckle, eh*—that shuts you up, eh?"

How dumb I was not to think that the police could easily trace me from the hotel to the bank. But what was the worst thing that could happen? They could deport me to Turkey, but they couldn't confiscate my money.

Two police officers arrived. Someone must have summoned them while I was being humiliated.

One officer grabbed my arm and pushed me to the corner of the room. The whole population of the bank, employees and clients alike, were watching and whispering, "*Youpin*—Yid?" "*Ouais*." Ya.

I dropped my book about the Dreyfuss affair on the floor. The first policeman kicked it away from me. The second policeman emptied the contents of my pockets on to a table. Dr. Lugner's prescription pad captured their attention: "What is your name?"

"*Docteur* Adam Zakir."

The first officer slapped me so hard that I fell to the floor.

"What's that?" he said.

"Adam Zak," I began, attempting to rise to my feet.

He slapped me even harder. My head hit the corner of the table, and I fell face down on the floor. Blood gushed from my nose and head.

"What?" he said.

I turned my head to the side. Through my hair, I saw the interrogator lift his hand threateningly. My head ached. I tried to stanch the blood from my nose with my fingers. Was he beating me because he thought I was hiding my Jewishness? Didn't they take my passport from Mr. Dökmejian at the hotel?

Shakily and slowly, I got to my feet, glancing at his hovering hand. "I can explain the whole thing," I babbled quickly. "I'm neither Dr. Lugner nor his son, Adam. Adam died in Jerusalem. I'm Turkish, a bastard son of Sultan Vahdettin. I'm not even a real . . ."

"*Tais-toi, tu te touches?*—shut up, are you nuts or something?" They stuffed my things back into my pocket and then threw me into a van with other people.

As soon as the door closed, four Jewish boys turned their attention to me, searching my pockets, taking whatever money I had. I was impressed by the quickness of their hands and the number of rings—some of which looked like women's jewelry—they wore on their fingers. I was struck with their aggressiveness, given the circumstances.

The older men in the wagon were having a good time watching the boys' ruthless insouciance and abusiveness.

～

The back door of the van opened.

"*Aufstehen*—Get up!" a large German officer angrily barked.

The youngest boy jumped from the van and assumed leadership of our group, yelling at us in German even louder than the officer:

"*Schnell, in die reiche*—Hurry up, get in line!"

The German officer allowed him to take over. We all lined up; I was at the front, as I had been the last to enter into the wagon. The youngest boy stood next to me as if he were a sergeant overseeing the process. Two French policemen, a German officer standing behind them, registered us newcomers.

"Name, address, occupation, citizenship, marital status."

The officer who brought me replied for me with the pride of having made a good catch, "This one is a physician, a filthy rich one at that." The officer turned to me.

"What kind of doctor are you?"

"General practitioner."

"You, the doctor, put all your belongings into this bag and write your name on it. List the valuable items. Claude!" he hollered, "*un wog*— young Arab-physician."

∿

Claude, a young officer in charge of the administration of the Drancy dispensary, grabbed my arm roughly and shoved me along toward the station. As we drew closer to it, he unambiguously explained to me how the place worked.

The dispensary was staffed by one other doctor and three nurses, and though Claude grudgingly acknowledged that the need was great, the unit's living quarters couldn't accommodate more than seven or eight people. "The need is greater at Auschwitz," he added with a sadistic smile. He went on to note that there wasn't enough medication for all the "silly aches and pains" of the people in the camp. I should use medicine sparingly. He instructed that I must remember that all the patients here were Jewish, that is, "hypochondriacs and malingerers." Only very severely ill patients who could be helped should be referred to the hospital—the Rothschild. Dying patients were not to be bothered with at all. He added as a cautionary note that the doctor I was replacing had been sent to a concentration camp for "being unnecessarily compassionate."

I was more worried about the Germans' discovering that I wasn't a doctor than I was about breaching compassion rules.

A young doctor in his late twenties wearing a woman's scarf around his neck clicked his heels to salute Claude as we walked into the dispensary. The doctor welcomed me with a sexually suggestive look and introduced me to two of the nurses—also young and anxious and exhausted. The third nurse, he informed me, "was sick in bed." All the staff was Jewish.

One small studio apartment was designated for the doctors, another for the nurses.

Claude, opened a closet door, reached in, and retrieved a white lab coat that he threw at me: "Did they tell you about the daily routine? Strict obedience is required if you want to stay here for a while."

～

You see, the terms of suffering are clear: an outer dissolution to escape the unbearable abyss of the self and an inner inquietude to fill eternal emptiness. The existence pain seeks no cure; if it did, it would find no remedy—it rescues one neither from living nor from dying. I must seek a stance of concluding elsewhere not in pain.

～

I quickly learned the routine. Every morning, thirty to forty patients lined up in front of the dispensary. Once in the office, they were asked to undress, were questioned about their complaints, and had their temperature taken by the nurses, who would judge if the condition required a physician's attention. If no further treatment were deemed necessary, the would-be patients were sent back to their rooms, occasionally taking with them a few aspirins or laxatives. The nurses wielded much power.

The young homosexual doctor, Herb, was happy to share the patient load. Herb's diagnoses were frequently overruled by the nurses, who had, as Herb explained, "Claude's ear and other organ." Claude regularly slept with each nurse, sending away to the camps those who rejected his sexual advances or simply bored him. I asked him about Drs. Lugner and Weinstock. "They were at the dispensary for about ten days," he said. "They couldn't hack it; both were nervous wrecks and got shipped out to Auschwitz."

Herb cautioned, "Try not to attract any of the nurses and don't be attracted to one. Always share any *pots de vin*—bribes—you receive with Claude. The doctor whom you replaced wasn't simply being unnecessarily compassionate, he was also being a little passionate with Nelli, the one who is sick. Claude didn't like that. Incidentally, you should take a look at Nelli . . . I'm not sure why, but her abdominal pain isn't responding to treatment."

﹌

As soon as one hundred or more detainees departed, an equal number of newly arrested people arrived. Herb and I alternated attending newcomer registration with Claude. During these initial interviews, we were to pick out those detainees who seemed to have potentially contagious diseases and isolate them for further examination. This wasn't an act of humanitarianism; the Germans were interested only in protecting themselves. Once, I pointed out a man with jaundice. He was quickly hustled back to the police van, and I never saw him again.

Each time a police van disgorged its cargo of newly arrested arrivals, the stench of unwashed bodies hit me. The emerging mass of people, speaking in many languages, often caused the German officers to become agitated. They wanted silence and obedience, and they blamed the French police for the chaos. The local police seemed rather bored with the whole scenario. Adults pleaded and protested; some with *peyes* and *tallis* and dark clothing started to pray and *daven*.

"Please kill me, just shoot me, I beg you," a young man with *peyes* wearing dark disheveled clothes pleaded to a French policeman about his age.

"*Merde alors,*" the policeman muttered and walked away.

Older people prayed, trying to understand the questions being fired at them.

An older woman, wearing one shoe, limped to the front: "I swear, I'm not a religious person. I'm not even Jewish in the real sense of the word. In fact, my son is married to a *shiksa*. I go to the shul only on high holy days, with the whole *mishpoche*—family—because of my husband; I didn't know that every Friday morning he went to the *mikveh*. He demanded that I shine his shoes and iron his suit. Believe me, if I knew that he were so religious, I wouldn't have married him. You know how it is, in my youth, it was always *shidden*—arranged marriage."

"Shut the fuck up you old bitch and get rid of that crappy shoe!" A chorus of laughter rose among the German officers and French police. She was dragged away by two French policemen and pushed into a departing bus.

A tall, elderly gentleman stepped up to the desk, dropped the card box he was carrying, tied loosely with string, and gave a soldier's salute.

"I served in the French army for two years," he said. "I am French. I was born in Paris." He held up a picture of himself in uniform. "Me and my family, we are Israelites, *"pas Juif*—not Jewish."

"What's the difference? A dirty, lazy Yid is a dirty, lazy Yid," came the answer. The French policemen pummeled and kicked him over to the bus.

A supervising German officer slapped a man who was protesting that his name wasn't Jewish. The man's *teffilin* fell off, and the officer pushed the man so hard that he fell onto the person standing behind him. Several others in line fell backward like dominoes. I couldn't help but laugh with the rest of the officers and police. Did my moral idleness bring me to the point that I was joining them?

◆～◆

I was lucky to be a "physician," sharing a studio with just one other person; the other detainees were warehoused six to eight people in a similar-sized space. Others were less fortunate. Hundreds, mostly male detainees of all ages, were piled up into an old, decrepit hall. The men cried, screamed, cursed, whined, and yelled in a cacophony of languages—French, Polish, German, Ladino, and Yiddish—mostly Yiddish.

Drancy was an unfinished, low-cost housing project, and most of its apartments didn't have running water or electricity. While we doctors and nurses had our food delivered to the dispensary, others lined up for hours in front of the common kitchen to receive their daily ration. Everyone was given an aluminum cup for water and soup and a plate for solid food, such as canned sausages and cheese. The inmates, which is what they were, regardless of the authorities' various euphemistic titles for them, such as temporary detainees, relocation contingency, and Drancy members (as if this were some sort of a club), were to wipe their plates clean with their equally dry bread; there was no water for plate washing. There was a group of inmates who regularly received food, cigarettes, and even cognac from outside contacts, their family members, and friends. Hence, there was a lively and open black market for those who had somehow smuggled in money, coffee, fresh bread, and ham; a bottle of Courvoisier went for one hundred francs.

There was another market, the market of Judas: this was of Jews informing the Drancy officials about those they knew were Jewish but not yet arrested. The informants revealed the potential hiding places and French names these individuals might be using. With each successful arrest, these *Chasseurs aux Juifs*—Jew hunters—were rewarded with a full meal, cigarettes, or a night's stay at the dispensary.

The medical staff was treated quite differently. We not only received the same type of food that the officers and clerks ate but also had plenty of it. This was because we also functioned as the medical staff for the officers, some of whom even brought family members for care and free medication or asked for certain drugs—tranquilizers, antacids, laxatives, and painkillers—for themselves.

The detainees of Drancy were a strange mix of people who never would have mingled in any other circumstances. There were aristocrats like Monsieur de Bologne—whose father apparently had changed his Jewish name. A dignified elderly man, he refused to come to the dispensary on his own, even when a small stroke justified a full visit. There were professionals—lawyers, teachers, and engineers—who were too shocked by their predicament to protest except to complain of indigestion, insomnia, and other bodily dysfunctions. There were shopkeepers, tailors, watchmakers, and dealers of all sorts of businesses. These were mostly the first- and second-generation offspring of immigrants who were thoroughly frightened. Then there were the unruly adolescents who, oblivious to the gravity of the situation, constantly preyed on others and manipulated the staff, including us. One of the kids, Saul, with whom I had been thrown in the van when I was arrested, showed up every morning with different ailments until he was admitted "to rule out appendicitis." Clearly the nurses were up to something: Saul had become Claude's newest lover, much to the relief of the girls, who happily obliged Claude's use of the dispensary's care room for his sexual needs. Now, two of the dispensary's beds were permanently occupied by Claude's lovers: Nelli and Saul.

The turnover among the doctors and nurses was much lower than that of the rest of the Drancy population, which was shipped out every four to eight weeks, depending on the availability of trains. It was quite unpredictable. Within an hour or two of an order, people were herded on buses—about fifty to a vehicle—to the train station. The occupants often sat atop each other or stood. I watched the process from the dispensary window that overlooked the loading area. Each time I was struck by the discrepancy between the demeanor of the German officers, shouting obscenities, and that of the detainees' resigned calmness.

At times, as they were about to depart, they were cooperative, apparently thinking they were doing something good for France. The detainees proudly sang the *Marseillaise* in defiance of the German officers. Meanwhile, the French police murmured the anthem while helping the Germans load the Jews onto the buses. What sort of macabre perversity was being played out?

⌇

After her initial resistance, I thoroughly examined Nelli and found that she was bleeding from anal fissures and torn hemorrhoids. She confessed that Claude forcefully sodomized her.

Nelli was also hiding a bag of diamonds either in her vagina or in her rectum, depending on her anticipation of Claude's choice. She was the daughter of a jeweler who, as the situation in Paris deteriorated, taught her how to wrap diamonds and tuck them. She promised to share the diamonds with me if I could "get her to the hospital" and gave me five stones in advance. They were all big and clear, like my mother's. "These are the rare diamonds: colorless, flawless, two carat," she said. "The other five, I'll give you in the hospital." I wondered briefly if the treasure in the Yıldız Palace contained diamonds.

That night I secured the diamonds in my rectum—not as easy a task as it sounds.

Nelli was hoping to escape from transfer to the hospital. I had two other female patients waiting to be transferred to the Rothschild Hospital, both with unrelenting, inexplicable high fevers. I asked Claude if it would be okay to transfer Nelli to the hospital for a gallbladder check. Claude agreed to her going after questioning whether she had any other complaints and was reassured by me that she didn't.

"Make sure nothing goes wrong," he said. "You know what I mean."

I nodded. The four of us and an officer climbed into the back of a small ambulance; a driver and another officer sat in the front. I knew the officer riding with us in the back from his many visits to the dispensary. He was a bit of a hypochondriac and asked about the maladies of the vehicle's other occupants. After we arrived at the Rothschild Hospital, he accompanied me to register the patients. When we returned to take the patients into the hospital, all three women were gone. Had someone else escorted them to the waiting room? Apparently not. The driver and the other officer sat in the ambulance's cab, smoking cigarettes and chatting. The officer and I scurried around to find them; there wasn't a trace. I understood that Nelli took the opportunity to run away, but how could the other two with fever disappear into thin air? The officer and I decided to go in different directions to search for them. I found myself alone, unsupervised, and in front of the entrance to the hospital. Many thoughts jumped into my mind: Should I run away? Where would I go? I had a nice place at Drancy; why mess that up? If I tried to escape and was caught, I'd been treated like any other detainee and stripped of privileges. Still, the idea of returning to Claude with the news of three missing patients—especially Nelli—didn't seem very promising either. I hesitated for a moment, glanced at the ambulance sitting about fifty meters away, threw off my white coat, and bolted.

I jumped over the low stone wall into the adjacent park and began to run as fast as I could from the park into a side street. I kept turning around to see whether anyone was running after me. Only momentarily convinced that no one had followed, I ran up other side streets, turned around again and again, and shifted from one direction to another to confuse potential pursuers. Meanwhile, I became totally lost.

Out of breath, my head throbbing, I bumped into people, fell over, got up, and again turned to check for hunters. Meanwhile, I couldn't believe that Nelli had cheated me out of five diamonds.

～

I registered at the Turkish consulate's front door, giving Cemil Karasu's identity. I explained the purpose of my visit: lost passport and the need to return to my wife and two children in Erzurum.

I waited for what seemed to be an eternity. I kept one eye on the entranceway half expecting Claude or an officer to walk in and pick me up. I worried about how I was going to pull this off.

A young man with a black mustache began to quiz me sternly:

"How could a grown-up man lose his passport? You didn't by any chance sell it to Jews, did you? Apparently you were given your exit visa just a month ago."

The officer looked into my eyes with a strangely resigned wisdom. There are people who would accept someone desperate's counterfeit coins all too knowingly.

F O U R

**Muhammad threatens me, shakes his finger, and makes me angry.
I want to fight.**

Istanbul

1941–1945

Nothing gives me the knowledge of eternal order.

I sat away from the window of the tightly packed compartment of the train and from a safe distance watched the French and German officers pacing the platform. Were they being so vigilant so that not a single Jew would escape? What a waste of energy and time was this immoral obsession for two of the most powerful nations in the world!

Until the train pulled out, I was sure that the officers somehow would find me out and drag me back to Drancy. My anxiety was so unbearable that I thought about giving myself up. Being at Drancy was by no means as painful as waiting to be picked up. Then the train shook on its wheels and slowly, too slowly, began to move. The German officers were looking directly into my eyes. Couldn't the train pull out of the station a little faster? As the train picked up speed, I was enormously relieved, and I let it rock me into a restless sleep.

As the train pulled into the Sirkeci station, I woke up and jumped from the train to the platform. After fifteen years, I was back in Istanbul. The sun was about to rise, and from the minarets of the Yeni Cami in the old Karaites section, the *muezzins'* calls of *Ezan* filled the Galata square, summoning people to morning prayer. I felt a sense of exhilaration. Then a profound disappointment came upon me. The *muezzins* were not chanting the traditional "*Allahu akbar*" but its Turkish translation, "*Tanrı büyüktür,*" totally flattening the cadences and meaning of the *Ezan*.

I bought a grilled fish sandwich made on one of the fishing boats. It was stale; nevertheless, it held the attraction of a homecoming. On the one hand, I felt as if I had landed in a country different from the one I had known; on the other hand, everything was familiar; it felt as if I had never left. It was organized chaos, and there were the earsplitting sirens of steamers and porters—carrying enormous amounts of baggage on their backs—elbowing the pedestrians out of their way by howling "*destur*—beware!" A childlike lightness came over me as I began to walk toward my old neighborhood. I smiled, clapped my hands, skipped, and received curious stares. I slowed down in Çağaloğlu to take a deep breath—oh yes, this was Istanbul, the air filled with the smell of fresh *simits* and coffee. But something else—the smell of exhaust fumes—almost choked me. I approached an old beggar sitting in front of an empty garbage can. He screamed at the top of his lungs, cursed me, and made a threatening gesture:

"*Gavuroğlu gavur*—son of an infidel, go away!"

I was taken aback. Did I look foreign? Suddenly I lost my bouncing walk. My smile froze on my face. I put my hands into my pockets and hunched over. I walked away.

The first thing I had to do was find somewhere to stay. Then I must sell the diamonds to have some money, then find the treasure hidden in the Yıldız Palace. Over the years I kept reimprinting in my mind the map I'd gotten from father's Italian concubine. In the Grand *Selāmlık*—men's quarter of the Mabeyin building—I was to face Mecca and walk directly to the largest panel. Could it be that simple? If I found the treasure I should look for that woman. But how? I didn't even remember her name.

The Hotel Claude Farrère was still there, though an additional floor was under construction. With some anticipatory anxiety, I entered the lobby; it looked brighter than I had remembered it. I asked for David. The man at the reception desk looked puzzled.

"He is the hotel owner," I said.

"Well, I don't know anyone by that name, sir. No one individual owns this place," the receptionist replied with an air of superiority. "The hotel is owned by a corporation.

"You're wearing an *ala franga*—foreign outfit. Have you been away for a long time? Now, if you want a room, I need to see your ID."

I gave him my passport. The receptionist's demeanor immediately changed. "Oh *affedersiniz*—I beg your forgiveness, Cemil Karasu *Beyeffendi*. We are most honored to host you, a Turkish lawyer from Paris! Let me help you to your room. Is your luggage in the car?"

I had to be careful not to forget my new name.

"My bags will be delivered later. I would like to rest for a little while."

My room looked over the Sultan Ahmet Mosque and the park in front of it. I could even see part of the Hagia Sophia if I leaned out the window and looked left. I stared out the window for a long moment, as if it were the first time I had seen these sights—maybe it was the first time I was really seeing them. I thought sadly about how, if I had been born one or two centuries earlier, I would have been given a building like this hotel as a minor gift, even if I were a bastard son of the sultan.

"Are you content with the room Cemil *Beyeffendi*—sir?" the manager asked. "If there is anything else you need, please let me know."

"Yes, thank you," I replied. "There is one thing. I need to borrow a screwdriver and a hammer."

I wondered what had happened to David, his family, the Kurds, and Schwarz, the ever-present Jewish manager of the hotel. Then I dozed off.

I must have slept the rest of that day and night, though I briefly woke up during the morning's *Ezans*. Of the three mosques surrounding the hotel, the smallest of them, the Firuz Aga, was the noisiest. When I finally roused myself and opened the hotel room door, I found a small sack containing two screwdrivers and a hammer. I took them in, went down to have breakfast, and picked up a newspaper. I couldn't read the first one, so I picked up another. The same! The alphabet had been changed! Arabic letters were no longer used, but Western ones had been adopted, though with some peculiar punctuation. Now I understood the confused look of the Turkish consul in Paris at my antiquated Turkish and why I had this Western-style passport. Seemingly overnight, the country had become European. Still, breakfast was the same as it always had been: sun-dried olives, goat cheese, bread, and tea.

I decided to sell one of my diamonds. I picked one, carefully cleaned and wrapped it in a Turkish lira (which carried Atatürk's likeness on it), and headed toward the covered bazaar. I passed by the Çağaloğlu and noticed that men were dressed in a hodgepodge of clothing, Western outfits mixed with oriental styles. They had adopted all sorts of headgear, but the traditional fez was not among them. Young women wore skirts and tailored jackets and sported colorful hats or no head covering at all. The older women wore long coats and covered their heads with subdued scarves. Meanwhile, I busied myself trying to read the signs on the stores, buses, and trolleys, which were all written using the new alphabet. Workers had put up new street signs bearing new names.

Suddenly I found myself in the middle of dozens of screeching high school girls dressed in navy skirts, white shirts, and navy cravats. They chased each other, laughing and teasing. They were from the Çağaloğlu high school, the same school that my Gülseren had attended. I remembered how she and the other girls had always walked quietly—heads down, shoulders pulled in, trying to make themselves invisible. I wondered what had happened to her. I picked up a white shirt from one of the vendors, ran my hand over the delicate fabric, imagined the swell of Gülseren's small breasts, then reluctantly, softly, dropped it back on the cart.

I turned left to Nuruosmaniye Street. Here I was in a familiar place. Both sides of the street were still occupied with rug sellers wearing *shalwar*—traditional baggy pants—drinking tea, rolling worry beads, eyeing passersby, and expertly identifying an easy mark to gently prod into their shops. The vendors called out as I walked past them:

"I have an extraordinary *Buhara*, one-of-a-kind, *Paşam*—my general."

As usual, the courtyard of the Nuruosmaniye Mosque was almost impenetrable because of the beggars and peddlers. White, black, gray, and rust-colored pigeons flew in and out. Males with their puffed-out breasts cooed at females and, in quick reversal of strategy, pecked the ground repetitively as if they were surprised to have found something to eat and could offer it to them. Female pigeons responded to the second scheme better.

Holding the stone firmly in my pocket, I entered the covered bazaar and walked toward the Old Bedestan market. I was looking for the man from Diyarbekir to whom I sold some of my mother's jewelry. His store was next to the *Kuyumcu Kapısı*—the jeweler's gate. I found it exactly as it had been, including the man himself, though old and gray. Should I inquire about Doğan?

He gave me eleven hundred lira for the diamond.

Meanwhile, I didn't know how little a Turkish lira bought, but I soon found out when I sat down to have lunch in a restaurant in

Zincirlihan, the inner-city caravanserai inside the bazaar: Two *lahma-cun*; spiced, ground lamb on flat bread; and one *ayran*, the yogurt drink, cost me ten lira. Fifteen years before, I could have eaten there for a whole week for that amount of money.

Now I've got to sneak into the Yıldız Palace and find the treasure before I go searching for Cemil, Sabina, and the children in Erzurum. But what if the whole map and directions had been no more than a cruel hoax? If there was such a treasure, wouldn't it have been found by now?

～

I left the bazaar and walked up to the *Sahaflar*, the old book market. I was looking for some familiar written words. Alas, the dozens of book-stores that lined both sides of the market were full of new books—mostly translations of French and English literature. I opened a secondhand *Jane Eyre*. I didn't understand a word. Turkish was now an entirely contrived language. The elimination of Arab and Farsian words, which made up 80 percent of the written language, had rendered me illiterate. Colorful magazines displayed pictures of seminude American and French actresses or drawings of seductively engaged long-legged brunettes with bosoms overflowing their diaphanous dresses. Every major newspaper—*Hürriyet, Vatan, Milliyet*—had a few pictures of İnönü, the president, diving into the water in Marmara. Each bore the same description: *Çiviledi*—nailed!—a word I understood. Next to it, they all showed a picture of a large number of German Jews being wel-comed by the minister of the interior.

I sat on a chair in the café in the courtyard of the Beyazit Mosque, which was surrounded by scribes squatting in front of previously dis-carded, rickety typewriters. The old magnificent plane tree, which shaded the whole courtyard, seemed altogether undisturbed by the sea of change in the country. I wondered when and by whom it had been planted. A pile of melons had been dumped on the small cemetery in the mosque. A man leaning on the *türbe* of the Sultan Beyazıd spat seeds onto the ground. Kids carrying tea in small glasses on their swing-ing trays called out "*Çay, Çay?*" That was the only sound competing with the rustling leaves of the trees. Turks in traditional outfits (minus the fez) were gathered in small groups around the tables, drinking tea and conversing. This place remained as serene and hospitable as I remembered it. An older man at the next table stopped me gently as I was paying for my tea: "No, no! You look like a stranger; we are honored that you sat here in our modest café. We couldn't let you pay. Come, join us; one shouldn't be alone."

My vision blurred with welling tears. What was one to make of this country?

～

Beyazit was as busy as usual. It's the trolley hub. From here the trolleys turn into the square, stop at various points, then depart again in all directions. Here again, time slowed for me. I walked toward the gate of the university; it was adorned with gold letters in the new alphabet, identifying it as the University of Istanbul.

The park between the gate and the main building was filled with students strolling or sitting on benches. Although there were many female students, they clustered in groups separate from the males, except in the café and the library. In these two buildings, which protruded toward the Süleymaniye Mosque, gathered seemingly upper-class students who intermingled quite freely with those of middle class. Gone were the days of the *Effendis* and their aristocratic attitude. The basement of the café was still used as a cafeteria for poor students. I looked inside. The workers were getting ready to serve dinner. I glanced at the corner table where I used to eat, and for a moment I thought I saw myself there all by myself. Was I more pitiful now or then? I left the campus from the same side gate that I'd used years before and passed by Gülseren's old apartment building. It looked run down. Old, dusty houses looked older and dustier. Women were still watching from behind grills of windows with rotting lattices. Walking down the street, I whistled our tune. The tune came out exactly the same as it always had. I stood in front of her window waiting for her to pull the curtains, tilt her head to one side, and smile shyly.

My old house had been replaced by a concrete apartment building; there was a restaurant on the first floor. They must have built over the old foundation because in the basement where my room had been (now converted to a kitchen) were the same narrow windows. I bent down and looked in. Had I really lived there? I entered the restaurant and asked the owner if he knew Sakız Hanım, the woman who had owned the house previously. He didn't.

"I used to live here, some years back, in the basement," I explained. He nodded. "Would you like to see the menu?"

～

I returned to the hotel and crawled into bed. I woke breathlessly in the middle of the night. My heart pumped so fast that I couldn't even count my pulse. I stayed quietly in bed. Perhaps a bad dream had caused an anxiety attack. I removed the diamond pack from my rectum. Maybe the discomfort it inflicted had caused my attack. I drank some cold water. I sat on the bed in the dark and realized that at any moment my heart might go into fibrillation, and it would be all over.

Then, on second thought, I wondered how bad that would be. I didn't exist for anyone. I was without a life witness; whether I lived or died had no consequences for anyone.

My pulse slowed to one hundred beats per minute, then eighty, then seventy. I must have dozed. I woke up about noon feeling exhausted. I didn't even have the energy to do my morning routine of cleaning the sores on my legs and putting some cream on them. I knew that increasing fatigue and dry skin were obvious signs of loss of thyroid function, unless, of course, they were actually manifestations of my pan-neuroses, which would explain why I had lost my interest in women. I couldn't remember even having an erection during the past few months. Had my libido been sublimated to survivor guilt?

I wondered why I kept bumping into people on the streets since I arrived. Was it because Istanbul was crowded, which I wasn't accustomed to, or was it because I was a little disoriented here? And what was I to make of last night's episode? Although I had been having anxiety-related episodes of tachycardia for over a year now, what could explain a pulse rate of more than one hundred and twenty beats per minute, especially in view of the fact that regularly I had a very slow pulse? I tried to remember what I had been dreaming about when my heart started to race. Oh yes, I remembered fragments of it. My mother's casket fell off the car carrying it. It was empty. Did this mean that I hadn't had a mother in a real sense of the word?

I ordered myself to get organized. I made a mental list: short term, see a doctor—oh, forget that, I'd just get some thyroid extract—and find the treasure.

∽

I must go on being.

I got a taxi to take me to the Mosque of Hamidiye, which was adjacent to the Yıldız Palace entrance. I thought that my destination would not arouse suspicion. The driver corrected me:

"You mean the shrine, *Yahya Effendi's Külliyesi*! If you really want your prayers answered, you should visit it on Friday nights, when *Yahya Effendi* communes with *Hızrilyas*, the saint of divine love."

I was really taken aback; I hadn't realized that it was possible to enter the Külliye, especially at nighttime! This bit of news was an incredible boon because the Külliye was literally inside the Yıldız Palace's walled park. The whole time I'd been wondering how I was going to scale those gated palace walls, taxis were driving through them. As the cab sped over the Galata Bridge and entered the ancient cypress-lined road that ran parallel to the Bosporus, I gazed at those once-frightening palaces and other structures. Here was Dolmabahçe, where I was brought to stand before Refet Pasha to be disposed of; here was Çiragan Palace, where other members of the sultanate were incarcerated. The driver pulled through the enormous iron gates of Yıldız and put the car into low gear to prepare for the steep climb to the Külliye. The shrine was filled with people, mostly older women in *tcharchafs*. I sent the cab away even though the driver suggested he wait to drive me back. This was to be my one and only dress rehearsal. There were no guards around, except for one old fellow by the saint's *türbe*.

I gave him five lira; he attempted to kiss my hands.

"*Ustacığım*—my dear master, is it all right for me to take a walk toward the palace?"

"Of course," he replied, "the place is totally empty. Some of the buildings are not even locked; you can visit them. My nephew is the only guard. He's there to make sure that people don't tear away the wood and stones—they do, you know, to use them to build homes, those beasts."

I walked uphill and passed soaring sycamore, linden, and chestnut trees and overgrown willows, plane trees, and cypresses. My heart beat hard. I entered the courtyard to the Yıldız Palace. The place loomed larger than anything else in the world for me: this was the source of the negation of my worth, my legitimacy, and even my very existence. I stood in front of the Mabeyin building. It was just a large wooden house with faded white and green shutters. I passed through into the second courtyard. The place was utterly neglected and run down. All sorts of vegetation grew through the cracks of the stone floors. The wooden shutters of the harem banged against the walls and windows.

"Kardaş ne arirsan—Brother, what are you looking for?"

A young man with the shabby uniform of a bekçi—guard—woke me up from my reverie of beautiful but sexually deprived concubines teasing handsome officers. A sultan could not have satisfied all the women in the harem. Now that I had some experience, I knew that if anyone needed more than one sexual partner, it was the woman.

"I was told by your uncle at the Külliye that you might show me around, of course with . . ." I pulled out ten lira and squeezed it into his hand. The bekçi immediately took his hat off as a sign of respect and said, "Başüstüne—your order."

"I would like to see the selāmlık—the reception room—if possible."

"The place is totally empty. I heard from my uncle that the day Vahdettin left the country, hundreds of people from the nearby towns of Beşiktaş and Ortaköy swarmed the place. For three days they ransacked it; they even took the mattresses out from under the sick Valide Sultan—Padishah's mother. Later the governor locked up the place and put it under police protection, but there was nothing much left to protect. So now it is just my uncle and myself. The government doesn't pay us enough for us to make a living. Allahaşükür—thanks to God—gentlemen like you help us survive. Anyhow, if you want to see the selāmlık, I'll be happy to show it to you. The governor doesn't want us to take visitors beyond the second courtyard."

"I am terribly sorry that the government doesn't sufficiently appreciate your devoted services," I said, extending another ten lira to him.

Across from the mosques stood the three-story-high sultan's grand palace, Büyük Mabeyn. Its selāmlık was the largest room I had ever seen, comparable only to the interiors of mosques, even plastered with the same color: yellow-white. Next to it there was an equally large hamam—bathhouse. I walked to the middle of the room, the heavily dust-covered floors squeaking beneath my feet.

"Which direction is Mecca?" I asked. I knew the instructions on the map by heart because I had repeated them so often.

The guard pointed the way.

I turned toward Mecca and looked straight ahead: a three- to four-foot wall separated two windows. I casually walked all the way to the end of where the prayer rug would be, as in the instructions. All the while I surveyed the wood panels. There were no differences among the panels covering the wall between the windows and those covering the rest of the room.

"Would you like to see the harem?" the guard asked.

"Yes, thanks."

The harem, in contrast to the *selāmlık*, had many small rooms in a row and adjacent dining and bathing areas. I imagined the women lying in bed in one of these rooms, waiting for Vahdettin to show up. At that time he had four wives and four concubines, so a weekly visitation schedule wouldn't have worked, and totally random visits must have generated much anxiety, jealousy, and envy. Maybe he visited different women at different times of day.

One of the rooms had a bed in it. The guard explained that he usually slept at the Külliye, where his uncle had a kitchen, bath, and two bedrooms. Occasionally on Fridays, visitors were allowed to pray through the night, and on those days he would sleep here.

"My mother was once a concubine to Vahdettin; she may have slept in one of these rooms. I wonder whether you would allow me to spend a night here, just for her memory. I'll pay of course . . ."

He stopped me. "*Siz emrediniz efendim*—your order, my sir, anytime. I am sorry, but for the bathroom you will have to go outside or come down to the Külliye. It isn't comfortable for a gentleman like you, but if it would give you some solace, who am I to argue?"

I felt a terrible unease by his quick, unquestioning acceptance. Was he accustomed to such bizarre requests that he simply went along with the gag as long as he made some money?

"Anytime? How about tomorrow?" I said and gave him another ten lira.

On the way to Ortaköy, I stopped a taxi, which returned me to the hotel. I didn't even have the energy to have dinner. I lay down on my bed and fell asleep, only to wake up in the early hours of the day with a headache the likes of which I had never before experienced. It felt as if my head were going to explode. I felt my eyes bulging out. To keep the pain at a tolerable level, I had to sit on the bed and press my eyes with my hands. Later I thought that maybe I needed some fresh air, so

I walked out to the *cirit meydanı*. The arena was still dark; there wasn't a single soul in the area, and the only sounds were the distant barking of dogs and the same screaming whistles of night guards.

~~~

I took the diamonds (putting them in my private safe) and got into a taxi. I arrived at the Külliye at sunset the following day. Both the young guard and his uncle were very cordial. They offered me some tea with real sugar—the gift of a wealthy guest. The uncle was a little bit more curious about me than the younger man: he wanted to know if I had any relatives in Istanbul, where I was staying, how long I was planning to be in Istanbul, and what business I was involved in. I became convinced that they were planning to do away with me. Was I repeating my boat incident?

The guard lit the gas lamp: "The door is unlocked; if you get scared or need something, just come down. *İyi geceler*—good night."

I threw myself on the bed. I couldn't even handle two peasants, I thought.

The room was very small. Did women stare at these walls and the ceiling when they had sex? Had they enjoyed themselves?

The nausea and headache that began when I first got here got worse. All of a sudden, I began to vomit violently, liquid splashing across the room to the wall. I must be a nervous wreck, I thought. Oh boy, Doctor Lacan would have had a field day with this! After an hour I felt better, dimmed the lamp, and took it and my instruments to the *selāmlık*. I went right to the wood panels between the windows. I presumed I had at least half an hour—it was the dinner hour—before they came around to check on me. I would have someone like me under guard, were I in their place.

There was the wood panel described in the map, twice as large as the rest covering the wall from the floor to the ceiling. I jimmied a screwdriver onto the side of the hammer and inserted it in the joint of one side of the big panel, which split right in the middle. I tried another smaller one, and the same thing happened. Wood chips cascaded on me as part of a third small panel came crashing down to the floor. This was not only hopeless but messy and dangerous. The noise I was making could alert the guards. I knew I must quickly pack my things and get out. As I pulled the screwdriver from the wall, with a sudden jolt, the last panel turned one hundred and eighty degrees, exposing a floor-to-ceiling closet space. There was nothing inside except a heavy manuscript. No gold, no jewelry. I was sort of relieved. Carefully, I began leafing through the manuscript. It was volume five of *Siyer-iNebi*, the original ancient Turkish version of the illustrated life and miracles of the Prophet. Suddenly I felt a powerful blow to the back of my head.

〜

Even though I was semiconscious, I knew that I was tied to a chair. My head throbbed. I heard conversation and vaguely saw images. After a few moments, they grew clear. Two men stood before me; one was a civilian, the other wore a police uniform.

"He has no identification on him. His clothes are of French make, and he was carrying lots of cash. Should we just call him another lunatic and send him to *Bakırköy* Hospital?"

It was time to open my eyes. Only at the point of drowning do I remember swimming.

"Where am I? Oh, my head. What happened to me?"

The two men looked at each other. One rolled his eyes. The other nodded.

"This is *Beşiktaş Karakolu*—police station—and I am the commissar. You have been arrested for damaging government property. The guards say you were looking for treasure."

"I am terribly sorry. May I pay for the damages and whatever is the penalty associated with it?" I said.

The civilian smiled at me.

"Who are you sir, where do you live, and where did you get the idea of finding treasure in the Yıldız Palace?"

"I am Adam Zakir. I live in the Claude Farrère Hotel at Çağaloğlu. I am the son of Sultan Vahdettin. Oh my! No, no. I am Cemil Karasu. Actually, I am a lawyer; I trained in Paris. My wife couldn't get pregnant, so Adam . . ."

The commissar attempted to interrupt. "How do you like that; he turns out to be a real lunatic."

"One more question: Did you find any treasure?"

"No! I think a door panel fell on my head and I lost consciousness."

"All right," said the civilian. "Take this man to his hotel, search his room, find his real identity, pick up his personal belongings, and transfer him tonight to *Bakırköy*. Now!"

~

"Wake up. *Bashekim*—the chief doctor—is here." Someone pinched my nipples. I wanted to sleep, but he kept up the pinching. I half opened my eyes; the room was filled with white-uniformed people. I knew it must be morning rounds. A young doctor presented:

"This is a second admission of Cemil Karasu, a forty-one-year-old manic. He gave different names to the police: Zakir, Adam. He was admitted last night. He was arrested by the Beşiktaş police for threatening the guards of the Yıldız Palace with knives and for damaging the walls of the Külliye with a hammer. He was heavily sedated on admission and is still somewhat incoherent. He just came back from Paris where he was studying Law. At the police station, he claimed that he is the son of the sultan Vahdettin. There are no signs of hallucination. He is under homicidal precaution, which is why he is tied to the bed. Diagnostic impression: recurrent mania."

I watched the physician in chief through the slits of my eyelids. He was my Dr. Mazhar Osman. He hadn't changed a bit from when I had met with him as a young man. He rubbed his forehead while staring at me with a troubled look:

"Untie him and bring him to my office right away."

~

I staggered to Doctor Osman's office. He gently reached out to me, held my hand, and led me to sit next to him.

"Adam, right? What is this all about? What happened to you? What is this breaking into the palace business, and why are you in Istanbul?"

I began to cry. I didn't want to, but I couldn't speak. Was it his kindness, the connection to my childhood, or was it finally being recognized by someone?

"It's okay, Adam, we don't need to talk right now. You'll be fine here. I'll get you a private room, and you won't be obligated to talk to anyone except one doctor—Ruth Wilmanns. She is wonderful, a Jew who escaped from Germany during the war. She speaks French. You work with her. I know you don't belong here, but it would do no harm for you to rest for a while, collect your thoughts, and discuss your issues with her."

∽

I told my story to Doctor Ruth Wilmanns. She thought I should write a book based on events in my life. I eagerly awaited her daily visits because I poured out my heart to her, and she shared her own problems with me:

"I feel very much alone here," she confided. "As soon as this war ends, I shall emigrate to Palestine or to America. You should do the same. These countries, especially America, will be the best places for Jews to live. Do you know who is lifting the lamp beside the golden door of America? Emma Lazarus, a Jewish poet."

Dr. Ruth Wilmanns tried to put my past into a productive use for the future: "You are familiar with a number of languages; why not be a translator in the Middle East? You could go to Palestine and help with the Zionist agenda: wouldn't that be what your mother would have wanted you to do? You know 'Adam' means 'out of red clay' in Hebrew—out of the soil of the Holy Land, where you should return."

∽

Dr. Mazhar Osman obtained a visa under the name Adam Zakir from the English embassy for me to visit Palestine—provided I buy a return ticket to Turkey. Dr. Ruth Wilmanns thought that I would fit well with the third *Aliya*. This immigration to Palestine was conducted primarily by ships passing through the Bosporus and carrying mostly Eastern European and Russian Jews. Although the British officially limited passage, hundreds, if not thousands, of Jews were regularly transported from the Black Sea and through the Bosporus to Palestine.

I am not sure how much my wanting to please Dr. Ruth Wilmanns contributed to my decision to embark on this new adventure.

Dr. Mazhar Osman definitely didn't want me to linger in Istanbul. When I told him that I wanted to visit my mother's grave before leaving the country, he offered an ambulance escort:

"Not that I am worried about your being a grave robber," he said teasingly, "I just don't want you to get arrested for being one."

A burly driver took me to the cemetery in Eyüp. The place hadn't changed at all, except that overgrown bay and pomegranate trees, honeysuckle bushes, and wild thyme were hiding some of the graves.

Humming bees frenetically flew from one flower to another. Was my life also reducible to an innate determination to live?

We passed the deserted and dilapidated mausoleums of Sadr-Azams and Ulemas. The graves, once protected by iron railings, were in disarray, a rummage of cupolas and broken columns. The headstones, decorated with fezzes for men and flowers for women, were scattered among the acacia trees and aromatic cypress groves.

The Jewish cemetery remained orderly and barren. The lamentations of beggars and the flutterings of ring doves filled the air. It took me a while before I could identify my mother's unmarked grave. I remembered it was sandwiched between *Haidi* Edelman and *Ethel* Cantor. I found those two markers, but there was a third one—another Edelman, *Judy*, 1935–1936—between them. Had I remembered the names wrongly? Had they removed my mother's remains or buried the year-old baby over her? I placed a few stones on the protruding thatch of grass covering the grave of Judy and returned to the car. A bunch of white butterflies followed me. As we drew by the Muslim cemetery, I thought of the story of the Eyüp Mausoleum, which perhaps illustrated the fate of all graves: Eyüp Ensari, the Prophet's standard-bearer, was buried on top of two sainted Byzantine doctors, Cosmos and Damian. What difference did it make where we were buried?

I asked the burly driver, "If something isn't lost, should it be sought?"

The driver shook his head. "Yes, sir. Whatever you say."

Now I didn't even have a dead mother.

~

"Please keep in touch; let me know what it is like there," said Dr. Ruth Wilmanns. "Make sure you see a doctor there for your headaches," and she kissed me on both cheeks. "*Başhekim*—chief of hospital—wishes you the best of luck and asked me to give you this envelope."

Did I see a few drops of tears in her beautiful sad eyes?

As the ambulance pulled out of the long driveway, I kept looking back. Dr. Ruth Wilmanns looked so solitary in her white uniform. She stood motionless in front of the administrative building's doorsteps.

We got to the Galata, where a number of ships were docked. They were big and brand new and surrounded by elegantly attired gentiles who, I presumed, were going to Europe or saying good-byes to travelers.

A policeman led us farther up the Bosporus. Suddenly, the look and the noise level of the crowd changed. A rusty, obsolete-looking cargo ship marked with a barely visible name, *Struma*, came into view. It was covered in peeling gray paint that revealed previous coats of grease-smeared, rust-stained, blue, red, and black pigment and was swarming with equally beaten-down people. People were piled up on an added flimsy structure built atop the upper deck. A policeman forcefully parted the crowd to make way for the ambulance.

The ambulance driver must have been instructed not to leave my side and to see me aboard the ship. After he double-parked the vehicle, he took the small bag that Dr. Ruth Wilmanns had given me in one hand, grabbed my arm with the other, and walked me to the gate. There he pulled a letter from his white coat and handed it to the British officer who was standing guard and checking passengers' tickets and passports. The officer looked at me contemptuously, handed me my return ticket and passport, and pointed me "in."

A shipmate took me down one level to a dark and damp dormitory crammed with people. I asked him if there was a mistake. I didn't think I'd bought a third-class ticket.

He tersely replied, "This is second class, sir. You don't want to see third class. Furthermore, be thankful of your luck; we were full to ship's capacity. If one person didn't die on the way, there would have been no place for you at all."

With that, he threw my bag onto the upper berth in the last row and left.

Men of all ages wore tattered clothes and hats and held tightly onto their swollen, battered suitcases, which were tied with belts. I was in a Tower of Babel; I didn't even recognize some of the languages being spoken. The men spoke in escalating, high pitches to hear each other. Some recited psalms, others shouted; a young boy practiced the *haftara*, the part of the Torah repeated at one's bar mitzvah. Orthodox Jews, wearing *tallis*, *teffillin*, and *Kipot*, quietly murmured while rocking back and forth. Still others in regular clothes ate with extraordinary ferocity. The whole area reeked of a mixture of potato knishes, onions, sardines, cheap cigarettes, sweat, bad breath, farts, excrement, and vomit. Gagging, I ran outside. Two tugboats hauled the ship from the dock. Except for a few women and a man in a white uniform, nobody congregated at the dock to see the ship off.

That day I had the worst episode of a headache and vomiting of my life. After quickly emptying the contents of my stomach on about two meters of the ship's rails, I began throwing up bile. My abdomen continued its spasmodic contractions, and I continued to dry heave, although I had nothing more left in me.

An old man with a pasty face put his hand on my shoulder and spoke in Arabic-accented Turkish. "Son, we aren't even at sea yet. You aren't one of those fellows who is going to Palestine to die, are you?"

His eyes glittered with some vague ingratiation. My nausea stopped.

The tugboats released their lines, gave a two-blast horn salute, turned, and sputtered back toward Galata. The sun was about to set as we circled the Sarayburnu, the point of land on which Topkapı Palace was built, and schools of blue-colored *lüfers*—bluefish—shimmered as they played on the surface of the waters around us. The Topkapı Palace, Hagia Sophia, and the Blue Mosque, embraced by the dark ruins of the Theodosian walls, were bathed in the pinkish sunset. At Gülhane Park, the ghosts of Emperor Constantine, Empress Eirene, and the sultans Mehmet, Ahmet, and Süleyman with their *gözdes*—most valued women—bumped into shadows of cypresses, umbrella pines, planes, and chestnut trees and into each other. Had those people really lived? They must have. I had seen their tombstones. The palaces, churches, and mosques they had built and lived in still existed.

The clouds and mist began to close over the Bosporus and the Sarayburnu. Would my odyssey end but never stop? Would I be thrown from one unreality to another? As Istanbul disappeared, I became aware of the envelope that I still clutched in my hand. I tore it open; it contained a note from Dr. Mazhar Osman and my hospital chart. His note was brief:

Dear Adam,

My advice is that you get rid of your passport with your name as soon as you land in Palestine. You should reclaim a new identity for better or for worse. The fact that your mother was Jewish entitles you to live honestly and legally in the Jewish land. You should present your professional situation to the Jerusalem Medical Society and try to obtain a license to practice medicine. With thousands of immigrants arriving there daily, they could surely make use of your skills. I wish you the best of luck. I know everyone is going to America or Europe, but you must remember our saying: "*Akıntının aksine yüzen kaynağı bulur*—the one who swims against the flow of the river finds his source."

My chart was only a few pages long and, besides the admission note, contained only a few nonspecific comments by Dr. Ruth Wilmanns:

"The patient is feeling better; his headaches are positional. Projectile vomiting may imply increased intracranial pressure; neurological studies are recommended. Patient requested to be, and was, discharged."

I hesitated for a long moment, put everything back into the envelope, and threw the packet into the sea. It floated and drifted away.

∽

My self has to be reassembled.

I was quivering at the edge of an abyss. The old man appeared again; he must have been watching me.

"Son, what was that you got rid of with such reluctance?"

"My unreal past," I said.

"You should get rid of your real past as well, son; the past is another time and another country."

"Is that why you are going to Jerusalem?" I asked.

He laughed. "No, son! I make a living by taking people to Jerusalem, those who want to find a future or just to forget their past. They get a new country, new jobs, new spouses, and even new names—mostly Hebrew names to confuse the authorities. What is your name, the one that you'll be using in Palestine?"

"Adam Lugner." I guess that is as good and confusing a name as I can choose and may even be true in some ironic sense.

"Whatever. I am *Hadji* Abdullah. I run this rickety ship, but don't worry, it'll get us to Palestine. And what do you do? Now, this is for real."

"I am a physician."

The old man's eyes brightened: "Oh, I see, that is why you came here with an ambulance and danced through customs. I was wondering how sick you might be to require an ambulance. You know, lots of people die on the way to Palestine. Listen, I usually have one or two doctors on the ship, but this time I have none—partly, I think, because I have fewer Jews on board, lots of Christians and Romanian Gypsies, though."

"You're taking Christians and Gypsies to Palestine?"

"Oh yes. Palestine is not for Jews only, you know."

"How do you make a living? These people all seem to be penniless."

"Ha! There you are wrong; they all have something hidden—money, gold, and diamonds hidden somewhere, including in their assholes. That is the safest place—I learned that from a real professional who always travels to and from Palestine using a different name each time. He is count of something—I call him Boris. Anyway, he advised me to check the assholes of dead passengers before throwing them overboard, especially if they were traveling alone. Guess what? One out of three times I found diamonds packed in their asses. God willing, if a few more good people die in the next couple of trips, I will buy myself a new ship."

Was there some moral mutation going on in the world that such a man and Dr. Lugner, who was the embodiment of wrong, could be totally comfortable with their obscene existence? Their casual sharing of immoral ideas and behavior with me had an "of course" quality, as if they were expecting my admiration. Was it because they had figured out that I was one of them? But my wickedness came with a built-in punishment—self-doubt; theirs didn't. They seemed to use their immorality to validate themselves. They didn't believe in God. There is no such a thing as a secular morality. I, at least, was looking for reasons and ways to believe in God.

The image of this man exploring my corpse's rectum—and finding some diamonds—passed before my eyes. Well, if I were to die on his ship, why not? Why should diamonds be buried in the muddy bottom of the Mediterranean? Was this a rational altruism based on the inevitable or a symptom of my not being unequivocally on my own side?

"You should make as much money as you can in the next five days. I'll even give you a private cabin so that during the daytime you can see patients and at night you can sleep there. Once you're in Palestine, you won't find a job as a doctor. There are more doctors there than there are patients. I know some doctors who work as stonecutters and fruit pickers."

That was simultaneously frightening and comforting news: I would be an unemployed doctor.

Hadji Abdullah quickly spread the news that a skilled doctor was on board and was receiving patients. To my surprise, people from the captain of the ship to third-class passengers all had some medical problem. Under the close administrative supervision of *Hadji*, patients lined up every morning in front of my cabin. It was like Drancy: the ship had only a few medications to offer. I listened to them, examined them, advised them. In return for my services, I had the privilege of a private cabin, ate the food prepared for *Hadji*, and listened to his philosophy and fantastic stories.

Meanwhile, the number of patients I received and the fee *Hadji* was charging went up. He said he would share the profits with me fifty-fifty. The word was out that I had been the chief of medicine at the Rothschild Hospital in Paris. I had only mentioned to *Hadji* that I had practiced in Paris and used to transfer patients for admission to Rothschild.

I didn't go out of my way to disabuse the rumor. I wasn't a doctor to begin with, so what difference would it make whether I were the chief of medicine at the Rothschild Hospital?

～

Dr. Lacan said I should be truthful to myself. Well, my truth was the totality of my lies. I can't be myself mainly because I cannot make sense of my own lies. Even if I can, I become only the sum of my own impersonation. I cannot even be squarely in a false position. Thereafter, I am not a lie until someone defines me as such. Then I need not convince others of the truthfulness of my lies.

We spent the next five days at sea steaming about three to four knots. Meanwhile, I had no headaches, no vomiting, not even mild nausea, though the sea was quite choppy, and the ship rocked all the time. At times it leaned too much to one side or the other and prompted the captain to gather people to serve as ballast.

If I ever had a question about my having a serious illness, it was resolved on this trip: being meaningfully occupied and filled with the hope of finding security and permanency took care of all my symptoms. Every evening, I joined *Hadji* in his cabin to dine with him. Afterward, we settled on a *minder*—cushion—and smoked *narghile*. He had very long fingers.

〜

Two days behind schedule, we could vaguely see the coast of Palestine. By early afternoon the ship slowed to a near standstill. People who had been traveling in the crowded, unsanitary quarters were eager to disembark and were getting impatient. Finally, the captain's announcement came (passed by word of mouth) that we were waiting for sunset so we could disembark and thus avoid the one-month quarantine imposed on all newcomers.

I found *Hadji* sipping his tea in the captain's cabin and asked him why passengers from Europe were to be quarantined when the plague was in Palestine. It made no sense.

"My dear doctor, come, sit with us to have tea. You see, this is the Middle East; here nothing makes sense. Presume that everyone is guilty until it is proven to be the case. The problem is that most of the passengers have no visa, no passport, no identity card of any sort. I only have a list of their names—mostly made up—and their country of origin. If we enter Jaffa, they would not be allowed to disembark, and I would have to take them to Cyprus or return them home. Neither option is desirable for anyone, least of all me. So, after sunset, we'll anchor at my favorite shallow harbor, and you'll all be transported by small boats to the shore; then you're free as birds. The British will never find you, and if they do, they'll never bother extraditing you."

What was the point of my getting a passport and a visa and worrying about their authenticity then?

Even before the ship anchored, we were surrounded by dozens of rickety boats, rowed casually by *fellahin* waving lanterns and hollering at the top of their voices, "Jaffa, Jaffa."

With the efficiency of a well-rehearsed evacuation plan, all the passengers were lowered one by one into the waiting boats and taken away to shore. There were a few quarrels about the fee for the short boat ride and whether it included *baksheesh*.

I went to say good-bye to *Hadji* Abdullah, who presided over the debarking as if orchestrating an invasion. I asked him, "How could such a spectacle be secret from the customs police? We can see the port from here, so they must see us."

"Oh my dear doctor!" *Hadji* spoke with an exasperated tone of voice. "Now, as a token of my appreciation, you'll ride with some of my staff, who will be spending the night at the port. They'll put you up at the hotel they are staying at if you like or arrange your trip to Jerusalem. Good-bye and good luck. Don't spend everything on Russian girls!" He put a bundle of money in my pocket. He'd given me no choice but to trust him. I was beginning to understand his mentality: he cheated me but was also generous, he was lazy but also strong-willed, he was frightening but also affectionate, he was merciless but also kind, and he was fanatical but also had an intelligent sense of humor.

∿

Jumping from a dinghy into the dark, shallow bay south of Jaffa would have been frightening if the scene hadn't been so comical: dozens of small boats bobbed up and down a few feet from shore. Groups of people tried to get off the boats with the help of the *fellahin*, and others fell into the water and pulled themselves ashore to their destiny. Some of the travelers yelled out names of friends and family, others cursed loudly, and still others, swimming away from shore, were redirected. Those who made it sat on the sand dunes shivering.

I had thought Palestine would be a hot country, but the chilly night air bit my body through my wet clothes. The water seemed to be warmer. Onshore we were greeted by a swarm of another group of Arabs—porters, drivers, agents for hotels, and even money changers who hawked their services.

"*Hawajah*—sir, good hotel! Good hotel, cheap!"

"Jerusalem, Jerusalem, safe, safe!"

Two men grabbed my small bag by each strap and seemed about to tear it apart; neither would let it go. I looked around for the men from the ship who were supposed to accompany me; they must have simply run off.

About fifteen of us passengers and thirty or more Arab porters began the long walk toward the town. We left a wet trail behind us. At the edge of Jaffa, we entered a street with roughly paved stones. The swinging lanterns the Arabs carried did little to make the holes in the road visible. The travelers, who tried to keep up with the porters, stumbled occasionally and lost grip of their possessions. Panicked, they got up and ran to catch up with the guides. I was at my stumbling worst; somehow, no matter how careful I was, I kept bumping into people on my right and left. It was as if the darkness obliterated my peripheral vision. As we walked up a steep hill, we travelers became winded and drew the caravan to a halt. I presumed the Arabs were eager to finish their work and go home and must have been unhappy with our pace. Or were they? They offered us a piggyback ride—of course, for a "modest fee." Now the reason for the twofold number of porters to passengers made sense: one man for the luggage, the other for the person.

One of the porters, a man I estimated to be in his fifties, knelt in front of me, signaling me to get on him. A horrible sense of shame came over me: I just couldn't—I gave him the money anyway. But he insisted on giving me a ride; he wanted to fulfill his part of the deal. The more he tried to cajole me with his gracious gestures—how easy it was and how strong he was—the worse I felt. The Arab wouldn't be turned down; I finally had to give in.

~~~

Before we had gone very far, we were met by an old, open farm wagon pulled by an even older tractor. We piled aboard. No one seemed to mind the crowding: we needed each other to keep warm. I noticed that none of the Jews I had met on the ship were with me. My wagon mates were Gypsies, Armenians, Russians, and Eastern European Christians. One portly Arab passenger wore a white cloth with a black headband and a red, fezlike hat—*tarbush*. He sat in front of the wagon and explained that the Jews debarked on the north bay. There they were met by Zionists who escorted them to *kibbutzim* or wherever else they wanted to go.

"But we are safer," he went on. "There are a lot of Arab rebels who ambush vehicles and rob and kill non-Arabs. The English soldiers would rather sleep at night than arrest illegal immigrants. So, does anyone here have European cigarettes?"

~~~

At daybreak we arrived at Jerusalem's Jaffa Gate. I was covered with mosquito bites. There was no kneeling and kissing the earth, prostrating, or weeping among the passengers. I saw anxiety in their faces and a little bit of disappointment; or were these just my own feelings reflected on them? I definitely did not feel the spiritual exaltation I had read so much about people experiencing on their first sight of Jerusalem. The Jaffa Gate was closed and plastered with ominous notices in English, Arabic, and Hebrew:

"Attention—Bubonic Plague—Keep Out."

The English guards patrolling the area looked very unfriendly. There were dozens of people, mostly Arabs, scattered in front of the gate. They waited for admission. The portly Arab on the tractor gently accosted me, offering to get me in for a steep fee, "unless you want to wait here with all these people and get the black disease!"

He took my bag, and we began to walk alongside the walls encircling the city. These impenetrable walls were built by my ancestor, Sultan Süleyman. Now I had to bribe an Arab to sneak me through them, I thought.

"We'll first try the Armenian Zion Gate; if that doesn't work, you'll definitely be able to pass through the Jewish—Dung Gate." The Armenian Gate was closed. We kept walking. My guide advised that at the next gate I would be better off if I were not seen with him. I should just walk to the gate and tell the guards that I was dropped off at the wrong bay.

"Tell them you are Jewish and there was no one there from the Zionist organization to pick you up, so you hitchhiked all the way from Jaffa."

He further advised that if I wanted an inexpensive, clean room, I should go to see his cousin, *Hodja* Nasir of *Tariq Bab el-Hadid*. I guessed that making the pilgrimage to Mecca from here was easy; this explained why it seemed everyone was either a Hadji or a Hodja.

The Dung Gate was guarded by Jewish police. There were a half dozen people in line. I just got on the line and greeted them. "*Shalom, shalom.*" That was it; things went as smoothly as my Arab guide described. I am an example of the survivor of the unfittest. A guard handed me a piece of paper with the address of the Chabad Social Service Agency on Jabotinsky Street. Could the world be so cruel? Would I end up begging in a street named after the person who ate and drank in our house and with our full consent was instrumental in the demise of the Ottoman Empire and consequently my own demise? The past is supposed to nurture the present; mine poisoned it.

∾

Wherever I go, there I am.

I entered the hot, dry, stone-on-stone city with a vague feeling of anxiety; I felt as if I were an intruder. I was engulfed immediately by a human river and carried away by it, my feet barely touching the ground of the narrow, winding, dirty streets. All of a sudden I was deposited in front of *HaKotel*—the Wailing Wall. Old, pale-faced Orthodox Jews, their canes covered in yellow dust, chanted psalms, kissed the stones of the wall, and caressed the tufts of wild capers that grew in its cracks. Nearby, Arabs with ripped clothes and swarthy faces yelled back and forth while their donkeys brayed. Arab women in an oxcart laughed and sang. English tourists haggled with Arab boys over souvenirs. *Müezzins* called the invitation to evening prayer at the top of their lungs; church bells rang incessantly; Jews clamorously banged their pots and pans to herald the Sabbath. The result was an unharmonious resonance in various keys. This wasn't a quiet land.

I staggered away, trying unsuccessfully to walk parallel to the walls of *Haram es-Sherif*, the Temple Mount, to find an entry door. In this walled city, all manner of places were again walled. I walked in the suffocating heat through a maze of ancient, dilapidated tenement-like buildings with white- or salmon-colored plastered domes of stone and ornate facades. These buildings walled both sides of the narrow streets with closely lodged, huge, smooth flagstones. Patrons of an Arab coffeehouse spilled out onto the street, playing cards and backgammon and smoking *narghile* and cigarettes. Some sucked sugar with their tea while swatting a swarming army of flies.

Ah, another old Istanbul, I sighed contentedly to myself. But the moment the men saw me, they stopped what they were doing and stared. Their eyes were hostile, and a cold chill ran up my spine.

"*Al-salamu' alaykum*," I offered. "I am looking for *Hodja* Nasir of Tariq Bab el-Hadid; his cousin gave me a ride from Jaffa. I need a room in which to stay."

The hostilities instantly melted away. I was pulled into the café, and they offered me tea and cigarettes, and someone patted me on the shoulder.

I had missed the cordial and affectionate reception of Muslims and their simplicity. The Albanians in the compound where I grew up were equally kind and generous people. They couldn't read the Qur'an or understand it. But somehow in their simple way they understood the essence of their religion: the love and faith in it. The chauffeur Abbas was the ultimate example of the wisdom of the illiterate. Once I asked him what was in the Qur'an that he always kept under his pillow. He said there were two dried violets from his hometown, Hasankale.

A robed man carrying worry beads said, "Please forgive us, we thought you were a Jew. This is the Tariq Bab el-Hadid, and *Hodja* lives at the other end of the street—the last house before the Gate to the *Haram*. Just walk toward that sound."

I followed the hollow thud of a tambourine to the front of a run-down stone house with moss and lichen growing on its walls, a house that nevertheless seemed somehow inviting.

↜↝

Hodja Nasir was about fifty years old. He lived alone in the old house of red- and cream-colored stone. Two *Ka'ba*, the black stone of Mecca, were painted on either side of the recessed door, at the edge of Bab el-Hadid.

Hodja walked me through the house, which was filled with the scent of rose essence. While he pulled on his rosettes, he explained that his only wife had died four years ago and his two daughters had married and moved to Syria, a safer place than Jerusalem. He had seven grandchildren whom he visited every Ramadan. He used to rent out rooms in his house. "Foreigners won't live in Muslim homes these days," he said. "They're afraid that Jews will come and slaughter them." Other Muslims didn't travel to Jerusalem anymore; thus, *Hodja* was poorer but not dispirited. I had the choice of the rooms, more than one if I wanted. In fact, I could use the whole house, as he spent most of his time on the flat roof or in the madrasah, where he was teacher, guardian, and caretaker, all rolled into one. Students no longer came from Egypt, Syria, Iraq, or other Sunni Islam countries. The Vakf endowment had run out of money for even maintaining the school, let alone paying for teachers. *Hodja* offered me use of his *madrasah jawhairyya*—his jewel *madrasah*—which was just a few minutes' walk away, if I needed a quiet place to sit or meditate.

Hodja's square face was almost covered by his long white-gray beard, mustache, and eyebrows. He wore a *kaffiyeh* and a long white robe. He shuffled along at a slow, swaying pace, leaning backward to balance his large belly.

He noticed my concerned glances at the irregular walls. Some stones protruded into the room, and the ceiling bulged so low at mid-room that I could touch it. He commented, "Don't you worry about the stability of this house. The houses on this street were built one thousand years ago for the loyal staff of an emir of Mamluk Turks. This house has survived earthquakes that destroyed temples and wars that wiped out empires. It will still be here long after you and I are gone. You see this emblem, the wine cup? It is the sign of ultimate trust: it means that the sultan would drink from this commander's cup without hesitation. Yes, we loyal followers, Mamluks, drank wine, sang, and danced until we were converted to Islam by the Ottomans. Anyway, if you honor me to live here, I'll be your most loyal cup bearer. I am also a very good cook. Do you like spicy food? You don't have to give me much money; whatever you can afford will suffice." He spoke with the hoarse whisper of someone who has smoked for years.

"I am not sure that you'd be so pleased to have me here if you knew that my father was an Ottoman and my mother was Jewish," I said. Why was I bleeding the truth all of a sudden?

A little startled, he reassured me that he had nothing against Jews, and, as for Ottomans, he prayed that they would come back, defeat the British, and bring some peace to the country again.

"During the Ottoman centuries Jerusalem was one of the most serene, calm places in the world, as a sacred city should be. Look what is happening right now: we are all fighting with each other—Arabs, Jews, British.

"You pick your room and bed and settle down; I'll brew some Sudan tea in the samovar."

I was strangely elated to find this house and meet *Hodja* Nasir. I picked a room that overlooked the Haram from the front window and an inner court from the back. In the courtyard, laundry, including underwear, was drying on crisscrossing clotheslines attached to acacia trees. Two women, one young, the other older, chatted—their hair, face, arms, and feet uncovered.

In one corner of the room, a mattress rested on the floor atop an old kilim: dark red hexagons alternating with green Jewish stars on a light-blue base. Mademoiselle Blanche would have loved it. There was an open Qur'an on a white-enameled and carved wood *rahla*—an X-shaped stand—and a lamp held up with wires. *Hodja* explained that the rainwater well and bathroom were in the inner common courtyard and were shared by two other families. I was to bring my own water in an *ibrik*—kettle—from a gigantic earthenware jug in the house; I was never to dip into the well and never use the bathroom or enter the courtyard during the day because at this time it was the dominion of the women. If I needed to go to the bathroom during the day, I was to go to the *madrasah*. I was to leave my laundry at the courtyard door; the women would wash, dry, and return it to the same place. I was not to speak to them; all communication was to be conducted through *Hodja*. If I saw their faces, I was to quickly avert my eyes. This part of the instruction came too late; I had already looked at the women, and both were beautiful. They didn't fit my image of Arab women: very dark skinned, overweight, and masculinely hirsute. Both these women were very feminine, thin, and tall and had light, pinkish skin and brown hair. I wondered if they, too, were Mamluks of north of the Black Sea and most likely a little mixed with the white Russians. But how could I ask *Hodja* about them without being thrown out of the house?

༄

The *muezzin* of *Al masjid al-Aqsa* was inviting believers to the evening prayer, and as we entered the *Haram es-Sharif*, the site of Solomon's temple, my whole body began to shake. What was I doing? I didn't belong here. But to my astonishment, when I entered the *Qubbates-Sakhra*, I heard Noah's flood roaring, which, according to legend, only Muslims can hear. *Hodja* matter-of-factly walked me to the *Sabil al-Sultan Süleyman*— a magnificent fountain near the gate of the chain, built about 500 years ago by one of my ancestors (I must have at least a drop of his blood). All of a sudden, I felt as if I belonged there, as if I were returning home from a long exile. With the same familiarity displayed by the other worshipers, I sat in front of one of the fountain faucets and performed ablutions, washing my face, my hands, and my forearms, right one first, up to my elbows.

I strode into al-Aqsa. I had been in mosques before but only as a spectator.

The moment I stood *i'hdāl*, poised for prayer; faced *quiblā*, toward Mecca; raised my hands; and said, "*Allāhu akbar*," I felt transformed— as if I had been a Muslim all my life and knew exactly what to do. For me the prayer ended effortlessly as I turned to my right, pronouncing my submission: "*al-salāmu alaykum warahmatu l-lāh*—may the peace and mercy of God be with you." I turned left, *Hodja*, just turning right, smiled. I repeated my submission.

As we walked out, I asked, "*Hodja*, did you negate the whole prayer by smiling at me? I know that you're not supposed to contaminate prayers with earthly gestures."

"The smile and all other signs of love and affection do not contaminate the religion, *aziz ah*—dear friend. The danger is in the lack of a smile and affection."

~~~

That night, after I ate *Hodja's* proudly prepared, delicious, spicy lamb stew, I told him my whole life's story in total honesty. I wanted so badly for someone to know all about me. He quizzed my eyes with his own the way that Abbas had. Why was I in Jerusalem? I didn't know, but there was nowhere else I could have gone. Here I had the opportunity to blend in peacefully, perhaps get a medical license, be married, and have daughters of my own. But for the moment, I wanted to write my life story, and I wanted to visit some old cemeteries.

Hodja ruminated, "Peace? Forget it, but cemeteries we have plenty. This is the only country, in fact, where more people die than are born. Jerusalem is the Jewish graveyard. They come from all over the world to die here. They don't even believe in an afterlife. If you like, I can take you to Damascus to visit your father's *türbe*."

Why was he buried in Syria? I wondered what happened to his wives and his son, Ertuğrul, my childhood nemesis?

I knew that my relationship with *Hodja* would be a special one. I offered him half the money I had earned on the ship. He refused to take it all but pulled out a few notes and stuffed the rest back into my pocket.

"Render it *Helāl*—clean!" he said. The man had nothing, wanted nothing.

"I've been looking for someone like you for a long time," I said. "Actually, *Hodja*, I am not sure what I just said is true either. I am not what I say. I live a surrogate life. I am not myself. I hide myself behind words if I can't hide through an elusive presence. I am all surface."

"First of all, no one is himself," he replied, smilingly. "If things you say are good, they are not lies. Secondly, the surface is as important as the depth. The innerness is what kindles the surface. You know that wine isn't made of peeled grapes. Most important, you'll find your way back to yourself by allowing someone to love you." I decided I would call him *Al-Amin, Sophos*—the wise man.

He exemplified good faith at its best, as an incarnation of non-longing. I was an example of bad faith at its worst. I was an unbeliever, a thief, a liar, a betrayer, and a promiscuous murderer of unborn children.

"You need to have some compassion for yourself," he said, as if he had read my mind. I don't even feel entitled to my suffering.

⌣

I liked the conviviality of the Arabs and their genteel way of accepting me. I would live with them; maybe this was my destiny—to come to Jerusalem not to be part of Zionism as my mother might have envisioned but to follow my father's faith. Living with Sophos was the ultimate opportunity to perfect my knowledge of Islam. An inner serenity came over me; I finally may have found my home.

I should have known all along. Islam is the faith to which I should belong. The Qur'an is the third revision of the Abrahamic religion. Why read the earlier versions? Furthermore, both Jews and Christians quarreled a lot with God before accepting his guidance. Muslims were eager to receive God's word. It is in the Qur'an: "The scriptures were revealed only to two sects (Jews and Christians) before us; we have no knowledge of what they read but don't say; had the scripture been revealed to us we would have been better guided than they."

⌣

Unfortunately, my newfound faithful joy didn't last too long. The following day was the first day of Ramadan, and Sophos reminded me that he would wake me up before dawn for *suhur*—the last meal—after which we would fast for the rest of the day.

I woke up to Sophos pulling my arm. "Eat your *suhur*."

There was a generous meal—falafel, lamb shank, rice, yogurt, dates, and bananas, all spread on a large copper tray in the middle of the room. Two enormous kilim pillows were arranged against the windows, and next to them were two gaslit lamps. Following Sophos, I dipped my bread on the lamb shank.

Sophos poured some dark liquid into my glass. I took a sip. It tasted of alcohol.

"What is this, Sophos?"

"It is fermented date juice, and it is not considered *hatîya-t mumayyita-t*—a mortal sin."

I felt the same profound sense of disappointment I'd felt when Dr. Lugner punctured my yearning to embrace Judaism.

"Yes, but Sophos, it is still a *hatîya-t*—sin. You'll go to *Jaannam*—hell. Why bother fasting tomorrow if we are going to drink alcohol now?"

"Dear Adam, neither eating nor fasting unites one with the Creator. Neither the avoidance of drinking nor the other *haráam* of the Qur'an nor the strict obedience to all its *shari'ah*—Islamic law—will bring you to the presence of Allah when you die. What matters is experiencing the presence of God in the present. The promise of eternal rewards in Heaven—virgins, gold, silk, water—should make an intelligent person like you wonder about the simple-mindedness of the exchange. Don't confuse the civilizing principle of religion with its spiritual intention. The latter is not a material at all but an evolution toward a blissful state—*bagā*—in dwelling in the divine."

"So you are a mystic man, a *sūfi*, not a real *Musulman*—Muslim," I said.

"This is how I practice my religion. I am not, as you disappointedly noticed, an ascetic—a secluded celibate depriving himself of all the bodily pleasures."

"So, what are you then?"

"I am what God breathed in me. I am part of the Creator. You can reach divine union with Him in this life through your own *tariqah*, your own path. There are no other requirements."

A *Hodja*, an *ulema*, a custodian of the most sacred mosque was committing *kabirah*, the unpardonable sin.

"Sophos, Islam declares unequivocally that Allah has no partners. Isn't what you are saying considered a *shirk*—sin—of the worst type? In Turkey we had the *Bektāshi* and *Mevlevi* orders who had similar ideas of *Zohar*; they believed in the love of One, everything is united in him, that God was love—love of wine and everything else."

"You disapprove?" he asked.

"I really don't know," I said. "A man like myself cannot play judge. If you remove all my explanatory props, you'll find only an acquired veneer of adulthood. I am confused more than anything else. When we entered the al-Aqsa mosque this morning, I had a great yearning to become Muslim in the true sense of the word. Now you are negating all of Islam's principles, leaving me nowhere, as I have been all my life. I don't know how to relate to what you are saying. If I relate to it, I will be further isolated. I hardly have any connections in real life. I need a God through whom I may belong with other people."

The night was ending. The white threads were becoming distinguishable from the black ones. *Al-Amin*—wise one—Sophos finished the rest of the wine. "I am sorry. All I can offer, *Saddikie*—friend—is the ever-incoherent truth, and it has no moral value."

I guess everyone suffers from the illusion of being understood.

I hardly slept. Is life easier at the shallow end, or is my soul too short for the deep end?

⌇

In the morning, Sophos walked into my room carrying a book—*The Guide for the Perplexed* by Maimonides—in Arabic—and sat in a chair across from my bed:

"All the Turks I know are quite charmingly irreverent. So let me hear which of your wish-beliefs I rattled last night."

"Well, the Prophet, between the ages of ten and forty, went repeatedly to a cave on Mount Hira and remained there for days to meditate. On his fortieth birthday, the angel Gabriel appeared in the cave and commanded, 'Recite.' And he recited the Qur'an."

Sophos laughed: "You are about forty, right? Neither success nor failure occurs overnight, *Saddikie*, never mind becoming a prophet. In fact, between the ages of ten and forty, Muhammad was taught by monks. He disappeared daily, at times weekly, to various Christian cells. His most influential teacher was a monk called Nestor, who taught him the notion of a single God. Because Muhammad couldn't read, he had to learn by rote. That is also why the Qur'an was recited over many years and not just as a single revelation. For each recitation, Muhammad had to go to 'the retreat' to be retrained."

Sophos was as good as Lacan. Yes, I had been hoping for some revelation. I had also been looking for a ground of reconciliation between Islam and Judaism. Hesitantly I said, "You know, the Prophet sought a covenant with the Jews. He even took to his home two virgin Jewesses, one as a wife, the other as a concubine."

Sophos laughed: "So, you can reciprocate by loving a Muslim woman. But Muhammad took Jewish women as wives and concubines not as a sign of peaceful rapprochement but as the spoils of war. He wasn't all that selective when it came to women. Let's see if I can remember all of them. I think Davidah, Safiyyah, and Juway-riyyah were Jewish; Mariyah and Sirin were Coptic Christians; Umm Salamah and Umm Habibah were Muslims; and Maynunah was an idolatress, as was his first wife, Khadijah, who converted to Islam. As for virginity, most of these women were previously married; only A'ishah's virginity was certain—of course, she was just a child when the Prophet married her."

I asked, "Is it true that those of you who have been to Mecca have the images of the *Ka-bah* imprinted on your inner eyes? There is Ibrahim's footprint on the Black Stone and his Arabic inscription on it, blessing your faith."

Sophos laughed even harder: "I have been to Mecca many times, and my inner eyes do not have any imprint of the image of *Ka-bah*. By the way, the inscription on the Black Stone isn't in Arabic; it is in Aramaic, a language used in the liturgy by early Christians, and it reads, 'I am God.' Next and the final question, I don't know about you, but I am getting tired."

"Well, the final question is about his end. Like Jesus, he ascended to heaven. Over the years, people schemed to kill the Prophet. The last plot was by a sorcerer Jew, Labīd. He procured a piece of the Prophet's hair, tied seven knots in it, and threw it into the *Zamzam* well. Immediately the Prophet's health deteriorated; he couldn't eat or drink. He grew weak and feeble. Gabriel came to the Prophet and told him to get on his mare, Al-Burāq, and all would be taken care of. Burāq took the Prophet to Jerusalem, where he prayed, and thousands of angels lifted them with their wings, and brought them to Paradise."

Sophos looked pained. "*Saddikie*, come to terms with your ending," he said. "Muhammad lived to age sixty three. Toward the end of his life, he suffered from severe headaches, not unlike yours. He couldn't lie down. On his last day, he went to A'ishah's house. He requested cold water from seven different wells be poured on his head, and he asked for a toothpick carved of palm branches. He appointed A'ishah's father,

Abā Bakr, the first caliph, the leader of the prayers, not to replace him but to lead the Muslims. The Prophet died in A'ishah's arms. A grave was dug in the room where he died; they found an empty old grave, and the Prophet was buried there. Do you know what his last words were?"

I shook my head no.

" 'Here is the sign of the coming end of the world: Two tall buildings.' "

Well, the last knot untied itself. My soul was excavated totally. I was a dead-again Muslim. I was hoping and expecting to find a purpose and meaning for my life through religion, but instead my fate was to be faithless in the middle of three faiths.

FIVE

God believes in me.
I want to love.

Jerusalem
1945–1947

If I can't find God as defined, I have to redefine God.

Even Moses disappointed God. Why should Sophos meet my high
expectations? Sophos is himself. He is an undetermined man following
his own steps. Is that peculiar? But isn't everyone a bit peculiar? Maybe
a man is simply the sum of his peculiarities. Why should he be a manifestation of my idea of an ideal person? There are neither normal nor
ideal people. Normal and ideal are just ideas. I must accept Sophos as
he is; I must accept the "is-ness" of everything.

Today I appraised my rectal bank's inventory again to get an idea of how
long I could continue to live on it. The prospect of selling some of the
inventory gave me an excuse to walk around the Old City a little. I
hadn't realized how small Jerusalem was compared to Paris and Istanbul,
yet it shared with those cities the same tension and foreboding quality.
There was a hierarchical presence of the religions as represented by the
height of the respective structures: mosques—the tallest, with their
minarets—next, churches with their bell towers. The synagogues were
the lowest, by law of Ottoman rulers.

On one building wall, a poster advertising a performance of Johann
Strauss's *Gypsy Baron* was juxtaposed with red graffiti declaring the

British murderers. Telephone poles were decorated with flyers from the health department urging people to visit the Hadassah Clinic at Mount Scopus to have their eyes checked—free of charge—for trachoma. Above that, a flyer announcing *Maccabiah*, a Jewish athletic competition, bore the image of a female athlete. Someone had gouged the eyes from the picture.

The town was full of clergy—rabbis, ministers, nuns, priests, and *muftis* dressed in long religious garments. British soldiers in short pants patrolled the long winding alleys full of bickering peddlers of trinkets, carpets, beads, bangles, waxworks, and assortments of knickknacks. There also were stray dogs, cats, and children who didn't seem to belong to anyone.

Above the narrow alleys hung rugs and copperware. The alleys themselves were crowded, especially around the Holy Sepulcher, with persistent beggars, the most dogged of whom were young, purposely mutilated children. Six-year-old Arab girls missing a hand or a limb convincingly flirted with foreign tourists to extract money; teenaged Jewish boys sold Zionist "Shekels" and stamps of the Jewish National Fund. Sinister-looking characters accosted passersby *sotto voce* and offered pieces of antiquities (some genuine) for sale. The Holy Land was an open and noisy bazaar.

It wasn't clear where the storefronts of the umbrella and shoe-tree makers, furriers, or coffee shops (with their loud gramophones) ended and the streets began. British Rudge motorcycles wove through the crowds; cars, too, rode through, particularly large Rolls-Royces and Fords, which required people dining at outdoor cafés to get up, pull their chairs to the side, and then grudgingly return to their spots. Some young Arabs shook their chairs threateningly toward the passing cars; one actually threw a chair at a passing car, which sped away as fast as the unpaved street would allow. Was this country Palestine, ersatz Israel, or the non-Arab, non-Jewish *Philistia*? Even a peculiar person like me couldn't feel safe here.

I stopped by one of the Hasidic jewelers (there were as many Jewish jewelers as Arab carpet sellers) and showed him one of my diamonds. While rearranging his black felt hat with each assessment, he offered a different amount for the gems in British pounds, French francs, or *megid-dos*, Jewish currency. "Your best bet is to sell it in Arab *bishliks*!" he said in a conspiratorial tone. I chose pounds. That evening, when I returned to my room, I found that a thick writing pad had replaced the Qur'an on the writing table. Next to it, on the floor, there were two plumed pens and an ink box, and a large *minder*-sitting pillow lay before the table. I had never gotten a better gift in my life. Being so well understood by this thoughtful and generous stranger elated me. I had a surge of warm feelings I had never before experienced. I sat on the minder, tucked my legs under me, took one of the pens, and dipped it into the ink. I was found!

∾

I am free of the tyranny of the already known, but still I am yearning for the illusion of knowing. I've stopped believing in God, but I still need a tune to dance to. Maybe I can dance to pure goodness. In fact, seeking God may simply mean seeking the sedimentation of the soul of God, that is, the divine characteristics of God, becoming not a god but godlike. That first requires finding your authentic self, which means making your soul visible, then making the quantum leap of losing it—that is spiritual condensation.

I was seeking God so as to make sense of myself. I needed to locate myself in an overarching paradigm. I needed God to give me a meaning for my life. What I found was that to seek the meaning of life is not relevant. The meaning of your personal life is defined by your approximation to your guiding principles and by having a life witness to your successes and failures in your efforts to remain loyal to them. There is no ideal self with corresponding ideal meanings. The task is finding your real self, and your own corresponding meaning will evolve from within. I found my real self by becoming totally transparent to Sophos, whom I loved, valued, and trusted. Could I have found myself in some other relationship? I might have, but only with another Sophos—a wise, kind, accepting person who knew himself, lived a simple life, and enjoyed it. I had to find my real self in a relationship with someone who had mastered the art of living but didn't pretend to be an expert on life.

∾

I happily settled into a routine in Sophos's home and life. We lived like birds, according to his healthy habit principals—sleep at dusk, rise at dawn. We had all our meals together, and once a week we went to the

Turkish bath at the Lion's Gate. We visited *türbes* and other Muslim cemeteries almost daily.

At Mount Scopus was a Turkish soldiers' cemetery. Under the overgrown weeds, scattered decrepit headstones, and shapeless and unmarked graves languished the once brave and victorious Ottoman army. Chickens and roosters pecked at the carcasses of cats and dogs that had been dumped on the land. I pondered the soldiers' lives and their fossilized dreams.

Now I understood the meaning of the old Kurdish song: "*Giden gelmiyor, acab nedendir?*—Why do they not return?"

The rest of the time I explored Jewish and Christian cemeteries—to which Sophos was reluctant to accompany me—or walls and gates, and I wrote.

Sophos agreed to come with me to find Adam Lugner's grave in the Jewish Cemetery at Mount Olive.

Before he would help me find Adam's grave, Sophos had to pray at the tomb of his idol, Mujir al-Din, an Ottoman scholar.

I was surprised to find the area overflowing with nuns. Sophos explained that Christians had mistakenly identified al-Din's mother's tomb, which was a few side steps away, as that of the Virgin Mary. "Now the Christians want to excavate al-Din's tomb because they believe that another holy Christian, possibly Joseph, is buried there as the tomb is made of carved stones dating to pre-Islamic ages. It is nonsense because reusing building materials is not uncommon here, and most of the buildings are made of ancient Byzantine and Jewish stones. One of the stones on the tomb has *XP* engraved on it and most likely came from a nearby ossuary, whose use preceded Jesus' birth. Some people insist that *XP* means Christianity, but it is simply a sign meaning "sealed" in Latin. On the walls that Süleyman built, you'll see real Christian signs because he used the stones of the Knights Hospitalier. *Qubbat es-Sakhra*—the Dome of the Rock—was built with material from Byzantine times."

Mount Olive was not a cemetery: it was a necropolis with acres of granite sepulchers teeming with insects. It was almost as big as Old Jerusalem itself. Neither Eyüp Cemetery nor Pére Lachaise even came close to it. They all hoarded history and claimed to be spots where humanity assembled to be judged by God, but Mount Olive was the most convincing—there, there was a faint sense of eternity.

༄

Although the Jewish cemetery seemed a sea of tombstones, I had no difficulty finding Adam's grave. The photographs taken by his family and their description of the grave's position in relation to the tomb of the Prophet Zachariah and the main gate made it very easy to find.

Adam Zachary Lugner
1905–1926
Cherished son and brother

I heaped a few stones on his gravestone. I recited whatever I remembered from a chapter of *Mishnah* that begins with the letter *D*. I wondered what had happened to Sara. I stretched myself across the grave, folded my arms, closed my eyes, and for a few minutes remained motionless.

Sophos pulled me up.

"Is it true that dead ones never existed?" I asked him.

"Do not keep tempting fate, my friend. You have already done that once by taking the dead man's identity."

That night I woke up after a few hours of sleep with a violent headache and spasms of vomiting. Sophos ran into my room, washed my face and my nightclothes, then held me in his arms.

"I guess I should stop feeding you calves' brains," he said with a look that belied his belief that it was the food that caused my condition.

༄

Newspapers headlined a story of a major disaster: my old ship, *Struma*, was refused passage from the Bosporus, at which point it returned to the Black Sea and sank with four hundred Jews on board. There were hateful editorials against the Turks. Sophos noticed my lowered, crimson face, shook his head and put his hand on my shoulder.

Are all people essentially something like myself? Do we each grow up to become a wretched creature who creeps on earth toward the same destination? Have religions deprived us from the antecedent condition of all being, the unitary ground of oneness?

⌒

Redefining God means defining spirituality without any connections to religion. Spirituality is a form of homogenized intelligence, a more precise form of knowing; it is a form of unknowing, a quantum unknowing—not learning but remembering. Spirituality is a way of being in the world, not another worldliness—above this world, rather, deeper into it. It is a form of purity, a more precise form of purity—the purity of intention. Spirituality is undifferentiated theism. Spirituality is a form of love; not a love that recognizes the value of its object, it is love without object.

⌒

The Russians contrasted sharply with Jerusalem's old Jews, who were just there to study the Torah and peacefully await the arrival of the Messiah. The Russians and Eastern Europeans were like a different species from the old, studied Jews, and they reminded me of the socialist Jews in Paris. These "Young Jews" who wore kerchiefs around their necks like Arabs were charming, energetic, and convincing. In the middle of the day, they got drunk on the undrinkable cheap local wine—Carmel Hock. A number of them tried to recruit me to various Zionist activities while I was casually having a *gazoz*—a carbonated sweet lemon drink—at the Center or playing chess at the coffeehouse. I joined the discussion of distribution of money by the *Khevrot-hagolah* societies and whether the ultimate blessing was to be dependent on another Jew.

Every day, newspapers announced terrorist activities against British properties, docks, and railroads and reported the arrest, trial, or acquittal of militant Jews associated with those crimes. *Doar Hayom*, a Hebrew newspaper, reported these events with the patriotic justification that people had no choice but to resort to violence to free their land from British occupation.

It was impossible to tease out the truth from the gossip. Did the Arabs actually kill all the settlers at Hebron and burn their houses? Who put arsenic in the dried figs? Had the Jews bombed a British officer's car? Did the British arrest a dozen militant Jews? One thing was clear: a major upheaval was brewing. Even though Arabs and Jews played chess games in the same coffeehouses and even though British soldiers dated Jewish girls and went dancing and drinking, there was an ominous mood of an impending disaster.

I wondered how it was that in the three countries in which I had lived, I always became embroiled in their turmoil and ended by getting displaced.

～

Redefining self means defining awareness without any connections to psychologies. Otherwise, your loneliness will cut deeper. Introspection is only an interim medium at best. My introspection was an awareness craze. Ultimately one must reach non-self-reflective awareness. All my life I kept the eyes of my mind wide open, and I almost missed what really matters.

I need to practice being useful to others—the undergirding of all existence. Sophos says I should be immersed in the matter in hand and absorbed in the present. He says my life should flow toward others—and flow cheerfully. Having a downcast spirit dries up the bones!

～

I decided to try to obtain a medical license. I expected to find a recalcitrant Jewish or English administrator at the health department. Instead, I found a bunch of easygoing, if not lackadaisical, Arabs sitting at their desks reading newspapers, smoking, and chatting.

They passed my credentials among each other numerous times, had me fill out a form, and then had me sit in the corridor the whole afternoon waiting to meet with the commissioner doctor in charge of licenses. They didn't know when or whether he'd show up "unless I wanted to visit him in his private office," one of the employees winked. I took the address and went to visit Dr. Abdul Ahmet Cellāli at his home office in Aqabat et-Takiya. He lived in an elegant stone house, a part of the Imaret of Haseki Sultan. An old man servant wearing a white *galabia*, red *shash*, and red *tarbush* escorted me into a large dome-vaulted room. There wasn't a patient in sight, nor was there any sign of a medical office. The room was ornamented from floor to ceiling with stone-engraved calligraphy. The windows were narrow, with open shutters exposing protective iron grilles. Outside, the rest of the walls were covered in blue-green ceramic tiles decorated with colorful floral motifs.

The old servant asked the reason for my visit, and I told him. He then informed me that the doctor's fee was fifty pounds. That was a hefty sum. Nevertheless, I nodded to the man that I agreed and quickly wrapped the fifty pounds in the application form and handed it over to him. As I waited in the palatial room, I admired the glass mosaics and tried to read the verses from the Qur'an written on the interlocked, glazed ceramic.

Finally the doctor, a short, fat, very dark-skinned man in his fifties, arrived. He was dressed like a European gentleman coming to breakfast, clad in a red smoking jacket and slippers. He smiled widely.

"Another Jew, ha! You'll never find a job with the government or in the hospitals, you know. There are too many of you whose credentials can't be verified. But given the situation in Europe, I'll give you a limited permit. You'll practice under the supervision of a fully licensed physician—me—for one full year. You'll report to me once a month. At the end of your provisional time, you'll be interviewed by the three members of the Medical Board—I am one of them—and if all goes well, you'll be granted the privilege of independent practice."

He returned my application, signed and sealed. I was now a legitimate doctor on paper!

∼

My purpose found me.

Sophos was even happier with my obtaining the permit than I was.

He said, "I am glad you allowed yourself to be taken in." A sense of exhilaration surged in me. Love must be the only human sanctuary.

Sophos thought the *madrasah* would be the best place for me to practice being useful. Of course, my services would have to be free of charge, but helping poor Muslims who couldn't afford to see a doctor would be serving God, though the rewards would be unpredictable. My self-doubts about my legitimacy notwithstanding, I actually liked the idea. It seemed that had been more or less my fate anyway. I had served Russians and Kurds in Istanbul, Eastern European Jews in Paris, and immigrants on the ship, so why not Muslims in a *madrasah*? I'd start Monday.

The first few mornings no one showed up, but I had my writing set with me, so I sat in a well-lit corner of the *madrasah* and wrote. Thursday, Sophos brought a patient, a mentally retarded, paraplegic young man. If I were not already a little skeptical of this idea, his compassionate gesture, compounded with the impossibility of the demand, would have totally discouraged me. Friday I didn't even bother going to the *madrasah*. Saturday morning, while I was in my room engrossed in writing, Sophos came in, out of breath and hardly able to contain his excitement.

"Hurry up! You have lots of patients waiting for you."

I ran down to the *madrasah* and I couldn't believe what I saw—there was a line of people in front of the school, extending all the way to the old Süleyman fountain. I walked into the *madrasah*. There was another surprise waiting for me: an ink stamp bearing the inscription Adam Z. Lugner. *Tabíib*—doctor.

A smiling Sophos finally caught up with me. He took me aside.

"I asked the imam to announce the arrival in our neighborhood of a Turkish/French doctor, who would help us without any charge. He said that if anyone wanted to make a donation to the mosque for your service, they could do so. He gave his blessing for something Arabs are already inclined to do—highly value foreign doctors and get free medical assistance."

Seeing the look of being overwhelmed on my face, he added, "This is it. You are licensed to practice medicine in Jerusalem. You and I know where you started and where you ended—your grave is well marked in the cemetery. So in between just work hard, however long or short it may be. You see, *Saddikie*, every man needs a mooring, a purpose, a reason for his existence. This is best obtained by lovingly devoting oneself to serving fellow humans. Only in giving yourself to others can you find yourself. We know why you are needed; you shouldn't worry about what you need. That'll take care of itself. The love of work will come back to you as self-worth. Without such a mission, life falters and dissipates to failing emptiness. You'll be unknown and unfound."

"I don't have a real self, Sophos. Mine is a fictitious self. My self is a precipitate of my subjective experiences. At best I could become the sum embodiment of counterfeiting."

"Every soul has a lie in its formation," replied Sophos.

Sophos's redemptive relation was transformative for me.

∽

It was midnight. I was bent over my writing pad trying to recall the name of the cheap local wine when Sophos ran in with such a wave of excitement that the wind from his flapping robe almost blew out the flame of my gas lamp.

"Sophos!"

"Don't be scared. I have good news. The grand *mufti* wants to meet you."

I shrugged.

"No, no, this is a great honor," he said in a serious tone. "The request for an audience always is made to him by a petitioner and is rarely granted. He heard so much praise of you and your service to the community that he initiated the visit. So let's go."

We entered the mosque of al-Aqsa, leaving our shoes outside. Mufti Haj Amin el Husseini sat with two other people on the floor next to the *mihrab*, the plaque that shows the direction of Mecca. Sophos bent over, kissed the mufti's hand, saluted the others, and sat. I followed suit. The *mufti* looked at me for a long time as if trying to figure me out. He had a penetrating stare.

"*Ebn elvez awaam*—little swan is a good swimmer," he said, in a voice that seemed subtly threatening. "We are happy to see you, son. These *fedais*, self-sacrificers, are two of the leaders of the Istiglāl Party and my most loyal companions in our sacred mission. We know a lot about you, and we find your altruism most convincing; we think we can trust you and hope that you'll put your noble blood in the same Islamic service that your ancestor Ottomans did."

He must be kidding, I thought. Weren't these the same Arabs who betrayed their own Muslim government and helped the British defeat the Ottoman Empire?

I stared at a pile of Ulster rifles behind him.

"You are curious about these, yes? Islamism is inherent in Islam, but the nationalism's inherent violence is time limited. You may already know what I am going to tell you, but it still may be worth my repeating. *Al-Quds*—Jerusalem—has been a Muslim city for more than one thousand three hundred years. Before then it was always Arab, for thousands of years, all the way to the beginning of time. There were always Jews and insignificant Semitic tribes, intermarrying with each other, losing their eyesight as a result. No one paid much attention to them. Their hero, King David, wasn't even Jewish. They claimed that the Western Wall was the remnant of their Temple, but the stones of that wall are as big and similarly placed as those of the pyramids.

"All the glorious structures that you see here at *Al-Quds*, Mosques, *Harem es-Sherif, Qubbat es-Sakhra* were built by Arabs. The old palaces and fountains are Ottoman gifts. Whoever controls *Al-Quds* controls the world. Jews are in an eternal battle with us to dominate the world. They have money, and we have Allah. Big nations like China and America one day will see the light and convert to Islam. That will be the end of the Jews once and for all. For the moment we seem to be losing ground. The money is pouring in from Europe and America, and Jews are being smuggled in by the thousands. We have to do something about it. Once the British hand over the government to the Jews, it'll take *Mehta's*—the Prophet's—coming to take it back.

"What we need is some access to the British thinking, so that we can plan ahead to take appropriate precautions. You'll be measured by your allegiance to Allah, not by your provenance."

I wondered what he wanted me to do. The *mufti* extended his hand for me to kiss to signal the end of the meeting. I asked Sophos what would bring peace to the region and stop the fighting between Jews and Arabs.

"Nothing," he replied. "The fighting is a historical game for us. *Jihād* means struggle; it has no end point. In the Jews we have found an eternal playmate; they also love to quarrel without any goal. Palestine is the perfect playground for attracting *Naṣarah*—Christian—spectators."

I guess we are all suffering from a profound sort of misunderstanding. I was interested in neither Zionism nor the Istiglāl Party.

∾

Anyone who steps out of the subjective world sends himself into self-exile. To be like Sophos, I need to rein in my mind, not in terms of where it lives but how it loves—the soft ascension to self-donation. I must rein it in at the sacred threshold of self-exile.

Finding self even in the form of losing it is not an answer to all life questions; it is rather the precondition for the answers. The question, "What is the meaning of my life?" may be responded to in the form of deeds.

∾

My Arab patients had the same problems as my previous patients, and treating them was as similar, with a few important exceptions. Women didn't take off their clothes. They had to be examined through their outfits and in the presence of other women. Some women didn't want to be touched at all, and I had to diagnose their diseases by listening to their complaints.

Another oddity: both male and female patients wanted to have injections—of any kind. If after the exam and/or interview they were simply given a prescription, they expressed their dismay quite openly. I routinely administered injections of vitamins, signaling the end of the visit.

In return, the patients were very generous. Rarely did anyone show up without a gift: eggs, live chickens, honey, yogurt, freshly baked bread, milk, natural gum, goat cheese, lemons, rose jam, pistachio baklava, halvah, fruits, pieces of old ceramics, beads, and ancient coins.

There were some serious endemic disorders: trachoma, seed infection of the eyes, typhoid fever, dysentery, skin infections, malaria with an enlarged spleen, and occasionally bubonic plague. Thankfully, the health department supplied, gratis, some newly discovered and very effective medications, such as disinfectant chloramine sulfonamide, DDT, penicillin, and quinine. They worked miracles and made me look like a miracle maker, which caused the line of patients to lengthen. Until now, even the Jewish doctors treated some of these conditions with cupping, bleeding, castor oil, lubrication of the gut, hypnotics, sedatives, small doses of arsenic, orders for smoking, and writing amulets. I sent the more serious cases and those in need of surgery to *Sha'arei Tzedek*—a Jewish hospital in Jerusalem. The patients preferred to go there, even though they weren't all that welcome.

~~~

My monthly report to Dr. Cellali consisted of my knocking on the door of his residence and handing an envelope, containing twenty pounds, to his old manservant. We repeated this monthly procedure wordlessly as he stood in the threshold and then closed the door in my face. It was a good thing I wasn't a real physician; if I had been, I'd have been terribly offended by such disrespectful treatment.

Despite these episodes, I had no reason to complain; the rest of the time I was so reverentially treated (equally undeservedly, I must say), that it all balanced out. I had a loyal friend in Sophos, professional satisfaction at the *madrasah*, quiet pleasure in reminiscing about my life while writing, and exaltation in catching glances of my young female neighbor, Şükran, whose courtyard activities had increased significantly.

I remembered how I'd felt, seeing Gülseren in the window of her house while I stood below it and whistled. I felt the same feeling of profound sexual tranquility.

Little by little, Sophos confided in me. It took him a year before he told me that he was in love with Şükran's mother Fatima; he brought me a message from her telling me that nineteen-year-old Şükran was becoming "lovesick" with me and that I should either stop staring at her from my window or do something. She preferred that I do something. Along with the note, Fatima sent a tray of pistachio baklava that she had made.

"Sophos," I asked, "didn't you warn me that Arab men would tear a man limb from limb if he were caught committing adultery with one of their women and that the woman would be stoned to death?"

"Yes," he replied, smiling. "It was a warning not to get caught," and he sank his teeth into the baklava. "*Saddikie*, you know a lot about being a doctor but nothing about life. Being is not something to be studied but lived. Take life on.

"Tomorrow night, when you see a flickering light in the courtyard, take off your shoes, and walk out there. Şükran's door will be unlocked. Just go in quietly; Fatima will be there to protect you both. Make sure that none of the men are in the courtyard using the bathroom and be sure to leave before dawn."

"Sophos, are you out of your mind? You told me that it was dangerous even to suggest the appearance of impropriety. Now you're setting me up to have sex with a married Arab woman and her mother is in collusion with this deadly affair?"

"She is just kindly reciprocating," Sophos said. "Şükran has been a confidant and best friend to both her mother and me. Now stop fussing about it; she is worth the risk, Adam. Şükran will wash your feet with rose water and dry them with her hair. I would lay my life on the line for Şükran if she were even mildly interested in me."

"I thought you loved her mother."

"Adam," he sighed in exasperation, "you can love one woman, then the other, then another. The source of love is God. All love emanates from that source. If you only love one person, that means you really don't know what love is."

That evening we ate one of my patients' gifts—eggplant stuffed with ground lamb, tomatoes, onions, and spices that burned the tongue—in silence. Afterward, we both paced the room, hands behind our backs. Soon I returned to writing, but I couldn't concentrate because of my excitement and trembling and the sound of Sophos' pacing. I'd never seen him so anxious.

Suddenly he stopped abruptly and turned to me. "Look *Saddikie*," he said. "You have been here for more than a year, and you have not bedded a woman or a boy. No man can live the way you do; fasting of the heart is not good for your health. You're the doctor, but let me tell you, your headaches, vomiting, bumping into people, the sores on your ankles are all coming from your backed-up 'water of life.'

"Are you waiting for the Savior—Messiah—dear friend? What? Eternal future? How about the eternal now? Life is just a succession of 'nows.' There is no afterlife, you know. It is here and now, and that is it. You can't be afraid of living all your life, Adam. As for women, why are you afraid of their love? I suppose you are scared of being hurt. Of course love can hurt, but it also heals. This may be your last chance to change. You cannot change by just observing. You have to jump into living. Life must be fully lived, not just endured. Yes, Şükran is married, but I know from Fatima that she loves you. Don't run away from her. And don't have any more fits like the one you had this morning. You scared me half to death."

"I had a fit?"

"I found you on the floor beside your bed, face down. When I lifted you up, I couldn't wake you and saw you frothing at the mouth. I cleaned you off and put you to bed. When I came back from the mosque, you were talking in your sleep, in some strange language. I thought you were possessed. Adam, you see patients all day, write all night, visit only cemeteries, and have no women. *Latin tábax wila tinshíwi*—you can neither be toasted nor roasted."

Why would I have had a seizure?

"Maybe one of the patients is putting poison into the food, or someone has been using hashish in cooking and then stopped bringing food, triggering a withdrawal seizure," I ruminated aloud.

"I think that is a bit far-fetched, don't you?" Sophos said.

"Or maybe," I continued, without answering him, "lack of sex is responsible for my symptoms. Dr. Freud said the same thing, and he's a very famous doctor."

"Then there would appear to be only one solution," he asserted.

"But Sophos, I don't even know whether I can do it. Making love is a sort of distant memory, not even my memory, as if it was the memory of someone else."

"Nevertheless, you must try. The candle is flickering. Yel-la—hurry—take your shoes off, no coughing, you lucky son of a bitch."

Is it the beauty that is convincing or the convinced third party? I stepped out into the courtyard. It was almost pitch dark, and I stumbled as I set my bare feet on the cold, uneven stones. I crossed the courtyard shivering. I stood in front of Şükran's door and for a moment pictured two Arab men running toward me with big, curved, flashing scimitars in their hands. I very lightly touched the door, half hoping it was locked. The door opened to an equally dark hallway. Someone grabbed my arm firmly and pulled me in. I nearly fainted.

Fatima walked me toward a dimly lit room in the back of the house. I saw Şükran's shadow; she seemed so tall. Fatima tugged me inside, then left, closing the door behind her. Şükran and I stood in the middle of the room. How was I supposed to behave? I felt as if it were my first time alone with a woman. I'd had this feeling once before, just before I kissed Gülseren in the hallway of her house in Istanbul. Şükran took off her slippers and pointed me to a *minder*.

"My father and the boys are sleeping in their house, my husband is at the village, and, as you know, my mother is watching over us."

She blushed. Her porcelain white skin took on the color of her pink dress and red *hijab*. Her hair was loosely covered by white lace that hung over her shoulders. The whole room was decorated with white lace—curtains, bedsides, tables, edges of pillows—and red silk or wool—bedcover, rugs, and pillows. Everything seemed soaked in heavy, sex-smelling perfume, especially Şükran. She wore a long gold chain adorned with dozens of gold coins around her neck. Both her arms were layered with gold bracelets that reached all the way to her elbows. The jewelry jingled with a self-confident melody at her every movement. She picked up a tray full of cookies and sweets, placed it on the floor near us, and sat next to me. In my life, I had entered enough deep waters, but in these I knew I could drown.

I held her henna orange–colored hands and lifted them to kiss. They were surprisingly rough. She shook her head disapprovingly and bent over to kiss my hands. I put my hands on both sides of her face. I couldn't read her dark eyes. It was as if I were looking into a well while suffering with a desert thirst; but I wasn't interested in drawing any water. Şükran didn't even blink her eyes as I pulled her face to mine. She averted her lips and instead offered her neck with a pure-hearted reserve. I tried to undo the top buttons of her dress. She gently retreated, softly put my hands on my lap, and began to undress me. She hung my clothes on the back of a chair, turned down the bed covers, and got in. I thought she was getting undressed under the covers, but when I got into the bed, I realized she had only taken off her panties and pulled up her dress. She kept moving her pelvis sideways, as if teasing me, but she looked too serious and too desirous for that type of play. I knew that even the most willing woman gets a little unsettled with the proximity of sex. But she also was giving me a disapproving look. I couldn't decipher what I was doing wrong. I didn't know if it was because of too much excitement or fear that I couldn't have a firm erection.

Finally, exasperated, she murmured, "Say it."

Now I understood. Women, whether Jewish, Turkish, French, or Arab, all wanted to hear the same thing before abandoning themselves.

"I love you," I whispered back.

"No," she laughed. "Say it."

"Say what?" I said, genuinely puzzled.

"Say, *Bismillah*—with God's permission—you silly goat."

"Oh! All right. *Bismillah*."

My earlier sexual hesitancy with her vanished. I lost track of time while making love to her. I guess this is the sex that Sophos exalts as the affirmation of love wherein the heart is its organ. We seemed to have unearthed our ancient belonging.

For once, even my shrunken penis performed. In fact, I seemed to have a strange, boundless new energy. She was beautiful, and I immersed myself in her long white neck and long brown hair. As for her, her passion was inexhaustible. Our tryst ended when Fatima knocked softly on the door. In whispers, Şükran and I pledged to meet again.

When I returned to my side of the courtyard, Sophos awaited me. He patted me on the head and went to bed. I was wide awake and agitated. I sat down to write; where was I in the journal? Oh yes, I had just met the grand *mufti*, but all I could write about was today. I ended with "God exists for the permission of sins."

∼

Ardor of my longings ends within myself.

Never mind that I love and feel loved; it is a miracle I walk on this earth. I am fully incarnate in my mind. I love my wounds and am happy in small ways. The sun and moon speak to me of the rhythm of the universe, and I know now that there is nothing to understand. I derive pleasure from things outside and am aware of their container of seeds of displeasure; I seek joy from within, which contains only its own joyful seeds. I don't believe in eternity—endless time—but I believe in "no time." I don't believe in remaining in my present or other forms, but I believe in formlessness.

∼

I needed to share my feelings with someone, but I didn't want to talk to Sophos about Şükran because he was a little too involved. Finally, I had no choice. But Sophos, drunk to his eyeballs, was more interested in how "it" was and kept peppering me with questions: "Did she fart? Did she bleed? Did she faint?"

"When can I visit her again?" I asked him.

"Not too often," he replied. "Don't make it routine or too organized; otherwise, you'll become complacent and get caught. The visits have to be random and infrequent. It will be safer and will also keep the fire alive."

The next day I stood glued to the window. I saw only Fatima hanging up wet laundry (she totally ignored me). I was worried that Şükran was sick or upset. Then she showed up, wearing a simple cotton dress that exposed her arms and legs below the knee. Her head also was uncovered. She lingered, smiling, while checking the dryness of the clothes. She bravely threw glances my way while simultaneously motioning for me to get away from the window.

∼

The gratification of lust in a lover is not to be gulped but sipped. Sexual desire contained in love is a tenderly sought, mutual source of pleasure. It should be savored in the service of generosity and culminate in the reverence of love. Of course, not just love but all feelings are symptoms of remembrances. If you had joyful memories, good feelings in love will be disappointing, for they are neither permanent nor convincing. If you had painful memories, bad feelings in love will remain permanent and convincing.

∾

My reputation as a physician exceeded not only my expectations (and my knowledge) but also my competencies and, more concretely, my capacity. Now I was *saghiir tabiib*—the small doctor—and for the first time I didn't mind it. By giving myself to others, not only did I accept myself, but I found myself. Being there for others brings out one's simpler view of life. A one-afternoon-a-week practice turned into three afternoons, then every afternoon, and even so, I still wasn't able to see some patients, who may have waited for hours. People from the nearby villages arrived at dawn to line up for a visit. Some of the problems were overwhelming and time consuming. One man had been kicked by his horse—his forehead literally was caved into his skull; another had an untreated subdural hematoma; a third had a small nail lodged in his eyeball. There were emaciated children, a breech delivery stuck in midcourse, gastrointestinal bleeds, and many hypochondriacal delusions that proved difficult to tease out.

As if those weren't enough, I began to get Christian patients, including the families of British employees, who were always accompanied by guards. Unhappy with the long waiting lines, they demanded (and were granted) exclusive time for their treatment from the mufti of the Haram es-Sharif. They had no problem buying the drugs I prescribed, no matter the expense. They wanted to reciprocate for my free services, so they invited me to their homes and clubs, invitations that I gently refused. I had neither the time nor the clothes to wear for such occasions. The British women were particularly appreciative of me because no matter what illness they had, thought they had, or pretended they had, they received the same prescription: "Go home to England."

There was no "civilized community" to which these women were accustomed; even colonial life didn't exist. Jerusalem was a "relic," one British female patient said. Once you had seen all the historical sites, which didn't take more than a few days, there was nothing to do. They were also worried about their security. They rounded themselves up behind barbed wire and now suffered from concentration camp–like distresses despite how luxurious and voluntary their stay. The Jews, whom they had helped to establish the country, had now turned against them. The British had no ally in this part of the world. "Why are we still here?" they lamented.

Having European patients further increased my standing among the Muslim population but attracted the negative attention of physicians in town. I received a note from the Association of Medical Doctors of Jerusalem to appear before an ethics committee for a review of my practice. There were claims that I had supernatural healing power and, it was rumored, that I did not charge patients for my services and thus that I created a damaging discrepancy of expectation for the rest of the medical community.

～

I believe people try hard to misunderstand each other so that they can suffer. I have myself as a witness. Suffering is a form of secular moralism; it provides a sense of cognitive security to the sufferer; it establishes subordinating dominance over others and makes all attempts to help futile by its indeterminacy. The sufferer belongs to the cult of being alive in the fearful eyes of others. But his painless inner deadness illegitimizes his suffering and makes his questioning of the mutation of the meaning of life irrelevant. We must live in the joyful eyes of those who are not afraid of dying. We must take residence only in being, without rescue, transcend the meaning-of-life question—while living in mere successions of moments not muffled by strivings. We have to learn to suffer better in order to be worthy of it, widen the circle of compassion—to suffer with. That is the irreducible communion.

～

The river, before losing itself in the ocean, traverses long stretches of land. I have traversed all three religions and feel as if I am about to reach my final destination—an unbroken, unfleeting, and eternal presence. It is said that he who has already drunk turns his back on the well. Well, I have already lived. I found a new observation platform—living out of time. From here every search for content looks hollow. I have no arguments for or against anything, only a deep and silent peace. I seek no power or position or wealth, only the tranquility of my soul. I ask for nothing. Yes, man can live by bread alone. I have no point of reason or rightness, only an invisible smile. I have no morality or immorality for the world to see, only benevolence and native filial instincts. I have no special goal or ambition, only that of pursuing truth. I have no framework for life, only framelessness. I have no questions, nor do I seek answers. Things are as they are, and all is self-evident. I had friends— Abbas, Sara, Sophos—whom I caught along the way through my confused journey. The same thing happened with my lovers: Tatiana, Gülseren, and Şükran. What if I had taken a different turn? Now my fear is not that life may end but that it may have never begun. One never becomes whole within oneself: others help one design a philosophy of life—a perspective—seeing things at once and in relationship to another, including between the noisy arrival to the world and the silent return to the inorganic state. This is not a last-minute self-indoctrination but a truth in the making—the reason I am speaking in the past tense is because I seem to be living in a posthuman existence. As for God, I believe in everything and nothing. But God believes in me; this paradoxically belies that there is really an "I."

Until this point I had written about what had happened to me. Now I was writing down what was happening to me as it happened. This was like simultaneously acting my life while scripting it.

I woke up this morning a little late. The sun streamed in through the windows. I took a deep breath of the dry air. A tray on the floor brimmed with cheese-filled, freshly baked pastry and honey in its natural comb. I saw two gold coins in the corner of the tray. During our morning walk and visit to the cemetery, Sophos and I talked about the coins.

"You don't need to return them," Sophos said emphatically. "She'll be hurt. It isn't a payment for your services or anything like that; it's a symbol of her commitment to you. She won't give you gold coins every time you sleep with her. This is all. Now you can reciprocate; you can give her one of your gems, or write her a beautiful poem."

We arrived outside the sprawling Jaffa Gate and sat on the ruins of an old windmill.

"Sophos, do you know why this gate is wider than the others?" I asked.

"Kaiser Wilhelm II allowed the Sultan Abdulhamid II to maintain huge deposits of money in German banks. He closed his eyes and ears to the Armenians' pleas, and in return the sultan granted the inauguration of a Lutheran church and opened a new wide gate in the walls of Jerusalem for the kaiser's cars to pass."

Sophos chuckled. "So they misled each other. *Saddikie*, happiness is arrived at through the narrowest gate."

Outside the city walls the houses had red brick roofs. Many houses had tin petrol cans with flowers in them lined up along their windows. We were surrounded by white and pink oleander bushes, red anemones, cyclamen, blue lupines, and many other wildflowers.

This is no arid patch of land as the Ottomans describe it. The signs of a blooming desert are everywhere.

"Sophos," I said, after I took in the vista before me, "Are gems and poems interchangeable in value?"

"They are," he said simply.

The diamonds have been in his safe since I moved in with him.

"Sophos," I ventured. "Did you look at my gems?"

"No, Adam."

I sighed. Here was a godly person whom all three religions urge man to become: generous, soulful, deeply caring, and joyful. He embodied the essence of religion without being religious.

We stopped talking and watched a crowd a few hundred meters away. Young Jewish women athletes finished up practicing discus throwing and now lingered playfully, perhaps for the benefit of the spectators—a few teenaged Arab boys and soldiers of the British regimental pipe band, who wore kilts and colonial hats.

Suddenly the games stopped: a rhythmic trembling of the land was followed by a large cloud of dust that slowly rolled into the arena. A herd of cows idled in front of us. Dozens of young Arab girls in the middle of the herd collected dung with their bare hands as the beasts defecated. They put the steaming heaps into tin cans, which they carried on their backs.

Seeing the horror on my face, Sophos explained, "Once the girls get home, they'll make dung cakes and lay them out on the roof to dry. Dried, these cakes make good heating or cooking fuel."

As the herd passed and the dust settled, the Jewish girls and British soldiers emerged from the whirlwind, covered in a yellow tint.

All at once, I felt as if I were falling into a hole, the hole enclosed in an even larger hole. "Even a hole is a hole in something. I know that I am a precipitate from a larger being," I was muttering.

"What is the matter, Adam, your foot is shaking! Hold onto me. Are you sick? I think you are having a fit again. Don't worry, I won't let you fall; I'm holding you. Adam, say something! Your eyes are rolling; let me get the foam out of your mouth; my hands are clean. Open your mouth, Adam—Oh, my God . . ."

᷾

Those were the last words I heard Sophos say, then everything slipped away. The next thing I remembered was feeling drugged. I lay on a stretcher, a belt across my chest, in a small area cordoned off by white curtains. Sophos was holding my hand.

"I had to bring you here yesterday; you kept having one fit after another," he said.

A young doctor came in, followed by a group of nurses and students. The doctor asked with an air of self-importance, "Why is this man here?"

The first nurse read from a chart. "It says here, 'First status epilepticus of unknown origin. No fever. No signs of alcohol or narcotic withdrawal. No history of trauma. Admit to rule out an intracranial space-occupying lesion.' "

"And who is this Arab?"

"He is the patient's landlord," the nurse said. "He brought the patient here. Incidentally, doctor, this patient is the famous Dr. Lugner of the Haram."

"You're kidding! *Sajah*—the false prophet?" he smirked. Someone among his entourage giggled. The young doctor continued, "I guess the miracle cure isn't self-applicable. Apparently every three hundred years a Sabbatai Tzevi comes into the world."

Now the entire group laughed. The joking went on as they looked into my wide-open eyes as if I were deaf and blind.

For the first time, Sophos spoke up, raised his voice, and used Hebrew for emphasis. "Tabíib is not the Messiah! He is a *Zaddik*—a superior being."

I smiled. They all looked at him.

The doctor said, "He knows Hebrew?" as if Sophos wasn't there either.

Sophos murmured, "*Ill maa yhárf is-sayar uishwíit*—he who doesn't know what a falcon is will roast it." Was I really a falcon as Sophos thought or just an ordinary bird for eating?

∼

I am in the Sha'arei Tzedek Hospital for a week, being studied for potential diagnoses. There is no doubt: I have increased intracranial pressure, which is causing the projectile vomiting. They have tapped into me with so many lumbar punctures that I wish I were dead already. The X-rays show a mass, sitting centrally midline on top of where my eye nerves cross. Now it seems to me such an obvious diagnosis—pituitary tumor—how could I have missed it on my own? It explains my bumping into people— peripheral blindness—chronic thyroid deficiency (the cause of all my sores, soft and shrunken testicles, and decline of my sexual desire), my size, and, of course, the seizures. Had I unconsciously denied it, wishing that it would go away or better, that it never existed? How could I have a brain tumor?

On the unit, I am well treated and regarded, even by some doctors. I have a special lamp, a table, and a chair and am able to continue writing. The nurses and aides are particularly attentive. They ask questions about "untreatable" medical problems afflicting their relatives and friends. Even other patients tiptoe into my room to take a peek at me. But there is something else—an aura of mystery—unrelated to the reputation that surrounds me. I can do nothing wrong. The food is kosher, but Sophos manages to smuggle in the fresh halvah and cheese puffs that Şükran prepares. Sophos tells me the poor girl blames herself for my condition. The hospital even tolerates the constant presence of Sophos on the unit. I must be dying. All my life I didn't want to live and tried to kill myself. Now that death is about to occur, I want to live. I wonder how my hero D'Artagnan would have died. Most likely he would have flung himself onto the sword of death. But then, he flung himself into life, too.

I wonder whether living or dying demands more courage.

"Don't hold too tightly to life," says Sophos.

If I could gently cradle myself to break free from time and space. Open my fist, and I'll be free from all fears, including the nameless dread of no longer being. I am entering some bleak hollow—"no longer being." As much as I complained about life, death is unimaginable.

Sophos kept talking. "Death is part of the cycle of birth and rebirth. The seeds of today blossom to flowers and become seeds again. Death is a reseeding. From death and only from death comes life."

My blurred self didn't need another opaque layer. "My death will visit me only once Sophos; I don't want to die the way that I have lived most of my life—in lies and cowardly rationalizations. Maybe I am simply afraid of dying, even in my attempts to kill myself. I should have lived as if I'd already died. Now, I want to die as if I've really lived. I don't long for some explanation, comfort, or promise. I feel better by feeling worse. Let me truly experience my ending, fully and honestly live my death. Just help me to hurt better."

"And how did you get there?" This was the first time Sophos asked a question to which he didn't have an answer already.

"Simply by understanding our sameness."

Sophos looked amused.

I continued, "I got here by unfolding into wholeness, by believing in immortal continuity and in primordial dissolution, and I accepted the dissatisfaction inherent in this kind of lack of permanence. Things are as they are. I got here by building my house on a fault line by believing in the creation, not necessarily in the creator, whether you call that Allah, Jesus, God, Yahweh, or some other name. Each grape is its own winery."

Sophos smiled. "Adam, you have a great winery."

"The reason I got nowhere until now is because my mind was never free from itself. For me faith is like my poetry and your music. After that, it didn't take a gigantic leap to realize that my death is not an extraordinary event; in fact, it's not an event at all. I no longer see things with earthbound eyes. The transcending life is a spiritual condensation, we are here."

Sophos kept smiling. "You make your own way by going."

He gently touched my lips with his.

I felt inebriated by his kiss. I looked at him and recited,

Dost-u hazandan sunulan mey pek hoş olurmuş
They say: Offer of spirit from the nostalgic cup is delicious
Aksaçlıdan buse alan sarhoş olurmuş
The kiss of a white hair makes one delirious.

The scent of eucalyptus trees came through the windows of my hospital room and flooded my senses. Sophos held up a flower and sang the words to a song, "Your tears are clear."

~~~

Sophos finally explained the mystery of the special attention I was getting. They pulled out my—or, rather, Adam Zachary Lugner's—chart from 1926. I forgot; Adam had been in this hospital too. Sophos further added to the confusion by telling the nurses that I was reborn many times and would be born again and again.

~~~

I have a deep and abiding sense of well-being.

In pureness of deceleration, I am no longer interested in my surgery or in living or dying. My childhood driver Abbas's recollections crowd my mind. It is summer in Hasankale. I am swimming in the Karasu River. All of a sudden, hundreds of white pigeons appear and fly toward the castle. Fehim, the oldest son of Ibrahim Hazretleri, stands by the old man, who whispers something in his son's ear. This time Fehim doesn't jump off the cliff. Instead, he walks down the mountain and leaves town. He goes to Jerusalem. I hear a joyful shout. My inner inquietude subsides.

I cannot tell whether this is the end or just the beginning. It seems like nothing has changed and everything has changed. Until now things were not so clear. You see, *bulanık suda, balık avlanmaz*— in muddied water, one cannot fish. Now I know clearly who I am; I am who and what I love, though I do not dare to be clearer; I concede the existence of another reality, though I cannot take the world as its witness; I've tasted insanity, though I can't tell what sanity is; I've understood the presence of things, though not the significance of their absence; I've witnessed the godlike existence, though not the existence of God; I've seen the path to sainthood, though not the path to adulthood; I know what virtue is, though not its verging on the sacred; I am aware of the underground river of wisdom, though I am reluctant to tap it with my own well; I am inebriated by love, though sober in its connection to sex. In fact, love is the pain of being truly alive.

This may all sound too vague and not promising of any salvation from inner discontent. But the vagueness is the best part of the promise, which I almost missed.

‿‿

The surgery is scheduled as the first procedure on Thursday morning. No one has discussed the matter with me. A calm and disciplined silence has blossomed within me.

Wednesday I was visited by the Canadian neurosurgeon, Dr. Rosen, and the administrator of the hospital. They wanted to talk to me about the confusion surrounding my identity. The administrator scratched his head and said, "How can this be? Adam Zachary Lugner was born in Paris, October 17, 1905, to Dr. Harvey Lugner and his wife Dorothy. He was admitted to this hospital on September 5, 1926, with the diagnosis of a pituitary tumor. He died in the operating room on September 7 from uncontainable intracranial bleeding. The same day his body was given to his family. You present exactly the same name, background, and history. You also have the same physical characteristics—height, weight, and hair color—and the same disease, except you're alive."

"I am not dying my own death," I reassured him. "I won't disturb the order of things. I'll try to have exactly the same ending. Tomorrow, please give my body to my family—Sophos—who is the only friend I have in the world."

The administrator and surgeon looked at each other. They quickly left the room. Sophos was crying.

"Are you crying because I am going to die?" I asked.

"No," he replied. "I am crying because you said I am the only friend you have in the world."

"Well at least and finally I have one, a real friend. I must have developed an embryonic sense of self."

It is about five o'clock in the morning, August 28, the day that the storks depart from Istanbul. An aide shaved my head. He gave me a mirror. I look like a newborn child, bald and wrinkled. A young female doctor walked in and inserted a catheter into my penis; she didn't even look at my face. What a sad last encounter with a woman!

"Can we now tie some loose ends?" I asked Sophos.

"Yes, *Saddikie*, only fallibly."

"I want you to give one of the gems to Şükran and keep the other two for yourself. Incidentally, they are unusually precious diamonds. The book that I have been writing you can send to Cemil Karasu in Hasankale, if he is still there.

"I'm almost up to date. I'll keep writing until I can no longer do so. Make sure you include the new pages as well. Obviously, as the narrator, I'll not be able to complete my story. A last request: if possible, bury me in Adam Lugner's grave. You see, I am giving my death a purpose: a poetic condensation of man's sameness."

Tears poured from Sophos's eyes. "Adam, Adam, I'll deliver your book in person." With a slight frown, he continued, "You don't need to give me anything. Love can be exchanged only with love; it has no other currency."

But I no longer heard him. An old Turkish song kept playing in my head:

Yolculuk var, Yolculuk var yarına—a journey, a journey for tomorrow. The world is to live in as well as to die in.

I stand at the granite wall of a castle. All of a sudden, hundreds of white doves emerge below me, weaving their wings into hexagons and rectangles, the same patterns and shapes as Erzurum kilims. I throw myself toward them . . .

EPILOGUE

∾

I AM AMITI. I discovered the fragments of this narrative among my
parents' treasured possessions after the death of my mother, Sabina,
in 1984. My father Cemil died twenty years earlier from a massive heart
attack. As one of the surviving characters of this story, I became curious about the fate of those others mentioned and embarked on my own
pilgrimage to determine what happened to them.

Bakırköy hospital confirmed that Cemil Karasu was admitted once
in 1933 for treatment by Dr. Mazhar Osman but denied having any
record of Adam.

Tevkifhane prison no longer existed. In its place stood the luxury
Four Seasons Hotel.

I found the sisters, Gülseren and Gülderen, in their late seventies,
living together in a small apartment in the Turkish seacoast town of
Yalova. Both sisters were retired teachers. Gülderen, the younger, never
married. Gülseren's husband, a lawyer, was long dead, and they had
no children. The sisters were delighted to meet me. They knew Adam
as Zakir and said they often reminisced about him. Gülseren even played
on the piano for me the tune Adam whistled to entice her to the window. As I left their building and turned back for a second look, the sisters were at the window, looking at me from behind the half-drawn lace
curtain.

Ertuğrul went to Egypt with the hope of reconstituting his status
there as the pretender to the throne of the Ottoman Empire. He died
at the age of 32 of an unknown cause.

Emmanuel Carasso was exiled to Italy. After his fortune was confiscated, he lived in penury in Trieste. The last ten years of his life, he was
blind in both eyes. According to *Archivio dello Stato Civile di Trieste*, he
died November 2, 1934, of unknown causes, at the age of seventy-two.

Emmanuel's blindness may have been related to a slow-growing pituitary tumor located at his *sella Turcica*. This raises the question of whether Adam was sired by Vahdettin; or was he in fact fathered by Emmanuel Carasso?

Tatiana (Ivanova), eighty-six years old and very ill, lived in the Gayrettepe section of Istanbul. She didn't remember Adam or David and wanted only to talk about some baroness friends.

Rabbi Nahum (Nahoom) became the chief rabbi of Egypt and died in Cairo in 1960.

Dr. Ruth Wilmanns Lidz (she was married to Theodore Lidz, a professor of Psychiatry) had, in fact, emigrated to the United States. She had taught psychiatry at Yale University in New Haven until her death in 1995.

Dr. Lacan became a very famous psychoanalyst and even formed a school of his own in Paris, only to dispense with it six months before he died there in 1981.

The French embassy, after long denying they had any knowledge about Mademoiselle Blanche, reluctantly provided me with an address in Strasbourg. When I went there, there was no Mademoiselle Blanche, nor did anybody recollect that such a person had lived there. In fact, the address belonged to a retired career diplomat whose family had lived there for at least four generations.

Sağolan—Soghoman Soghomonian ("Komitas Vartabed")—died in 1935 after having spent the last fourteen years of his life in the Hôpital Villejuif, a public institution for the mentally ill, located on the outskirts of Paris.

Sara, Gerald her husband, and the Lugners were all killed at Auschwitz.

I found Denise's son in a run-down group home. A seventy-year-old veteran with alcoholic breath, he welcomed me in full military regalia. He told me that his mother, Denise, married Dr. Lavalle, who died within a few years of their marriage. The widowed Denise spent time in and out of hospitals before eventually succumbing to cirrhosis of the liver. Her son couldn't remember when she died.

I found Abbas's only son in Erzurum. He owned a makeshift bus that operated between Hasankale and Erzurum. He showed me his father's memorabilia: a picture of him standing next to a Mercedes and another photo showing Abbas carrying a rolled-up kilim and standing behind a "European woman." She was Mademoiselle Blanche. He was pleased to show me a clay Hittite tablet given to his father by a boy who may have been "an illegitimate son" of the last sultan.

When I knocked on the door of the *Hodja*-Sophos's house in Jerusalem, I found a man a few years younger than I—a short man with light brown hair and Asian eyes. He was blind. I was stunned as I stared at him. It was as if I were looking at myself in a mirror. Yes, he had heard the story of the old *Hodja* and the Turkish doctor from his mother. The *Hodja* had given his house to Şükran, the young man's mother, before he, determined to die there, set out for Turkey.

When I asked him whether his mother Şükran was alive, he told me she died years ago. I was looking at his eyes, the same hazel color as mine. I ventured to ask him if his name was *Zakir*, and he nodded. He said he was surprised that I knew. Only his mother had called him *Zakir*.

He was obviously the son of Adam, my half brother, by Şükran.

When I tried to reach him the following year, I learned that he had died of an untreated brain tumor.

My sister Nevim vaguely remembered an old Arab man visiting us when she was about seven years old and that he brought a package, the contents of which she never saw. But she remembered vividly the two gems that the Arab also brought. The man said he was carrying out the will of a doctor friend who had died in Jerusalem. He adamantly refused to take the gems for himself and requested that should he die, he be buried in Hasankale. The next day he was found dead at the bottom of the granite cliff of the castle. "He must have fallen off while visiting the cave," people said. My parents had him buried behind the castle in a grave marked "Arab," for no one knew his name. My mother gave the gems to my sister, explaining that they were glass. "No diamonds can be so big, clear, and shiny," she declared. My sister had no idea what happened to the gems.

I found the "Arab's" grave in a remote corner of the castle's cemetery. Digging through the packed soil of the long-abandoned site, I removed his remains and carefully carried them to the part of the cemetery where the elite and *ulema* (sages) lay in their eternal rest. I reburied them in my father's grave, turned the inscribed headstone inward, and somewhat clumsily carved on the now-outward side of the stone: "*Sophos.*"

In 1996, I was diagnosed with the same type of brain tumor that Adam, Emmanuel Carasso, and Şükran's son, *Zakir*, had. I was operated on, and the tumor was partially removed.

Amiti
11 February 1999

About the Author

T. BYRAM KARASU, M.D., Silverman Professor and the University Chairman, Department of Psychiatry and Behavioral Sciences at Albert Einstein College of Medicine and Psychiatrist-in-Chief of Montefiore Medical Center, is the author or editor of fifteen books, including the seminal *Treatments of Psychiatric Disorders* and two best-sellers, *The Art of Serenity* and *The Spirit of Happiness*. He is currently the editor in chief of the *American Journal of Psychotherapy* and a Distinguished Life Fellow of the American Psychiatric Association. Dr. Karasu is a scholar, renowned clinician, teacher, and lecturer, and the recipient of numerous awards, including the American Psychiatric Association's Presidential Commendation. He lives in New York City and Westport, Connecticut.